THE SCHWARK

A Novel by Derek Meyer

For all of the Schwarks in our lives

The Fire
The Otter
The Forage
The School
The Fox
The Art Therapist
The Premonition
The Necklace
The Gift
The Sea
The Ants
The Ship
The Captain
The Ghost
The Crows
The Black Hole
The Donation
The Portrait
The Nightmare
The Dock
The Astronaut
The Plan
The Amanita
The Last Day
The River
The Mission
The Atoll
The Promise
The Schwark
The Sequoia

The Fire

In through the darkness crept the subtle, almost imperceptible hint of a fond distant memory. A gradual warming sensation gripped his mind and wrapped it up inside the heaviest of his Grandmother's knitted wool blankets. It was reminiscent of the surreal comfort of basking in the musky haze that enveloped him while his Father enjoyed half a cigar on their front porch in late October - of the first mouthful of his Mother's Sunday-morning sourdough pancakes laced with freshly warmed maple syrup. The memories and feelings and emotions and sensations entirely overwhelmed him. It was the smell. A single, faint olfactory stimulus, like a candle at the end of a long, dark tunnel - beckoning, calling, enticing every desire to seek more, to venture inward. In his half-sleep stupor, he inhaled deeply through his nose and held his breath.

The sudden explosive rush of understanding electrified his entire body and mercilessly tore him away from the promises of a deep, dream-filled sleep. His eyes shot open, but darkness remained. And there it was - the ghost, the spirit, that which was responsible for teasing his dreary mind with thoughts of love and safety, only to viciously supplant those with a flavor of anxious, palpable fear of the unknown. Dancing along the wall in a slow-motion waltz, the amorphous ghost-spirit rose and dove to its own song, a silent melody, only known to creatures whose existence was pure ephemeral.

It was evidence of the spark of life, of a perfectly roasted marshmallow, of a cheesy circus magic trick, of a night under a sea of fireworks. It was also the belch of a chimney at the crematorium, the furious exhaust of an overloaded semi-truck chugging up the mountain pass, the final mutterings of a lingering cigarette butt at the bowling alley. Which was this spirit, that which floated from his open window, swimming down across his closet door, drifting over his wooden bin of stuffed animals, spiraling up and up over his bed, into his nostrils, towards his brain, melding with his dreams and fears and hopes and confusions. Heads or tails, black or white, good or evil - which was this smoke?

"Who are you?" the Boy inquired, not daring to make any sudden movement, except with his eyes - his wide-open, new-moon eyes. No answer, except for the synchronized dive and rise and swirl of the Smoke, which rose on its haunches and turned to face the Boy.

"*What* are you?" the terrified Boy dared through the sheets. His thoughts raced through the possibilities: had his Father lit the fireplace?

Had there been a barbecue? A bonfire? No, none of those. His mind clouded as neurons flooded with overwhelming animalistic tendencies - raw emotion and pure, perfect fear. He knew this Smoke's name. He knew what this Smoke was before it spoke.

"I am death," hissed the Smoke. "I am the Great Change, the Balancer, the Reset, the Bringer of Fire, the Equalizer. I have always been, and always will be."

The Boy stared at the Smoke spirit as it loomed giant over his single twin bed. Arms outstretched, it wore a gray cloak that effortlessly and hauntingly drifted over the comforter and glared at him, two small softly glowing orange embers in place of eyes - the Smoke was alive, and it had come for him. In each passing second, the Boy's room began to take on the lighter flickering shades of sunrise: of bright blood-drenched reds, nauseating yellows, and hurricane pinks. The Smoke stared at the Boy as harsh notes of crackle and pop and sizzle filled the room.

Erupting from his bedsheets and tumbling onto the hard, granite-cold oak floor of his bedroom, the Boy began to crawl towards the last bastion of safety, the last place on Earth that trouble dared - his box of stuffed animals. As he swam into the confines of his beloved Bear, Whale, Otter, Wolf, Shark, and Fox, fear briefly faded into nothingness, as an imagined safety net fell snuggling around him.

"I'm okay," whimpered the Boy.

"You're okay," replied the Whale and Shark.

"Glad you're here, pal," answered the Otter.

"Just a bad dream," confided the Fox.

One breath. Two breaths.

"Open your eyes," commanded the Wolf.

Three breaths.

A cough, a burning sensation in the back of his throat. A terrible itching underneath his eyelids. The creeping of liquid fear injected straight into his bloodstream. Peering upwards, he searched for what he knew was there but wished was simply a nightmare. He began to taste the saltiness of his own sweat beads accumulating at the corners of his lips.

The heat. What had begun as building, oppressive warmth, suddenly crescendoed and erupted through the cracked bedroom window as a tidal wave of terrible, enveloping heat. Ticks and cracks and rumbles of freshly consumed woods and pine needles flooded his ears. The walls were ablaze with schizophrenic blurs of fire aura - oranges fighting purples and battling blues only to yield to massive flashes of yellow that temporarily blinded the Boy. Above the chaos hovered the Smoke, thicker and heavier and more gigantic than ever. It's unblinking, judging eyes of flame searched the Boy's soul and held his mind in a perpetual state of simultaneous awe and terror.

"You cannot run," purred the Smoke. The Boy starred, clutching his animals and the impossible hope they suggested snuggly to his chest. "You are from fire, and to fire you shall return," announced the Smoke, its great many arms creeping forward.

A pounding at his bedroom door. A crash and sudden disfigurement of the Smoke as a shadowed figure rushed towards him, coughing violently and waving its frantic arms in desperate windmills at the onslaught of death that poured in through the window. His Father.

"Get up!" screamed his Father. Two massive hands came down on the Boy's shoulders and plucked him from the confines of his stuffed animal safety shield. As his Father carried him through the upstairs hallway, the Boy's senses quickly faded - vision blurring, sounds fading, feelings sublimating from his fingertips. The world floated and sank, bobbed and gasped and rolled and flailed into the swells of impossibly thick smoke as his Father whisked him downstairs, through the living room, out onto the porch, onto the driveway, and set him down onto a rough patch of gravel and concrete. His tunneled vision widening, the Boy blinked away ash-crusted tears.

"Stay here! I need to get your Mother," explained his Father between hacking gasps, flexing his charred fingers that were now dotted with salmon-pink patches of raw flesh. Paralyzed from fear, the Boy could only observe as the figure of his Father stumbled and coughed and flapped as it made its way through a barely recognizable doorway, back into an unknown and unforgiving hell-scape. A miniature forest of blue and orange flames quietly and quickly enshrouded the cedar-planked siding, as quivering tongues of curious death slithered into what was once the Boy's bedroom.

Searching for escape, the Boy's mind found reprieve in the darkness beyond the glowing embers of his house. Back there, in the thicket and brush dwelt an unimaginably green and dense, alive and earthen forest of ferns and firs and fungi and life, endlessly dripping with morning dew and afternoon mist and evening rain. Through closed eyes, he envisioned all of this - the vibrant saltiness of an ocean breeze, the jarring tappity-tap of a woodpecker at dawn, the beams of sunlight onto the leaf-strewn trails he walked with his Mother on the way to catch the school bus.

A sudden tickle at his nostrils ripped him back to the present, where two menacing orange eyes growled mere inches from his face.

"It has always been this way, this will be no different," growled the eyes. The Smoke bellowed forth from the surrounding forest, belching fire beneath every stone and twig, as the woods became aglow with the luminosity of a thousand suns. Marching forward in synchrony to the deafening roar of bark and leaf and moss boiling from the inside out, the Smoke raised its arms toward the sky and blotted out the stars, leaving the blood moon alone to choke behind a cloud of ash.

Desperation exploded in the form of sudden shrieks and cries and terrible, wrenching moans from the periphery of the raging bonfire that was part of his Home. His Mother. His Father. Their voices, their tears, their screams. The Boy clamored to his feet as the chaotic figures emerged from the hottest flames and the darkest smoke. One carried the other, collapsing to a knee. Rising, falling, coughing, crying, crashing in a heap of sweat-drenched skin, Smoke-riddled clothing, and fire-singed hair.

"I-I...," stammered his Mother, "couldn't find the necklace," she finished, clutching an empty space at her neck. His Father's answer was the harshest of wheezes and gasps - no words articulated, only the breath sounds of struggle and poison and defeat reverberating upwards into the apocalyptic atmosphere that descended all around them.

Scanning the glimmering treeline in desperation, the Boy searched. Unimpeded by the furious pounding of his heartbeat at his eardrums, he allowed the jet-engine roar of the forest fire to dissolve as he intensified his focus. His gaze suddenly fell onto the faint ribbon of basalt rock lining an overgrown path of blackberry and rhododendron. His family's trail - down and down, away from the Smoke, to the creek, to the water, to their salvation.

"Mom, the creek!" the Boy exclaimed. As they hobbled into a half-eaten forest of haze and grief and otherworldly heat, the Boy glanced back to steal a final look at the only house he had ever known, memories of utter happiness and restfulness and love - now burnt to ash. As he gazed upon these prior dreams, his eyes recorded the most traumatizing event he would witness for the rest of his human life.

Massive, sweeping, angry arms of roiling, impatient smoke suddenly grasped their family's house with menacing hands of liquid, ferocious flame and squeezed, and choked, and strangled the last drop of life from the structure's throat. In a final gasp, his house shuddered and collapsed and incinerated into nothingness, becoming Smoke itself. Rising into a cataclysmic plume, the ash barreled down the trail after its former inhabitants, the Smoke snarling as it assimilated this new-found death. Glancing over his shoulder as he ran, the Boy saw the two unfathomably bright burning suns beaming down upon him from beneath the mountainous hood of sickening Smoke.

"Leave us alone!" screamed the Boy.

"I will always be with you," crackled the Smoke.

"No! No you won't!" the Boy sobbed.

"In time, you will understand what I am - what this is," finished the Smoke, suddenly dissolving into the scorched trees, revealing the speckled light of the Milky Way standing watch above him.

"Who are you yelling at?" his Mother moaned. She was stumbling down the path while supporting the weight of his Father, the trailing, nauseating odor of burnt flesh and cloth wafting behind.

"The Smoke! It did this!" The Boy replied. His Mother stopped abruptly, carefully lowering his Father against a tree as she gasped for air. Kneeling beside the Boy, she clenched his shoulders firmly with both of her calloused hands, the whites of her eyes trembling with every human emotion.

"No. No one did this. No human, no monster, no spirit, no god," she said, shaking the Boy.

"But I saw the Smoke! Its eyes!" he pleaded. Her brow furrowed. Her lip twitched. Her grip tightened into a tetany of trauma and love and resignation.

"Enough!" she barked. "Enough with your fantasies. Let me tell you the reality: the house is destroyed, my necklace is vapor, your stuffed toys are dust, and if we don't get your Father to a hospital soon…," she hardened her face and stood, fists trembling at her sides. "Do you understand me?" she whispered, "Home is gone."

The Boy stared at his Mother as hot tears rolled from the corners of her eyes, leaving behind troughs of dark ash on the sides of his cheeks. He hugged her as tightly as he could, even though deep in the fabric of his life, he knew she was wrong. Their house, their material things - those things may be gone. But Home?

Home was never gone.

The Otter

Around the circular cedar card table, the two figures sat in silence, laser-focused at the task in hand. Around them, the thick purple fog of nothingness floated by, windless and silent. Where or when they were, was anyone's or anything's guess. Upon the table lay hundreds of small building blocks - a full kaleidoscope of colors, a cornucopia of shapes and angles. The two creatures worked furiously, silently, snatching up a block here and there, disassembling and reassembling as manic ideas swirled inside their minds. After some time, the Boy set his art piece down and heavily sighed. The Otter raised its dark eyes to peer at what the Boy had been creating - it appeared to be some sort of house - a cabin perhaps.

"I have a story I'd like to share with you," began the Otter, "something to perhaps cheer you up." Shrugging in response, the Boy opened his mouth to speak, but instead sighed once more. The Otter continued. "Once, when I was very young - just a pup actually - barely able to hold a rock between my flippers, let alone crack a wizened mollusk - a sudden, terrible thing happened to me, too." The Boy stared back, eyes immediately more enthralled.

"What was it? An undersea volcanic eruption? A rabid white shark? A massive oil spill? A monster from another universe that can only survive off of fresh otter meat?" he suggested. The Otter chuckled.

"No. None of those things, thankfully. And you read too many comic books, Boy!" he lightheartedly scolded. "It was a storm - a storm for the ages, of legend. A maelstrom that came so fast and terrible, our estuary became a floodplain. Undersea currents so strong, that our kelp forests uprooted and floated away. Ravaging tides so strong, that the mollusk and clam and oyster and scallop beds were totally mutilated. Chaos. Pups separated from their mothers. Water flowing over wooden docks and down asphalt streets. Otters and people swimming for their lives," continued the Otter, setting down his building blocks. He appeared to be making a spaceship of sorts, not of human standards, naturally, but more of the sea dwelling mammal type. Either that, or he was making a very large replica of half a clam shell - it was difficult and too early to tell, one might suppose.

"What did you do? Did you get lost? Did you lose your toys, too?" the Boy inquired. He was rapidly assembling some sort of fortress, complete with cannons and barricaded walls and blockheaded guards at the ready. Homeless building blocks floated aimlessly around their drifting table, but the Boy adeptly and masterfully plucked the perfect pieces from the misted air with his left hand, and without a pause, pushed them into place with his right. The Otter eyed the Boy's transforming creation with great interest and some subtle jealousy, for otter flippers are a bit clumsy for these types of things. Clearing its throat and ruffling its whiskered jowls, the Otter continued.

"The first moments were pure terror. I can't remember much, honestly," it began. "The first thing I remember was tumbling uncontrollably through a gigantic swell, holding my breath and not knowing which was was up or down. In that horrible moment, for whatever reason, all I could think about was my pet snail that lived under the abandoned dock," the Otter recalled, setting down its building blocks blocks to rub its eyes, clearly filling with emotion and memory. "I mean, I'm about twenty-five times that snail's size, and I couldn't paddle against the current worth my life! Imagine a tiny snail! The horror!"

"Where did the storm take you?" The boy had quit plucking his plastic blocks from space and instead clutched his building blocks semi-masterpiece firmly, eyes intensely set on the Otter.

"When the rip and pull of the storm surge finally released me from its maniacal grasp, I slowly rose to the surface, half-alive, half-conscious, but fully aware that I was going to take another breath and discover an unfathomable ruin. My head broke the brown and soupy froth and I gasped a lonely and terrible small breath, for I could have inhaled the world and more." The boy gulped, setting down his fort, analogous memories stirring up inside his own mind as the Otter continued.

"I remember opening my eyes and seeing the vertical rows of seaweed somehow above the water, rising forever upward into a blood red sun, spiraling outward with limbs and arms and needles outstretched. All around me, these green giants loomed above, as I floated on my back. Trees. Surrounded by trees! Douglas Fir, to be exact. I was *inside* the forest - the floods must have carried me through the tidal swamps, over driftwood dams, and clear across the estuary embankment, into the deep coastal woods - certainly no home for a sea otter!"

"Were you scared?" whispered the Boy. The Otter nodded.

"At first, oh yes, of course! And then the waters calmed, pinecones and bits of kelp intermingled in small eddies, fish nipped at bobbing mushroom caps, a crab navigated aboard a small raft of clumped tree moss and mangled sword-fern - and me? I simply floated on my back, staring up at the glorious fir trees, marveling at their stoic simple swaying in the post-storm breezes." The Otter hugged itself as it spoke, eyes closed, reveling in the moment once more. Suddenly, it opened its black marble eyes and pounded the flimsy card table with its flippers, tossing building blocks aimlessly into space. "And then, something truly incredible occurred! Down through the branches, a silent rustling. A ghost in the tree. Then the eyes. Two small midnight eyes staring at me. Upside-down! Or perhaps... right-side up? A 'tree-otter' - or you - you might call it a 'Squirrel.' It had wandered down its trunk, and was now nose-to-nose with me at the base of the tree I happened to float against." Rubbing its whiskers and wriggling its rubbery black nose, the Otter, smiled and paused, taking a deep breath before it continued.

"I cannot tell you how long we stayed that way - locked into each other's gaze, me on my back, the Squirrel balanced precariously on the side of the fir, breathing each other's smells, seeing each other's faces, and *knowing* - knowing that despite such loss, such great devastation and turmoil, everything was in its right place. I was not scared, I decided. In that moment, I was in *awe*, for how quickly the world had changed! How beautiful the world adapted. How *strange* to be alive! Just alive! How strange!" The Otter grinned through closed eyes - a toothy, ecstatic grin blending together past and present, fear and love, real and unreal. The Boy thought he felt the subtle inklings - the faint understanding of how the Otter felt, but wasn't certain.

"What about your mom, your dad? Did you stay in the forest?" the Boy stammered, tears of something that was neither sadness nor joy building up along his lower lids. The Otter sighed.

"As I drifted along between ravines and glades, soft oranges and weary blues hinting of night, I watched as a crescent moon revealed itself behind fading storm clouds. The surreal novelty of floating through the forest quickly subsided as I found myself welling up with a deep anxious swell inside my chest," said the Otter, folding its rubbery dark flippers across its furry chest. "A chill within my bones not stirred by cold, but rather fear of the unknown, set its teeth, and I began to whimper and cry. Alone. I was alone... and then I heard it." Slapping the side of the metallic folding chair with its tail while slapping the wooden table top with a flipper, the Otter replicated the sound.

Whump-whump-tickity-tick-*whump*.

"A barely perceptible echo through the massive trunks and rolling hills of flood and fern," whispered the Otter, barely twitching a whisker from the sides of its rubbery lips.

Whump-whump-tickity-tick-*whump*.

Whump-whump-tickity-tick-*whump*. The Otter gazed at the Boy, enjoying the reaction he had stirred.

"A bear? Was it a whale? A bear riding a whale through the woods?" exclaimed the Boy. He was now standing over the table of half-formed building block creations, barely able to hide his excitement. The Otter opened its eyes and shook its head.

"My family's call. 'Whump-whump-tickity-tick-*whump*.' Before I knew my name, I knew this beat," explained the Otter. "You see, you need a very precise, wedge-shaped piece of shale and an adequately rounded mollusk shell. You place the shell on your belly and knock it twice with the wide part of the rock - 'whomp-whomp' - then quickly turn the stone over and tap the mollusk with the pointy end - 'tickity-tick' - and finally roll the stone over once more for a final strike, louder than all the others - 'whump.' The call of my family. *My* family!" roared the Otter, balancing on its tail to match the Boy's widened eyes.

"So I followed that beat through the moonrise and the dawn, over the edge of the estuary embankment, and into the newly formed bay. It was there that I found them, floating calmly" whispered the Otter. "My Mother. My Father. Aunt, Uncle, Grandmother - all of the otters - all beating out the call, just for me. I was Home again," it finished, slowly sliding back into its seat, eyes blinking away fresh tears of remembered joy. The Boy's mouth opened, inhaled, and slowly closed. His eyes shut. He smiled the smile of exhausted relief, seemingly living vicariously in the Otter's tale.

"Did you tell them where you had gone? What you had seen? What you had learned?" asked the Boy. The Otter cleared its throat and nodded softly.

"That next morning, as we floated next to each other through a crop of surviving seagrass, I reenacted my encounter with the Squirrel and the feelings of contentment I had experienced. They nodded and smiled, scratched and groomed my head, knocked rocks on clams and fed me my portions - but deep down, I felt that they did not truly know what I had felt. 'Shock' some said. Disappointment began to drip into my heart, but was thankfully soon supplanted by the knowing - the understanding - that perhaps… maybe not everyone has to feel the same way about these things. These feelings and emotions and perceptions that occur when our lives border on impossible," finished the Otter.

"I think... I know... what you mean," the Boy replied, mind half-in, half-out of the present.

"I think you do, too," replied the grinning Otter. "In fact… I *know* you do." Snapping the final brick into its sculpture, the Boy saw what it was the Otter had been meticulously building all along - it was an ant - an ant riding the back of a bird - a crow, maybe. Gaze drifting to meet his furry friend's, the Boy allowed a faint smile to stretch across his lips. The Otter blinked, one eye a flaming hazy sunset, the other a crystalline yellow full moon.

"Let your mind float amongst the firs, Boy," he said through that eternal, enchanting grin, "and now… now it begins. Wake up!"

The Forage

Her voice. "Hey... wake up." Bursting into life as a pale yellow and orange blurred fireball alight behind his tired eyelids, the day began. He sighed and shifted beneath the heavy down comforter his GrandMother had made for him last winter. It was a subtle calculated movement meant to convey that perhaps he was still asleep and dreaming. She was no fool, however. She had played this game before, and a sly knowing smirk slid across her face with pursed lips holding back that impulsive giggle.

"Nice try! I know you're awake! Do you know what we're going to do today?" she said as she flung open his cocoon from his feet to the waist. A sudden burst of chilled forest air swept in, sending a brief convulsion of shivers up through his shoulders, flicking his eyes open ever so subtly, but enough to tip his hand.

"Mister! I saw that! Now get up! There's an adventure to be had!" she announced, backing away from the small twin bed, arms crossed. She grunted - lovingly impatient. "And... pancakes," she teased, revealing the ace up her sleeve. That trump card - *pancakes*. The Boy's eyes shot open as he exploded out of the comforter, only to find himself becoming more intertwined and wrapped up in the sheets in the most peculiar of ways. His Mother laughed at the ridiculous sight and decided to escalate the hysterity even further, as was her typical style. She pounced on the entrapped Boy and began tickling him ferociously without mercy.

"Ha! No! Stop it!" the Boy pleaded, flailing in convulsive fits of flying fists and feet and sheets and pillows until he found the edge of the bed and chaotically tumbled off the side straight onto his back. The two stared at each other, sharing in that sudden silence that only a parent and young child could know after such a minor accident or fall, where neither knows the extent of the injury or pain, each attempting to interpret the drama, feeling their own hurt - usually more mental than physical.

"Good morning!" she exclaimed with her sadistic yet ever-loving smile.

"Pancakes, huh?" was all the Boy could answer, massaging his rear end. Nodding rapidly, His Mother helped him out of the mess of strewn about bed matter. Squatting next to her, the Boy gazed up at his minuscule bedroom window, cracked an inch or so open. The morning fog was drifting into the room and slowly, calmly, lazily settling onto the uneven wooden floor, dispersing upon impact in slow-motion, carpeting his pile of stuffed animals with velvety smoke-kissed tendrils.

"Can Wolf come to breakfast?" he pleaded to his Mother.

"Well, as long as he chews his food with his mouth closed," she responded, with a gentle stroke of the Boy's hair and a soft squeeze of his shoulder. The Boy hugged his Mother, who he loved with all of his might. Before jetting out of the room, he grabbed Wolf and hurdled down the stairs of their forest home into the kitchen, following the whiff of fresh maple syrup heated over their small wood-fired stove.

~~~

"Well Hey-oh, kid! Sourdough pancakes with marionberry jam, maple syrup, homemade, fresh whipped cream? That sweet tooth's gonna creep up on ya, pal!" chided the Wolf to the Boy. "But I'll say, you are one lucky son of a gun, you know that? All I'm gonna say is, where's the meat, man? Where. Is. The. Meat? A Wolf's gotta eat, Boy!" howled the stuffed beast.

"We are vegetarian, you know that, Wolf!" began the Boy, plunging a forkful of breakfast into his mouth. His Father chuckled between gulps of coffee.

"Sounds like your Wolf woke up a little hungry today, huh?" said the brawny, bearded man.

"Yeah, I guess. I thought he ate pretty well last night, but maybe Otter or Whale stole some - actually, probably Shark," the Boy replied. The Wolf gasped.

"Nahh, man! Otter and I are cool. Whale and Shark, too. Just had to pay 'em back for that one time out on the river, you know. Saved my whiskers, man. Saved my whiskers." recalled the Wolf.

"Yeah, you should have stayed in the boat," reprimanded the Boy. His parents glanced at each other, holding back snickers. His Father couldn't help himself - he had to join in his son's morning make-believe.

"So was it Wolf's fault? Or the person who decided to bring *all* their stuffed animals on our overnight rafting trip, hmm?" he gently scolded, wagging a finger at the Boy. Getting up to clear the dishes, his Father joined his Mother at the sink. The Boy thought he heard her whispering, but the rushing tap from the sink faucet drowned out hidden voice.

"I hope he grows out of this someday - for his own sake," the Boy would have heard her say softly to his Father. Picking up his Wolf from the
~~~

table, the Boy scampered back to his room, shouting to everyone and no one in particular.

"I wonder what adventure we're going on today!" he said out loud. He had been homeschooled for four years now, and everyday was a new lesson, a new adventure, a test, a reflection. With Nature as his classroom, the forest and beach and creeks as his classmates, he never felt entirely alone. His Mother, the teacher, principle, and coach - his beacon. His parents, on the other hand, were beginning to think he could use a bit more contact with the same species.

"The *Fox*!" exclaimed the Wolf, suddenly. " Now that I think of it, maybe he *did* steal some of my dinner!"

~~~

"Tell me - what do you remember about the weather this past week and what does it mean?" his Mother asked, sitting across from him on her favorite fire-pit stump. School had started. With her first question, the bell had silently rung. Teacher, pupil, and a small stuffed Wolf sat in a tight semi-circle. Clearing his throat, the Boy recollected his thoughts.

"Sunday was daylight savings, so we slept longer, and the mornings are brighter now, but the nights longer," he began, stirring the soil at his feet. "The rains started on and off last week, but are now steady in the afternoon. The temperature dropped a bit, but yesterday was warm and dry. The leaves are falling and the salmon are finished with their runs. We can still grow radish and kale and potatoes. The tomatoes and strawberries finally gave up, but I saw one more tiny berry hanging on. The air smells of pine needles and Earth." His Mother smiled.

"Very good!" she replied, "The rains started and then stopped. And then it was warmer yesterday. What do you remember about that, in particular? What grows in the Fall when that happens?" she prodded. The Boy stopped kicking at the soil and stared at his feet, sinking into his memories and lessons of prior autumns. The Wolf spoke first.

"I'll tell ya what grows - my appetite! You gonna get me something to eat or what, kid?" growled the furry canine.

"Quiet Wolf! I'm thinking," said the Boy out loud. Had he glanced up at his Mother, he would have noted a very pronounced sarcastic eye roll. Squeezing his lids closed, the Boy silenced all sights and sounds and smells around him and focused his attention to the Earth. Grabbing the Wolf, he took the deepest of breaths and dove.
~~~

As small as the tiniest filament of freshly branched moss, the Boy entered the soil and burrowed down, down, deeper and deeper. Layers of moist forest debris - ancient bark chips, sappy pine needle clumps, shed fern leaves in various states of half-decay, newborn leopard slugs squirming and writhing in a state of stuporous newborn life - the underworld surrounded him. Near the roots of the tallest coastal fir trees, he encountered the threads of an unusual species. Branching in all directions and performing biological alchemy in symbiosis with the other underground attendees, these white fibrous tendrils twitched and vibrated and glowed a dull blue as the Boy approached.

"Who's that guy?" asked the Wolf, caught in the warmth of the glowing threads. The Boy scratched his head until his 'ah-ha' moment arrived.

"I think that's mycelium!" he announced. "I remember my Mother telling us that it grows in this sort of way shortly after the first rains in the Fall, especially after the soil warms for a few days."

"What the heck's a 'my-seal-ee-um?'" snorted the Wolf.

"Like a mushroom! Or, part of a mushroom," explained the Boy. "If the cap is the 'apple,' then the mycelium is like the 'tree.' This is the living, breathing, *alive* part of the mushroom. And this mushroom? This one lives a special life," he continued, dragging the Wolf to a place under the Earth where the mycelium met the roots of a great fir tree. "See Wolf? This fungus lives *with* a Douglas Fir. They are friends! They give each other stuff, and make each other happier because of it. Sort of like trading, or a double-birthday, or a marriage," he finished, content and proud of his answer. The Wolf hacked up a bit of soil-crusted phlegm and shook his head.

"Mushrooms, huh? Never could eat 'em - taste all sorts of weird, ya know? It's the texture. Like a dead whale or something,'" it grimaced. The Boy frowned at that suggestion.

"Should we tell Whale about that comparison?" he warned.

"Nah man, no, no. I mean, Mushrooms are cool. Whale's cool. Just forget I said that, okay? Sheesh," sighed the Wolf. Holding back his laughter, the Boy nodded. He loved the Wolf, especially for his immature speak-before-thinking remarks.

"The Chanterelles are rising," said the Boy, his mind re-emerging from the soil to stand next to his Mother. His voice was softly confident and glimmering with excited hope. Clapping her hands, his Mother beamed her radiant smile down toward him as she knelt, stroking the mossy carpeted forest floor.

"Yes, they are about to pop! The great recyclers of our ecosystem are up and at it. Today's a wonderful day to go say 'Hello,' don't you think?" she suggested, her eyes twinkling a bright purple, her exhaled breath misting through the canopy of sparkling fir needles and soft cedar leaf. The word carried through that frosted air - 'Chanterelle' - that golden, beautiful gem of the woods. The Boy's favorite. Almost on cue, a minuscule patch of mycelium erupted from the duff and gently wrapped his Mother's feet - a plume of warm musky air pulsing across the bark chips. As his goosebumps settled, the Boy swung his backpack onto his shoulders, mushroom knife in hand, Wolf in the other, and stood at attention in front of his Mother, vibrating with the anticipation of the hunt.

"I'll lead," he announced.

"You'll lead," she repeated with a subtle proud nod.

"'King of the mushrooms', today, eh? I don't get you people!" murmured the Wolf, as the Boy proceeded into the fern-thickened woods, dew on his eyebrows, dirt under his fingernails, utter joy and ecstasy fueling his morning spirit.

"North-facing slopes are colder and better this time of year," he remembered to himself. "Pine-needle forest floor with sword ferns - not too thick with secondary growth but not totally barren," he recalled in his mind, changing trajectory slightly. "Look for a small, vase-like, beautifully pale yellow gem," he heard his Mother say many forages ago.

"Fungus-amongus," he whispered out loud. He loved that saying - his lucky mushroom mantra.

"The heck?" barked the Wolf - it was riding upside-down in the Boy's backpack and couldn't see a thing. The morning's fog was lifting, and the afternoon autumn sunbeams shone through the fir trees and onto the single-track game trails in scattered rays arranged suspiciously synchronized. Spider webs glistened on the periphery as the Boy's face broke through haphazardly arranged silkworm chord and stray branches blown down by earlier storms. He slowed his pace and squatted, allowing the forest's energy to sift through - that subtle warmth and earthen spice that permeated pores and saturated souls.

"One. Two. Three. Four," he counted, turning his head a full one-hundred-eighty degrees.

"What you countin,' kid?" asked the Wolf.

"To ten," explained the Boy," Gotta get into mushroom-time. Real slow-ow-ow like," he exaggerated.

"Five." A breath.

"Six." Heartbeat rising.

"Seven." Wind ceasing.

"Eight." Eyes drawn to the base of a gargantuan fern alongside a towering redwood.

"Nine." Hands separating the sagging fronds.

"Ten." At the base of the glistening green plant, he began to find his friends. Little brown Galerina umbrellas spun up to greet him. Massively stemmed bright pink Russula caps burst onto his retina. Angel Wings and Pig's Ears. Candy-caps and Fairy Rings.

"Hello there," smiled the Boy, as he meticulously dusted and cut the choice edible species at their stipe, careful not to disturb their 'tree' of mycelium. His Mother looked on proudly, collecting her own cache simultaneously, asking questions of the Boy every so often.

"Sure it's an Oyster? That tree's dead - they don't often go for that," she would prod.

"Well, we can do a spore print back home,' the Boy would respond, tucking his prize into a separate section of his backpack reserved for the questionables. Coincidently, the Wolf was also placed into this compartment.

"How do you know it's not toxic?" his Mother would ask about a separate find. Instantly, the Boy would respond, the knowledge ingrained into the recesses of his memory.

"It's gills don't fork. And we can see if it glows in the dark back home!" He loved taking freshly picked mushrooms into his bedroom closet after a foray. He always hoped some would start to fluoresce, even though that would mean he would have to throw them away. The mysticism of their glowingness seemed so intriguing. Only once had it ever happened - a Jack O'Lantern mushroom disguised as an old, wisened late-season Chanterelle. It filled his entire closet with bright blue-green fluorescence and seemed to laugh in a slow, baritone haunted-house like manner that both terrified and delighted the Boy. Caught up in this memory, the Boy suddenly tripped over a fallen branch, landing face first in a soft patch of freshly decomposed elm leaf at the base of a colossal old growth fir. Clearing the detritus from his eyelids, he gasped.

"Mom! I found one!" exclaimed the Boy. A few paces ahead, tucked under a fern, the golden gem of the forest glistened a sunset yellow. Clambering to his feet, the Boy leapt over a pile of decaying branches and ducked beneath a bundle of super-saturated moss, careful to dodge the prying thorns of a stray blackberry vine. Kneeling before the mushroom, the Boy caressed the underside of its ridged cap as he deftly sliced its stipe with his mushroom knife in one fell swoop. Turning the fruit over in his hand, he admired its smooth, impossibly golden cap that hung lazily at the ends in great curled edges. Bringing the thing to his nostrils, he inhaled deeply. The dank, citrus odor penetrated every cell of his being, as he suddenly found himself launched beneath the soil once again

~~~

"She worked hard to make that!" bellowed the voice. All around the Boy, surrounding him in a vast net of fibers of various calibers and colors, were the roots of the great and ancient Douglas Fir, their tips vibrating and hissing at him.

"I... I know," whispered the Boy, a bit shakily.

"I have known Her many generations before your time, Boy! She has given me so much! And I, I have given her my gifts in return. What have you given me - her - *us,* to be able to take so freely the fruits of our love?" echoed the roots, decidedly agitated, but testing. The Boy blinked. Sudden guilt and unsureness entwined his mind, reluctance replacing confidence. Silence was not the answer at this moment, and the Boy knew this. How to respond to such a noble Fir and its Chanterelle mistress? The Wolf nudged the Boy in the ribs.

"Better say somethin' kid, or we might be stuck down here awhile," it suggested through its gritted teeth. The Boy swallowed, held his breath, and exhaled slowly.

"I... I give you a promise," started the Boy. The roots shifted in impatient silence. "I will tell the world of your life - of your love, your needs, your gifts, and of your friend, the Chanterelle. I will protect you as best I can. I will live my life like the Fir and the Chanterelle when it comes to making friends, to taking care of each other. Especially when two beings are so seemingly different, but so similarly needing," said the Boy, his
~~~

heart in his throat. A blink. A breath. The earth around the Boy and Wolf erupted. Darkened, battered roots and bright frenetic mycelium raced around each other in a chaotic lovers embrace, catching the Boy and Wolf in their grasp, launching them upward through the soil, through the duff, and back onto the forest floor in a great explosion of leaf and dirt and bark and mist.

~~~

Opening his eyes, the Boy lay with his arms outstretched, supported by the softest of baby ferns, legs cushioned by heaps of foam-like sprigs of moss. His Mother hovered above him, slowly shaking her head from side to side, a look of resigned disbelief worn on her sleeve.

"Well, well. Look at you," she smiled.

"Did the Fir and Chanterelle accept my offer?" the Boy asked, eyes wet with tears and hope.

"Kid, sit up and look!" howled the Wolf. As he rose, the Boy smelled the incredible richness on the afternoon forest breeze - that slight lemon-scented, earthen odor he so adored. Around him, arranged in a massive circle, were hundreds upon hundreds of bunched yellow chanterelle caps - the golden treasure of the woods. His Mother's mouth gaped.

"Never in my life have I *ever* seen so many!" she gasped, "How did you find this?" A warm, hot tear of knowing and love fell down the Boys cheek.

"I made a promise," he whispered.
~~~

The School

A heavy knock at the bedroom door.

"Wake up in there! I have to drop you off early so I can get to work!" stormed the muffled voice. He opened his eyes and watched her shadow retreat from the artificial light below the off-kilter door frame. The sun had not yet risen but he could not tell, for the brackish yellow haze of city lights perpetually crept into his room, eroding time and sucking away any semblance of a peaceful night's rest. Glancing over to where his old bedroom's window should have been - had been - his gaze was met by a completely blank, yellowing wall. Had the painfully fluorescent lights in his room been on, he would have noted the faint brownish streak running from the ceiling through the beige wallpaper - likely from a shoddy roof, or a loose hot water pipe, or maybe just an ancient skid-mark from the room itself. The lingering odor of sweaty underwear with a hint of cheap lemon-accented air freshener would suggest the later.

The Boy's eyes adjusted to the dark as he sat up in his creaky single bed frame, mattress coils protesting every subtle movement with dramatic moans. He took in the tiny apartment bedroom in a single frame: one small rectangular window high above his bed, three blank walls, a hollow faux-wood door, an empty closet, and most distressing of all, no toy chest. A box of broken crayons and a rusted slinky lay haphazardly in the corner, but these things hardly counted to him. He missed his Whale, his Otter, his Wolf, his Shark, even Fox. He wondered if they had somehow escaped the night of the great Fire. Wolf and Otter would have been the most likely of the bunch - Whale was sort of a lost cause in that respect, though - hopeless tiny flippers, and significantly top-heavy. He imagined his crew forming a rope of knotted bedsheets and flinging one end out of the second story window, tying the other to the Boy's bedpost, shimmying down prison-style to freedom. Someone would have to have helped Shark - the Boy very much doubted it could have made its way down clutching the rope with its teeth, as that would have certainly have been the end of their escape efforts.

"Hey!" came the pounding at his door. "Get out here! Now!" His Mother had not been in the best of moods since their move into the city's apartment complex. Neither had the Boy, for that matter. Sulking through the mold-tinged hallway, the Boy yawned his frustrations, his anxieties, his exhaustions, and his remorse into the stagnant air. He wore the only armor he could don to prevent his stress-induced retching in that very moment -

the subtle hint of the breakfast his Mother had made, wafting in from the hallway, waiting for him in the tiny kitchen. He sauntered over the creaking floorboards and emerged weary-eyed at the table.

Sitting over an ancient folding table with uneven legs that bobbled back and forth, the Boy poked at his lukewarm pile of gelatinous plain oatmeal with a cracked spoon. His first breakfast without sunlight, his mind unfortunately reminded him. Glancing through the living room window - slightly larger than his bedroom's - he frowned at the gray stagnant scene of miserable steel and glass and concrete leviathans that obscured most the view of any sun, or moon, or star, or even sky for that matter. A taxi horn squealed excessively longer than it should have. A police siren screamed into the distance. The steady roar of traffic coming and going over the highway bridge not too far from their complex exhaled a disgusting moan. A motorcycle revving up. A car alarm. A barking dog. The cacophony was mind-numbing and depressing for the Boy. He closed his eyes and imagined the morning sounds from the forest: the breeze through the fir needles, the musings and chirpings of jays and ravens out hunting for breakfast on the forest edge. The sound of his Father turning the newspaper and scratching his beard in consternation. His Mother humming along to an old jazz tune while slicing an apple. And, on some days - if the wind carried right - the distant crash of high-tide waves upon the rocky seashore down the hillside.

"You need to eat this," she said flatly. "There's not much for lunch today. I'm sorry," his Mother stated, plainly and gloomy. "I'm going to get groceries after my second shift tonight. I'll pick you up before it starts, okay?" she announced. No mushroom foraging today, the Boy realized.

"Sure," he mumbled, coldly and bland. He ate the cooled stale oatmeal, and stared out the window.

"Are you excited about today?" she asked, mild enthusiasm lacing her sleep-deprived speech. The Boy did not reply. The idea of 'school' had always meant lessons with his Mother in the forest. Of course he had learned to read and write, and his math skills came naturally, but it was the lessons of ecology and stewardship and exploration that meant the most to him. Going to *a school* was an abstract thing in his mind: kids sitting in rows in a single room, inside and not out, with an adult at the front dictating a lesson - a bland one at that. Repetition, memorization, test-taking - things he was certainly not accustomed nor attuned to. Concepts he very much would like to avoid, if possible.

"You're *going* to make friends - it's *going* to be good for you," his Mother said, poking him playfully on the shoulder. Deep inside the fibers of her heart, despite her own personal anguish, she really did want the Boy to have a go at this new life.

"I *had* friends back home. I miss *those* friends," replied the Boy, speaking into his empty bowl. His Mother sighed.

"I'm talking about *human* friends. You had one - maybe two - real, flesh-and-bone, human friends back there. Your toys do *not* count as friends either. And by the way - this is 'home' now," she said with motherly finality as she hurriedly cleared the clunky table and prepared her apron for her first shift. Waitressing at the greasy spoon grill and dive on the city outskirts, near the highway truck-stop was the last place she wanted to be - other than homeless, which was the very real, and very possible alternative.

"When are we going to see Dad?" asked the Boy. His flat affect and dreary eyes made him seem ten years older in that gray morning light. His Mother abruptly stopped smoothing out the stray hairs springing out from behind her ears and looked at the Boy as if he was a mile away. She held her breath.

"I'll take you tomorrow. After school," she replied, head slowly falling forward to examine the new shoes she had purchased from the thrift store yesterday. The sole was coming loose from the side of the left shoe already, despite several sloppy super glue applications.

~~~

A light rain had begun to fall, and the silver sun had disappeared behind the scattered steel stalagmites of rectangular monstrosities surrounding him. The Boy realized he had yet to actually see the sun since their move to the city, as the rainy season's clouds seemed fixated on their mission to keep him in a perpetual state of gloom. Dressed in one of his only two outfits provided to him by the thrift store, he walked down the city sidewalk with his Mother. The sweater he had donned was particularly warm and had a funny zigzagging swath of purple and green running across the front and back. His khaki pants were a little too baggy, but that was the 'style' his Mother had explained. He found himself daydreaming about the previous owner of the clothes - who was that boy? Did he live in the city with his family? Did he like it here? Did he ever wear other boy's clothes, too?
~~~

"You'll have to shimmy the door handle, it's stuck again," his Mother interrupted. The Boy walked to the passenger side of their old red station-wagon and touched the rusty door handle, suddenly paralyzed as his mind transported him back into the night of the Fire…

~~~

Circling over the car, the Boy watched as his family emerged from the creek and sauntered down a forest access road to a small clearing where their car was parked. Allowing itself to float down from the treetops, the Boy's memory replayed an image of himself tugging and beating on the back hatch until it suddenly flung open, sending him spiraling to the ash-laden ground. The back seats were quickly pushed down to make room for his Mother to position his badly burned and semi-conscious Father down onto his back. Inside the car, he relived the sound of the engine protesting ignition several times, his Mother cursing and crying with every frantic turn of the key. The hiss and puff and grumble of the old six-cylinder machine kicked into gear, smoke pouring in around the tiny vehicle - part exhaust, part apocalypse. He reimagined the jostling of his body on their way down the washer-board dirt road, his Father moaning with ever bump and grind. Away they went - away from the Fire, away from everything they had known. Their station wagon had been their escape pod that terrible evening, and was essentially the only major item from their prior lives that was saved.

~~~

"It's stuck," the Boy replied, mind replanted into the present. The handle was especially stubborn today.
"Let me try," his Mother said, her words palpable with impatience and frustration. "Okay. Fine. It's broken or something. You'll have to get in the backseat and crawl over to the front, I guess," she resigned. Two hard starts and a moment of panic later, and the station wagon clunked and clicked and clacked down the city side road adjacent to their apartment complex, heading off toward its first destination that morning - the Boy's new school.

~~~
~~~

Sweating palms, flushed cheeks, leaping heartbeats, slight nausea. He had only felt this way on exactly three other prior occasions. Once, when he had to wait with his pet labrador at the veterinarian while the technicians prepped several vaccinations. A second, when his Father had driven him into the town clinic for his *own* immunizations. And finally, when his family had escaped down the forest road blanketed in thick smoke, leaving their home and all of his stuffed animals behind to burn. Today was to be the fourth time.

They walked down the blindingly white, overly waxed main hallway together, hand-in-hand, the Boy gripping his Mother's palm intensely with white-knuckled apprehension. Sensing his reluctance, she squeezed back in confident reassurance. His shoes squeaked with every step, and he imagined every kid in every classroom suddenly gawking and grinning at him through the brick walls as he made his way toward the Principal's office. Blue-white fluorescent lights hummed and ticked above, and Fire-truck red, metallic lockers reflected his distorted, faceless reflection back at him, ambivalent and disinterested to his presence. Stumbling through the half-opened hazy-glazed glass door, the Boy came to halt.

"You must be our new student," chirped the Principal's Secretary. Purple lipstick, excessive eyeshadow and rosy foundation. Oversized glasses and a plastic pearl necklace. She typed furiously at a keyboard, making quick strange glances up at his Mother between sentences. Beyond her stood a set of heavy-looking french-doors of darkly varnished cedar. The Boy envisioned the Secretary as some sort of benevolent clown guarding the entrance to the circus, or of a troll protecting a treasure-laden cave, or perhaps a witch occupying a haunted house. Either way, he was certain he did not want to enter through those particular doors anytime soon.

"Let me introduce you to the Principal," the Secretary smacked. Prying her fingers from the keys, she scurried to the massive doors and carefully swung them outward, revealing a dark room smelling faintly of mildew and leather. At the end of the squat room sat a curious man behind a meticulously carved mahogany desk. Bald head, well-groomed black curly beard, dark purple business suit, pointy red pleather shoes. The desk was littered with small idols and statues and miniaturizations of various deities and creatures. The Boy noticed several similar figures clustered together, one made of jade another of copper or brass, identical in their rotund bellies and massive grins as they sat with palms raised in meditation. A small totem pole of intricately carved menacing faces with birds' beaks. A minotaur juxtaposed to a unicorn. A plastic leprechaun probably from a cereal box or fast-food restaurant was positioned squatting over a small stone statue of a bearded man wearing a bedsheet, a halo over his head. A blue-skinned, four armed humanoid sat cross-legged wearing golden pants. Tiny plastic soldiers with ridiculously dramatized biceps and monstrous cannons and launchers stood frozen with cartoonish grimaces and scowls wiped across their faces. The Boy estimated that there were perhaps one hundred characters scattered across the great desk. A deep exhale from the man that sat opposite him broke his trance.

Slowly raising his gaze to meet the Principal's, the Boy nearly gasped. A partially closed window had cast a shadow across the bearded man's face, allowing only the top of his face to be seen. The Principal was staring back, his eyes focused and intent on the Boy. Suddenly, the eyes began to slowly rotate up and outward, revealing a ghost white nothingness that sparkled blindingly bright in the afternoon light. Sensing the Boy's momentary fright and convulsion, the Principal, barely concealing his knowing smirk, silently passed an open palm across his forehead, hovering over his brow. With a quick snap of his fingers, he revealed his full face from the shadows and chuckled softly. Two pupils gleamed down at the fear-stricken Boy. No ghost eyeballs. The Boy swallowed hard - had he imagined it all?

"Welcome!" the man began, his pointed beard stabbing through the air as he spoke. "My sincerest pleasure to meet you two. I know you've endured much grief and loss, and I want to assure you, ma'am, that your son will find our school to be like a new home for him," purred the Principal, extending his well-manicured hand out towards to Boy's Mother. Hesitantly, she stepped forward.

"Thank you. I hope for that, as well," came her soft reply.

"This is *not* home," murmured the Boy. Although he was fixated on a small replica of a long-necked brontosaurus facing off against a tyrannosaurus-like creature, the grinding of his teeth suggested his thoughts were elsewhere. He felt a firm hand on his shoulder and a powerful, commanding squeeze.

"Don't do this, not here!" said the silent squeeze. The room was stale and quiet for a moment, before the Principal cleared his throat.

"I know how much things have changed for you, son. For that, I am truly sorry, and I know this place must seem *very* different." Standing to face the open window behind him, the man seemed to fixate on the passing taxi cabs and rain-coat enshrouded passerbys, rushing this way and that. "But I believe you will come to really love it here, if you give it a chance," smiled the Principal, turning to face his newest pupil. Searching his face, the Boy surprisingly saw sincerity and tenderness broadcast across the man's face. Still, the Boy bit his lip and doubled down.

"How can this be a home or even a place to learn if there aren't any trees? What about the breeze? Where are the snails? There are no mushrooms, no crows, no bubbling creeks or scaly fish, no blackberries to pluck, no wood to collect, no seeds to plant, no weeds to pick, no rain to wipe away from your face, no sunbeams radiating through the pine needles?" protested the Boy, his eyes glistening with passion and fear and forlorn memories. His Mother, now close to running late to her first shift today, clearly had no time for the Boy's philosophy on education, and, grabbing him by the armpits, proceeded to reel him inward an inch from her fire poker face.

"Listen. I know this is tough, but you need to understand," she started.

"No!" the Boy snapped, fighting against her impossible strength. The two grunted and hissed and stamped as the Principal warily looked on. A deep exaggerated sigh echoed through the room.

"Ma'am," interrupted the Principal, "May I share a story? I promise to be quick. I think it will resonate with your son quite well." Both Boy and his Mother stared at the man and said nothing. In their hearts and minds, they both desperately desired to return to their forest home and resume life the way it had been. Both were also coming to understand that that was simply never going to happen anytime soon. Cracking his knuckles, the Principal beckoned his two guests to sit with him on a large rug laid out in the corner of his office, small pillows dotting its surface. Several silent moments passed before he began.

~~~

"When I was your age, I woke up before the sunrise every morning to help my Father milk the goats. Have you ever milked a goat?" the Principal asked, raising an eyebrow to the Boy. Both were squatting cross-legged on a thick multi-colored rug that was simultaneously soft and scratchy. The Boy shook his head.

"Oh, it's really quite satisfying!" clapped the Principal, "and the goats are quite thankful! One moment you are yawning and barely able to
~~~

open your eyes, the next, a happy goat is trotting up to you, asking for a hand in relieving the swelling in its udder," he mimed, squirting invisible nipples out in front of him. "Such a remarkably rapid relationship you build with those animals! Anyhow, just after finishing with the goats, my Mother would call for my assistance in collecting eggs from the coop and putting out fresh feed and water for the hens. Then it was off to help repair some barbed wire in the perimeter fence with my brother, all before the sun had risen. The day would go on and on like this until sunset, when my family would all convene for a massive dinner together under the altar of exhaustion and hard work." The Principal was staring at a figurine of an angel alongside a caricature of a cartoon devil. His mind had clearly transported backward several decades in time.

"I learned so many valuable lessons back then," the older man signed. "I'm sure you have your own favorite stories of the forest? A daily routine?" he asked.

The Boy held his breath and nodded, feeling the memory strings tug at his synapses from every direction and dimension. He refused to give in and swallowed the urge to share.

"Yes." whispered the Boy - it was all he could manage.

"Well, like you, my life drastically changed, too. One summer, the drought was so bad, that all of our crops died. Our animals became ill. We spent our last dollars caring for them. And then, one evening around a very meager supper, my Pop, he sat down and simply said, 'We have to sell the farm.' And that was that. The next morning, my Mom, she packed up our van, and we moved to this city. I was devastated. No goats. No fresh apples to pick or hop cones to harvest or fences to mend. My parents sent me to school - not unlike this one. You see, I was homeschooled, too, up until we sold the farm. At first it was difficult to adjust, but I found that kids in the city could be just as fun as kids in the country - they just had different games to learn, different things to like, different jokes to tell. I learned to love the change, to relish in adaptation, to grow from the differences I had with them. Change is scary - I know that. I can feel how scared you must be of everything changing around you so quickly. But I want you to know, that if you are strong, and smart - which, if you were raised like me, I know you are - you are simply going to love this change. But it will take time." he finished.

The Boy was listening. He had never milked a goat, but he understood that it must have been as satisfying as feeding hay to the rabbits in their hutch, or pulling out the first bright red radish of the season from their garden. He had never mended a fence, but he imagined it similar to unclogging a gutter or cleaning out the cistern - not pleasant, but satisfying in its completion. He knew he was strong. He knew he was smart. He exhaled, lifting his heavy head to nod in agreement with the man, his Principal.

"There will be hard moments, but many more good ones to outnumber them, you see. If you are having a hard time here at school and can't seem to shake it, come talk with me. You have an 'all access pass,' - I'll let the Secretary know," the Principal said with a wink. The Boy decided he liked this man, even with his strange pointy shoes and bizarre collection of creatures erratically arrayed on his desk. He and his Mother shook hands with the Principal and walked back out to the hallway. The Secretary followed, humming a funny tune that suggested both impatience and aloofness. His Mother knelt by the Boy's side, a thin smile creeping across her cracked morning lips.

"I'll pick you up later this afternoon - around 4 o'clock. There's an after-school program where you can meet more kids, play games, and do schoolwork - things like that," she said quickly. The Boy's eyes suddenly widened with the stark realization that he would be spending most of the day in this foreign land, this school.

"Be out front right at four, because I've got to make it to my second shift by five and traffic is supposed to be bad at that time, or so they say," his Mother explained. With that, she hugged his rigged body until he placed his surrendering arms around her torso. With that, she rose and hustled through the entry doors out into the morning mist. She was gone. Slowly pivoting in place, the Boy turned to face the Secretary.

"Well wasn't that sweet!" she said through strangely pursed lips. "I bet you'd like to meet your classmates, wouldn't you? Follow me - Room 103 on the right," she snapped, quickly striding down the linoleum with a click and clack of every heel. "All of your classes will be in here. It's almost time to switch periods, so wait for the bell, and we will go in and introduce you - won't that be special!" she clucked.

~~~

A skull-splitting, exaggeratedly drawn out steel-on-steel ringing howled down the hallway, leaving the Boy's eardrums painfully vibrating for several seconds after the murderous hammer ceased to beat. A muffled slamming of heavy paper books and a scurry of a million frantic feet
~~~

scuffing against freshly waxed floors erupted from all sides. Suddenly, six bright yellow doors burst open with children of all ages pouring out into the hallway in an incomprehensible mob of laughter and strange sounds bites that whizzed all around the Boy.

"I think your brother likes my sister," whispered an older student to another, through concealed giggles.

"I like can't believe she, like, didn't even notice that, like, piece of gum, like, totally stuck to her butt!" announced another shrill voice, loudly enough for most to hear.

"I'll trade you PB&J for that salami and cheese thing your mom always makes," offered another.

"Its my turn to sleep over at your house this weekend. I want to play that video game you've got," declared a particularly authoritarian one. The Boy imagined he might as well be a ghost in this foreign land, with the indigenous population waltzing right past him, talking in unknown languages, dressed in bizarre clothes, practicing rituals and cultural normalcy that were totally impossible for him to understand. Except this was just a regular school in a regular city at a regular time. The Boy knew then - he was truly an outsider.

"Alrighty, come with me, mister," squealed the Secretary. Children were funneling back into their respective classrooms and some turned a curious eye to the Boy, examining him from nose to toes. His heart began to race. In through the door that stated '103' in large block numbers, he slinked against the wall behind the Secretary as his eyes rapidly scanned the room and the thirty odd faces of children staring back. They were his age, sure enough, and all one by one, were gazing at him and waiting, some smirking, some giggling, some with a totally flat affect.

"Hello students!" began the Secretary, "This is your new classmate." Turning to introduce the Boy, the stifling silence was pummeled by the terrifying rapid-fire percussion of the school bell, signaling that another period had begun. Tripping backwards over his feet, the Boy slid into the chalkboard in a soft explosion of white dust as erasers tumbled to the ground. The class laughed as a singular organism, sending the Boy's already maximal embarrassment to unparalleled levels. Helping him to his feet, the Secretary finished his introduction and demanded that the class say greet him in sarcastic unison, appeasing her standards of supreme cheesiness and cookie-cutter platitudes.

"Now, please be friendly to our new student - he has been through quite a bit and this is his first time in a *real* school." She finished, reveling at the word 'real.' In his mind, the Boy saw himself standing tall, deriding this false school, announcing that he was returning to the beauty of his forest classroom, and the *real* world that had surrounded him there. Taking a deep breath, all he could manage was a sad, dusty cough and a resigned sigh.

"Right!" came a new voice. "Well, we are happy to have you join us - take a seat right over there and you'll find your literature book under your desk. We are on the second chapter," his Teacher announced. She was a cheery woman with tomato cheeks, thick black glasses that magnified her cartoonish eyeballs, and a lengthy brown skirt that constantly swirled around her in amorphous shapes as she floated between the aisles of students.

"Psst, hey, kid!" hissed a student behind the Boy. "You've never been to a school, huh? Do you even know English?" Snickers broke out around them. "And why is your hair so long? Like, are you a boy or girl?" More stifled laughter. The Boy was equally exhausted and mortified and simply stared at his closed literature book. The Teacher called on a student to begin reading the chapter aloud.

"A-and, th-th-then Ja-ja-James s-s-said..." stammered a child from across the room struggling at every instance to recite the words, but not hesitating a bit. Several antagonizing minutes later, he had finished the paragraph, incurring no chastising or bitter laughter from any of his comrades.

"That's very good. Now would our new student like to try reading the next paragraph?" the Teacher's question burst through his bubble of denial and caught him completely off guard. He looked up at the woman, his eyes lost in space and time. Seeing his abysmally distressed look, she simply drifted over, opened his book up to the exact page, and pointed to the paragraph with a tap of her finger. Swirling her dress, she squatted next to him and simply smiled, an effortless maneuver meant to provide comfort and confidence to the otherwise hopeless Boy. He bore down upon the words.

"I've sailed all the five seas. From the land of Bora Bora to the icy shores of Tripoli. Commodore Centipede, they used to call me," The Boy began. He raced through the first three paragraphs before the Teacher could gather his attention and solicit his pause.

"Wonderful, fantastic pronunciation. I see you're no stranger to a good book. Let's have another student pick up from there," she segued. The Boy caught a smirk and nod from her, not unlike what his Mother would signal when he was exceeding at a task she had challenged him with. He felt slightly proud in that moment, the singular light in what was otherwise the darkest of days.

"Hey. Hey new kid!" came the voice behind him again. "So you're a nerd or something, huh?" it chided. "I could tell by that sweater. Looks like the sweater I donated last year to the thrift store."

~~~

Lunchtime. The Boy was assigned to a table of random classmates, but no one really wanted to ask him any questions - instead, they were caught up in a card game the Boy did not understand. When it was discovered that the Boy had never heard of the game, all forms of communication were cut off. He ate his sandwich and carrots in silence, wishing he were anywhere else but there. Gathering rotten cedar in a downpour would have been more enjoyable he decided.

The shriek of the bell, another miserable sixty minutes of sitting at a desk, forced into scribbling through endless simple math problems. As the sun moved to the other side of the sky, a final series of bells rang out, and students departed in hordes - some to buses, some to walk home, others to their awaiting families in minivans and sedans. The Boy sat. He did not know which bell was his, nor did he know what happened at 'after-school,' as his Mother had called it. He cautiously looked around the nearly empty classroom to find five or six other kids muling about in their backpacks, shuffling books in and out of their desks, staring out the window at the rain that was falling diagonally.

"Alright after-schoolers," started his Teacher, "Leave your things here and we'll all head over to the gym for the next hour." Falling into line, he marched behind the other students, shoe-gazing the entire way to the end of the school's single hallway. The Boy had never seen anything like the school's gymnasium before. Buffed and waxed wooden floorboards ran seamlessly together, with stacks of stairs on wheels flanking the main central court, as monstrous hanging cages of fluorescent lights dangled and hummed above. Kids of all ages ran everywhere. Some shot basketballs in a strange line, some others mingled in a circle, dribbling a soccer ball back and forth, with the youngest group playing what appeared to be a game of freeze tag. The Boy swallowed his anxieties and steeled himself to try his best - he loved games, and figured he had his best chance of making
~~~

friends here and now. As he approached the gaggle around the basketball hoop, an errant soccer ball thwacked him in the side of the head.

"Ha! Sorry kid! I said 'heads up' though!" shouted the owner of the stray shot. The Boy felt tears building. He joined the back of the basketball game, sniffling away his embarrassment.

"May I join?" he whispered to the child in the back of the line.

"Hey, uh, sure - it's a new game anyway," replied a boy his age. "Let's do something longer than the word 'Horse' though," he suggested to the rest of the crew.

"How about 'Idiot?'" another boy joked, followed by a chorus of laughter.

"That's the same number of letters as horse," stated the Boy, looking at no one in particular. He had never played Horse, but he did know how to count.

"Yeah, wow. Aren't you a genius," responded the other. "What do you suggest then?"

"How about... 'Giraffe?'" offered the Boy. He imagined a giraffe playing basketball and decided it would likely be just as awkward as he imagined. Certainly no worse than he had been that day, though.

"Okay, fine, let's start," announced another player. The game began with the Boy in the back. He quickly realized he had never shot a basketball before, and as he watched the technique of the other kids, he desperately wanted to quit. The girl in front of him sank her shot on the first try, as another child rebounded the ball and bounce-passed it over to the Boy, who surprised himself by catching it with both hands and not his face.

"C'mon, kid, shoot!" stammered the impatient player behind him. The Boy cocked his arms behind his head and launched the basketball like a catapult. Flying over the transparent backboard and into the aluminum bleachers behind, the cacophonous crash echoed around the gym. The game abruptly stopped as several kids began laughing.

"Woah, you are worse than my sister!" ribbed one of the players. "Better go get that ball before you get the first 'G!'" The Boy scampered over the bleachers and found his basketball wedged between the footrest and lower bench. By the time he pried it out and returned to the court, he discovered that he was, in fact, the proud owner of the letter 'G' - the boy behind him had made a basket after just two attempts. As the game progressed, the Boy was awarded an 'I,' 'R,' 'A,' and an 'F' before most other players had their 'G.' He started to believe that giraffes were, in fact, probably terrible at basketball, their gangly legs attempting to dribble and shoot were likely no better than his own. Another wild shot later, and the Boy was declared out.

"Don't I have another 'F?'" protested the Boy.

"What? No! G-I-R-A-F-E. One F. You're on 'E' - so you're out, new guy!" replied the previous game's winner. There was no argument by the other players on how giraffe was spelled, nor was there any rebuttal from the Boy, who knew otherwise - he had had enough. Sauntering away in defeat, he found himself behind the aluminum bleachers, out of sight of everyone in the gym. Slowly lowering slinking to the ground, he hugged his knees and began to silently cry.

~~~

Between stifled sobs, the Boy quietly spoke to the musty air around him.

"Where am I?" he pleaded. No answer.

"Where am I?" he whimpered again. Muffled, sporadic laughter of other children panged into his soul.

"Where am I?" he spoke into his palms, resigned to the terror of silence.

"You're under the bleachers! And you're right in the path of my *project*," chirped a slightly annoyed voice. The Boy cracked his eyes. A shadowy figure squatted several yards away and was beginning to slowly creep toward him.

"Your... project?" The Boy repeated, wiping tears and snot into the cuff of his donated sweater.

"Yeah. Ants!" announced the voice - a softer, slightly squeaky voice - a girl. "I'm studying ant behavior, actually. I'm a scientist," she declared matter-of-factly, her face emerging from the shadows of the bleachers. Her silky black hair was tied into a messy ponytail and held together with several hair clips shaped like butterflies. Her eyes were wide with excitement and pride, the whites of her sclera highlighting the contrast of her dark brown irises. Her skin was darker than most of the other kids in the school, thought the Boy. Sort of olive-toned, a soft-brown, reminiscent of the cap of a porcini mushroom, he imagined.

"What sort of behavior are the ants… doing?" inquired the Boy. For once, he actually found himself interested in something inside this school.
~~~

"Well, let me tell you," began the Girl holding up her palms in exaggerated fashion. "These small black ants - 'sugar ants' my Mom calls them - live in big colonies outside. They all go out looking for food, and not just sugar, as you might think," she explained. The Boy knew all about sugar ants, but he liked the way the Girl dramatically explained the creatures to him, her arms and legs scurrying around like a small insect. The Boy began to fantasize as she spoke, and suddenly found himself shrunk down to ant-size, following her in single-file as she spoke. His lopsided antennae dangling in front of his ant-face as he stepped in time to each of her six legs.

"So I followed them to this stack of chewed bubble gum here under the bleachers," continued the pony-tailed mushroom-skinned ant-Girl, oblivious to their transformation, "and then I conduct the experiment! I either block their way with a couple big books, or I clean up the gum and see what happens. And you know what? They are so smart!" At that moment, the Boy's dreamscape was filled with a massive shadow, as a meteor-like math textbook fell from the sky and thudded into the earth with the density of a hundred skyscrapers - an impenetrable mountain range.

"If they get blocked by something - like this book - they go into a frenzy at first," the Girl explained, as sugar ants burst into a chaotic scramble all around them. Antenna and legs brushing up against his own, monstrous pincers clicking back and forth, six-eyed, tear-dropped heads full of tiny hairs examining him briefly but thoroughly.

"Then, someone finds a way around, or over, or through! And I think they tell everyone!" the ant-Girl exclaimed. "But ants can't talk or anything. I think they might do it with smells, like a dog at the dog park, except I can't smell anything when I check," she hypothesized - she was sniffing several close-by ant rear-ends to the dismay and annoyance of the insects around her. From his periphery, the ant-Boy observed as a distant rogue scout paraded around the side of the massive book, out of sight for a few moments, only to return to the group at a furious pace. Antennae frantically entangled with other antennae as the message was passed at an exponential rate. More ants joined as the single-file line reformed. Marching around the side of the humongous book, the ant-Boy swore he detected a faint whiff of something - something like dirty socks and cinnamon.
Just then, the Girl poked the Boy's shoulder with a very human finger.

"Hey, you okay? You were gawking pretty intently at that book on the ground there," she said, through a very human mouth without pincers or antennae. "So did you hear what I said?" she asked, testing the Boy.

"Yeah. A smell. To communicate. I think you're right. And I think I smelled it. Dirty socks and cinnamon," The Boy nonchalantly announced. He was not afraid if this Girl judged him, he was finally able to act more like himself in her presence. As the Girl began to giggle at his ridiculous statement, the Boy was surprised to hear his own chuckling along with hers. Sitting under the bleachers, imagining himself as an ant, sending out scented signals of dirty socks and cinnamon - the hilarity of the situation ignited the Boy's spirit and he began to laugh hysterically. How quickly his day had changed. As the two caught their breaths, the Boy noticed that the Girl was massaging her chin quizzically, caught into a deeper though.

"I think you are on to something. We should try to replicate that smell and see if the ants will follow it!" she suggested, to the shock of the Boy. Was she serious? She was looking at him wide-eyed, eager for a response. He nodded quickly, unsure of what else to do.

"Good! Great!" she clapped, "Next time then. I'll bring the dirty socks, I have lots of those. You want to bring some cinnamon-smelling thing?" She was incredibly excited by the idea and smiled with a huge grin at the Boy.

"Sure, meet... *here*?" he asked, undecided if his confusion was due to her desire to actually attempt such a silly experiment, or if it was her uniquely charming spirit and unbridled friendliness that had his heart singing. She beamed at the Boy. A bell shrieked in the distance.

"Yup! Okay! Its four o'clock - time to go! My family is going camping this weekend. I'm hoping to see more ants in the wild! See ya later! Don't forget the cinnamon!" she said, waving to him as she sprinted out from behind the bleachers, losing a butterfly clip in the process. The Boy picked it up and placed it in his pocket. He decided that maybe he could try one more day of this school.

The Fox

Through yellow sunfire eyes, the Fox squinted and scrutinized the four upside down cards, wrinkling his trickster snout into a sly upturned grin. The back of the cards was coated in a reflective coat of magnificent royal blue that seemed to glow in the haze that blanketed the small table on which the two players floated alongside.

"You can look at two cards, and *only* two cards, remember," said the Boy, keen to observe the Fox for any foul-play. It wouldn't be the first, second, or fifth time the Boy would have caught ol' Foxy at his sly games within games again.

"I know, I know," smirked the Fox, "What do you call this game again? 'Dumb?' 'Slow?' 'Boring?'"

"It's called 'Golf,'" sighed the Boy, "some people call it 'Stupid,' "but I don't like that name. I like... 'Member?,' like 'Remember,' but the name is a question, so you have to say it like that, get it?" Cocking a single wiry orange eyebrow up conspicuously, the Fox slowly rolled his head back and yawned.

"You're a strange fellow," said the Fox, picking up the first two cards in front of him and placing them back down without a show in the world as to what they might represent. "But I like you," he smiled. Likely satisfied at his draw of cards rather than his reflection on their friendship, thought the Boy. Softly hued pink and yellow translucent butterflies spun and tumbled drunkenly around their heads. The small circular table tilted this way or that depending on how one placed weight on a certain edge - a confusing phenomenon to the Boy, as the table seemed to float on nothing but mist and a dream. The butterflies occasionally landed on table legs and chair backs, their beating wings creating miniature contrails in the thick haze. Continuing in silence, the two players studied the down-ward facing cards in front of them.

"So school's not your jam, eh?" started the Fox. Picking up from the deck, he lazily studied the card and changed it out for one of his face-down cards - a Queen of Clubs - a good move. Clacking softly in delight with himself, the Fox let his pointed ears shiver. Sinking into his seat, the Boy stared out into space while an errant butterfly landed on his shoulder, its purple eyes luminescing up at his own. As the table revolved slowly through the foggy blank soup, the Boy imagined himself in several locations: could this be some sort of strange eternal purgatory, or was he socked in atop a great mountainside? Perhaps it was simply some ephemeral moment in time and space where one might believe life to actually be one big dream. He decided he would never really know.

"I like *school*," the Boy sighed, "I don't like *the* school I'm at, though," he clarified. "I mean, reading is fine. Math is okay. But we aren't really learning the important things. We aren't spending time to understand how the world *really* works and lives and breaths. It's weird, I guess." He picked up a card - a Ten of Hearts - no good. Discarded. He continued his diatribe as the Fox took his turn.

"This school is mostly about teaching enough to do well on homework and quizzes, memorizing things one month, only to forget them for a new set of things the next month. I bet *no one* there knows how to start a fire, or tie a fisherman's knot, or identify a hedgehog mushroom, or thin a patch of baby beets." He drew an Ace of Spades - a low card - and replaced it with an eight of spades. The Fox grimaced - more likely at the discard than the Boy's description of things.

"The kids there? They just talk about video games or movies or things from TV. They don't seem to know anything important." The Boy was on a tirade, free-flowing his repressed thoughts from the day - thoughts he dare not share with his Mother, for her patience had worn thin. It felt good. It felt bad. He didn't know how it felt. The Fox let the Boy continue, more-so to keep his focus off the Fox's quick moves rather than out of consideration for his stress. Flipping a King of Diamonds on the discard pile, the Fox nodded towards the Boy, who seemed to be a world removed from their floating island of nowhereness.

"Why don't you pick up a card," whispered the Fox. The Boy realized that his reminiscing of school had led his memory astray, and he could no longer recall which of his four cards was which. He drew a Jack of Hearts - zero points. The Jack was the best card there was, so the worst he could do was replace it with another Jack from one of his four... and that was exactly what happened.

"Ho Ho! Not paying attention, are we? Not… 'membering,' eh? I'll be taking that!" announced the Fox, cackling with delight as he deftly snatched the Boy's discarded Jack for his own. As he replaced it for a Queen, the Fox reclined his rickety wooden chair back and kicked his back legs up onto the card table, sending a gaggle of butterflied into a chaotic flurry. He was surely in the lead at this point.

"So tell me," purred the Fox, "have you make any acquaintances? Any *human* acquaintances, I might add?" he asked, half sarcastically. The Boy noticed that the Fox's right paw was suspiciously close to one of his unturned cards, vibrating with anxiety - had Ol' Foxy forgotten what card lay there? The Boy covered his knowing grin with a palm.

"No. Well, yes, actually," started the Boy, drawing a Two of Spades and replacing it with a King - a good move. "The Principal of the school collects small strange statues and trinkets and idols - all sorts of things. Mermaids and angels and werewolves and gods. He told me a story of how he lived on a farm when he was my age, and I think he and I would have been friends back then." The Fox cocked his fury head to one side and shut his eyelids in pretend dreariness.

"You're not supposed to like the Principal, Boy. *No one* likes Principals." A pale orange butterfly flew onto the Fox's nose as he murmured, causing him to half-sneeze, half-convulse in a fit of ticklishness, Suddenly, all four of his unturned cards spun atop one another in disarray. In a fit of panic, the Fox frantically tried to position his cards as they had been, his rubbery black lips curled into a grotesque snarl of frustration. Catching his breath, the Fox smoothed down his wiry whiskers and quietly drew a card - a lame Seven of Hearts. Hurling it onto the discard, he huffed back into his chair, paws crossed tightly over his chest. The tides were changing, thought the Boy.

"Well, I also met a Girl under the bleachers," revealed the Boy through squeamish closed teeth. He knew how funny it sounded, but it was the truth.

"Now we're getting somewhere!" grinned the Fox, his pointed ears now standing at attention, his yellow eyes and sharp oval pupils yearning for further details. The Boy picked up another Jack, this time replacing it with a 10 of spades. The Fox barely noticed the switch.

"She's not like a lot of the other kids there. She's more like *us*, I guess," the Boy reflected.

"Heh. More like *you*, anyway," replied the Fox. "Me? I'm as cool as a cucumber, pal. You? You're just a pickle, buddy. A little on the fermented side, always a bit salty. You know what I mean, jelly bean?" he taunted. The Boy could have sworn the Fox had just peaked at another face-down card, but it happened too quickly, for his mind was caught up in a daydream - as an ant-Boy. The Fox had likely taken advantage of this pseudo-time-travel moment away from the game, if ever so briefly, drew, and discarded, his gaze still transfixed on the Boy.

"You'd like her Fox, I know you would. She sees the living world in detail. She seems to understand the bigger picture, much more than the other kids." An emerald green butterfly with purple pulsating wings sat atop the pickup deck - the Boy looked at it and smiled, letting it dawdle for the time being. "She's weird. She's friendly. She says she's a scientist, too." As he spoke, The Boy realized how much of an impression the Girl had made on him in such a brief instance together. The butterfly departed the table, flew a quick lap around the Boy's head and rose into the swirling mist.

"Sounds like you're on the verge of a friendship there, kiddo," suggested the Fox, drawing a card and interchanging it for a Five of Diamonds. The Boy was certain the Fox had replaced all four of his cards at this point and was ready to knock. "So you're ready to go back on Monday - to this school?" The Fox inquired, tendrils of fog pillowing his reclined chair, paws draped behind his neck. He was obviously confident in his hand, and equally confident that that Boy was still terrified of the new world he was forced into since the great Fire. Swallowing an impossible lump, the Boy sighed.

"I am. I mean, I want to," started the Boy, drawing an Ace. "I think I need to give it time. It needs to give me time." He realized he had forgotten the identity of his final unturned card. "We need to give each other time to appreciate what the other has to offer, I guess. The school and I, that is," he finished, not entirely sure who or what he was talking about now. Holding his breath, he swapped out the final mystery card for his Ace - a King - a massive stroke of luck! The Boy decided he might just do alright after all.

The Fox knocked.

The Boy nodded back.

The Fox smiled.

The Boy smiled in reply.

"Did you know I'm dead?" asked the Fox, matter-of-factly. The Boy had one last turn, but he was frozen in time and space, even if neither existed around him at the card table at this moment. He looked at the royal blue backs of his four unturned cards, and then at the Fox. He thought tears should have formed in the corners of his eyes by now, but he instead felt a blanket of calmness and warmth fall around his shoulders. Several of the butterflies now swarmed around their table as it stopped rotating and started to slowly drift upwards.

"I... I know," the Boy quietly replied, "and I'm sorry, Fox. I miss you. But it's good that you're still here, still with me... in this way. I'm not sure what exactly this *way* is, but I'm grateful," he finished. The Fox smiled and softly clacked his teeth.

"It's simple, son," began the Fox, "I'm dead and I'm not. I'm here and I'm there. I just… I am." Transfixed in each other's presence, the two players nodded in their mutual understanding of the way things were to be, had likely always been. The Boy felt his heart warm ten times over as the thinning fog around the table reciprocated back with pulses of sunrise red and sunset orange. Closing his eyes, the Boy imagined the crash of distant waves upon his favorite forested beach.

"Flip on three," announced the Fox, "One... Two... Three." The Fox had two Jacks and two Aces - a score of two. The Boy had two Aces and two Jacks - a score of two.

"Well how about that!" clapped the Fox, his whiskers shimmying back and forth. "A tie!"

"You and I always tie, Fox," reminded the Boy. "But I'll play you again. And again. Because I like you. And I like our time together. But you'll have to stop peeking at your cards one of these days," he ribbed with a wink. The Fox gave the Boy a sideways glance, his snout twisting into a maniacal knowing smirk. Their eyes locked into a well-meaning stare-down.

"I like you, too, Boy," said the Fox, unsure of just how much trickery the Boy had truly noticed.

A thousand butterflies flooded the table, landing on hands and paws and cards, making shuffling impossible. Both players lost their gaze on the other and erupted into full-throated, gasping bellows of laughter. Neither Fox nor Boy had felt this much joy in a great, long while.

The Art Therapist

"Wake up, you," whispered the tired and tattered voice. A drawn-out yawn as a gentle hand wearily floated toward his shoulder - it smelled faintly of ashtrays and spilled beer, despite the best efforts of the cheap hand soap. He was only slightly awake, in between worlds of dreams and reality, not exactly sure which was which in the present, yet he was likely more lucid than his Mother that morning. The Boy opened his eyes and looked up at her. Dark circles beneath her heavy eyelids, the Boy's Mother managed a dreary smile and blinked so slowly the Boy thought she might fall asleep sitting just like that at the edge of his bed. She looked gaunt and thin - although she had always been relatively thin, but also fit and toned by her day-to-day forest chores. Here, in this city, where she worked double-shifts almost daily with minimal, fragmented sleep in between, she seemed to be slowly dissolving.

"I... I made breakfast for us. Come. Eat," she said, sighing as she kissed his forehead, pulling off the covers. The Boy placed his feet on the cold, boring hardwood floor and glanced around his dull, empty, blank bedroom, void of color, of toys, of morning misty sunlight, of morning dew smell. Sulking into the kitchen behind his Mother, he never registered that it was the weekend. On the flimsy card table beneath a single, dimly lit dusty lightbulb sat a pair of chipped pale grey dinner plates with an unusual circular-shaped object in the center of each. At the center of the table stood a translucent sculpture of a miniature woman with some sort of brown viscous substance inside. The kitchen smelled faintly of burning and cardboard. The Boy clumsily sat down in a mismatched purple wooden chair, its seat too low for the card table. Picking up a bent fork, he poked at the spongy matter on his plate.

"What's this stuff?" he asked, probing its innards with a butterknife. Squishy, somewhat bready, with perfectly spaced squares pressed into the interior.

"It's a waffle. Sort of," his Mother replied, her back bent over the sink scrubbing a stubborn stain on her apron. "It's an 'Ego' - like a... like a space-waffle, I guess," she quipped, spinning to sit down across from him. "If I could afford to make *real* waffles for us I would, but this will have to do," she huffed, clutching the plastic idol of a woman, flipping open her scalp, tipping her upside down over the space-waffle. "The syrup isn't the same that we're used to either. And I'm not sure if there's actually any *real* syrup in there, so I guess it's sort of space-syrup. So there you go, a real space-breakfast. Welcome to the future, kiddo," his Mother said with a tired wink. He could tell she was trying to be funny, but the tone revealed hidden disappointment and longing for their typical weekend meals together.

"Thanks Mom." The Boy poured some space-syrup onto his space-Ego and dared a small bite. The incredible sugariness of the combination was overwhelming to his palate, and caused a reflexive cough and gag. The texture of the Ego definitely placed it into the space-food category. Is this what kids in the city ate every weekend, he wondered? He watched the syrup congeal into the square nooks of the Ego and imagined how happy the sugar ants at school would be to discover such a ridiculous thing. Perhaps the Girl could conduct a taste-test experiment. He smiled at that thought. He smiled at his Mother.

"I know it's no sourdough, but it's what we have - for today, anyway," his Mother apologetically announced, chewing through her own Ego, poorly disguising her grimace at the terrible sweetness. She smiled at the Boy. They ate their Egos in silence and day-dreamed of past lives.

"Have you made any friends at school?" his Mother asked. The Boy shrugged. He started tracing small nonsense designs with pooled space-syrup puddles, trying to avoid any topic regarding school. She set down her silverware abruptly.

"It will take some time, I know. Just be yourself and you'll find friends," she suggested. "You have a lot of different experiences from them, but they have many of their own to share with you, too. Keep an open-mind, okay?" Her desire for him to fit in - to assimilate - to adapt - was clearly obvious to the Boy, but he appreciated her for allowing him to not have to say anything else about the topic. He nodded once and finished his glass of water.

"Can we go camping sometime?" he blurted out, nearly choking. What he really wanted to say, though, was, "Can we go back to the forest and never come back?" Examining him quizzically, his Mother squinted as she understood his words, both said and unsaid. Sighing, she slowly leaned over the wobbly card table.

"Maybe someday," she spoke into her coffee cup. It was all she could confidently reply. Drawing a breath, she continued. "But not today. Today, we are going to visit your Father." The dingy dining room held its breath as the lightbulb flickered its dissidence. Staring out through the small living room window at the grey sky looming over the grey buildings

hovering over the grey noise of the city that flooded over the beating of his
and his Mother's grey hearts, the Boy frowned.

<center>~~~</center>

Chugging up the comically steep, pot-hole-ridden hill, their station
wagon curly-queued up and around the fir tree canopy that now spread out
beneath them. Turtling his head into his shirt and closing his eyes in fate
accepted, the Boy exhaled deeply as he greeted the rotten inklings of
nausea. He always did at this point, about half-way up. Unsure if it was the
steep, sharp turns of the car or the anxiety of heading to the hospital, he
had come to decide that it was probably both. A fine morning mist sprayed
down from the sky, too slow for his Mother to switch the wiper blades to
automatic, but enough so that she would have to intermittently flick the
lever from time to time. The wiper blades were very old and in need of dire
replacement. Each random swipe resulted in a ridiculous squeaking
"Errreeeekkk" as the blades protested their to-and-fro. An ambulance raced
up behind them, sirens blaring erratically, red and blue lights convulsing
furiously in every frequency. His Mother jerked the station wagon off to
the side of the road, precariously close to a steep drop off guarded by and
this swath of overgrown sword ferns. That was the last straw.

"Mom," was all the Boy could manage before projectile vomiting
onto the rubber floor mat. He stared at his partially digested space food -
chunks of waffles and syrup swirling in a pool of bubbly water, saliva, and
pale bile. He thought it basically looked unchanged in form, and wondered
if he could actually reassemble the Ego like some macabre jigsaw puzzle.
In silence, his Mother put the clutch into park, opened her creaking door,
and tip-toed around the sword-ferns over to his side. He opened the door,
beads of rain dribbling onto his chin, as she swiftly removed the floor mat
soaked in space-vomit and dipped it into a puddle of muddy runoff. it in a
puddle of standing muddy water in a nearby drainage ditch. Tossing the
wet mat into the back trunk, she got back into the driver's seat, popped the
clutch into drive and turned back onto the gleaming asphalt. Had she taken
a breath? The Boy wondered if she would even remember doing any of it -
that endearing robotic dutifulness of cleaning up a child's spontaneous and
explosion excretions - only a Mother's love.

The monstrous concrete parking garage loomed in the distance.
Behind it, an ivory tower of perfectly reflective glass, a cylinder stacking
twenty or more stories into the granite gray clouds which swirled and faded

45

around its dull form. Several elevators floated and sank along its midline. The Boy could see a helicopter perched near the entrance - a nearby sign warned, "Emergency" over massive automatic sliding doors. The station wagon crept into the garage and searched for a place to hide. In the dark and dingy fluorescent orange parking lot light, they crept up and up, each floor sardined with rows and columns of cars, but no space for their own. The Boy wondered if this was how sugar ants felt when they returned home to their hive. He bet they felt much different - full of excitement, of homeliness, of safety. He felt none of those feelings as they parked.

They rode the elevator to the twenty-first floor. Various people joined and departed en route, some dressed in flowing white overcoats, discussing numbers and values and topics with other people dressed in baby-blue pajamas complete with little booties to cover their shoes and hair nets over their scalps - probably cooks, the Boy imagined. Pagers beeped, phones rang, and a calm woman announced over the intercom "Code Blue Room 681" - perhaps a call to afternoon tea? Floor twelve, Floor thirteen. The elevator slowed, and opened slowly to allow a tall man dressed in a sleek brown three-piece suit to waltz aboard - a bronze-studded stethoscope dangling around his neck, a fog of intense cologne wafting around his aura. He smiled and winked at a group of younger women clustered behind the Boy - they were all wearing shorter white coats - most likely waitresses, the Boy was certain. The elevator stopped again, and the man departed, his pointed shoes click-clacking across the linoleum. The waiters giggled and whispered. The elevator lurched upward again and for a brief second, the Boy thought everyone on the elevator was going to get a chance to examine a sample of his space-vomit. Floor twenty. The waitresses departed and a chirpy flock. Now, the elevator was empty, save for two souls who held each other's hands tightly as the elevator announced, "Twenty-first floor - Burn Unit."

<center>~~~</center>

In perfect silence, they watched as their distorted images in the stainless steel doors suddenly peeled in half as the maw of the elevator effortlessly yawned and waited. Neither Boy nor his Mother made any movement. Hearts held still as breathing ceased. Perhaps the world had frozen completely, thought the Boy. Maybe that would be better, he pondered. An almost inaudible sigh pierced the stillness as her foot trepidatiously tiptoed onto the twenty-first floor.

"Why hello there, you two," hummed an elderly woman behind a small desk draped in plump succulents and dusty philodendron. "Good to see you again."

"Hello," replied his Mother, scribbling mindlessly onto the sign-in sheet.

"Today's the thirteenth," stated the concierge woman. She was knitting a pair of tiny purple mittens. His Mother flipped back a few pages - four days since they had last been here. Time seemed to have sped up and slid past her - four days. Traversing down the pristinely clean hallway, surrounded by blips and beeps and puffs of ventilators singing in quiet chorus, the two visitors gripped each other's hands fiercely. The microcosm of the hospital swirled around them: smiling nurses carrying rolls of gauze, squiggly lines leaping and diving on over the overhead row of television monitors, bags of clear fluid hanging from glimmering steel poles clustered together in a corner, the smell of bleach, of sterility, of nothingness waxing and waning with every few steps. The Boy prepared himself.

Four days ago, the Boy sat at the end of the bed staring at a figure that his Mother said was his Father. The Boy was not entirely sure that could be possible. He would have believed anything but that. In fact, he would have found it more believable if someone had told him he was watching a modern day mummification process. Almost entirely wrapped in bright white gauze, with tubes of various sizes entering at the elbow, in the neck, near the groin, through the nose, and inside the mouth, the figure lay entirely still. Slightly propped up in a bed that occasionally rocked from side to side with inflatable cuffs around its legs, the only motion came from the intermittently inflating and deflating accordion-like machine that filled the figure's lungs with air every few seconds. It was terrifying. It was boring. Depression unlimited. It was very much the worst part of his new life since the fire. Being in that room drained the Boy of his boyhood.

Four days had passed. The Boy had resigned himself to another silent and lonesome visit with the comatose figure known as his Father. Yet as he rounded the final corner and peeked into the room, he immediately felt the hairs on the back of his neck stand in shock - something was amiss. The room had somehow grown significantly larger. A midday sunbeam glistened through the partially drawn shade and cast a glow on the foot of the bed, where the Boy vividly recalled being the home of the monstrous ventilator machine - now gone. In its place, a humble reclining chair and a vase of lilies.

"Dad?" whispered the Boy. His Mother clasped her hands over her trembling mouth. The two stood and stared, hearts beating furiously, eyes blinking and fluttering back fresh tears, veins surging anxious adrenaline. A single tube of clear fluid snaked into his Father's right elbow. His face and arms were newly uncovered, his pink scarred flesh marbled and fragile. In incredibly slow and purposeful motion, the Boy watched as his Father's hand rose to grasp a small gray remote with a single black button on the top. As his thumb slowly depressed the trigger, a cautious and mellow 'beep' emanated out from the machine looming over the bed. Had the Boy dared to stand closer to his father, he would have seen two pupils tiredly retreat and shrink back in painless bliss. His Father sighed. The Boy floated next to his father and cautiously touched the warm hairless skin of his forearm. Am almost invisible smile pressed across his Father's burnt lips.
"I love you, Dad," the Boy managed to finally say, tears rolling down both cheeks. His Father's smile widened - 'I love you, too' it seemed to silently convey. As he ran his hand from arm to his leg, the Boy found that his Father's legs were still heavily bandaged in thick gauze smelling faintly of iodine. The Boy allowed the minuscule weight of his hand to slowly come to rest on his Father thigh.

"Uhh!" came the muffled yelp, accompanied by a sudden jerk of the legs and wince of the eyes - his Father was obviously still in excruciating pain. Thumb pressing the button again, his Father anxiously stared at the morphine drip above his head, begging the 'beep' the hum out its approval. The Boy backed away as his Father's squinted eyes relaxed and fell asleep under an opioid-induced fog of dreamlessness.

~~~

"We removed the breathing tube yesterday," explained the very tall doctor, stroking the white stubble of his short beard. A pristine, impossibly white laboratory coat hung tightly across his bony shoulders. "His airway still has a long way to go in recovering from the burns and smoke inhalation injuries. He's been carefully instructed to not speak for a couple of weeks - he needs to rest his vocal cords, you see," the physician continued, running his lanky fingers along the sides of his bulging Adam's apple. "The burns to his legs were very severe, but the good news here is
~~~

that the skin-grafts are slowly taking. Once his pain is controlled, he can return home with you," finished the elderly man, placing a gentle and heavy hand on the Boy's shoulder.

"When… when will that be?" whispered the Boy, unsure if he could tell the difference between days and years, for it seemed as if time had simply melted away. The doctor paused and considered the question thoughtfully, his eyes examining the Boy's Father from head to toe in a careful and calculated manner. He cleared his throat.

"One week," he replied with a confident nod.

"One week," parroted the Boy. The doctor smiled and knelt down to meet him at eye level. Removing his thick-lensed glasses, the Boy watched as the creases in the corner of his tired eyes began to fold into grins.

"In the meantime," the physician began, his voice suddenly upbeat, "we have something special for you this morning," announced the doctor, with a mysterious sparkle gleaming from his eyes. "Do you like to paint, son?"

~~~

Around her waist spun a kaleidoscope of psychedelic spirals and swirls of every color and pattern. She wore a light blouse decorated with images of a chaotic Milky Way melting into an Amazonian jungle canopy. Around her neck hung thick hemp necklaces laden with hazy green crystals and burnt amber ingots that dangled down to her belly. Rings and bracelets of every metal and every design jingled and jangled. As she pulled up her sleeves, tattoos of spiders, wolves, and intricate native designs of fishing nets and dreamcatchers paraded across her olive skin. Swaying to a silent melody or perhaps an ocean breeze, the Art Therapist helicoptered to the floor, quietly landing cross-legged on the carpeted common room, her smile stretching ear-to-ear in earnest, child-like enthusiasm.

"Come. Sit," she beckoned to the Boy, her inviting hand extended out to him, fingers playfully tickling the air. Her turquoise rings sparkled and clanked as she removed several containers of paint and bundles of small brushes from her canvas backpack. The Boy noted that the bag was decorated in a tapestry of various patches depicting gods and goddesses - some he knew, others totally unknown. As he slowly slinked over to her side, his eyes fixated on the tattoos across her knuckles - 'L-O-V-E' on the right hand, 'L-I-F-E' on the right. A single tendril of patchouli oil tickled
~~~

his nose from the small incense candle she lit and positioned between them. Humming a pretty and simple song that the Boy did not know, she softly laid out blank pieces of thick paper and pressed their edges flat. Mystified and comforted, the aura of the Art Therapist reminded the Boy of his Grandmother - the confidence of body-language, no need for spoken word to convey intentions. She handed the Boy a small brush and opened several vials of beautifully tinted super-saturated colors.

"I'm going to paint a picture without even thinking," she started, dipping her brush into a satin red. "It's just whatever I want to paint, however I feel, right now, sitting in this room - next to you." The Boy watched as she began to make several strokes over the top of the paper in no particular form or function, no certain pattern. She hummed her song as she did this, swaying her shoulders back and forth as if slowly engaged in a rhythmic dance with the paper she was painting, a shared energy passing between the two.

"If you like, you can try it to," she suggested, her free palm upward, extended toward the Boy's blank paper. He watched, mesmerized, as she effortlessly selected a bright orange hue and began mixing it into her streaks of red without a moment's hesitation. She swirled this onto the crimson red that was drying on her paper - A sunset? The Boy's imagination began to take flight. Cautiously picking up a flat brush, he paused, unsure of which color to start with. Sensing his hesitance, the Art Therapist began to chant in a slow, melodic, sing-song:

> *"Let go of your mind,*
> *And put trust in your heart.*
> *The brush goes where it goes,*
> *There's no end, nor no start."*

He closed his eyes and inhaled the deepest of breaths, as if to dive beneath a double-overhead swell, deeper than any of his fears could possibly lurk. One by one, his stressors and anxieties peeled away - the school, the city, the apartment, this place - the hospital. One by one, he removed these shackles, and watched them ride away into the deep blue current of nothingness, leaving behind only pure and unadulterated present, calm mind. His heart suddenly surged with raw ecstasy and limitless energy, as all of this fell away.

A perfect pitch black stood centered and firm. Forest-fern greens and old-growth-bark brown melded at the periphery of the great darkness

in intertwined amalgamations. Suddenly, a bright orange and yellow
erupted from this inner spiral, furiously stroked, extending outwards, paint
piled on top of itself in great glops and splotches. Oranges became yellows
became blues and purples. As the daggers of darker colors spiked and spun,
an abrupt whiteness - a nothingness appeared at the edges of the paper. The
Boy finally set down his brush. Minutes passed, perhaps hours. Fading
back into his reality, he sighed deeply and satisfyingly. A bright shadow
hovered above him - humming joyously. The Art Therapist was stretching
her arms out overhead, an approving smile woven across her face.

"You've discovered something," she both asked and suggested,
eyes closing in satisfaction and knowing. The Boy nodded, not uttering a
word.

"And how does that make you feel?" she said quietly, opening her
eyes, moist with happiness. The Boy looked at his art piece. He could feel
the oppressive anxiety and fear banging at the door of his consciousness,
but found it inexplicably trapped in the beyond, banned from this world of
quiet, simple, inner peace. Relief rushed over him like a freshly lit bonfire.

"Calm," he replied to the woman. She nodded and began to hum
again, adrift in world unto herself, a world that the Boy now shared. He
decided it was probably the most wonderful world of all. Glancing over at
her painting, his mouth slowly began to gape. On the periphery rose swirls
of orange and yellow and red in a massive fiery storm of furiously stroked
lines and swathes. This gave way to an inner layer of quiet, almost
invisible blue hues that then gave way to darker, thicker, richer purple and
eventually, greens and browns and blacks intertwined in color symbiosis.
And then, suddenly, a perfect circle of pure white - no color, no nothing -
standing central and pure. Hers was an almost complete opposite of his
own art vision. In that moment, he felt her hand gently press upon his own.

"You see,' began the Art Therapist, tracing the outer bands of the
Boys's painting with a soft finger, "if we let it, the fire will burn down and
down, deeper and darker," she continued, fingertip spiraling into the dark
center he had created. "Eventually, there will be nothing." The Boy sat
motionless and swallowed, nodding slowly in his understanding of her, of
himself, of his unconscious now made conscious. She stroked the top of his
hand.

"There is another way," she segued, positioning her art next to his
own. "If we keep what we love at our center, our heart - pure and clean and
clear and free," she continued, moving her palm from the central white
sphere of her piece, up to the Boy's sternum. "If we can keep this centered,

we will be protected, infinitely happy, no matter how intense the fire rages on the outside," she whispered, her hand rocking rhythmically with his own pulse. As his gaze shifted between the paintings laid side-by-side, the Boy understood. For the first time in a very long time, he felt at home within himself. Happiness, he decided, was a decision he chose to make. And at that moment, he promised himself to always choose happiness.

The Premonition

"Hey sleepy-head! Wake up, I've got a surprise for you," came the echo of his Mother drifting through the apartment. Rubbing his eyes, the Boy yawned and searched for an exit from the pile of blankets stacked on top of him. Had it all been a dream? He couldn't recall leaving the hospital, or even eating dinner, for that matter. He had been riding a wave of unimaginable bliss filled with exploding swirling colors and scents and sounds. Rising from his bed and extending his arms toward the cracked ceiling, he stretched his muscles along with his smile and inhaled a great breath of comfort of happiness.

"You're looking chipper this morning - sleep well?" his Mother observed from his bedroom doorway. She was wearing a rucksack and had on her old pair of rain boots. The Boy nodded and stared wide-eyed at her feet.

"Are we going camping?" he asked in disbelief. A sly smile and a slight shake of her head suggested otherwise.

"I had a peculiar dream last night," she replied. "Come eat and I'll tell you about it," she teased, drifting out of his room toward the dim light of the kitchen. The Boy leapt from his bed and scurried after her.

~~~

She stirred her coffee methodically as the Boy sloppily pasted chunky peanut butter on his toast. Slicing an unripe banana, he positioned the soft discs carefully atop the spread – one of his favorite new breakfasts since living in the city. He looked up at his Mother patiently before taking a bite, for the nourishment her dream-stories provided surpassed any food he could eat that morning. Since he could first remember, he had loved her morning dream-stories – and this was the first she was willing to share in a very long time.

"I was lost in the woods," she began, "in the middle of a moonless, cloudless night - but there were no stars or constellations to light the forest. I could feel the trees and ferns around me but I could not see them. I could hear the trickle of our little stream, but I could not tell in which direction it lay. I tried to walk and find our trail, but I kept tripping on ruts or wandering into blown-down branches. I was scared." The Boy sat motionless on the edge of his short chair, his attention glued to his
~~~

Mother's retelling of the dream, his breakfast still untouched. She took a sip of her coffee and continued.

"I fell a final time and as I lay face down in the pine needles and moist duff, I started to cry. I thought I might be kept in that darkness forever. And then, suddenly, the hair on my arms stood up as a chilled breath of ocean breeze crept through the fir trees," she whispered, the Boy feeling shivers on his neck.

"I sat up and faced the wind as it began to blow with more and more energy - it started to actually *push* me," his Mother continued, standing up from the table to face the apartment window.

"At first, I fought it - I gripped the soil and the roots and the ferns with all my might. But it was so strong - I began to slide across the dirt, twigs and leafs whipping past my face," she spoke, voice trembling, arms outstretched in front of her, blocking invisible pine cone and wood chip missiles.

"Was it going to blow off a cliff? Down a ravine? And then... I felt this funny feeling." The Boy's eyes focused intently on his Mother's as she stared back at him wide-eyed, a sly grin curled on her lips.

"I felt this presence around me, and... *inside* me," she gasped, hands to her chest. "It almost said, 'go with the flow' - like what your Father always says. So, I did! I let go. I let that wind push me and guide me whichever way it wanted. My feet rose off the forest floor, and I sailed through the woods and over creeks and rivers and down gullies and up over high passes, faster and faster. I started laughing! I didn't even care where we were going, that wind and I. I didn't even worry," she sighed, collapsing back into the clumsy dining chair.

"And then," she paused, her hands clutching a mug of lukewarm coffee as she swallowed a sudden bolus of trepidation, "the wind stopped. And do you know where I was?" she asked the Boy.

"Where were you, Mom?" the Boy barely managed, his heart leaping with excitement, of fear, of worry, of joy. She replied with a wild smile.

"I was standing in the middle of where our *home* used to be, on top of our hill!" she clapped on to the table, a small eruption of coffee skittering across its surface. "A full blood moon blazed above me, and, impossibly, the brightest ribbon of the Milky Way I had ever seen, right next to the moon!" she depicted, tracing the apartment's ceiling with her outstretched finger. The Boy gazed up with her and nodded.

"The trees around me were all burnt, but the air somehow smelled of lavender and pine. I expected to find the ruins of our home all around me, but as I slowly spun, there was nothing there at all. Just grass. Just grass, and..." she stopped abruptly.

"And what? And what mom?" The Boy was standing at the table now, beneath the blood moon glare of their single solitary kitchen light bulb.

"A mushroom. Unlike any I've ever seen. A soft purple glow emanated from below its golden, sparkling gills, and at first, I thought it was a Jack O'Lantern or some strange type of Amanita. I laid down on my stomach to check its stipe and veil, and the mushroom did the strangest thing!" she spoke, now crouching below the dining room table, examining its unfinished, slightly moldy underbelly. "The mushroom - it bent down, too! In fact, it copied *every* movement I made!" she mimicked, arms waving at her side. The Boy, now tucked under the dining room chair, smiled as he rocked back and forth on his haunches.

"And then I saw the eyes," his Mother continued, her voice a ghost "The cap had two burning red eyes that I swear were looking at me. I stood back up and watched in disbelief as the mushroom grew and stood as tall as me. But I was not scared - oh no. I nodded to the fungus, and a faint glow from the mushroom started to pulsate, like the flickering of Venus or Mars on a clear night. I just stood there, staring at the mushroom, as it stared back at me."

"Did you pick it?" the Boy whispered. His Mother was always incredible cautious with wild fungi, but she knew how intrigued the Boy was by new species, so she would often pick specimens to bring back and show him so he could practice their names and their characteristics. He was hoping she had somehow picked it from her dream-world and brought it back across to their breakfast table.

"That was the strangest part," said his Mother. "Just as I felt that strange knowing to just 'go with the flow' of the wind, a voice inside my dream-mind softly spoke and told me 'take it or leave it' - another one of your Father's favorites," she said. "I *knew* that this mushroom wanted me to pick it, and as I stooped to cut the stipe at its base, the mushroom's luminescence exploded into a fluorescent bright green strobe!" She exclaimed, twirling back into the kitchen, the Boy hopping after her.

"The light was so bright, I could barely see. As I squinted through the brilliance, I blindly extended my hands and took a step forward," she said, with a stumbling step toward the Boy. "And suddenly, my fingers brushed upon a velvety soft mushroomy veil. And do you know what happened next?" she softly asked. All the Boy could do was blink.

"I felt the mushroom actually *squeeze* my fingers back!" she gasped, her hands clasped around the Boy's own. The Boy trembled as his heart strummed wildly. The air in the kitchen began to warp and pulse. The glow of the lightbulb erupted into a white phosphorus supernova. The smell of pine and lavender flooded his sinuses.

"As delicately as I could, I knelt and cut the mushroom at its base, careful not to disturb its mycelium, which glowed with their own orangish hue beneath the soil. Just as I plucked the fruit, a soft purple aura rhythmically pulsed from its gills. Without a second guess, I placed the mushroom into my mouth and swallowed it whole. A sudden, incredible warmth poured over every inch of my dream-body - I was so comfortable, so at peace, so... at home." The Boy stood next to his Mother, tears at the corners of his eyes. Tears of knowing, of happiness. He hugged her mightily.

"I... I think that we... we need to visit our old home today, " she revealed, a hand gently stroking the Boy's hair from his face. "I think there's something left for us to find."

The Necklace

A delicate but persistent afternoon mist obscured most of the drive up the winding forest service road. His Mother drove their station wagon slowly, for the soaking late autumn rains had created hidden craters in the unpaved gravel - a slight lapse in focus could result in a broken axle - and an impossibly expensive call to the towing service. As they headed deeper into the forest - their wilderness - the odor creeping in through the air vents of their car subtly changed from that of dew and mild earthen decay, to that of an old flannel shirt soaked in campfire smoke. Higher and higher they rose, accompanied by the whine of the car's boxer engine that struggled to change from gear to gear. Bursting above the fog, the barren giants appeared, naked and barren to the elements, stripped of bark and leaves and forest floor companions. A burn. The Burn. Their Burn.

"Oh," his Mother quietly gasped as they coasted to a halt. Sitting in silence, the two passengers could staring straight ahead, trembling in their battle to suppress flashbacks of that night - *the* night. With simultaneous inhalation, and subdued sighs, they kept their masks in place as the station wagon lurched forward, croaking up the desolate mountain. A final turn - an all-too-familiar bend in the road - and the car rumbled to a stop amidst charred stump and ashen leaf. Their driveway. Almost unrecognizable, except for the internal knowingness - that sixth sense that felt the heavy pull of gravity near a place as special as Home. The two opened the wagon's doors and stepped onto the once native, now alien, soil. The overpowering and unpleasantly pleasant smell of bonfire maliciously invited itself inside their nostrils. Both frowned deeply at its terrible significance.

As they shuffled up their old driveway, contrails of ash swirled from each step and wafted into the chilled afternoon mountain breeze. The Boy, feeling the urge to glance backward, noted the two sets of footprints - one small and uneven, the other larger and confidently pressed - meandering upwards from the station wagon. A sort of poorly choreographed reenactment of the moon landing. There would be no flags to plant or throngs of cheering crowds to welcome them back from this journey, however. Summiting the drive and crossing the horizon, the two figures stood at the foundation of what was once a beautiful home, meticulously cared for, lovingly revered, and now... unfathomably ravaged and nearly unrecognizable. What was this place, this chaotically arranged bundle of burnt planks and fractured support beams, charred bricks and blackened steel? Surely this savaged skeleton was not the same body that had held his dream-filled nights under his Grandmother's quilt, his hearty and soul-warming meals with his parents, his adventures and misadventures in the basement and attic with his friends and stuffed animals... was it? As an almost resoundingly horrible answer to his silent question, the house wheezed and sputtered in the wind and let loose a dozen tumbling broken bricks from the free-standing, lonesome chimney. He hugged his Mother and closed his eyes as tightly as he could.

"Wake up, wake up, wake up" he chanted into his mind. Stillness. He opened his eyes and accepted that he would not be awakening from this lucid nightmare, this gravesite of his previous self. His Mother cleared her throat and wiped her moistening eyes, leaving a tight smudge of grey ash across her cheeks.

"I have to go inside. There is something here for me," she spoke - her voice a cautiously quiet, powerfully certain commandment - to him or the ruins of the house, the Boy could not tell. She pivoted to the Boy and kneeled in the cremated remains, sending a plume of particulate that stained the glare of the sun a hazy orange and fiery red hue. She grasped him by the shoulders and locked into his knowing eyes.

"It's too dangerous for you to walk in there with me. You'll have to stay here" she patiently instructed.
The Boy slowly nodded, for he was utterly undecided if his heart and mind dared enter into through the mystic and otherworldly boundary of this surreal spirit, this shattered skeleton of a home. Benevolent or malevolent? He took no sides in this thought, and instead sunk into the earth and sat, fine dust bathing his feet. He would decidedly wait for the heroine who was his Mother to cross over and retrieve whatever it was she knew awaited her in that carcass of their past.

~~~

One step. One strident, confident, step that only a strong woman such as herself cold possibly take. Into the ash, the roast, the decay of prior joys and happinesses. She thought nothing of those things as she slowly marched under crossbeams of smoked death, over molten carnage of unrecognizable prior items, however useful or useless they may have once been. A refrigerator, an oven, maybe the steel chandelier the Boy's Father had welded together for her birthday many summers ago? She felt the ghosts of these memories reach out for her skin and her recognition and her
~~~

sympathy, yet her resolve beamed too brightly from her unwavering gaze - she persisted forward. An almost mystic force guided her through the tangled mess - she simply knew where it was she must step, and where her hand must reach to recover what had called her from the depths of her unconsciousness, that other dimension of dream-worlds. Near what was once the peaceful confines of her and her husband's bedroom, she suddenly stopped. Feeling the subtle warmth emerge beneath her feet, the soft purple glow of the ash, the Boy's Mother became very still. Her breath - caught in her throat - her hairs - electrified at their follicles, her pulse - quickened and ready - she knelt. As she carefully swept away the detritus, a pair of softly lit red eyes emerged from the blackened char and stared back at her. Withdrawing her hand, she gasped as the eyes lifted from the ash and rose inch by inch atop a pulsing purple haze.

~~~

Sitting quietly and crossed-legged at the bones of his Home, entranced in his Mother's traverse, the Boy shuddered as his ears began to pop and ring - the pressure atop their hill suddenly plummeting. A harsh, chilled breeze draped around his shoulders, as he shivered and rose from the ash. A cloudless, pale blue sky, without a hint of storm, and yet the wind suddenly howled from everywhere and nowhere, furious and confused. The Boy stood and backed away from the house as the resurrected smoke and odor of fresh burn began to circulate counterclockwise around the blackened cornerstones of the deadened structure. The figure of his Mother blurred into shadow as a pillar of spiraling midnight black ascended into the sun - an ashen dust devil. Scuttling backward, he slipped on an exposed Fir root, and fell sideways into the penetrating soot. Pushing himself to his knees as his lungs protested in coughing spasm, the Boy rubbed his eyes and squinted through the chaos of the storm. Extending his arms, his hand vanished through a wall of roiling dust, its caustic taste coating his lips. As he stumbled forward, arms and legs grasping for any familiar purchase, he had the absurd notion of feeling like a naked hermit crab on a beach with no shells, wandering aimlessly - hopelessly. He shook his head and stopped, tears whisked into the air before having a chance to coat his cheeks. Sinking to his knees, he closed his eyes.

"Wake up," he whispered into the dust. Suddenly, unexpectedly, the wind around him completely stopped. Refracted beams of light golden
~~~

sun zig-zagged through the ash that drifted back upon the Boy. Comforted by the warmth and stillness, the Boy dared to lift his head - and gasped. Rising from the chest cavity of his Home - directly where his mother had been - stood the impossible sight of an infinitely tall ashen tornado, silently howling in onto itself. Its hollow, pitch black core intermittently burst pulses of purple as the burnt chimney and stone corners of the home glared orange and red.

"No! It can't be!" the Boy sobbed. Clamping his eyes shut, his thoughts immediately flew to his art work in the hospital. *His* art - the darkness in the center.

"I won't let it!" he commanded himself. As he forced his frantic breathing to slow, a soft, glowing melody emerged from the periphery of his mind - a familiar, comforting tune. Rhythmically rocking back and forth on his heels as he hugged his legs tightly to his chest, he began to hum.

"Let go of your mind… and put trust in your heart…" Chanting as he swayed, the Boy imagined a brilliant white light encircling his Mother - a shelter in the storm, a candle at the end of a tunnel, a center of light. He focused, and drove out the fear. He inhaled, and opened his eyes.

~~~

Silence. Perfect, awful silence. Darkness. Unreal, terrifying darkness. She had seen the rapid progression of the funnel cloud ascend from the earth, had captured that final expression of worry and anxiety on the Boy's face. The storm was all-encompassing around her, yet, inside the bones of her home lived an undisturbed, unnatural tranquility. Her hand remained outstretched, but as she looked beyond, she could not delineate ashen layer from fleshed fingertip, for the darkness was pure and unforgiving. The allure of the purple glow had vanished, the red eyes beckoning her every emotion now extinguished.

"No, I will not," she whispered into this nothingness. Closing her eyes, she focused on her dream - her premonition. She replayed the moment she plucked the golden-gilled mushroom, on the sensations immediately felt upon swallowing it whole. She basked in the knowledge, the knowing, the unparalleled self-peace and gentle power she had felt. She inhaled as deeply as she dared, a faint purple pulse illuminating the curtain of her eyelids. A sudden expansion of her senses - the faintest sound rising and falling beyond the veil of the blacked whirling beast that spiraled
~~~

silently overhead. An unknown song carried to her from a familiar world. A soft, fearless humming. She joined it in harmony, gracefully swaying from note to note. Smiling amongst the nightmare, she plunged both hands into the cold, burnt charcoal and grit, clasping her trembling fists around that which had drawn her so deeply to this place, that calling, beckoning thing - her lighthouse from another universe. As she roused it from its resting place amongst the layered soot, a blinding light emanated from its skin as it materialized out of the black - a phoenix newly risen. Clutching her treasure to her chest tighter and tighter, she proudly rose, humming the tune louder and louder. A single hot, clear tear burst from her eye and fell upon the earth... and with that, the tentacle of the storm released its grasp and receded into the calm, autumn sky, leaving a fine mist of gray ash that rained back down onto surrounding fern and Fir.

~~~

He saw her there, breathing softly and surely, rising from the dirt. A victorious, set jaw, her eyes tired, yet satisfied. As she stood triumphantly and faced the Boy, he noticed that every remaining crossbeam, panel, two-by-four, and brick-wall had crumbled or disintegrated. The only burnt bones that remained standing in the face of such a merciless darkness were, of course, the burnt bones of his Mother. She glided towards the Boy, and he noticed hardly a footprint behind her, her figure as light and airy as an Osprey's downy feather. Her hands were clasped over her sternum, her eyes fixed to the horizon beyond. She looked down at the Boy and softly smiled, uncovering her hands one at a time. A flash of light so fierce, it momentarily dazed the boy. As he rubbed his startled eyes, he noticed a heart-shaped image slowly fading from his retinas. A silverish glimmer, like the back of a grey whale glistening in the distance as it surfaced for a great breath. His vision cleared, and he held the breath that he had forgotten to take.

"Mom…" he whispered. At the center of his Mother's chest was her most prized possession, an heirloom of incomparable significance. Generations of past love, loss, and everything in between represented by a single, simple thing - her armor and her shield. Her necklace. Her Family's necklace. Perfectly preserved and pristine as the day it was forged, it was seemingly immune to flame and fury. She clasped its heavy fasteners behind her neck and knelt beside her son, holding the heart-shaped locket in her palm. As she placed a soft hand upon one of his cheeks, the Boy felt
~~~

the simultaneous sea-breeze on his other, the warmth from both enveloping
him in comfort and love - his Home. As the two walked back down the
drive toward the station wagon, The Boy could not help but notice the
curious purple-hued aura that now surrounded the figure of his Mother.

The Gift

The first thing that struck the Boy's eye was her long, heavy rope of thick, scraggly, gray hair that stretched into a single braided ponytail, swaying deep down below her thin waist. Hand-woven hemp ties separated the great knotted mess into uneven segments, each highlighted with its own meticulously concocted strand of golden wire that shimmered bright in the late afternoon sun. Silently standing sideways to the Boy and his Mother, she gazed mile-long over the rolling hills of towering Douglas Fir, contemplating something far beyond the Boy's comprehension. Upon her sun-weathered skin, the mysterious woman wore a thick, tattered, black leather jacket with frayed fronds down the sleeves - some missing, some cut and knotted at various lengths. On the back of her jacket, two large, golden butterflies lived as intricate patches stitched onto either shoulder blade. Sun-bleached, cracked leather boots with golden eyelets concealed the ends of the tight black denim pants she wore, completing an ensemble that both blended and contrasted with the ashen wasteland all around her. Casually lighting a hand-rolled, half-smoked cigarette, the woman allowed a half smirk as she sensed the Boy's apprehension and simultaneous curiosity. She turned towards the two approaching figures.

"Think I've got something for you, kid," said the stranger, her voice a rough low-level grit that sounded to the Boy just as his father's weekend whiskey-scented breath smelled. The Boy saw that she carried a crumpled brown paper bag in her left arm, with some sort of oblong object concealed inside. His Mother strode ahead.

"Pardon me, do we know you?" she started. "We have... we *had*... very few neighbors, and I'm afraid I've never met you before." His Mother's cautiously polite voice replied. The pendant of her necklace pulsed with soft white and purple waves. A sheet of low clouds had lazily floated in front of the sun, draping a shadow over the three of them. The leather-jacket woman took a long drag on her half-cigarette, extinguished it on the side of a blackened stump and tucked it back into her front pocket. Exhaling slowly, she released several small silver smoke rings that seemed to flap and flitter around her head before rising into the soft mist that was filling the upper limbs of the forests' corpses.

"You might say... I'm a traveler," she cryptically replied, her voice a gravely smoke, haunting yet familiar. She blew out the last few remaining delicate smoke creatures from her lungs and smiled widely at the Boy again - teeth as white and brilliant as a sun-bleached antelope skull in the high steppe.

"And where is it you are traveling?" his Mother replied, growing impatient. "Surely not here, unless you enjoy visiting hell" she chided. Shifting her stance and crossing her arms, she was clearly irritated that the wave of incredible energy from the act of finding her necklace was now receding into this strange interaction. The leather woman beamed.

"Heh heh heh," came the reverberating, deep-throated chuckle from the Leather Woman's closed lips. As she gave her head a slight shake from side to side, the Boy could see that she was considering the question for a few moments. "Actually, ma'am, hell is most likely where I, in fact, am from," she answered monotonously. "Hell is where I'm going, and the hell I could tell you why that is!" she shrugged. "I'm a scavenger - always drawn to this sort of death and destruction, searching for any sort of life, or evidence there of, I guess you could say. Remaining things - knick-knacks, photos - that sort of thing," she explained, aimlessly drawing random dusty patterns with the toe of her boot. The Boy could sense his Mother's disapproval.

"Right," his Mother began, "knick-knacks - not jewelry.. or small safes or vaults... or precious gems or metals. Certainly not those things, I'm sure." His mother's sarcastic and biting tone embarrassed the Boy, but he could understand how this Scavenger might be considered a thief, - a robber of memories, at the least. What if she had discovered the necklace? Had she found other things of theirs before he and his Mother had arrived? Furrowing his brow, the Boy took a step closer to his Mother.

Sensing their skepticism, the Scavenger leaned against the front bumper of their station wagon and crossed her legs, dragging a plume of fresh ash that blew around her in perfect circles. She could have been born from the fire, thought the Boy. He did not fear her, he decided.

"Sometimes I find a thing here or there that makes a buck," began the Scavenger, tucking her hands into her high-waisted jean pockets. "Gets me a greasy meal or two. Maybe a quarter tank of gas for my bike. Sometimes a cheap bed at a broke-down motel. I'll tell you one thing, though," she said, abruptly raising her gaze and pausing to sigh.

"I know," the Scavenger smirked. "I know if the things I find are alright for me to have, or if they need to stay in the grave, so to speak. And sometimes, I know that I'm the one that's been charged with returning them to their proper owners," she continued, her left eyebrow raised in the Boy's direction. "Which is why I'm standing at your drive this afternoon," she finished, pulling out the cigarette and relighting it with her other hand in one fluid motion. Creaking softly as she peeled away from the bumper of the station wagon, the Scavenger's leather jacket molded around her stocky frame as she began to approach the Boy and his Mother. Charcoal-laden dust from her boots and tobacco smoke from her nostrils spiraled into one another around her ponytail, intimately dancing and intertwining like two long-lost friends reunited. The brown-bagged bundle in the crook of her left arm was noiseless and perplexing to the Boy. Stopping a few paces away from the the two bewildered figures, the Scavenger lowered to one knee like a recently returned knight bowing in respect to the king or queen. The Boy unconsciously stepped forward, his Mother silent in neither protest nor approval. The Scavenger cleared her throat and placed the paper bag down into the ash.

"As I said, kid. I know… and I know *this* is yours," she said, patting the crumpled bag. "I knew you would be here. I knew *when* you would be here. Don't ask how, don't ask why," the Scavenger continued. "So... I've brought it here… take it," she instructed, slowly offering the bag forward. The Boy could not help but notice how soft, how tranquil, how empathic the Scavenger's eyes appeared, her irises a fluid shifting grey tone that lightened or darkened seemingly dependent on how deeply she smiled. Taking the paper bag in both hands, the Boy's eye-contact unbroken from the Scavenger's. As she touched the bag, a sudden gush of familiar energy flooded into his fingertips, up through his arms, into his mind and body, filling him with supreme comfort like an old, warm, woolen blanket.

"Open it" encouraged the Scavenger, "I think you'll be pleasantly surprised" she winked. A faint, echoing laughter materialized seemingly from every direction around the Boy. He thought some of the animalistic cackles actually sounded strangely recognizable, but he couldn't be entirely sure, as they blended and bled together into a zoo-line ensemble. As he opened the top of the boring brown paper bag, the laughter swelled into a cacophonous roar, sending a tremendous chill down the length of his spine. Quickly crumpling the bag shut, the Boy retreated as the drowning voices shrank back into the depths of his consciousness.

"Don't be afraid," whispered the Scavenger, placing a heavy hand upon his shoulder. "Disaster - and especially fire for that matter - changes things, makes them look and seem different on the outside. But if you search deep beyond the coal, you'll find that same love. You'll savor that same friendship. You'll relish that same fondness of shared memory. You just have to be strong," she grinned, "and you look plenty strong to me, kid," she finished, her eyes twinkling a thousand various colors, red to violet.

"Okay," the Boy replied, nodding with gained confidence. He swallowed and took a breath of fresh autumn forest air. Glancing at his mother, the Boy saw her crack a relaxed smile - not at him, but the stranger - the Scavenger. His gaze fell lower, as the necklace glowed softly - a pulsating yellow and orange. The Boy's ears began the sense the building laughter that emanated from the brown paper bag - more childlike than before, more playful and inviting. He grasped the top of the bag and unfolded it gingerly. The great swell of laughter peaked and crashed over him like a rogue wave, drenching him in a pleasant, ticklish warmth. As he gazed into the bottom of the bag, a luminous rainbow of infinitely alternating colors greeted his eyes. Thrusting his hands inside, he immediately felt a rough tuft of wiry hair, a flat fleece-like coat of scale, a stream-lined mid-section with sharp polyester edges and fins at the caudal end. What was this… thing? No, he thought. He had felt this before - a thousand times before. Lifting it from the bag, the Boy's heart leapt from his chest. Time completely stopped, save for the steady pulsing spectral colors of red, green, yellow, blue, and purple from the spiraling hole atop the thing… the *creature* - a small blow-hole?

"Whale!" exclaimed the Boy.

But the sharp ragged dorsal fin.

"Shark?" the Boy yelped, overwhelmed with ecstatic confusion..

The tuft of wiry red hair and sharp ears atop its head.

"Fox!" he joyously erupted.

The set of furry flippers and whiskery snout.

"And Otter!" the Boy pronounced, hugging the thing to his chest.

It was all of these things, and more.

As the Boy examined the creature, turning it over and over in his arms, he came to see every single one of his beloved stuffed animals somehow amalgamated into this one singular beast. His eyes filled with tears as he rapidly relived the death and resurrection of his childhood.

"When I came across the ruins of your home, there was this huge iron chest with wooden accents that was still slightly smoldering in a corner," the Scavenger began. "It drew me. It called to me so deeply and loudly. Almost like... laughter..." The Boy opened his eyes and stared at her. He could hear it - the giggling, the suppressed snorts of snickering - more clear and crisp. It came from the creature, he suspected.

"I flung open the burnt lid of the chest, and low and behold, there were about ten or fifteen stuffed critters in there," explained the Scavenger. "'Some kids toys,' I thought. 'Must be important,' I felt. Can't tell you why. Thing was, all of them were pretty worse for wear from the fire. Missing limbs, burnt hair, lost eyes - the whole nine yards. I'm sure you could imagine," she finished taking out a fresh sheet of rolling paper.

"I decided to take them all back with me to a little place I was renting out - down the mountain, middle of nowhere I guess you could say," she continued, licking her newly rolled cigarette closed. "Lady I was renting from, she's real good at stitching, real crafty-like, you might say." The Scavenger paused, taking a long drag and exhaling an impossible double smoke ring from her nostrils. She continued on.

"This lady has all these dolls and things she's made - 'back from her times on the island' she likes to tell me. Used to be a priest or priestess for her people. Anyhow. I asked her to salvage what she could from the mess of critters I brought in - maybe make up some sort of new toy for a certain kid I suspected would really want it. I expected her to charge a fee - ten or fifteen bucks, but no siree!" the Scavenger stood, shaking her finger in mimicry of her seamstress acquaintance. "I came back a few days later, and what do I find? Lady handed me that… thing," she said, pointing to the Boy's creature. "She says, 'It has been blessed. One day, you will know,,' and walks away - and I never saw her again!" The Scavenger exclaimed, leather-bound arms raised overhead to accentuate the story. "So, I kept it with me for a few days, until I had the strangest dream. That toy - that *creature* - it came to me - in my dream!" proclaimed the Scavenger, jumping into the air, sending ash and smoke swirling into a volatile explosion overhead. "It told me I had to be here. *Here! Today*! So here we are, kid," she exhaled in final conclusion. Smoke - sweet and dank - drifted over the creature, who's blowhole suddenly pulsed in every color, seemingly in approval of the circumstances. The Boy's eyes had never been wider - was this a dream? Certainly not, he decided. A compulsory sensation filled his heart just then - leaping from the earth, the Boy ran to the Scavenger. Throwing his arms around her, he buried his head in amongst the rough leather jacket, its dangling fronds scratching the back of his neck as the scraggly woman draped a heavy arm around him.

"Thank you," he whispered.

Their eyes meeting over the top of the Boy, the two women stared at each other and slowly nodded in unison, smiling their approval of each other's mission, however mysterious or confusing. Sunlight burst from the clouds and enveloped the three at the bottom of the burnt of drive.

"Of course," replied the Scavenger. "May your new journey be filled with good luck and fortune," she finished. Rising to a creaky stand, she nodded and announced that she would be headed back down the road a quarter mile to her motorcycle. The Boy and his Mother stood side by side, hand in hand, watching the leather-clad, smoke-blowing, ash-kicking woman casually but stylishly disappear down the gravel, amongst fresh forest mist and charred Fir. The Boy wondered when they would cross paths again - here… or elsewhere.

The Sea

"Well, howdy, buddy! Pleasure to see you down here, pal!"
bellowed the slightly goofy but earnest voice. Floating a few feet below the
surface of a magnificent undulating coral reef, the Boy quickly discovered
that he could breathe just fine underwater - simply inhale and exhale, a few
bubbles, a slightly salty taste in his mouth - no big deal, really. Swimming
through the swift current proved equally as easy - a few flaps of his arms,
and he was off. Brain corals the size of boulders, stag-horn formations
stretching twenty or thirty feet tall, fans and sponges ebbing and flowing
with the rhythm of the sea - all danced to the unheard beat of the ocean's
maestro. Occasionally, a humongous surface swell would rise high above,
drawing the Boy up and under its turmoil of rolling undercurrent - a
favorite free ride of leatherback turtles and bottlenose dolphins, alike.. All
around schooled and swirled constellations of technicolor creatures of all
types and sizes. The tiniest clownfish, hiding anxiously amongst the
confines of its poisonous anemone brush, poking her snout out from time
to time to investigate the inquisitive Boy. The rock lobster, clicking and
clacking and probing, sampling the debris drifting past his humble
limestone cave, enjoying the free lunch kicked up by the Boy's awkward
swim strokes. The barracuda, its menacing open-mouthed wolf-fangs
protruding in all directions, its set of terrifying saucer eyes, patrolling the
periphery, well away from the grateful Boy.

"Pretty neat, huh?" said the funny voice. The Boy couldn't tell
where it came from - perhaps out in the open royal blue depths beyond the
barracuda, where he dared not swim just yet.

"Um, it's great," replied the wary Boy." Who are you, exactly?" he
inquired - towards the clown fish, lobster, barracuda, eel, turtle, and
everyone and everything in between. He realized he didn't feel wet, or
cold, or necessarily scared in the depths of the ocean - a familiar warmth
permeated his bones and draped him in a feeling of relaxed homeliness.

"Guess I should introduce myself!" announced the Boy's
mysterious underwater host. Out from the infinite abyss beyond, a subtle
multicolored haze began to pulse brighter and brighter as a monstrous
shadow lazily approached the Boy. The rainbow of color rose like a
flashlight in a mineshaft, until it shone upon the reef, illuminating the life
under a shower of beating light. The clownfish burst from the anemone and
joined hundreds of other previously secretive clownfish in a great
synchronized circus of loops and barrel rolls between the protective

branches of stag-horn. The lobster stood on his tail and clicked his claws in time with the pulses of purple and red and green. The barracuda closed their mouths for once and appeared quite dapper. An underwater festival of frenetic joy and dance had erupted upon the reed at the anticipation of the massive, mysterious creature's arrival.

"Hello friends! Hey! Haven't seen many of you in some time!" said the beast, bowing to the reef in a hilarious, over-the-top, matter. The animals and coral reciprocated the salutation in simultaneous gestures - tail-fin curtsies, waving antennae, synchronized bursts of bubble. The beast was slightly larger than a school bus, but as it swam near the coral, its gargantuan form disturbed hardly a grain of sand from the ocean floor. Twirling to face his guest head-on, the creature's great luminescence emanating from its blowhole blinded the Boy momentarily.

"Well, woah! Sorry about that, friend!" exclaimed the beast, its dorsal light-source dimming rapidly. Opening his eyes, The Boy could just make out the outline of what appeared to be a set of pointed red ears atop the creature's head. And what was that, on its underside? A pair of furry flippers? Whiskery face... pointed dorsal fin...

Whale.

Shark.

Fox.

Otter.

His stuffed animal hodgepodge resurrected from the ash of the fire and gifted to him from the Scavenger and her priestly landlord seamstress. The Boy grinned from ear to ear and threw open his arms, a stream of frantic bubbles burbling from his mouth and nose. The creature lurched forward, swimming within a few feet from the Boy, hovering in place effortlessly. A few whiskers twitched back and forth, tempting a single brave lobster to extend a testing claw from the edge of the reef. The creature chuckled and extended a furry otter flipper towards the Boy.

"Well, heck! Pleased to meet ya!" it exclaimed, the blowhole erupting in pinks and yellows and purples and whites. The Boy grabbed the edge of the huge flipper and gently shook it up and down. "Why don't you climb on up? I'll take you for a grand ol' tour of this place!" declared the beast, rolling ninety degrees onto its side to display a cozy-appearing nook between blowhole and dorsal fin. The Boy's hesitancy was apparent, and before he could make a decision, a slippery fur-studded appendage scooped him up from underneath, lifting him skyward with frightening speed, carefully tucking him into place aside the massive jagged fin.

"That'a Boy! Hang on!" announced the creature. The Boy thought its voice was a mixture of something between a talking horse and the sounds narwhals probably make when they've had too much to drink. Either way, the creature's comforting demeanor made the Boy smile mightily and instilled a strange sort of confidence. He clung to the soft, sticky skin of the thing - careful not to go poking too close to the blow-hole - and suddenly, with a single powerful stroke of its tail, the patchwork beast and his Boy jockey launched across the coral reef, clownfish and barracuda waving farewell.

Rocketing across the underwater ridge-line, the Boy could make out strands of fire coral intermixed with lovely pink sponges and schools of tang and tuna on their daily patrols. The creature seemed to know each and every one of them, and both turned to acknowledge the other in passing.

"This part's a little rough, might want to ready yourself up there, partner," warned the beast. The Boy grabbed a few loose strands of red wiry hair protruding amongst the pointy fox-like ears and dug his heels into the sides of the whale-shark-fox-otter.

"Ha! Ho! Hey! That tickles, buddy!" The creature shuddered and jolted with convulsive fits that sent the Boy nearly tumbling off into the deep blue nothingness. Relaxing a bit, the Boy gave into the playfulness of the situation, letting a few chuckles out between the sudden dives and lunges. A few moments later, the sea darkened as the two entered into a murky kelp forest, thick with seaweed, miniature barnacles, bright yellow and purple starfish, playful, curious seals, and stalking, toothy white sharks- the later of which caused the Boy to tuck deeper into the dorsal fin of the beast.

"Scared of those guys, are ya?" sensed the creature of the Boy. "Nah, I'll tell ya what - very misunderstood, those ones! Very misunderstood. Good pals of mine, actually. Just part of Ye Ol' Food Chain, you know what I mean?" the beast continued. "Someone's gotta be at the bottom, someone at the top - it's the only way it works, really!" it philosophized. "So no need to be a pickle-chicken, my main man!" Sticking out a furry flipper to 'high-five' a particularly large white shark passing on their starboard side, the beast was at home. The Boy swore he saw the huge shark smile and wink at him as they swam past each other.

"Hey, Mister, um, fish-thingy? What do I call you?" asked the timid Boy, unsure if such a creature could even have a name.

"Oh, Me?" replied the fish-thing. "They call me 'The Schwark' around here, Boy," answered the beast.

"Ok. Mr. Schwark, you seem to know everybody, huh?" said the Boy.

"Ha! Just 'Schwark' pal - no misters in these parts! Ho! Ho! Yeah, I know all these guys and gals, everyone in these parts here is a good friend - a good buddy, you might even say," said the Schwark, pitching and yawing between ocean pinnacles and valleys as he spoke.

They dove deeper. Heading into the darkening chasm, the blowhole began to glow a soft, pleasing orange amber, as angler fish and octopus politely parted for the Boy and Schwark to descend. They passed underwater volcanoes belching thick smoke and spewing lava that advanced and hardened in seemingly slow-motion. Long-legged, spindly shrimp and bright red tube worms crowded around the geothermal vents, warming their appendages like kids around a late winter's bonfire. Suddenly, an incredibly huge squid emerged in front of them, its eight arms splayed out in a perfect enveloping circle as two monstrous tentacles lashing out in front of its menacing black beak. As it grabbed the sides of the Schwark, the Boy hung on for dear life as he swung violently from side to side. He screamed.

"Hey, my man! No need for that!" answered the Schwark, steadying its dorsal fin to better support the panicked rider. "Don't be such a pickle-chicken! This is one my girls, pal!" chuckled the Schwark. He slowed and pitched upwards, wrapping his large furry flippers around the squid, whiskers twitching madly about the squid's body. All eight legs began to wrap around the Schwark's pudgy midsection as the blowhole began emitting rapid pulses of purple and green.

"Her favorite colors," whispered the Schwark to the Boy. The squid began to reciprocate in its own luminescence back at the Schwark until both pulsed in harmonious frequencies of purple-green-purple-green-purple-green. Amongst intertwined flipper and tentacle, the two massive creatures floated slowly through the fantastic perfect blackness of the deep sea, solely transfixed in the presence of the other.

Slightly embarrassed by his previous fear, and by his proximity to such intense love, the Boy sheepishly smiled and turned to bury his face into the Schwark's dorsal fin to allow a bit of privacy. He soon realized the futility of his efforts, as out from the periphery of the abyss emerged a thousand softly strobing angler fish, each drawn to the intense purple-green luminosity of the two pulsating creatures. Slowly circling the Schwark and squid like a flood of lightning bugs at dusk, the angler fish encircled the their attraction, forming a massive stadium. In perfect rhythm, the fish began to glow a singular wave of purple and green that danced around the Boy's head and into infinity. The warmth of the Schwark and squid's embrace penetrated the Boy's heart and mind - was he himself also glowing purple and green? Clasping his hands in front of his face, he brought them to his eye and slowly opened his fingers. Floating in the near perfect black danced a nearly microscopic plankton, synchronized to the Schwark and squids' dance - purple-green-purple-green. As if on cue, an entire orchestra of bioluminescence grew to a blindingly bright crescendo all around the creatures - a plume of plankton. Pulsing faster and faster, the cumulative colors coalesced into a chaotic beating of singular white light. Temporarily blinded but completely overcome with emotion, the Boy slunk into the soft flesh of the Schwark and buried his face in its crop of coarse red hair.

"Don't wake up," the Boy whispered into the Schwark. Suddenly, he could feel the water around them become seemingly lighter and lighter, brighter and brighter. Peering between wiry hairs, the Boy glanced to his side and saw the ferocious velocity at which the Schwark was ascending - contrails of bubbles and blurred shadows of sperm whale and blue whale and humpback racing past. The Schwark's tail beat side to side with insane power and intent, the furry flippers plastered to its side, the fox ears tucked backwards into full-steam-ahead mode.

"Hang on, pal," warned the Schwark. Bursting from the fluid confines of the sea, the creature breached in a supremely magnificent manner into the glare of a high noon sun. At their apex of the launch, Boy and beast felt time slow to a near halt. Refracted rays of light gleaned off salty droplets shed from flipper and fin, arm and leg. The Schwark turned its heavily lashed eyes upwards towards the Boy and smiled.

"Here's where you wake up, buddy," it winked.

The Ants

Gasping for breath, the Boy awoke, flapping his arms wildly, expecting some sort of fluid resistance and finding none. Failing and kicking maniacally, he held his breath with cheeks bulging like an irritated puffer fish - perhaps the last breath of his life, he thought.. Naturally, he fell out of the single bed with a very earthy, very solid thud that knocked his entire lungful of air our in a mighty cough. Laying on the cold, dark wooden boards of the apartment, he respired loudly and thankfully. As he crawled up to a seated position at the head of his board-like mattress, his hand found the familiar patchwork texture of the beast - the Schwark - lying peacefully to the side of the pillow. Smiling and wincing in mild discomfort, the Boy gently picked up the mutant stuffed animal and hugged it mightily. A light came on in the hallway. Steeling himself, the Boy clutched the Schwark and strode into the bathroom to brush his teeth - to start the day. Monday morning. School.

<p style="text-align:center">~~~</p>

His Mother served him oatmeal with apple slices, humming softly to herself while she glopped small haystacks of the gelatinized sludge on her own plate. She was wearing the silver necklace and every so often, touched the heart-shaped amulet unconsciously. The Boy had not seen her so at peace in the early morning hours since before the great fire.

"I found you something the other day - at the thrift store down a ways," she casually mentioned, stirring a pinch of cinnamon into her oatmeal. Cinnamon. The Boy's eyes grew large at the spicy aroma - he had almost forgotten his mission. His Mother laughed.

"Now don't get that excited, I just wanted to save it until today - to celebrate," she hinted. "Your second week at school, after-all!" Dashing off to her bedroom, she emerged with her hands behind her back, holding a slightly bulky, mostly boxy thing.

"Close your eyes," she instructed the Boy. She lifted his arms into the air and slid cloth-like straps down his shoulders. A subtle weight fell against his back. As she awkwardly ratcheted down the buckles with great herky-jerky pulls and tugs, he nearly fell off the rickety kitchen chair. A slow-moving zipping commotion that was just out of site traveled from his right ear to his left with dramatic stereo effect. Taking a step back, she paused and clapped her hands.

"There! Go look in the mirror," she chirped. Shuffling into the bathroom, the Boy turned sideways and gawked. A backpack. Forest green canvas with mushroom-brown trim, its single zipper unveiled a maw-like gapping lid at the top. The bottom was reinforced with double stitches around placed around a base of thick worn leather.

"Your favorite colors," his Mother reminded. "Should be sort of rain-resistant, so you can put your books and lunch and things in there - like the other kids." He had never had a proper backpack like this before. Gathering wood or edible fungus in the forest, the Boy always lugged around a burlap or hemp sack. He hugged his Mother, face pressed into the surreal warmth of the metal amulet. His heart pulsed along with hers - he felt empowered this morning, for more reasons than he could count.

"I'm going to get ready for work. Pack up your things and we'll get going soon," she said, scratching the back of his head. As she turned and headed to the bathroom, the Boy scrambled back to his room. The Schwark was no longer on his bed, however.

"What the..." started the Boy, turning over sheets and pillows to his great dismay.

"Over here pal," said the goofy voice. Jumping six inches out of his skin, the Boy exploded off the mattress, caught his foot in a stray bundle of sheets, and for the second time that morning, toppled onto the cold apartment floor, landing completely sprawled out on his chest.

"Hey-oh! Zero for two today! Sheesh! Musta woken up on the wrong side of the bed or something - get it?" mocked the voice. The Boy's eyes drew to the small rectangular window up above his bed. The Schwark seemed to be sunning itself through the blinds, though it did not seem capable of moving. How did it get up there, the Boy wondered? More incredibly, was it really making noises?

"You look like a lost starfish down there, buddy. Come enjoy this sunshine for a second. Probably gonna rain the rest of the day - smells like it, anyway," said the Schwark.

"You... you can talk?" was all the Boy could whisper.

"Of course I can talk!" the Schwark replied incredulously. "I can burp and fart and hack loogies bigger than a sea cucumber, too - interested to see?" teased the creature. It was a very loud creature, decided the Boy, who looked over his shoulder towards the kitchen in panic - surely, his Mother would be wondering about the strange voice bragging to her son about all these bodily functions.

"Nah. She can't hear me pal. Only you and I have this... 'special relationship,' so to speak, if you catch my drift, wink-wink," the Schwark elaborated. Reaching to the window sill, the Boy plucked the animal from its perch and stared at it.

"I don't think I really know what you mean by 'special relationship,'" the Boy began, "but I was wondering if you would like to go to school with me today?" he asked timidly. The Schwark seemed a glow yellow for split second as it snorted and laughed.

"Aw, heck! I love schools! Tuna, herring, salmon - I could probably do human. Let's go" replied the Schwark as the Boy placed him carefully into the bottom of the new backpack. He didn't have the heart to inform the Schwark that this sort of school was in a boring room void of fish and coral, and not the plethora of jacks and barracuda he was used to swimming with.

"Alrighty! Let's get going, kiddo!" called his Mother. The Boy ran to the kitchen, and as his Mother turned to put on her heavy raincoat, he pocketed the small shaker of cinnamon from the spice rack and slipped it into an unzipped corner of the backpack.

"Ah-ah-choo!" sneezed his hidden hitchhiker. The Boy snapped to see if his Mother had heard the monstrous noise, but she only looked at him impatiently and nudged him on through the open front door and out into the foyer. Back into the bowels of the city, this landscape seemed a little less foreign and frightening in just the past week, thought the Boy. Humming to himself, the Boy skipped towards their station wagon as a light drizzle released from the grey blanket of low clouds above.

"I choose to be happy today," he silently announced into the depths of his mind, which glowed with golden confidence that morning.

~~~

"Please turn your text to page 326 and complete the first ten problems," announced his Math Teacher, who was also his English, Science, History, and Literature Teacher. He plopped open the massive book, and glanced at the assignment. A few minutes later, he was doodling absent-mindedly, having finished the overly simple problems in the span of several breaths. His classmates, however, seemed to be much slower. No matter - he let his mind wonder and his hand create. A series of small black dots laced around the notebook paper - ants. Ants carrying socks, and
~~~

cinnamon shakers, and butterflies, and mushrooms. Circling into themselves in a great spiral, the ants marched on into infinity.

"Ahem." came the exaggerated clearing of the throat as his Teacher leaned in over the Boy's left shoulder, examining his blatantly obvious disregard for math problems. He startled and jumped, jamming the sharpened pencil tip into the paper, fracturing the tip in a sickening crack.

"I've finished the problems," he softly stated, without looking up.

"I certainly hope so. Why don't you come on up to the chalk board and show us how you found the answers to the first two or three?" the Teacher passive-aggressively taunted. She was clearly in no mood for half-time art projects.

"Man, she's feisty, huh?" said a muffled voice from the depths of the Boy's backpack. "Heh heh, well, good luck, pal! Knock 'em dead! Break a leg!!" The Boy squinted at the backpack - was this Schwark supposed to be friendly? He wasn't entirely sure. Nonetheless, it's antics inspired the Boy to prove the creature he wasn't scared - he was going to march up there in front of all of these strangers and show them how simple this was. Screeching his chair on the linoleum floor, the Boy strode up to the green dusty board, picked out an orangish half-broken piece of chalk and wrote out the problem - a simple long-division series, requiring the carrying of a few left-over digits that his kept track of in his mind. He wrote the answer and turned to face the class.

"Thank you" stated his Teacher, her arms crossed, her lips pressed, forehead wrinkled. "And, please, now show how you arrived at this answer," she finished. The Boy stood silent for a moment and frowned.

"I... I don't understand. That is the answer." The Boy shuffled his stance - what more did she want? A few kids in the back of the class began to snicker.

"The proof. You couldn't have simply just known about the remainder of seven. Show us the whole process - it is, after all, *long* division" his Teacher insisted. More laughter from the cheap seats. The Boy blinked.

"But…" he started, "I just do," he mumbled. That's how it was. That's how it always had been with math - the answer just floated around his head like a brazen, bright blue butterfly suddenly landing on his nose, long enough for him to count the spots on its symmetric wings. That was the answer. How could he possibly explain this to an entire class of his peers? Laughter and sound-bites of "cheater," "weirdo," "idiot" permeated from various trajectories around the room.

"I think you can have a seat now," his Teacher growled. "Would anyone else like to to show us how to actually do this problem?" she asked sarcastically. The Boy, head hung low, ears tuned-out from reality, slunk back to his chair and sat. Pencil broken, heart heavy, confidence crushed.

"Sorry buddy," came the voice in the backpack. "They don't really get to you, though, do they?" it said in a last-ditch effort of condolences. The Boy stared at his circular ant portrait. They were all headed into a black hole of nothingness. Perhaps that's what school would be for him - follow the ants, follow them in their ridiculous circular pursuits of proofs to math problems, identification of gerund or infinitive phrases, how to properly shoot a basketball. He could honestly care less. What sort of education was this, anyway? Scores on tests paled in comparison to the knowledge and experience of the living world that none of his classmates seemed to appreciate - save for one. He sighed out loud. The Girl was staring at him from across the room and he caught her glance. She smiled. He reciprocated, semi-forcedly. Was she the way out of here? Out of the black hole? He was hoping so, anyway.

"Looks like maybe someone at least thinks you're an okay guy," quipped the Schwark. "I mean, someone *else*, because I also think... you know... oh, never mind," said the Schwark, slightly embarrassed. The Boy smiled again, a bit bigger now. The bell rang. Lunchtime. The Boy's heart sank. He had remembered the cinnamon. He had remembered the Schwark. He had a new old backpack. He had no lunch.

~~~

"You brought it, right?" she asked, sitting down next to him at the adjacent empty desk.

"Of course. Did you bring the... the socks?" the Boy tried to hide his smirk.

"Wearing them right now," the Girl said matter-of-factly, "three days straight! I think that will really get the ants attention! Don't you think?" she proudly exclaimed, pointing her shoes back and forth.

"Cool," the Boy made a mental note to hold his breath once the experiment commenced. A few desks down, a classmate had brought out a bright pink polyester lunch container that caught the Boy's eye. Ripping open the side zipper voraciously, the student removed several plastic-wrapped items: celery sticks, a small sandwich in its own baggy with the crusts removed, an apple, a metallic-looking space-juice box with
~~~

disposable straw, and a plastic pack of chocolate cookies. Plastic wrapped in plastic wrapped in plastic. The Boy thought about the time he found a dead baby seal at the beach, strands of plastic fishing net wrapped around its flippers and neck - its eyes bulged in asphyxiated torment. He shook his head rapidly to dislodge the image, but as he looked back at the Girl's shoes, he only saw the pair of black rigor mortis seal eyes staring back.

"Hey, you OK?" the Girl inquired. "Didn't you bring a lunch?"

"I'm not that hungry, actually" the Boy monotonously replied, stomach queasy from both hunger and disgust.

"You forgot it home, didn't you?" she said, immediately upending her purple lunchbox onto her desk. Several handfuls of bright red rotund radishes rolled every which way, a small Tupperware of soft white cheese, a bundle of celery sticks tied together with hemp, a paper napkin with a small stack of thinly sliced dark rye bread folded up neatly inside, a small Twix candy bar. She gathered up her bounty, and immediately began separating items into two even piles. "Survival" she stated, plainly, pushing a stack of food his way. "Hope you don't mind radishes - most kids don't for some reason. I don't think they've actually tried one, though" she finished, taking a crisp bite out of a particularly bright red and pink root. The Boy did not object - he was hungry, and the fresh vegetables were what his body and mind craved.

"Thanks," he timidly mustered back. The Girl was a good person - his first real friend in this new world.

"Hey. Buddy. Pal," a grainy voice from under his desk chair cat-called. "Got anything for your ol' Schwarky?" The Boy was stuck. He couldn't actually answer the Schwark - his new friend would think him mentally unstable. She may have already thought that, the Boy contemplated. He devised an alternative approach - a thought experiment.

"Here's a weird question about food," he began, "If you took a whale, and a shark, and a bunch of other animals, and combined them all together... into one big thing... what would it actually eat?" the Boy finished, polling both Girl and Schwark. The Girl responded first.

"Hmm. You're talking about an evolutionary funnel, where all the animals start creating hybrids because of stress from the environment! I read a science article about it - lions and tigers making ligers. Horses and donkeys making mules." The Girls' eyes sparkled as she recalled these details and facts. After a moment of intense thought, she continued, "I'd say such a creature would eat... chicken? Just like everything else - it would seek some sort of protein. We would need to conduct an experiment to be sure, though. I'm a scientist, so I sort of know these things," she finished, stamping her authority on the statement.

"Chicken? She nuts?" stammered the Schwark. "Well, I'm a vegetarian! Heck! I'm a fruit-itarian! You know what I want - no - what I *need*, right now, pal? A big ol' bowl of bright red, super-ripe, extra-sweet.... cranberries!" The Boy stared at his pack of half-eaten cookies in disbelief - a fruit-itarian, Schwark beast? Was this real? He felt he had no choice but to put this to the test.

"I think it might actually like to eat cranberries," he suggested to the Girl, a whiff of false confidence underscoring his theory." She seemed to be considering his answer, though.

"Cranberries, eh? That's interesting. I'll think about that and get back to you" replied the Girl, the scientist. They ate the rest of her lunch in silence. The Schwark went hungry.

<center>~~~</center>

Seven deafening bells rang out overhead.

"Holy Geez! That's the most terrible thing I've ever heard!" the Schwark moaned and groaned. "It's worse than that time a whole pod of bottlenose dolphins sung me 'Happy Birthday,'" he lamented. "Just a whole bunch of 'E-e-e-e-e! E-e-e-e-e! E-e-e-e!' for over three minutes! And on top of it all, they thought I was older than I actually was, too! Adding insult to injury, those guys… Dolphins - such pranksters!"

"It's not so bad, I think" replied the Boy. He liked dolphins, anyway. He thought the Schwark was probably being over-dramatic. The school bells were growing on him, he decided. They signaled the end of the boring part of the day, and onto the more exciting portion - the adventurous side of things. He stuffed a book into the backpack, careful not to smoosh the Schwark, and sprinted to the gymnasium, clutching a small shaker of cinnamon in his right fist. Slinking around the back of the bleachers, he stopped under the wad of bubblegum from three days ago and strained his eyes in the dim fluorescence that barely penetrated through the fenestration of the aluminum stairs above him. No movement. No ants. He furrowed his brow, and searched the darkness beyond for signs of his subjects.

"Psst! Down here!" said a soft but forceful voice down at his ankles. The Girl was flat on her stomach, examining at a dark patch in the waxy wood surface of the gym floor. The Boy squatted and saw that she was counting a series of black specks on the ground. They didn't appear to

81

be moving. "Dead" she whispered. "I think the janitors sprayed something down here. No more ants." They patrolled the back of the bleachers against the wall and found evidence of the genocide - several small black plastic ant-traps sitting squatly against a crack in the brick-wall that ran vertically through the mortar for several feet. The Girl handed the Boy the somber death chambers and motioned for him to smell it.

"Licorice" she surmised. "I really don't like licorice," she scowled. "I guess the ants do, though. They take it back to their nest and poison each other - terrible thing." The two sat facing the brick-wall in silence. The research project seemed to have taken a morbid turn for the worst. The Boy sympathized for the ants as well as the Girl. Deep inside himself, though, he felt a small bright flame burning with happiness at the realization that he had found another human that also felt sad when ants died. A stray basketball ricocheted over the back of the bleachers and chaotically came to rest nest the the two mourners. An older boy with blonde hair strode over and stopped abruptly upon seeing them sitting facing the wall.

"What is this, some sort of seance for weirdos?" he grabbed the basketball and spit on the floor next to the Boy. "Losers," he hissed under his breath, dribbling back to the court laughing as only a bully could - a supremely arrogant and ignorant sound, the Boy thought.

"Forget that guy," said the Girl to the Boy, "he's just scared about seeing something he doesn't understand."

"Forget that guy," said the Boy to the Girl "he doesn't want to understand."

"Forget that guy," said the Schwark to the Boy, "he's probably inbred anyway." With that, the Girl removed her shoes, pulled off her tube socks, yellowing with grime and dead skin and sweat, and stacked them against the crack in the wall. The stench was impressive - a sharp, rotten, cheesy vinegar odor that burnt the sinuses and made the Boy's eyes water.

"Holy moly! What in the heck is that?" said the Schwark, its voice muffled, presumably pinching its Otter nose with a furry fin. The Boy held his breath and unscrewed the lid to the cinnamon. Leaning over the pile of putrid socks, he vigorously shook the spice out until a fine brown layer coated the exterior of the laundry. The surrounding air devolved into a perverted sort of scented holiday candle set inside a trash can. The Schwark sneezed. The Girl fixated on the crack in the wall. The Boy scratched his head, happy to just be present behind the bleachers with his friends. They sat and sat, observed and waited. Minutes upon minutes went by, but no ants.

"Maybe the whole nest is dead," thought the Girl out loud.

"Maybe they sealed off the crack when they put these traps down," suggested the Boy. "My Father used to seal cracks in our cabin to keep the outside animals outside." The Girl sighed.

"Hmm. Well, what should we do then? I mean, ants are an altruistic and highly socialized," she explained. "They have a hive-mind. If some of the survivors are sealed off behind the wall, then they must be reforming a colony over there. So, it must be outside!" The two reached the same conclusion simultaneously, staring wide eyed with excitement at the other. She grabbed the spicy socks and stuffed them into her backpack, frantically tying her shoes back onto bare feet. The Schwark groaned.

"C'mon pal! It's probably raining out there!" it complained. "Let's look for ants somewhere else. Actually, let's just forget this whole ant deal and find some cranberries instead, what do ya think?" squawked the Schwark.

"No, we're going to go find them!" announced the Boy, suddenly realized he had just spoken out loud in response to the Schwark. He looked at the Girl and swallowed hard. She glanced at him side-ways and half-smirked, "Didn't say were weren't!" she replied. Bolting through the gymnasium backdoor, the two ran wildly and ecstatically out in the dingy, dusky city lights.

~~~

A fine mist drifted between buildings as they found their way into an alley adjacent to the school that the Girl believed followed the same miniature fault line in the brick and mortar they had seen from behind the bleachers.

"Look!" the Girl exclaimed. In between two huge rusting dumpsters stuffed to the brim with cardboard and garbage bags, a very faint static shimmered along the gravel up against the brick - the ants! Thousands and thousands of them, scurrying single file from one dumpster to the other. "It's perfect!" clapped the Girl. "We can do the experiment right here!" she announced, donning her figurative scientist jacket and goggles - which in this case, consisted of emptying out a pile of disgusting socks onto the wet gravel amongst the garbage dumpsters in a musty alley. Loving every moment of this incredibly strange adventure, the Boy dramatically brought out the cinnamon shaker, spun off the lid, and spilled the entirety onto the damp socks. Clumps of wet cinnamon congealed and
~~~

rolled down the cotton strands, forming dark brown expanding circles on the pale fabric. The odor was fantastically rich and stomach-churning. As they squatted in eager anticipation of any change in trajectory from their insect participants, a sudden congested, phlegmy hacking from behind them sent them scrambling into the gravel..

"Ha-ghh, Flo-pff!" A fat wad of speckled green and black sputum landed near the Boy's feet with a sickening smack. The two scientists turned to face a pair of saggy grey eyes staring at them from under a large cardboard lean-to propped against the side of a corrugated stairwell.

"What you kids doin' out here, eh?" Like a hard start on an old truck, the voice sputtered and grinded, attempting to catch spark and carry the sentence over groans of rusted vocal cords.

"Nothing! Just… uh... school project," replied the Girl, between frantic heartbeats and shallow breaths.

"Looking at ants and things!" said the Boy, immediately embarrassed by his honesty. The man in the box said nothing. Instead, he clumsily rose and loomed over the two, and rubbed his scraggly dark beard free of stale pizza crust crumbs. As he adjusted one of the three soggy sweatshirts he wore on top of one another, a piece of newspaper extruded from his left cuff, and he lazily tucked it back into place.

"Hard life," started the Schwark, "living out here, like this. Must be pretty down on his luck." Hearing the Schwark without taking his eyes off the box man, the Boy took a breath, forced a smile, and said, "Would you like to watch? I think its about to start." Pointing behind him towards the pile of socks, the Boy's smile became genuine as the Box Man canted his head to the side and grinned back.

"Alright," the gruff man replied, taking a seat next to the Boy. As the three unlikely scientists squatted around the cinnamon-soaked socks in silence, a funny thing began to happen. The ants were subtly and slowly turning. At first, it was just a few brave adventurers - scouts. Breaking off from the main assembly line of six-legged machines, hauling back organic shenanigans from the cafeteria dumpster, back to their abode in the cardboard recycling bin it appeared. These particularly brave bugs summited the mound of cheesy, spicy nastiness like wolves drawn to a week-old antelope carcass. Waving their antennae wildly, they raced back to the masses with the incredible news. The smell on the misty breeze through the alley seemed to intensify and change slightly.

"I knew it," whispered the Girl.

"Cool!" whooped the Boy.

"Sort of gross," lamented the Schwark.

"They're hungry," suggested the Box Man. Everyone looked at him, and slowly nodded in agreement. A few moments later, and the mastiff of wet tube sock was completely covered in a pulsating, undulating sea of black bodies, completely hypnotized and engrossed in the find of their lives, no doubt. The Boy, sensing the wave of building energy, closed his eyes. What would it be like to be one of those ants, he wondered?

~~~

Shrinking down a thousand-fold in his mind, he sprouted a pair of antennae and fell into place. An assembly line worker - caught up in the party of the century. Gazing around from the side of the soft, stinky mountain, he witnessed ants afar making the pilgrimage from the dumpster, gaining speed the closer they came to the great mount. Layers of arthropods, linked at the legs, dancing and swaying, rubbing and secreting their own old sock and cinnamon odors to share with each other, exponentiating the experience to a level of ant ecstasy the Boy had never known.

"How amazing!" he thought into his ant-mind. "To be alive in such a way - like this!" Holding onto the ants in front, behind, below, and above, he vibrated his exoskeleton in synchronized rhythm with the collective being that was the sum of their whole. He decided he could stay here forever and be happy - a most blissful place.

~~~

A burst of red and blue pulsating, angry, strobing light. Muffled, flat voices calling over a hollow-sounding bullhorn. Sirens blaring and honking and ripping him from his lucid fantasy amongst the ants. Opening his eyes, the Boy saw the worry in the Box Man's face.

"Thank you kids," the man said quickly. "That was interesting! I've gotta run, though - literally have to run." He sped off down the alley, his laceless oversized boots slapping the wet gravel. He was very thin, thought the Boy. "Down on his luck" he recalled. Two large men decked out in dark blue raincoats, caps, waving oversized flashlights out ahead of their blank faces approached.

"You there! You kids! What are you doing out here? You live here?" A funny question, thought the Boy - if he was an ant or a Box Man, then, why yes, he did live here.

"These cops think you live with the box guy," said the Schwark. He was probably getting wet in the canvas bag by now - the mist had turned to a steady diagonal rain.

"No, sir?" started the Boy, "we were just doing a school project."

"In a garbage alley? Why don't you come with us, you two?" the other police officer said flatly. It was not a question, decided the Boy. Red and blue strobing light refracted from microscopic raindrops into the Boy's eyes - he squinted the entire way towards the police car.

The Ship

Starless, moonless, perfect darkness extending in every direction - below, above, within. Black sea merged and melded with black sky - a continuous nothingness, terrifyingly beautiful. Bobbing on the surface in what he imagined to be the center of a black hole - maybe the center of the universe itself - the Boy could feel the undulations of waves, the fine saltiness bursting from white-caps, and the familiar, plush softness and felted sturdiness of his massive stead - the Schwark. The Boy could feel the energy pulse through the Schwark's body as it casually swam through the space-sea, headed in seemingly every and any direction simultaneously. Blowhole completely dark, the Schwark forced the Boy to abandon site and simply feel the wind, taste the sea, hear the sloshing water all around them. As the sea grew rougher, the Boy gripped onto the wiry hairs of the fox ears, his stomach lurching as the Schwark rose and dove with every crest and trough. Eventually, curiosity got the better of him.

"Where are we?" the Boy's voice was but a squeak amongst the mighty forces of nature that seemingly conspired to drown him out, figuratively and perhaps literally, he imagined.

"Somewhere far, far back," came the cryptic reply of the Schwark, who sighed in a melancholy manner that startled the Boy. He hesitated and stuttered as he thought the answer through.

"Like, far back... from the coast? Far back... from the city?" he yelled into fox ears.

"Nope!" rumbled the beast. "Different sort of direction, you might say!" The Boy rode on sildently for several moments.

"Far back... long ago? Far back... in time?" Perilous confusion filled the space between the Boy's words, and his self-realization of the likely conclusion made his head pound.

"Yep," the somber Schwark murmured. "I thought we should visit this place. Both of us. Something very important about it. You'll see." A faint pinprick of red light peeped and eked itself out onto the horizon and disappeared so quickly, the Boy thought he was hallucinating a floating angler fish. Again - a flash. This time, a hazy blue pulse, then nothing - darkness. Every few seconds the light would appear, bobbing lower, rising higher, distorted by the wave heights that seemed to be growing in size and power by the minute. Red-blue. Red-blue. Brighter. Closer.

"A boat!" whispered the Boy into the salty sea air. A fishing trolley, rocking and twirling madly in the violent seas around it, like a pinecone caught in a recirculating eddy - an endless loop of chaos. The alternating red-blue light atop the mast beat steadily, wearily, in all directions.

"They've been out here awhile," began the Schwark. "Fire on their boat. Engine's out. No radio." Narrating this tale of doom as he swam along the starboard side of the almost toy-like fishing boat, the Schwark's blowhole began to beat in synchronicity with the red-blue of the boat's silent and desperate distress beacon. At that moment, a massive swell pounded the port-side of the vessel, and almost brought the keel up into the midnight air. A door from the ship's cabin flung open, and a bearded man wearing a dark sweater tumbled out, miraculously grabbing ahold of the strained steel cables that were his last line of protection from certain drowning. In the glare of the beating blue light, the illuminated face of the haggard Captain stared bleakly over the bow and spat - a deep, guttural, drawn-out phlegmy hack - into the mouth of the greedy sea, who's arms and legs lashed and thrashed for its next meal, its next victim.

"Can't have me! Not yet!" the Captain bellowed, wiping his chapped lips with the soaking sleeve of his salty sweater. A maniacal grin spread across the man's face, and the Boy watched in horror and disbelief as he held himself steady on the cables with one hand, and undid his pant's fly with the other. The Captain cackled and hooted and roared into oblivion as a dark yellow steaming arc of whiskey-tinged urine hissed into the waves below. As if in protest, the storm surged and roiled and shot foamy salvos of cold ocean foam onto the sagging bow from all directions.

Red. Blue. Red. Blue. Time between the rise and fall, ebb and flow, peak to trough became increasingly longer. Near the bottom of one such trip, a vertical wall of water seemingly a mile high appeared, cast as liquid fire in the fluorescence of the red light from the boat. The Boy screamed.

"Hold on tight," the Schwark instructed, as it duck-dove beneath the tsunami, the thunderous rumble of water crashing over their heads. Pointing back up at the boat from a hundred feet below the surface, the two watched in near slow-motion as certain death approached the Captain and his forsaken ship. Like a hand casually swatting a gnat, the wave sent the boat tumbling end-over-end, capsizing once before rolling back onto its keel, capsizing again, the unyielding red-blue-red-blue calling towards deep space one moment, towards deep sea in another. The sea steadied and calmed, assessing the carnage it had dealt. Schwark and Boy rose back to the surface alongside the capsized vessel, the water beneath pulsing in eerie red and blue - attracting a few brave white-tip sharks, eager to greet the spoils of the storm.

"Ahh-hacck!" A great sputtering cough. A desperate drunken moan. Like some ancient barnacle, the Captain lay on his stomach, plastered to the stern of the boat's keel, his sweaters in tatters, thick trickles of blood navigating down his scalp. Flipping himself onto his back, the Captain sat up slowly and considered his fate. He awkwardly stood, feet wide on the shaky broken keel, which now stood higher at stern than bow as the boat slowly succumbed to its mortal wounds. The sea sat flat as glass now, the glow of red-blue lighting up the Captain's eyes, wide and beating, perhaps reviewing every moment of his life leading up to this moment. The Boy swallowed, his face moist with sea and tears. The Schwark sighed, its blowhole dark blue and purple with sympathy. The Captain laughed - a deep, soul-shaking bellow that stood the Boy's arm-hair to full attention. A crescendo of unapologetic and raging energy, culminating into a full-throated battle cry that sent spittle and sea flying from nostrils and lips, eyes wide and bulging in fury. As a great exhalation left his condemned chest, he panted and closed his eyes, resigned and exhausted.

"Can't we do something? The Boy cried, tugging at the Schwark's dorsal fin, desperate to have the creature intervene. Surely, there was room for two aboard this beast?

"We are both here and not, kid. These things have happened. There is no intervention," answered the Schwark. Frowning with forlornness, the Boy decided the mystery in mystique of this place was as much a blessing as a curse.

"Keep watching," instructed the Schwark. Turning his eyes towards the hopeless figure on the sinking, capsized ship in the middle of the universe, in the place between sea and sky, in the nothing, in the dark, the Boy caught his breath at the sudden sight, Between red and blue underwater strobes, the Captain stood perfectly still on the very end of the boat - nearly naked and glistening with sweat, and blood, and salt, and oil. Arms and face raised up towards starless space, he spoke his final decree to the air and sea, gods and ancestors, givers and tormentors, friends and foes.

"Well, you know me," the Captain began, in an ironically mild-mannered and sarcastic tone. He spat a mouthful of curdled blood into the night. "You know I gotta do it my way, even here, at the end," he continued. "You didn't really think I'd give *you* that honor, did you?" he cried. "I'll die on my own terms, thank you very much!" he finished with a sly, smug smirk and quick nod. With that, the Captain faced the blank black sea, sighed, and exploded into a mighty leap off of the now upside-down stern, gracefully diving into the ocean with barely a splash.

The Schwark submerged itself as the Boy whimpered. The two slowly dove beneath the ship to find the Captain hovering near the pulsating red and blue mast. Suddenly, the man erupted straight down into the empty darkness, breast-stroking and kicking at a steady and purposeful rhythm, eyes focused and locked forward with unknowable intent. Boy and Schwark swam alongside the Captain, the red-blue pulsating haze dulling in the depths. The Captain slowed his strokes and allowed himself to simply drift in the soft underwater current. Every so often, he let out a stream of bubbles that flew towards the still surface - the only indication of which way was up, and which was down. The Captain closed his eyes.

The creature and Boy swam directly in front of the drifting naked man, mere inches from his scruffy beard that bobbed and weaved around his face. That face - a very familiar face. The Boy knew this face. As if on cue, the Schwark began to emit a soft red-blue-red-blue luminescence from its blowhole, casting a steady light upon the Captain... upon... the Box Man. Gasping and choking on a mouthful of seawater, the Boy nearly fell off the dorsal fin saddle, overwhelmed with confusion and shock.

"Impossible," he breathed. A man whom he had just recently and very briefly met in a dreary, rain-soaked alley... a man who had just watched a pile of socks become consumed by a horde of ants... a man who the Boy had just seen running away from the red-blue strobe of the police lights... who had just jumped from a sinking ship... was now face-to-face with the Boy, about to die a hundred feet beneath a moonless sea and sky.

"Is anything truly impossible?" answered the Schwark.

"I don't know," replied the Boy, to himself, to the Schwark, to Captain, to the nothingness. The Schwark turned a fur-lined eyeball up towards the Boy.

"Well, I know," he started, "And guess what? I know him, too. That's why I brought you here." Bubbles floated from the Captain's mouth as his chest fully collapsed. Turning shades of purple and darkening blue, his lips slowly began to tremble. Moments from embracing his liquid grave, the Captain's eyes shot open and stared straight at the Boy - an unbreakable gaze, penetrating the Boy's mind and body, filling it with terrible fear and sudden infinite connectedness.

The Captain knew the Boy then, and smiled.

The Boy knew the Captain then, and smiled back.

Time and space, dreams and reality, consciousness and
unconsciousness - were these so opposite, so polar, so black and white - or
was there something else in between? In that moment, as he watched the
Captain, all the Boy could decide was that he knew he was truly alive.

91

The Captain

Searing into his dreamscape, his Mother's heated gaze from the bedroom doorway woke him abruptly and uncomfortably. He kicked off the sweltering quilt and sat, looking at her red eyes burning back at his. After she had picked him up from the police station, and mostly after hearing his excuse of some bizarre science experiment involving ants and socks and the cinnamon that they no longer had in the cupboard, she had grown quite upset. It wasn't until he finally told her about the Box Man and his many sweaters that her emotions boiled over. From the doorway of his bedroom, he could see her narrowed eyes, her pursed lips, her fierceness building and climaxing and filling him with regret and embarrassment. Unspoken words were more effective in conveying her disappointment and frustration, and this tore into the Boy's heart with the sharpness of a scalpel. Neither had spoken much since coming home late last night. It appears as if this trend was to continue this morning.

"She's not too thrilled, eh?" yawned the Schwark. The Boy ate his soggy breakfast in silence. The strange chewing sounds from masticating the space-waffle filled the void with an unpleasant gurgley sloshing. Only the buzzing of the dim fluorescent bulb swinging above the card table was slightly more annoying.

"Make your lunch," were his Mother's only words, as she pushed off from the flimsy table and proceeded to prepare herself for another double-shift day. Grease-stains were now a semi-permanent fixture of her apron, despite her best efforts to scrub and bleach them. Her hair often smelled of stale cooking oil, one hundred second-hands of cheap cigarette smoke, and strangely enough, pickles. The pale purple circles around her eyes refused camouflage despite her best intentions to mask them with make-up. Tired was just the tip of the iceberg.

Spongy white bread, mustard, lettuce, tomato, tofu - the Boy laid out the ingredients and stacked them into a thin sandwich before wrapping them in aluminum foil he had been recycling day to day. He picked out a bruised apple with four stickers declaring it 'on sale.' A handful of carrots and a small glass jar of peanut butter. His Mother had insisted that they attempt to at least eat more vegetables, even if it often cost much more than a box of crackers or chips - foods most kids in his class ate regularly. He did not object - carrots with their tops still on reminded him of their home in the forest, and he loved to stroke their fine fibrous green fronds and smell their gritty earthiness. His classmates often looked on as if he were some strange animal at a zoo. Actually, he though, they looked at him like that regardless, but he felt a secret knowledge when they watched him eat carrots, and that made him smile unto himself. As he packed his lunch together, he stared at the items and felt a particular sense of forgetfulness, of sudden emptiness, of vague selfishness. One sandwich, one apple, one bunch of carrots. One lunch.

"I think that would be a reasonable thing to do, too," suggested the Schwark, calling from down the hallway, still laying in the Boy's bed. How did it always know what he was thinking, thought the Boy? No matter, the Boy was in full agreement. He opened up the fridge and set up his operation for round two, keeping a careful eye turned and ear tuned to his Mother's room, in case she were to catch him in the act.

~~~

"Four o'clock today, sharp. I'm working a second shift soon after, so make sure you're out front then," his Mother said, flatly. The Boy nodded blankly, looking down at his scuffed brown faux leather shoes, wishing she could understand that everything was a big misunderstanding, hoping she would realize that certain things were real, others unreal, and some things in between. He wanted to burst out and tell her about the Schwark, about his dreams, about the Captain - the Box Man - the Girl, everything. He said nothing, and instead closed the door to the station wagon with a creaking rusty crunch. As the car puttered away, a plume of bluish exhaust belched up into his nostrils, the carbon monoxide and sweet, sickly smell of burnt hydrocarbons sending him into a slightly woozy, lightheaded sway as he made his way up the steps to his school. He made his way to his classroom door just as the warning bells sounded and signaled another ten hours of survival for the survivor.

Morning classes flew past, around, and over the Boy. Math and vocabulary quizzes: one-hundred percent perfect. Homework assignments: one-hundred percent absent. A rumor that he was cheating. A lie that he was "special," or "autistic," or "foreign,", or maybe just from another universe. Between these stinging sound-bites and affronts to his confidence, there was the ringing of bells, the pitter-patter of rain on the windows and ceiling, the extra-weight in his backpack of twice as many sandwiches, apples, carrots, and of course, the constant banter of a hungry Schwark creature incessantly requesting a bowl of cranberries. This was his life now, for some reason. The Boy sighed. He made eye-contact with
~~~

the Girl, who smiled at him. Her socks were less yellow today. The lunch bell rang.

"Wasn't it amazing?" the Girl shrieked. "You were right! Cinnamon and socks! All those ants! I'd say our science experiment validated our hypothesis!" The ecstatic Girl proclaimed, between intermittent mouthfuls of radish and pickled herring. She nearly choked twice, once coughing a small partially-chewed pickled fish head onto the Boy's desk. He was amazed that he did not vomit all over the Girl in that moment.

"Yeah, it was pretty cool," he agreed. "Even the Box Man seemed pretty interested." The Boy remembered the underwater Captain bubbling and drifting and drowning and felt a bolt of shivers run up his spine. The Girl appeared confused.

"The who? The hobo guy?" she asked, eyebrow cocked, "Um, yeah, I guess" she dismissed, "But I thought of another experiment we could try!" she revealed, eyes flickering with a different, daring energy.

"Underwear, nutmeg, and... spiders? Old shirts, cracked black pepper, and... stray dogs?" the Boy sarcastically replied, annoyed that she was not the least bit interested in the Box Man. She looked at the Boy with her mouth gaped open, partially chewed rye bread and farmer's cheese visibly lodged in the pits of her premolars.

"Close!" she stammered, "I think we should find scents, flavors, sounds to attract all those things - rats, dogs, cats, moths, butterflies, flies, birds, bees, and even people! Maybe there's a certain something... I don't know... a *Thing* that would make everything that's alive move the same way - change their directions, you know... come together!" she finished. The Boy nodded. A *Thing* - for everyone, for everything. He liked the Girl, her desire to put her intuition to the test, to hold up the standard that the world - that life - just might be entirely connected to itself.

"I have to go do something right now," announced the Boy, abruptly. "If anyone asks, I went to the bathroom, okay?" His eyes conveyed the importance and urgency, and the Girl did not hesitate in her silent acknowledgement and support. The Boy pushed his half-full lunchbox into his backpack and briskly strode out of the classroom and towards the side-door of the school, into the cardboard alley.

~~~
~~~

Rows of dumpsters, stacks of collapsed cardboard boxes, odors of mold and cat urine intermingling - the alley was much less exciting than the Boy remembered from yesterday. The steady blubbering and apneic gasps from a dark corner revealed the not-so secret mobile abode of the Box Man. Approaching timidly, tip-toeing through shallow puddles of stagnant rain water and garbage water and liquids that maybe weren't water at all, the Boy saw the pair of laceless boots protruding from the back-end of a refrigerator box and frowned.

"Not too far off from the galley of an old nasty fishing boat, in my opinion," considered the Schwark. "Maybe it's just like home for him," it said in an unusually nasally voice. Was the creature pinching its nose? The Boy couldn't be sure. Standing over the Box Man, the Boy saw that he had placed a battered dark blue trucker hat over his face to block out the sporadic headlights from passing cars and trucks, his unkempt curly and grease-slicked hair flung in all directions around it. The Box Man snored louder and louder the longer the Boy stared, perhaps unconsciously sensing the uncomfortable proximity of another human being. Suddenly, the Box Man let out a tremendous flatulence that seemed to shake the entire alley, reverberating off the soggy brick walls and accenting the terrible smell already present with an especially nauseating touch. The Boy grimaced and held his breath. The Schwark burst into throws of laughter. The Box Man awoke into fits of stammering confusion.

"Wh-who go-goes th-there?" the Box Man blurted and chortled, scrambling to his feet while shadow-boxing non-existent foes. Stepping onto a putrid banana, the innards oozing out in a molten puree of filth, the Box Man slipped in cheesy comedic fashion, landing on top of his shoddy boxy shelter, collapsing the entire shambled wreck underneath himself. Huffing and swearing a thousand curses at once, he glared at the offending fruit, tracing the shadow of the Boy with crazed eyeballs until he met his pair of faux leather boots. Snarling like a feral dog, the Box Man raised his curled-back , dry lips to meet the intruder.

"Captain," whispered the Boy. recognizing that wild ferocity and fiercely unique independence in the man. The Captain blinked, his gnarled tobacco-juice-stained remaining teeth slowly disappearing behind a gradually softening face.

"Captain, we've met, remember?" prodded the Boy, exponentially growing in confidence. The alley man - the Box Man - the Captain - spit a monstrous gelatinized load of sputum against the side of a steel dumpster with a smack.

"Huh," he grunted, "Ant Kid. With the socks and whatever. Weird Ant Kid - yeah, I remember." The Boy blinked and stood with is mouth apart.

"Ha! He's got you there!" chided the Schwark.

"No. But yes…" stammered the Boy. "From yesterday, right. But, no... not just yesterday. We've met at another time. Under the sea." The Boy stared at the Captain and imagined him floating a hundred feet deep in the cold black sea, a pulsating red-blue-red-blue illuminating his figure from above, beard flowing, body at peace, mind at rest. The Captain's tired eyes burst into surreal recognition. He remembered a Boy atop a massive furry shark-like whale creature on the night that he died. Almost died. Should have died. Did he die?

"What in the...." he gasped, sprawling backwards on hands and buttocks, backing up against the alley wall, covering himself with cardboard scraps in a frantic futile manner. "Gah-get out of here! You, you ghost!" Was he trying to escape his memories - his past? Or his future? The Boy could not know.

"Yep, he recognized us alright," the Schwark glibly thought aloud.

"Captain, it's alright. I wanted to just... to just say 'hello,'" said the Boy, squatting to meet the terrified man at eye level. "I just wanted to see if maybe you wanted... wanted some lunch or something?" the Boy awkwardly offered, lowering his backpack to the ground, unzipping the cover, and placing a foil-encased second lunch in front of the trembling figure covered in trash. The Captain stared at the Boy, at the lunch, back to the Boy. Licking his lips, he crawled forward like a stalking lion, snatching the lunch sack and retreating to his stack of cardboard. Examining the contents, his eyebrows raised at the carrots, and a genuine smile appeared across his weathered skin. He looked back upon the kneeling Boy.

"I... I don't know how you've found me, or who you are, or what you want... but... thanks." With that, he tore into the food and didn't say a word until every last crumb was devoured.

~~~

The Boy and Captain spent the hour revisiting the night of the storm, of the capsizing, of the swim to the depths of certain death. The Captain could not recall how he had gotten into such a predicament, other than his crew had escaped on a small dinghy at his behest. He was determined to ride out the storm - a fool-hardy plan in retrospect, as he
~~~

revealed to the Boy. The Boy, for that matter, could not understand how he had been in that place at that time - a question for the Schwark, no doubt. The Captain, to the Boy's surprise, accepted this impossibility without a bat of the eye. He didn't even ask about the Schwark, for that matter. The Boy thought the Captain had likely seen many strange things in his life.

"How did you... survive?" the Boy finally asked. The Captain peered over the Boy's shoulders in a thousand-yard stare, recalling faint details and impossible memories.

"I am not sure I did, Boy," he finally answered. "Sometimes, I think I did die, and this is a new life. Or a different life. A different timeline. Sometimes I think maybe I was saved." Picking up a handful of gravel stones, the Captain began to toss them into an old tire. "I have the strangest memory, or dream, or something in between, of being carried by a pod of dolphins back to the coast. Of crawling up the sand dunes into the tall grass and being kept warm by a herd of elk for several nights. Of making my way along a stream and being fed mollusks and small fish by a family of otters. Of following a huge butterfly up a ridge line to a forest road, that eventually led to a highway, where I collapsed. And awoke - in a hospital here in this city. I know - its totally crazy, right?" The Boy did not move. The Captain tossed another pebble.

"I believe it," the Boy finally replied, tossing his own stone into the tire. "Maybe some things just can't really be explained." The Captain snorted.

"In that hospital - I'm not sure what was real then, I panicked. For many days and nights, I couldn't see the sun or the moon. I was sedated and strapped to the bed rails. 'Schizophrenic' someone said. 'Delusional' someone else explained to me. I thought that was partly true, at least. When they let me free, I had no place to call home, no sense of where that might even be. I was lost in my dreams, nightmares, memories - real or unreal. I sleep here, because its warm. Because it's down the street from the hospital, and I am too scared to leave. Because you kids throw away so much food. Because there is a near-endless supply of cardboard and other things for me to shelter under. Because no one bothers me here." Nodding along the entire time, the Boy empathized with the Captain on more levels than he thought possible. The two tossed a rock into the tire at the same time, the black gravel pieces colliding in the air, skipping off the rubber of the tire's edge. They laughed.

"I don't feel at home anywhere now either," replied the Boy, to the Captain, to the Schwark, to himself, to the alley ants. "I sometimes don't know what real is either, but most of the time, I think I do. I have a friend that is sort of helping me to start to understand that it's alright to feel that way," he continued, nudging the backpack a bit.

"Aw, shucks, kid," came the typical half-sarcastic Schwark response. The Boy smiled and continued.

"I've been learning that if you try really hard to see things through the lens of being happy, of staying positive, then more good things will start to happen. You'll meet more good people. Home might actually start to take a new shape." The Captain had set his stones down. He was facing the Boy, listening carefully, his lips tight and eyes focused.

"But so many hard, disheartening things will happen along the way," the Boy sighed. "The toughest part is keeping your chin up and going with the flow, knowing that this rocky road is taking you somewhere wonderful, if you believe it will," the Boy finished. These were the feelings and thoughts that had been swirling around his mind for days, finally realized and vocalized and believed. He had never felt so strong. The Captain considered the Boy's words, mulling them around and chewing on the fat and sinew of their meaning as it applied to his existence. He chuckled and shook his head.

"Yeah, kid. You're right. Guess I just need to take the plunge... again," he half-joked. The Boy and Captain laughed at that - a morbid, dark, real and unreal laughter shared between two very unlikely new friends.

~~~

A creaking, groaning bell tolled from the bowels of the old brick building, signaling the Boy's return to loathsome lessons and lectures on boring topics with seemingly endless piles of homework that he never really completed anyway. He did well on the daily pop-quizzes, weekly tests, and the occasional spelling bee. Although, he certainly disliked the spelling bee the most, for it was usually just an opportunity for his peers to torment him by way of making faces or snickering at his embarrassment of having to stand in front of the class. Never mind the fact that he won every single spelling competition handedly - that fact only further propagated the legend of his strangeness, his nerd-dom, his 'otherness.' Sulking back to the classroom, the Girl burst from the shadows of a side hallway and began a rapid, manic interrogation of his lunchtime adventure with the Captain.

"What did you two talk about? she exclaimed.
~~~

"Uh... who?" the Boy asked, playing dumb.

"Oh come on!" she begged, "I'm a scientist! I make calculations and I easily deduced and reduced and concluded that the only reasonable thing you could possibly be doing with your extra lunch was to share it with somebody, and the only other somebody who would want it would most definitely be the guy in the alley from yesterday!" she stated.

"Oh," replied the Boy, his eyes darting back and forth, considering what he might decide to share with the Girl. Certainly nothing about his existential experience under the sea atop the Schwark creature where he first met the Captain from another time. "He is - was - a Captain of a ship... once." The girl skeptically considered this, as she recalled the image of a scraggly man examining the pile of ant-covered socks in the garbage alley. Her brow furrowed, she nodded in agreement with her thoughts.

"Of course," she said. The Boy suddenly saw a thousand little thought bubbles spring from her head like a Saturday morning comic strip in the newspaper. "What sort of ship? Where did he sail? Was he a fisherman? Why is he in an alley?" Before any of these bubbles manifested in the Girl's mouth as words, though, a steady, intensifying 'stomp, stomp' approached from behind the Boy. Thought bubbles popped and exploded in a million hues of pink and purple and gray and white, the words sublimating and dissolving into a fine mist around the two. The Boy watched the reaction of the Girl, her eyes becoming saucers, a massive grimace and slight gasp as a pair of calloused, firm hands clamped up, over, and upon his shoulders, fingers latching down in an assertive vice-grip of no-nonsense 'you-are-in-trouble' power. A faint smell of roses, chalk dust, and cleaning solution filling his nostrils. His Teacher.

"Bound to happen eventually," mumbled the Schwark

"You," the Teacher bellowed, her fingertips digging deeper into the Boy's clavicles. "Come with me. Right now, mister" his Teacher instructed through gritted teeth and snarling lips. An incredible gravity that seemed to suddenly triple in force glues his legs to the waxy linoleum, yet this was still no match for the powerful hands as they began to drag him backwards. Leading him down the packed hallway in a macabre sort of parade of the condemned, his Teacher and apparent executioner kept a firm grip on his moist sweater, tugging it upwards as if the Boy was a scruffed puppy. He avoided the faces and stares of the children to his right and left, for he already knew what sort of terrible things they conveyed. Past the lecture rooms, the gymnasium, the bathrooms, to the front of the building, a sudden right-hand turn that sent him reeling into a fake palm tree.

Suddenly they were in a waiting room. A purple-lipped secretary smacking stale bubble gum with an open mouth, drawn up in a perverted grin, silently greeted him. A set of heavy wooden double doors opened into the office with the desk lined with strange little caricatures of heroes and gods and creatures, as a squeaking leather roller chair spun slowly around in dramatic fashion - the pointy faux-leather boots tapping the ground, the mustache twitching ever so slightly.

"We need to have a chat," started his Principal, his face blank and gray.

~~~

His Teacher revealed she had seen him leave the classroom - had thought maybe he went to the washroom. How strange that he didn't ask or take the hall pass. When he didn't return in due time, she searched the bathroom, the gym, thought perhaps he was hiding. When the bell rang, she stayed in the hallway a little longer, caught him sneaking in through a side door, from an emergency exit near the garbage alley, dripping with raindrops. The Principal cleared his throat and stood, taking the interrogation baton from the Teacher. He started with the obvious questions:

"What are you doing out there? Do you ditch class and lunch all the time? Do you meet with somebody out there" The Boy replied with a shrug, a shake of the head, a still silence. Then the strange questions:

"Do you smoke cigarettes? D you drink alcohol? Do you buy drugs? Why don't you ever do homework? Why don't you ever take textbooks home?" Again - a shrug, a shake of the head, a still silence. The Boy's mouth refused to betray him with words. A rummaging through of his backpack. More questions:

"What is this thing, this funny-looking shark-dog thing?" More silence from the Boy.

"You're going to need to start telling me what is going on here, son." The Principal was firm in tone, but soft in facial features. The Boy noticed he was clutching a small figurine of a muscular turtle holding a sword, was it a ninja? It certainly looked to be a ninja of sorts. The Principal placed the turtle down next to the Schwark, examined both, and sighed.
~~~

"Hey. Listen," the man began, "I expected this to be tough for you. Adapting. I get it. But part of adapting requires you to follow the rules."The Boy saw that the Principal seemed to be fixated on the Schwark.

"Think he likes me," chuckled the Schwark. "Funny guy - likes toys, I see," he finished. The Boy plucked the Schwark from the mahogany desk and quietly tucked it deep inside his backpack, zipping it shut. He looked at the Principal and swallowed - still, he could not speak.

"You have to start doing some homework, son. You're going to flunk the grade if you don't start," explained the Principal. "Tests and quizzes are only part of it. I know you are smart, but proving you can put in the work is also important," the Principal lectured, gently shaking a bony index finger at the Boy. "And also, you can't leave class without an excuse, without a pass, without telling your Teacher. And you most certainly cannot leave the building. If that continues, we might have to consider expelling you from school. Just too dangerous. If you were to get hurt out there, we might be considered at fault." The Principal's theory was lost on the Boy.

"Expelled?" the Boy croaked, an expression of confusion forming on his face.

"Kick you out. Can't come back. Done. That sort of thing," replied the Principal.

The Boy said nothing. Ambivalence, fear, and joy jumbled through his mind in that moment, as several timelines of possibility flew in all dimensions around him. No more school - was that such a bad thing? No more adventures with the Girl or new-found friendship with the Captain - not such a good thing. Then there was his Mother.

"Go back to class now," the Principal ordered. "This is a warning today. A final warning. I want you to succeed. You want to succeed. So prove us both right, son, and make good choices," finished the man, standing at his desk, his pointy shoes click-clacking across the floor.Opening the doors for the Boy, the Principal followed him through the waiting room, smiled at the Secretary as she filed her maroon colored nails, and led him down the hallway back to Room 103. With a pat on the shoulder, and a hand on the classroom doorknob, the Principal fired his final salvo:

"By the way, I'll be letting your Mother know about the circumstances today and what we agreed upon. Enjoy the rest of your day," he smirked, opening the door to thirty devilish faces itching to irritate the Boy.

"Don't remember you agreeing to anything," murmured the Schwark.

~~~

Her silence betrayed her roiling rage. An aura of fierce fire red and orange enveloped her figure as she stood at the side of the station wagon in the steady rain, fists clenched, eyes black and terrible. Anticipating the meeting with his Mother after extended-day, the Boy had decided to continue his oath of silence to himself. No answer was better than a lie - was much, much better than the truth. Driving home, he tried not to stare at her ghost white knuckles as they strangled the steering wheel in a desperate attempt to delay her eruption. The Boy held every breath, releasing it as slowly as possible, preventing any possible noise or cough or gurgle or hiccup from triggering certain death. He managed to survive the parking of the car, the walk up to the apartment foyer stairs, the opening of their front door. Not long enough, though, to make it to the sanctuary of his bedroom, for her fuse was not infinite and would not extinguish, even in this downpour. Pulling his soggy sneakers off, he grunted ever so slightly. It was enough to break the deafening silence, enough to break the dam holding back her fury.

"What is in your backpack!" she bellowed, the heat and sudden pressure of her breath beating down upon the Boy like belched dragon-flame. He froze to the hardwood floor, time slowly, his heart attempting to leave his chest in apparent mutiny. He said nothing.

"Give me your backpack!" she exclaimed, yanking it off his shoulders in a single, surging motion. He did not resist.

"Not good, pal!" a frightened Schwark said, as the zipper flew open above it and a trembling terrible claw descended upon its face.

"Why do you bring this... this *thing*... everywhere!" his Mother hollered. It was more an accusation than a question, decided the Boy. She knew why he carried the Schwark everywhere - she was there when the Scavenger gifted it back to him. She knew its importance, but had also now forgotten. Tossing the Schwark violently across the living room and into the leg of a cheap coffee table, she peered into the near-empty backpack, dropping the last remaining item - his lunch-sack - on the kitchen counter.

"Where are your books! Where is your homework?" she hissed through closed teeth. The Boy shrugged. He said nothing.
~~~

"Your Principal called me at work! Told my boss that he needed to speak with me! Told me you went back into that alley the police found you in! Told me you are failing because you never do any homework! Told me you might be cheating! Told me!" Tears formed at the corner of her eyes. The Boy took a breath and held it.

"Say it," moaned the bruised Schwark from across the room. The Boy's eyes met his Mothers as he answered in a perfect unwavering, tone.

"I get perfect scores on every test. It's not my fault that it's too easy. It's not my fault that its too boring. It's not my fault that they don't teach anything important anyway. It's not my fault!"

They stared at each other in silence. His Mother's necklace glowed a deep purple. The Schwark's blowhole illuminated a slowly pulsing spectrum of rainbow. The Boy felt his own aura of forest green and cedar brown curling up from his fingertips. The tiny apartment melted into a sea of dueling shades and hues and contrasts and saturations. Mixing and matching, yellows intermingled with greens, purples danced with reds, a great conformity materializing amongst the great many colors and emotions and thoughts circulating and ruminating between the three figures - Boy, Mother, Schwark. All at once, a terrific, blindingly white light filled the living room - colorless and calm. A great understanding agreed upon in silence. Gracefully stepping over to the Schwark, his Mother picked it up from the dusty floor and returned it to the Boy. The Boy removed a piece of lint from the Schwark's left fox ear, looked at his Mother's forgiving face, and hugged her waist, a tear rolling down his cheek onto her grease-laden shoe.

"Play by the rules," she whispered. "It's not your fault. I'll talk with your Principal later this week."

The Boy nodded in acknowledgement. In this new life, making his Mother happy was paramount for their survival, he realized. Turning to his bedroom, Schwark held tightly under his arm, he headed towards sleep, an escape to dreams. And then…

"One more thing - a new rule," she began. "You cannot take the creature to school anymore. It's distracting you. Leave it home." And with that, she pivoted on her heels to her own bedroom and turned off the single dim kitchen light bulb. Her footsteps retreating, but the crippling last words repeating on endless loop in the Boy's mind.

"Leave it home. Leave it home. Leave it home," echoed the curse. The Boy gazed down at the Schwark. Its blowhole had gone dark.

The Ghost

Through the closed upstairs window of the two story suburban cookie-cutter home, they watched as a tall man with a finely waxed mustache sat on the edge of the short bed and read a small bald man a story. They could not hear the tall man's voice, but instead observed his mouth dramatically enunciate each word, arms waving around wildly as he recreated the plot in imaginary fashion for the small man. As the plot came to an end, and the book closed, the tall man leaned over and kissed the small man on top of his hairless head and turned out the light.

"Did you see that?" said the Schwark, sitting next to the Boy on the neighbor's roof. The moon was full, and the outline of the bed was still visible across the small yard separating the two identical homes.

"I think it's a boy in that bed - a boy with no hair?" queried the Boy. The Schwark shrugged and scratched its whiskers with a furry flipper as he shifted on his massive tail, tucked awkwardly beneath him. The Boy was amazed that the shingled roof could support so much weight. Maybe the Schwark didn't actually weigh that much. Perhaps it was a sensitive subject anyway, thought the Boy. As he gazed up at the night sky, the half-crescent moon seemed to wink back at him before suddenly racing off across the stars, dipping below the horizon and out of site faster than the Boy could comprehend. He gasped. The sky began to quickly brighten - black giving way to dark blue and purple, making room for hazy red and orange and yellow, before a blinding sun sprang from the opposite end of the Earth and chased away the last remaining stars. A cloudless blue sky carpeted the heavens and everything became still again. The Boy had taken but a breath.

"Did time... just fast-forward itself?" asked the Boy out loud. The Schwark yawned and motioned for the Boy to look back to the window - the bald child was awake and sitting on the floor of the bedroom. He appeared to be very thin, and very pale - dark circles beneath his eyes evident even from hundreds of feet away. Scattered around him lay an impressive array of action figures, plastic monsters with movable arms and legs, miniature replicas of famous mythical creatures like minotaurs, dragons, and yetis. Cereal box toys and race cars. Rubber bugs and alien beings. The bald boy was playing with two muscular-appearing figurines - turtles, by the look of the shells on their backs - as the bedroom door opened and the tall man appeared once again, carrying a steaming plate of eggs and oatmeal and toast.

"Breakfast in bed surrounded by ninja turtles - that's the life." The Schwark whistled as he laid back, flippers behind his ears, his blowhole beaming a fluorescent green.

"You know those guys? Ninja turtles?" asked the Boy.

"Oh yeah, great guys," remarked the Schwark. "Most people think they're just imagination stuff, but I'm here to tell you that it's based on a true story. Real turtles, buddy. Real ninjas," the creature finished. The Boy didn't exactly trust the Schwark, but decided it didn't matter. He turned back to the window. The tall man had retreated to a different room - his own bedroom - and was changing into a set of work clothes: a purple blazer. A pair of pointed faux-leather shoes.

"The Principal?" blurted the Boy in frank disbelief. "He... he looks about ten years younger. This must be before he moved to the city." The Schwark just shrugged again, clearly bored. It was having a hard time trying to pick its nose with the flat furry flippers, and instead, ended up tickling himself so badly he sneezed so harshly, that the entire roof shook, nearly knocking the Boy into the thorny rose bushes below. The Boy blinked, and the moon was once again hovering overhead. He blinked and rubbed his eyes, as the sun replaced the moon. An entire day had passed. Turning toward the Schwark, he saw that it had fallen asleep and was now lightly snoring, its rubbery lips flapping and slobbering with every exhalation.

Night.

Day.

Night. Day.

Night-day. Day-night.

Now rapidly: night-day-night-day-night-day. The Schwark continued to sleep, the deeper he snored, the faster the alternation of light and dark around the Boy. In the branches of the maple and elm trees around him, leaves burst from swollen buds, expanded in great green polygonal shapes, faded and withered to burnt orange, released themselves from the branches, and dropped to the golden grass in a span of seconds. Rose petals flourished and blossomed and died. Rain, snow, hail, sleet, and sunshine fell seemingly all at once upon the earth around him. An owl assembled a nest, roosted, raised a small clutch of fat and fluffed babies, watched them tumble out of the tree, and off into the wild.

"Hey! Wake up!" the Boy nudged the Schwark near the blowhole, which exploded into a fit of red and silver light. The protective membrane retracted over its huge black eye and looked annoyingly and the Boy. The sun slowed and floated over the sky and for once, stayed in place.

"Man, I was having a *fantastic* dream about the Squid and I - *deep* under the sea. We had a family and everything. And you just had to go and wake me up, huh, pal?" the Schwark growled.

"Everything was going way too fast! I was getting worried" the Boy confessed. The Schwark stretched its flippers and uncurled its dorsal fin.

"Ain't nothing to worry about my Boy. Time that is. Slow, fast, medium, backwards, forwards - it's all the same really. Your type gets caught up in the slow slog forward, like there's no other alternative. I'm here to tell you, that just ain't how it is, buddy. And don't ask me to explain." The creature gazed up at the burning sun and furrowed its hairy eyebrows, its blowhole replicating the blinding yellow starlight. The Boy had never been more confused in his entire life.

"Woah, look," pointed the Schwark, back towards the Principal's home. The bald boy's bedroom was dark and empty - no bed, no toys, no nothing. On the first floor, in what used to be the living room, a massive bed dominated the space. A stack of television or computer monitors stood nearby with squiggles of red and green bleeping and blipping across their faces. Poles of gold-tinged fluid hung from steel poles, and the Boy traced one of the pig-tailing tubes into the frail, bruised arm of an impossibly thin figure laying quiet and still in the center of the huge bed.

"He's sick. Like my dad," whispered the Boy.

"I think he's a lot, lot sicker than your dad, friend," replied the Schwark, its voice turning sympathetic and sad, the blowhole fading into twilight. Arranged in a semi-circle around the small, bald, sick boy stood a phalanx of action heroes, helicopters, airplanes, dinosaurs, and four ninja turtles tucked under his right arm. The Principal came in just then and sat next to the small, bald, sick boy and gently stroked his hand. A very pretty red-haired woman joined the Principal at his side. Her make-up had run down her face in streaks, and she blew her nose every few moments. Closing his eyes, the Boy thought of his own father, still at the hospital. It had been a few days since he had visited, and he missed him greatly, he realized. Flickering wildly behind his closed eyelids, the Boy knew what was occurring. Day. Night. Day. Night. Almost fifty cycles, he estimated. He felt a gentle, furry tapping on his shoulder, and opened his eyes to a blood moon taking up half of the sky. The house across from them was motionless and dead, save for a single faint light in the bald boy's old bedroom. A tiny tea candle flickered against the glass of the closed window, its flame lapping up the few remaining moments of life from its minuscule waxy reservoir. In the shadow of the flame, slumped against the closed bedroom door, sat a dark figure, head in hands, still and silent and forlorn. Almost imperceptibly, the figure slowly grasped a glass bottle of caramel-brown liquid. Raising its head to the candle, the Boy saw that the typically pristine mustache had gone ferrel - a scraggly beard now in its place. The Principal took a long swig from the bottle and grimaced. Staring down at his feet, the Principal began to convulse into deep heavy sobs, his hands pressed into his face.

The candle blew out.

The Schwark sighed.

The Boy whipped a tear.

The roof they sat upon began to creak - footsteps.

~~~

"Hi-i-i ya-a-ah!" came the high-pitched, blood-curdling scream from the top of the roof. A small, dark figure stood slightly crouched, arms held out in a karate-like attack pose. A bright cloud of dark blue, purple, orange, and red encircled each of his arms and legs. He suddenly leapt forward towards the terrified Boy and Schwark, who held each other in trembling arms and flippers.

"Aha! I've caught you! Spies! You are under arrest!" announced the small, cracking voice, its face coming into the moonlight. Curly red hair, freckles, pale skin. It held a small figurine of a human-like turtle in its left hand.

"The small, bald, sick boy," thought the Schwark and Boy into each other's minds simultaneously. Except, this boy was neither bald nor sick-appearing.

"I'm just kidding! Hi! I saw you looking at our house. My dad is pretty sad, huh," frowned the Principal's son, taking a seat next to the Boy as if they had always known each other.

"How did you see us here?" asked the Boy, still holding onto the Schwark for moral support.

"Easy! I'm dead now," answered the Principal's son, matter-of-factly, "so, I can do a lot of stuff I couldn't do before - like seeing you guys on this roof," he elaborated. "You're in my dad's school, aren't you?" he asked the Boy.
~~~

Nodding in disbelief, the Boy realized he was talking to a ghost in his own dream-scape. He felt the hair on his arms prickle up at the thought.

"Wish I could have been around when he moved to the city," remarked the Ghost. "He's going to really like it there," he reflected. He peered up at the Schwark, staring at its whiskered face, sharp dorsal fin, and muscular tail. "You're cool!" said the Ghost, beaming up at the creature. "I liked it when you made your blowhole glow like a rainbow."

The Schwark, gloating in the child's admiration, released a fantastic luminescence of every color imaginable into the night sky, sending his audience into applause and fits of unhinged laughter.

"What a neat toy you have!" exclaimed the Ghost to the Boy.

"Hey! Not. A. Toy, pal..." The Schwark suddenly dimmed the light show, and crossed his furry flippers, frowning a bit at the comment. The Boy stood and kicked a leaf off the roof.

"Your... your dad," he began, "he... he keeps all of your toys on his desk at school. I... I think they are yours, anyway," said the Boy.

"Really? Does he have my whole set of army guys there?" asked the Ghost.

The Boy thought carefully, and nodded.

"Wow! How about my dinosaurs?" the Ghost's eyes grew as big as the blood moon above.

The Boy nodded again.

"Aliens? Robots?"

Double nod.

"That's so cool. I'm glad he kept them." The Ghost stood and walked over next to the Boy. The two peered into the empty upstairs window, its candle smoldering. The Principal had moved to his bedroom and sat alone at the bed.

"My mom left soon after I died. She and my dad just couldn't bare to see each other without crying. I guess it's for the best," the Ghost revealed. "He moved to the city a little after today. He still visits where I'm buried - on Saturdays. He always leaves a new toy for me. I have a lot now!" he finished. The three beings sat off the edge of the neighbor's roof, feet and tails swaying into the midnight breeze. After some time, the Ghost turned to the Boy.

"Would you mind doing something for me?" he asked softly. The Boy blinked, opened and closed his mouth, and instead simply nodded. A favor for a ghost? Why not, he decided.

"Could you give him this?" he pulled out a ninja turtle with an orange bandana across its eyes, a slice of plastic pizza in its left hand, a pair of nun-chucks in the other.

"This one's my favorite. Dad buried him with me, but I want him to have it back. He needs it more than I do now. He has the other three turtles, but not this one," the Ghost explained, placing the figure gingerly into the hands of the Boy.

"When you give it to him, say, 'Cowabunga, dude' - that's what I always said to him before he turned out the lights in my bedroom," the ghost instructed.

"Cow-a-bung-gah?" repeated the Boy, carefully. He was so far down the rabbit hole of confusion, that he had decided to 'go with the flow' from here on out.

"Yeah!" affirmed the Ghost. "Oh. And tell him I love him, too. And that I think he's doing a great job as a principal. And that he should listen to you more." The Boy looked at the Ghost quizzically.

"Don't worry," the Ghost winked. The moon sank into the forest beyond, and the sky went pitch black. Darkness slid over the earth like a rapidly incoming tide. It enveloped the roof they sat upon, and shrouded the Boy in palpable nothingness so thick he could no longer see his hand in front of his face.

"Cowabunga, or something" muttered the Schwark.

"Cowabunga, I think?" said the Boy.

"Cowabunga, dudes!" whooped the Ghost.

The Crows

As the bell rang, the Girl strode past his desk at a brisk - almost comical - clip, and tossed a crumpled piece of paper next to his feet. Taking her seat a few rows forward, she turned her head to the side and slowly winked. The Teacher began scribbling various math problems on the board as the rest of the class scrounged into their bags for their homework. Motioning for him to open the balled up notebook paper, the Girl was now fulling facing him, miming a person reading a newspaper. So hilariously inept at being subtle - he smiled at that thought and leaned over to pick up the note. Unfolding it, he examined its contents. Words and diagrams were written chaotically all over the paper. Cartoons of black birds sitting on a telephone wire, some holding black things in their beaks, some flying towards the garbage alley, eating apple cores and other riff-raff, some others swooping towards the side-walk and street to examine a cracked up rock or egg or nut of some sort. Arrows and numbers directed the sequence in which he was to decipher the mess.

"Number One: The Problem," he silently read at the bottom of the note. The Girl's cursive was flowy and bubbly and so symmetric it almost difficult to read. "The guy on last night's news says that the crows around here are getting sick from eating garbage, because there aren't enough regular crow foods for them." The Boy scratched his head and looked over at the Girl - she was beaming ear to ear, making bird-beak impressions with her hands. He looked back down at the paper.

"Number Two: Observation: crows in my neighborhood like to eat nuts. They drop them on the concrete or asphalt and fly down to eat the insides. They love it. Plus it gets rid of all the annoying nuts that land in my backyard that my dad makes me pick up." The Boy had seen ravens due a similar thing with snails - letting them crack on the ground to eat the flesh inside.

"Number Three: Hypothesis: if I bring all the nuts for the crows to eat here in the city, then they won't eat garbage, and I won't have to spend the weekend racking nuts in the backyard!" The Boy shook his head. The Girls was clearly weird, but he loved this weirdness. He smiled at her. She pointed excitedly to the window.

Outside, on a slack power-line across the busy street, sat a murder of six crows, crowded next to each other, chests puffed out, necks tucked into their feathers. They looked like old miserly men waiting for the bus. Most of the crows were missing feathers in various patches, and they all seemed to be continuously preening themselves, itching their face, pecking at a wing. They didn't look well, thought the Boy. As he looked on, all of the bird beaks suddenly turned and followed a business lady as she exited a building, a small sac of trash in her hand. Tossing it haphazardly and towards the maw of an open receptacle on the street before diving into a taxi, she inevitably missed, letting the trash roll into the street.

"Caw! Caw! Caw!" came the chatter, slightly muted through the school's thick paneled window. In a matter of milliseconds, six hungry birds were upon the greasy sack, squawking and cawing and fencing each other for prime sack investigating real-estate. One particularly brave bird picked up the entire piece of trash and ripped it apart like a buccaneer slashing his sword upon a foe. French-fry butts, gobs of bright red ketchup, soggy hamburger bun crusts flew into the air, sending the animals into a rabid frenzy. The Boy observed that some crows seemed to stumble or limp on their legs, some flew awkwardly. Weaker birds were shunned to the side, outmaneuvered by the more crafty, more experienced crows. The disgusting battle for leftover fast food concluded as quickly as it had began, as the bloated, grimy murder returned to its post on the power line, twenty feet overhead. One of the more severely mangy-appearing crows suddenly sat very erect, as a large sputter of white, congealed poop shot out from between its tail-feathers, splattering over the front windshield of a pristine sports car below.

"Ha! What a shot! Guy's got talent!" admired the Schwark. The Boy thought he saw a few of the birds snicker, if birds could do such a thing. He looked at the Girl and nodded. These crows were gross, but they didn't need to be that way. They were becoming sick because of people - people moving in, taking their territory, chopping down their trees, giving them opportunity for different, poor quality, non-crow foods. He decided that he would like to play a part in fixing that.

~~~

"Did you bring an extra lunch again?" the Girl asked, looking over his smattering of items - a small apple, a hummus and tomato sandwich, a small thermos of soy milk.

"I couldn't - I got in trouble yesterday," the Boy sulked. "But my mom doesn't know exactly what happened. Still, I don't think I can pack
~~~

extra for the Captain - this week, at least," he sighed. As he finished, a second brown bag plopped onto his table.

"No worries! I made one!" she beamed, her mischievous eyes encouraging the Boy to examine a name scrawled in loopy cursive on the side of the paper sack - "For the Captain!" it read.

"Ready?" she grinned, pushing up from the table, "You ask for the bathroom pass, and leave first. Then, I'll tell her I have to go real bad and can't wait for the pass to get back. We'll be real quick, just say 'Hi' and 'Bye' to the Captain. And I'll take a quick look at some crow things..." she said, the plot unfolding in front of her eyes like a master battle plan.

"Ah, brother. Here we go again," quipped the Schwark.

The Boy gulped down the apprehension building in his throat, and let confidence swell in his heart. He couldn't let his friend, his teammate, his adventure buddy, down - he was all in. Striding over to the Teacher's desk, he plucked the bathroom pass from its holster.

"Five minutes," growled the woman from behind her tall desk, her thick-rimmed leopard-printed glasses reflecting the fluorescent ceiling lights like laser daggers aimed at the Boy. Her lips puckered sour. "Why are you bringing your backpack with?" she demanded. The Boy froze.

"Eh, well, I have to exchange some books at my locker," he replied, forcing a smile. Seconds that could have been hours passed. She crossed her arms and squinted her eyes.

"Hmph," was the woman's only reply. The Boy nodded and skipped out of the classroom, vision blurry, palms sweaty.

"Hey, pal, nice work there! Thought you might be leaving me behind," the Schwark complimented.

"Couldn't do this without you... partner!" replied the Boy to the empty hallway. Moments later, a squeaky pitter-patter approached from behind, as the Girl sprinted to catch up with him before they both exited the side door into the garbage alley. Extra lunch in hand, hearts beating wildly, minds ablaze with thoughts of the curious unknown that lay outside the confines of the classroom, the Boy and Girl laughed at themselves and at each other as they stepped into the cold rain.

~~~

Leaning casually against a steam pipe, he was nearly unrecognizable. Clean denim jacket with white fleece lining, black tight jeans, steel toed boots - with laces - a yellow beanie cap, a freshly lit
~~~

cigarette lazily perched in the corner of his mouth, the Captain grinned and shook his head as the Boy and Girl approached. He had managed to trim his beard neatly, and his ferrel hair was tucked back into a tight bun under the beanie.

"You must be the Captain," began the Girl. "You look a lot different today!" she blurted, handing him the brown paper bag, loaded with radishes, white cheese, rye bread, and a can of sardines. Inspecting the contents, the man's eyes lit up at the sight of pickled fish, and he beckoned the two to sit next to him on a neat stack of dry cardboard, which they did immediately without hesitation.

"Yeah, well, I took the 'plunge' you might say," he slowly began in response to the Girl. "Went to the shelter last night, got some fresh clothes that had been donated. This city's got great donation sites. Lots of hipsters," said the Captain, between slurps of soggy silver fish. "But anyway, this morning, I decided to go to one of those same-day labor signups down the street. Got talkin' to one of the other guys, mentioned workin' down at the port. Guess they're buildin' a big new harbor and need a bunch of help. So joined up. Moved a bunch of boxes around all morning, and got my first paycheck in years." His newly recovered pride filled the alley with a soft glow of orange light. The Captain took a long drag on the cigarette and let fly a string of several perfectly circular smoke rings that hovered in the alley and floated out onto the street, where several crows took notice, squawking their approval. The Girl's attention was torn in half.

"Congratulations!" chirped the Boy. "Are you going back tomorrow, too?" he asked. The Captain considered his questions as he spread some cheese onto the rye, laying a few herring on top as a garnish. The Boy never imagined the Captain was an open-faced sandwich type of guy.

"Well, still got my certification as an arc welder. Back before I piloted ships, I used to build 'em, you see. They're lookin' for welders down at that port, and the pay's not bad. Think I'll see what I can do, maybe work there for awhile." The Captain announced, inspecting a radish and soft white cheese with great consternation. The Girl glared at him, as if he were about to commit a sacrilegious act. He took a bite of each and chewed incredibly slowly, as if he were going to choke at any moment. To his surprise, he liked the strange combination, and quickly finished the Girl's gifted lunch.

"Heh... remember your little welding accident?" the Schwark chimed. The Boy remembered, but wished he didn't. Back in the forest, inside his work shed, his Father often welded. A "flux weld" - messy, smokey, but would "get er' done," as his Father would say. Repairing fence posts, various tools, or making his Mother a strange piece of art for their garden, his Father seemed to enter another world when he flipped down the welder's mask and let the sparks fly, joining metal bits together in an impossibly bright fury of fire and smoke. The Boy had once looked directly at the spark, despite his Father's constant warnings not to do so. For the rest of the day, his eyes burned, as if there were particles of sand lodged under his eyelids. His vision gradually returned the next day, but not before he was formally banned from the work shed for a month.

"So will you still live here then?" asked the Boy, rubbing his eyes reflexively, hopeful for both a 'yes' and 'no' response from the Captain.

"Think I'll start staying at the shelter for a bit. It's warmer. Might visit here every now and then, but you don't need to bring me lunch anymore. You've already done so much for me, Boy. Changed my life, I'm fairly certain. I give you my sincere thanks. Maybe one day, when I get a new boat, I'll take you fishing," the Captain said, flashing a significantly more pearly white smile. The Boy considered that and smiled back. To be back near the sea, on the sea, even in the sea, would fill his heart with the energy he so desperately sought since leaving the forest.

~~~

"Caw! Ca-Caw!" came the call from down the alley. The Captain and Boy turned to watch the Girl feeding the murder some sort of round object. She would toss out a handful of the dark spheres, and the birds would swoop down, examining the orbs, pecking at them awkwardly, before flying back up to their power-line sanctuary - some took the detour to the trash dumpster to inspect for stale pizza crusts or molded cheese bits. The Girl was obviously disgruntled and stomped her feet in frustration.

"They don't know what to do with the walnuts!" she yelled back at the Boy and Captain. "We have to teach them!" she exclaimed, racing over to the nuts strewn about the alley, grabbing a handful and running out into the city sidewalk. The Boy swallowed his anxiety - they were risking being caught again. Had it been five minutes since he left the classroom? Of course it had, he decided.
~~~

"Better help her out, son" suggested the Captain. They strode over and watched as the Girl yelled up at the crows.

"Watch, you birds! Watch!" The disinterested murder seemed to simultaneously turn their feathered backsides to her in ambivalence, a few sending white globs of poop in her direction - an utter mockery of her experiment. One particularly scrappy-looking runt crow continued to watch, however, cocking a dark glazed eye towards the Girl and her handful of nuts.

"That one's at least watching" she muttered. She rolled a nut on the sidewalk towards the street. The runt crow coked its head intently. The Girl squatted, fists tucked into her armpits, elbows extended as she mimicked a pair of wings. Hobbling and hopping forward on the sidewalk, she cackled and cawed and bobbed her head in bird-like fashion as she courted the stray nut. Passerbys gave the Girl a wide radius, clearly irritated and frightened by the very altered homeless Girl pretending to be a chicken or something. She was oblivious to their judgements, and supremely focused on the mission at hand. The Runt hadn't missed a beat..

Reaching the nut, the Girl actually bent down and picked it up in her teeth, her hair flailing around in the afternoon mist-kissed breeze. Gripping the teeth between incisors, she raced over to a pile of stacked milk crates, and, hopping up to the highest one, suddenly flicked her neck and flung the nut as high into the air as she could. Tumbling back to earth, the nut exploded on the asphalt, perfectly split into two halves. Almost immediately, the Runt dropped from its cable and crash-landed next to the broken nut. After several probing pecks and close-calls with passing taxi-cabs, the bird pulled the fresh walnut flesh from its exposed interior and choked it down into its gizzard.

"Squawk! Squawkity-Squawk!" it chirped, dancing and stumbling from mangy leg to mangy leg, delighted at the nutritious meal newly discovered.

"Yes! That's it, little guy! Good job!" cheered the Girl from the sidelines, now back in full human-form.

"She does a pretty good bird impression, I gotta admit," commented the Schwark.

"She's a strange one, eh?" added the Captain.

"She's a scientist, I think," said the Boy.

The Girl handed the Boy and Captain a nut and commanded them to gently toss them towards the same spot on the sidewalk. As the three nuts landed, the Runt and one of his chubby buddies flew down to inspect the calamity. Unopened, uncracked, the nuts frustrated the other crow, who flew back to the cable. The Runt seemed determined, however, having watched the Girl carefully. It picked up the nut in its mouth and flew to the stack of milk crates. Astonishingly, it flicked the nut high into the air, and took off, joining it in flight to the asphalt below. A satisfying "crack!" sounded from the street, and the clever little bird helped itself to second-lunch.

After a few more rounds of rolling nuts and cheerleading for the Runt, the Boy, Girl, and Captain looked on in amazement as the entire murder one-by-one, quickly caught on to the act. The chubby bird had even returned to give it a try. The Runt rapidly ascended from pupil to master, and soon, a pile of shells grew near the curb of the busy city street.

"Tomorrow, I'm going to bring a whole backpack full of nuts! We'll save the crows!" the Girl professed, arms folded over her chest in an "I-knew-it-all-along" sort of demeanor. The Boy did not have nuts to rake or food to share, but he was determined to be there as a witness, for the Girl had taught him more about the ecology of a city than any textbook or math problem. He looked for the Captain to gauge his approval with the experiment, but instead, felt a cold wind roar up from the alley - the Captain had disappeared.

A shadow emerged from the side-door of the alley.

A sickening feeling strangled the stomach of the Boy.

A quaking sense of doom struck the heart of the Girl.

"Nice knowing you both," whispered the Schwark.

~~~

Sitting in the oversized chair in the waiting room, the Boy imagined where he might go after they expelled him. Another school? Jail? He had a hard time deciding which would be worse. The nauseating sweetness of the secretary's peach-tinged perfume nearly caused him to vomit up his hummus sandwich.

"Might be funny if you do puke," encouraged the Schwark. "Maybe it'll get that lady with the purple lipstick over there to hurl all over her computer screen in one of those hilarious pukey chain-reactions," chuckled the creature. The Boy kicked the bag lightly. He was in no mood for jokes, for he was certain that if this school did not end his life, his Mother certainly would. The set of double-doors opened and the Girl
~~~

walked out between them, face stoic and flat - it was the saddest and least animated she had ever been since he had known her, thought the Boy.

"Caw," he whispered as she sailed by. She stopped, and without looking up, made her arms into tiny wings and gave a few small flaps. The Boy's face remained unchanged, but in his heart, he smiled mightily, for he had known that even in the worst of times, you could count on a good friend to beat back the darkness and crack open a sliver of light with a good joke. He was thankful for his friend. He would miss her greatly, he decided.

"Your Mother's here. I'm buzzing her in. Then you'll be seen by the Principal," the nasally voice of the Secretary declared. His Mother had left work to be here? A death sentence.

~~~

"In less than twenty-four hours, you managed to leave the school building without permission twice, ditched multiple classes, and put yourself - and now a little Girl - at tremendous risk," began the Principal. His resigned Mother, whom he expected to be at near-nuclear levels of anger, sat quietly next to the Boy, a defeated and bruised expression worn across her brow.

"I gave you an ultimatum yesterday. I wanted you to succeed. And we agreed. Play by the rules. And what do you decide to do? The very next day, no less? You decide to break the exact same rules. And with an accomplice now. I don't know what we're going to do with you, son," The Principal's face was earnestly sad, his typically well-waxed mustache fell limply at the ends, his faux leather shoes less shiny today. The Boy noticed that the Principal held a ninja turtle in his left hand, below the desk, as he spoke. It had a blue bandana over its eyes. Elsewhere on the desk, a turtle with a red bandana, a turtle wearing purple. No orange bandana though.

"We were just doing a science experiment. About crow behavior," the Boy explained, slurring his words together between sniffles and swallows of guilt and grief. He felt his Mother's hot gaze upon him. "I just like being outside - I miss it," the Boy continued. The dark and musty room filled with deafening silence for several moments. Eventually, the Principal sighed and placed the ninja turtle he was anxiously holding back onto its space on his desk.

"You like science, huh," the Principal observed out loud. The Boy nodded.
~~~

"I just like learning about the real world, in the real world, with my hands and my feet on it, my eyes and my ears surrounded by it," the Boy elaborated. "It's just not real here. It's like a jail for your mind here," he finished, adrenaline surging through his veins with the realization that he had spoken so bluntly, so truthfully about how he felt in this place - this… school. To his amazement, the Principal nodded intently and earnestly. Did he agree, wondered the Boy? The tall man stood slowly and faced a glazed-over window. Opening the blinds, he was met with the outline of a small black bird that stared back. He smiled and shook his head, turning to face the Boy and his Mother.

"I'd like to tell you about a special place - a place in this city that might suit you much better than ours," he explained. "It's called the 'Forest School,' and while it has the name 'school' in its title, let me assure you that is the only similarity it has with our school. Classes are outside no matter the weather. You'll still learn Math and English skills, but everything is taught through nature, with a heavy emphasis on science."

The Boy's heart stopped. Time froze in the cramped room. His Mother's eyes were wide and white with the expression of 'How-have-I-never-heard-of-this?'

"You, of course, would certainly enjoy it," continued the Principal, "but there is a catch: It's a private school. It is not free to attend." Hope sublimated from spirit as his body slumped into the wooden chair. His eyes, once watered with utter excitement, now released a stream of tears fueled by despair. His Mother could barely afford rent, let alone a new lightbulb for the kitchen. There was no way he would ever attend Forest School. He wished at that moment that the Principal had never mentioned such a thing.

"We can't afford it," his Mother replied bluntly, matter-of-factly. She had felt the Boy's energy build and burst in a matter of seconds, and she placed a hand on his shoulder in sympathy. The Principal slumped back into his chair, clearly aware of the angst he had just stirred up.

"I know how hard you work, ma'am. I am frankly inspired by your determination to make things work here in this city, for yourself and your son. Especially since your husband is still recovering," he said softly. His Mother bit her lip and looked at her feet.

"And," he continued, engaging the Boy this time, "I can clearly see how much the outdoors mean to you, son. If that is where you need to be to learn and grow, then it is my job to make that happen. It's not going to happen at this school, however. So. I have a proposition for you - and experiment, really," the Principal stated, his voice dropping a level as he creaked forward in his chair. The Boy watched as the man unfolded his hands and picked up the purple-bandana turtle.

"Another experiment, it never stops, huh," moaned the Schwark.

"The experiment goes like this," the Principal began. "You are going to pretend like you've just crash-landed on an alien planet. The aliens look similar to you, but do things very differently - not the way you are used to, not the way you enjoy. You have two options: *resist* the aliens and do things your own way - possibly getting into serious trouble - or, you can pretend to *join* them in their culture - at least until your mothership arrives to pick you back up."

"I take it back, whispered the Schwark, "I think I'm starting to like this guy." The Boy's wide eyes conveyed his intrigue in this idea - it was a matter of survival, really.

"Son, the planet is here - it is this school," the Principal explained. "Myself, your Teacher, your classmates - we are the aliens." The Boy grinned maniacally at that thought. "So, you can resist and fight and see where that gets you - or, you can pretend to be one of us, at least for a little while." The Boy wondered if the Girl was an alien, too - or maybe she had crash-landed like him and was stuck here? He'd have to ask her. Either way, he knew which path he would choose.

"I'll pretend," he answered confidently, "but when do I get rescued?" The Principal held up his hands, motioning the Boy to slow himself.

"Ah, wise decision. If you are going to join us, and be like us, then that means a few things," started the Principal, holding up his bony index finger. "It means taking textbooks home, it means doing your homework, it means not leaving the building unless you have permission, it means doing well on your tests - which, by they way will be a bit more challenging in your new grade," he added with a subtle wink. His Mother abruptly stood.

"Excuse me, sir. New grade?" she asked in disbelief. The Principal grinned. "Yes, ma'am. He's too smart for Room 103. I've consulted with the Teachers and we believe he can begin two levels higher. His homeroom Teacher in Room 103 was the most adamant about the change, as a matter of fact," he said with a chuckle, shaking his head.

"Nice work, kid. Moving up in the world!" remarked the Schwark. The Boy's mouth gaped open. He immediately missed the Girl.

"Let me continue though," said the Principal. "If you can pretend to be like us, the aliens - at least for a little while," he was now clutching all three of the ninja turtles as he spoke, "then... it will give me enough time to hold a fund-raiser for you. To pay for tuition at the Forest School, at least for next semester." Everyone in the room was standing, an aura of glowing green and blue pulsed from the three figures. A rainbow of bioluminescence filled the backpack at the Boy's feet. His Mother began to silently cry.

At that moment, a great sudden energy filled the Boy as he kneeled and slowly undid the zipper of his backpack. He reached a hand inside as the Principal looked on quizzically but with a curious smile. Although he had only packed a light lunch and the Schwark that morning, the Boy had an otherworldly knowledge of what he knew he would find at the bottom of the pack. He removed the figure and gingerly approached the Principal's desk.

"This is for you," he whispered, placing the ninja turtle with the orange-bandana in the center of the cedar desk. "Your son says that he loves you and that he thinks you are a great Principal." Color instantly left the man's face, as both of his hands began to tremble. Falling backwards into his chair, pupils dilated into a pair of black holes, tears welling in his eyes, the Principal reached a cautious hand towards the impossible thing, and gasped as his fingertips brushed against its shining plastic shell.

"How?" the man croaked. The Boy smiled at the Principal.

"A peace offering from another world," the Boy suggested. "I come in peace," he said, raising two fingers up into the air. The Principal shook his head in loving disbelief.

"Well then... welcome," the man replied, raising his own two fingers into the air. There was one final thing to say to the man, the Boy realized..

"Cowabunga, dude."

~~~

As they drove home through the gentle rain, his Mother touched the Boy's hand. She had so many questions for him. She was exhausted.

"We're going to pick up your Father tomorrow. You two can spend the rest of the weekend together while I'm at work. It will be good for you... both," she added. The Boy smiled wearily in reply - he knew he should be ecstatic about such an idea. He knew the weekend was what he needed after such an extraordinary day. His Mother frowned at his lack of enthusiasm, her eyes drifting to his backpack.
~~~

"So, mind telling me how you came by that toy? That turtle? Your Principal seemed shocked to receive such a thing," she inquired, attempting to hide her suspicions and conspiracy theories.

"I had a dream about it," the Boy replied, looking out the foggy car window at a wall of moss-covered fir trees in the far distance, daydreaming about the Forest School.

"Do you... do you have a lot of these sort of dreams?" his Mother carefully inquired.

"Just recently" answered the Boy, half-listening, half-pretending to be studying woodpeckers and snails and mushrooms with kids like him.

"Since... since we moved here?" his Mother pushed deeper, sensing roots running far deeper.

"No. I think... I think since I got the Schwark," he casually recalled. His Mother frowned and did not reply immediately. The Boy removed the Schwark from the backpack and placed it on his lap.

"Don't know if you should be revealing all this, buddy," warned the Schwark, its blowhole pulsing a steady red-blue warning. The Boy felt confident, though, why would his Mother care now?

"That's why I take it everywhere. It helps me see things differently. Makes school more fun," he finished. His Mother gripped the steering wheel suddenly much tighter as her lips pulled back into a flat line, her eyes narrowing.

"I see," she whispered.

Red-blue.

Red-blue.

Red-blue.

The Black Hole

Like a cache of newly hatched deep-sea jellyfish, the ten trillion pinpricks glimmered and winked and pulsed in the inky black soup. Two creatures, one atop the other - an unusual symbiosis - slowly orbited an infinitely massive purple-armed starfish that spun its glittered hazy tentacles in perfect curved radii, its center an impossible white ball of light that blinded and beckoned. As the two organisms gently barrel-rolled towards the galactic mass, they began to feel the pull of its immense gravity upon their stomachs and their spines. Nearer and nearer they drew to the outer bands of star-laced fingers that whisked and whipped past them as soundless giants engulfed in flames. Momentum gaining, anxiety building, respirations increased - the creatures tumbled forward, eyes wide, hearts in synchronized terror.

"I'm scared," said the smaller naked creature, clutching the furry and scaled much larger creature, a pale red-blue pulsing light emanating from a hole near its dorsal fin. Suddenly, the perfect orb of pure white energy at the center of the starfish galaxy silently exploded in a blinding, gargantuan pulse.

"What's happening?" the frightened smaller creature screamed into the pointed red ears of the larger.

"I'm... not sure. I've never... never been here," the larger replied. Deep inside the marrow of their skulls, an uninvited guest began to knock and rattle - a bottomless deep baritone vibrating their sinews and eyeballs, building and crescendoing as the white orb entirely filled the space above and around them. A steady, deafening hum roared from the orb as it spun on its axis at impossible speeds, palpable gravitational waves ebbing and flowing around the two creatures, crushing them under swells of invisible, terrible energy.

"It's getting closer!" exclaimed the smaller.

Meters - then centimeters - now millimeters from the surface of the spinning wall of light, the creatures gazed upon its glossy surface in mesmerized trance. They watched, as a single point on the ghost white orb - no larger than a quark - began to dim... and darken... Spreading out, shrinking back, fluxing out, and reeling in, the shadow grew and grew - the blackest of black, a light-eating thing that soon took on the exact reflection of the two creatures outlined in front of it, mimicking and copying the two creatures helpless, flailing motions. In agonized intrigue, the two creatures each extended an appendage towards their shadow selves, the harsh screeching and vibrations of the universe rising up in protest the closer they came to physically touching.

Three.

Two.

One.

Contact.

In what may have been a nanosecond, or perhaps a millennium, the shadow stepped out of the orb and melded seamlessly with the two creatures. In that instant, the white sphere, the wall of near-infinite white, stretched and twisted and flattened. A pinpoint of painfully bright light exploded from where the shadow had escaped and began to frantically devour what was once the center - the heart - of the living starfish galaxy. Both creatures were ripped one-thousand light years forwards and backwards, existing everywhere and nowhere all at once, as the ravenous light cannibalised itself. When the last speck was eaten, the pinprick of light began to pulse long-steady vibrant colors- violet, indigo, blue. Longer pulses. Green. The light growing faint. Yellow. A pause. Orange. A high-pitched ringing in their ears. Red. A creaking and a snap. Black. Thrown into a whirlpool of spiraling ferocity, the two creatures suddenly separated, their outstretched arms and legs growing and shrinking as the incredible flux of gravity stretched their forms and minds and spirits.

"Schwark!" screamed the smaller creature, its words pulled into the newly birthed black hole faster than they were mouthed. The larger creature hurtled towards the event horizon of perfect darkness, its eyes fixated on its smaller friend.

"I am with you. I will always be with you, pal," the eyes said. The eyes vanished.

Into the void.

Gone.

The Donation

"Hey! Its okay! You're okay!" echoed the voice from a faint corner of the universe. Lost in his nightmare, forever stretched and torn in the outer orbits of a dark, Schwark-less dream-world, he screamed from his dream-heart but out of his real-mouth. Dream-body still and silent in perfect blackness, real-body thrashing and kicking in dingy gray bed sheets. He screamed, and screamed, and screamed. Grabbing him by the shoulders, she shook out the shadow that had crept inside and brought him back into the safety of the light, of the real.

"It's okay!" she said again - his Mother. His real eyes meeting hers through squinting disbelief. He had never felt so grateful to see those gray, peeling walls and splintered hardwood floor.

"Some nightmare you had there," his Mother sniffed, her tired smile forced and only slightly reassuring.

As his hands explored the confines of the small single bed, a sudden terrible nausea flooded into his veins and made his head spin to the left in a flare of vertigo.

"Where is it?" the left hand frantically said to the right. "I don't feel a tail or a fin or a whisker over here!" replied the left. The Boy ripped the covers off, nearly knocking his Mother off the end.

"Hey! Easy there, kiddo! You're awake now, remember?" she yawned.

"No, no, no..." was all the Boy could mumble, as he turned over every square inch of the bed, before diving underneath it into a pile of dust-bunnies that had coagulated over the past few days. Sneezing, he arose and stared at his Mother in disbelief and fury and terror.

"Where is it!" he demanded, eyes wide and shaking in their orbits.

"Where's what?" she replied flatly.

"Schwark! Something happened to the Schwark! It went into the shadow!" His tone both explanatory and accusatory, his expression hardening.

"Oh. That thing. You know, I think you've become too attached to that stuffed animal - that voodoo doll mutant whatever." His Mother broke his gaze and looked up into the small window as she spoke.

Palms filling with cold perspiration, neck hot with untempered rage, the Boy's lip began to tremble as a bright red glow curled from his nostrils. His Mother went further. "I asked you not to take it to school anymore, and what did you do? Your principal asks you to start doing homework, and

what do you fill your backpack with? And finally, you say this Schwark
was the one that helped you find that toy for your Principal - where did you
really get it, hmm? I'm not sure what attachment you developed with this...
this thing. But its not healthy, okay?" she said through lecturing eyes that
half-questioned her own logic, tongue betraying the incomplete confidence
she held.

"You don't understand," pleaded the Boy through gritted teeth, "I
didn't even chose the Schwark. It chose me." His Mother's eyes raised at
that, her bottom lip tucked back under her incisors in a sincerely worried
expression. The Boy continued. "If it weren't for the Schwark, I don't think
I could even stand school. I don't think I would have learned anything, or
met anybody interesting, or had any friends at all." He began to cry, not
harshly or out of fear or sadness, but sheer frustration. His Mother softly
and cautiously moved a conciliatory hand towards his, and momentarily
touched him before he withdrew his hand as if bitten by a brown recluse.
He stood and beamed lasers into her chest with his pupils, vaporizing any
attempt at an explanation. He was her son, and this was an ancient dance -
she, the master instructor. Matching his posture in a slightly less aggressive
manner, she deepened her voice and firmed up her tone.

"Come me with. Now. I want to show you something." A
command. She had transformed; was no longer the reassuring, sympathetic
Mother, but rather, the authoritative, protective sort. Her necklace
illuminated a hard, dark purple and pushed the Boy's flaring orange aura
back into a corner. He followed her to the kitchen. On the rickety card table
sat a small heap of fabric, folded neatly and curt. A pair of dark brown
corduroy pants. A green checkered flannel. A mustard yellow beanie. On
the underside, in black permanent marker, the name "Ranch" was scrawled
in all capital letters.

"Who's Ranch?" asked the Boy, holding up the clothes. They were
his size exactly.

"You slept in this morning, so I decided to get us some new clothes
from the thrift store," she explained, holding a new purple sweater for
herself up to the reflection in the microwave window. "I worked a few
extra shifts, so we can afford it. Plus, today we is a very special day," she
paused, turning to face him with an exhausted smile. "Today, we are
bringing your Father home from the hospital."

The Boy had forgotten. Had they told him at the last visit? Yes, he
decided - they had. Where had time disappeared to? His Father was coming
home. After weeks in the hospital, and so many visits, he was finally

leaving that strange and sterile cell. Holding the new clothes in his arms, he suddenly felt every emotion a Boy could possibly feel pour over him like close-out wave on the break. He held his breath. He wanted to hug his Mother and tell her how much he loved her. He wanted to hold his Father's hand and find something broken that needed his expertise in repairing. He wanted to escape with the Girl and teach the crows how to be crows again. He wanted to give the Captain a sandwich and hear about his day at the docks. He wanted to show the Principal that he could be a dutiful alien, and complete his homework. He thought about the Forest School. He held the new clothes and looked at his Mother.

"Where's Schwark?" he whispered.

Silence. Pressure in the room warped and spun as the heat of disbelieving fury rose inside his Mother. The lightbulb fizzed and hummed and grew explosively brighter before dimming out completely, its last breath of life an afterglow of burning red wire filament impregnated onto the Boy's retinas. Blinking away the tracers in his vision, he refocused on his Mother and... asked again.

"Where's Schwark!" he demanded, dropping the clothes on the floor, pounding his bare feet into the hardwood, a reverberating echo knocking the newly filled glass of cinnamon off the kitchen table. Shards shattered like a million raindrops. A miniature brown mushroom cloud plumed upwards and coated the green flannel shirt lumped at his feet. Neither Boy nor Mother broke their antagonizing gaze.

"Your Father is coming home today," her lips barely moving, "and all you want to know, is where your little creepy Schwark toy is. You're about to be expelled from school. You can't seem to make any friends. You get brought in by the police. You don't follow any rules. I buy you new clothes and what thanks do I get? All it boils down to, for you, is 'Where's Schwark?' 'Where's Schwark?' You are too old for stuffed animals!" Sitting slowly down into the collapsible kitchen chair, she wore the deepest frown he had ever seen, upper lip quivering, forehead and eyebrows forming a perfect downward 'V' - her anger and disgust had reached a new level, and he was ashamed and embarrassed and forever saddened that he had created this storm.

"Where's Schwark." His final words, timid and powerless and defeated. His Mother was correct in everything she observed from the outside - but, the Boy decided, she did not understand how things were for him on the inside. Perhaps one day, he would tell her everything. For now, he just desperately wanted his friend - his connection, his ally, his vessel on which he navigated the confusing and overwhelming waters of the mind - both his own and the world's. He needed it now. She sighed deeply, covering her face with both palms, shaking her head from side to side in grief, in frustration, in anger, in everything. She could also use a Schwark, the Boy thought in that moment. Dropping her hands, she and looked at him blankly in the gray morning light that crept in between the broken plastic blinds of the living room. Her face half-shadow since the lightbulb's demise, she swallowed and blinked. As she opened her mouth to speak the two words he knew were coming - the words he already knew to be true - he finished them for her.

"It's gone," he said, shocked and sharp and dying. In an instant he was riding under the sea surrounded by hundreds of anglerfish to meet a giant squid in the name of love, and he was sitting upon a roof in another time to witness the birth of a Ghost, and he also watching a Captain make his last stand only to be given another. The memories flooding over him, down his throat, filling his stomach and mind and heart with everything he had ever needed.

"It's gone," she repeated, emotionless and plain and dead. "This is what you needed," she added. "It was holding you back." Tears rolled down the Boy's cheeks and pooled onto the cinnamon-dusted flannel he held in his lap. Lost. Robbed. Scared.

"When I picked out your clothes this morning, I donated the Schwark," his Mother revealed. "So, now, another little Boy or Girl will get a chance to play with it." A means to console him? To justify her actions? The Boy did not know.

His Mother did not understand.

The Schwark was gone.

The Boy did not understand.

His Father was coming home.

The Portrait

A long, silent drive up the serpiginous asphalt ribbon, to the top of the hill overlooking the city.

A long, silent ascent up the sleek steel glass elevator, to the twenty-third floor in the clouds.

A long, silent scribble up the side of the sign-in sheet, to satisfy the secretary of the burn unit.

A long, silent scuffle down the meticulously clean hallway, to the cramped single room of his Father.

A nod from the Nurse.

A smile from the Doctor.

A Father healing.

A Mother relieved.

A Boy with a giant hole in his heart.

"His grafts have taken very well, and he has regained most of his mobility," announced the Doctor, displaying his Father's lower legs, tight with knotted scar tissue like the gnarled trunk of a fire-scorched Douglas fir. "He will continue his home physical therapy routine, but will need to return to our office every week to check on his vocal cords. Until then, he's agreed to absolutely *no* talking - not even a whisper. Needs to heal proper, I'm sure you can understand," the Doctor finished, patting the Boy's Father on the hand. His Father smiled back graciously, the burn marks of his neck stretching awkwardly. His Mother leaned in and kissed his Father on the cheek. Beckoning to the Boy, his Father opened his arms and winked. Hugging his Father, the Boy began to cry. One tear for his Father returning home, the other for his missing friend, who he wished could have come with for this moment. Grabbing a piece of scrap paper and a pen, his Father wrote out a few lines in neat, precise cursive:

"I've missed you. Are you feeling okay today?" said the letter. At first, the Boy nodded slowly, then paused, and shook his head. Dismayed, his Father put a hand on the Boy's arm and mouthed the words, "I love you." As the two looked at each other, a gentle, melodious tune came drifting down through the hallway and settled into the hospital room, filling their ears with curiosity. A tendril of patchouli wafted into the room, as a soft aura of orange and purple filled the doorway. A familiar humming grew louder and more energetic the closer it approached. A hand on the doorframe with knuckle tattoos - "L-I-F-E." The Art Therapist flitted into the room like a hummingbird that had finally found its favorite flower, her eyes and smile beaming and infectious. Under her arm, she carried a canvas bag of hodgepodge items - brushes and pencils and paints precariously poking their bristles and tips and lids out over the edge.

"Hello again, my friend." Her voice a deep mystic rustling of leaves and bonfire smoke, the Art Therapist's hazy red shawl, a dazzling design of elephants and mountains and a foreign script written into the shape of a sun, draping loosely around her neck. "We have one more project to complete together" she revealed.

"I'm going to get a coffee - I'll be back when it's time to go," his Mother declared, a hint of annoyance in her tone. Walking briskly out of the hospital room, the Boy felt a sense of guilty relief. The Art Therapist removed several brushes and paint tins and scattered them about the foot of the bed. Placing a blank canvas in front of the Boy, she began to whistle softly. He felt a hand on his back, and smiled at the warmth of knowing his Father was there, too. As he glanced at the table near the bed, the Boy was pleasantly surprised to see a second sheet of blank paper there as well - apparently for his Father.

"Today, right now, in this moment, I ask the two of you to clear your minds," began the Art Therapist. "Now, look down at your blank sheet of paper - nothing there, totally empty," she continued. "With meaning and purpose, close your eyes, but keep the image of that plain canvas." Closing his eyes, the Boy could feel that his Father and the Art Therapist had done the same. He could sense the Art Therapist swaying gently from side to side to an invisible rhythm, and he joined her in this silent dance, no stranger to her inviting energy.
The Art Therapist spoke again, her chanting words beating along in time to the invisible song. "You have both been through so much in the past few weeks. Now, you will return home, to a new home, a new life. This exercise is to help ground you - to allow you to deepen your roots - to let them extend and grow and flourish in foreign soil." She sighed. His Father shifted on the hospital bed. "Throughout our lives, from birth to death," she continued, the cadence and intensity of the words increasing, "there are no stronger, no safer roots than our families. Our most beloved. A world can flip entirely upside down, a body can be wrecked from the inside out, but... with our family by our side, we are invincible," she finished. The Boy's neck hair stood on end, a warmth gathering in his chest. His Father squeezed his hand, and a peace settled like a massive down jacket upon his mind.

"Now, with eyes still closed, imagine your family: who are they?" the Art Therapist asked. "What do they look like? Where do they live?" she said, pausing and allowing the silence to concentrate the powers of imagination. "Open your eyes, and look at your canvas," she instructed. "Draw your family."

As the Boy thought about her questions and examined the blank white sheet in front of him, he watched as a small grove of Fir trees materialized in the distance and began to creep forward. As they approached the center of the vast white nothingness, the trees spread out in a perfect circle, forming a perimeter and allowing the soft green grasses of a coastal meadow to rise up from the center. Spidery sword ferns wiggled free from between the great trees' trunks and took up home amongst the forest floor. Above the canopy, a raven flew through a blue misty sky. A high sun released its rays through the soft fog, that dribbled through the needled branches and tickled the ferns with long tendrils of golden yellow. A porcini mushroom peeked out from around a hollow stump, fleshy cap expanding up and out. A small creek began to fill the ravine off on the left side of the page. His Father sighed.

Glancing over at the table beside the hospital bed, his eyes widened at the sight of his Father furiously drawing and coloring and painting his own depiction of their family. The Boy was mesmerized and worried - how would his Father draw him? A breath beside his ear carrying the odor of ginger and fresh pine pulled him back to his canvas.

"Now, who lives there?" whispered the voice, returning to its hypnotic humming sway. Within the forest meadow, the Boy watched as his a miniature version of his Father materialized. He wore sturdy work boots, a red button-up cotton shirt, a well-kept brown beard. In his right hand, a shovel - in his left, a handsaw. Always working, always dedicated to the duty, to the notion that once a job was started, it was his to finish. His art-Father smiled a pleasant smile at him through the canvas, as a mellow burnt orange hue filled in around the figure.

Off on the opposite side of the portrait, the Boy watched as a smaller person began to fall into place. Black rubber boots, brown corduroy pants, a green flannel, a yellow beanie. It was himself, he realized. He wore the same backpack. In his right hand, he carried a brown lunch bag, larger than it should be (for it likely carried two lunches, he thought). A faint forest green aura rippled around his art-self. He was frowning in the image. He was frowning out of the image.

Between the two beings on the canvas, a much larger figure rapidly constructed itself, line by line, shade by shade. This figure donned an apron with splotches of blood, dirt, and tears. Its arms muscular and folded. A face appeared, dark circles under the eyes, brown hair tucked up into a tight bun. Around its neck, a bright silver chain with an amulet in the center of its chest. A mythical purple glow encircled the necklace and radiated outwards in tight spirals. This was, of course, his Mother. She was twice the size of his Father in this rendition. A straight line across her face, she was the definition of stoic, strong, and dedicated. The Boy sighed.

As he sat back to consider his art-family, a great shadow burst forth from the royal blue sky above the forest meadow. Holding his breath as the outline of the figure sharpened, the Boy's heart began to race in anticipation. A massive figure, the length of a bus. It had a huge horizontal tail, a sharp dorsal fin, the pointed ears of a fox, wiry whiskers protruding from its face. The Schwark! Grasping the canvas, the Boy gasped as the blowhole erupted into a perfect rainbow of colors, cascading downwards upon his family, showering them in every combination of shades. Upon its face, a huge insane grin, its square teeth hanging goofily over it furry lips. Next to the figure of the art-Boy, a small bowl of cranberries appeared.

"Schwark," the Boy mouthed silently. The Schwark was family, the Boy understood - he missed it terribly, just as he missed his Father. As he wiped away a stray tear from the corner of his eye, he noticed that his hands were covered in paint. Looking at his hands, he suddenly realized that he held several brushes. Had he been painting this portrait? He had thought he was simply imagining it - like the Schwark would have him do in his dreams. Slightly confused, he set the tools beside the Art Therapist and examined the finished product. This was his family, he decided. This was exactly who they were to him at that moment in his life.

Chanting a verse of lyrics from another language, culture, space, or maybe time, the Art Therapist clapped her hands once and fell into silence. Standing, she picked up the portraits from both Boy and his Father and, in examining them, exhaled deeply with a soft smile. She set them side-by-side on the foot of the bed on which she had been sitting.

"Now, without speaking, look at how each of you envision your family. What is similar? What is different?" Her inviting tone lingered in the air as the two painters considered her questions. Gazing at his Father's representation of their family, the Boy was so pleasantly shocked at how similar it was to his own, that he almost burst out laughing in simple joy. On the top of a hill, dotted with mature pine and fir, his Father had drawn himself on the left-hand side, wearing the same clothes, but instead of a shovel and saw, he held a welding gun and a pair of pliers. On the right, he had drawn Boy - wearing, of course, what he was wearing now. In his hands, the Father had placed a school book and calculator. His son was smiling in this rendition. In the middle of the artwork, a tall woman stood, holding her fist high in the air, a red superwoman cape on her back. She was similarly larger than life. The Boy pointed to his Mother in his Father's painting.

"She's pretty strong, huh," he said. His Father smiled, placed his hand around his son and nodded deeply. His Father then pointed to the Schwark in the Boy's picture.

"What is that?" he slowly mouthed. Unsure as to how to explain to his Father the story of the Schwark, he instead looked to the Art Therapist and silently pleaded for her help. Sensing his hesitation and anxiety, she gracefully knelt beside him and smiled so earnestly into his heart, that he felt the panic melt away.

"Everything in your artwork has meaning," she comforted. "That meaning is unique to you and to you alone, but you can do honor to its meaning and significance in your life by sharing memories about it with others." Bringing her hands together over her heart and opening them up in front of the Boy. He could have sworn he saw a neon pink butterfly flutter out into the hallway.

With that, the Boy took a deep breath, looked at his Father's curious and caring eyes, and told him everything. He explained how the Schwark advised him while in school, encouraged his adventures outside of school, helped him make a new friend, helped him avoid several bullies. The Boy recounted its origin as told by the Scavenger, just after his Mother's harrowing retrieval of the necklace. He told his Father about the Schwark-led dreams: about the Captain, who was the Box Man, who is now the Captain again. About the Ghost, who was the son of his Principal. He explained how he was pretending to be an alien so he could eventually attend the Forest School. He even revealed the nightmare - the black hole - his Mother's rage and decision to take the Schwark away forever.

"It was my fault, I realize now," finished the Boy to his Father. "I broke the rules. I couldn't help it. I just... I just see things differently than other kids. I needed the Schwark to guide me, to help me teach myself - to learn from others. And now, because I broke the rules, the Schwark is gone." He laid his face into his Father's chest and closed his eyes, fighting back the sadness. Stroking the Boy's hair, the Father lifted his son's chin and kissed his forehead with tight chapped lips.

"It will be okay," he mouthed to the Boy, his Fatherly confidence radiating from tired eyes. It was enough to bring the Boy back from the darkness. But *would* it be okay? The Boy decided he didn't know. Grabbing a small notebook and pen, his Father began to write a few lines as the Boy patiently waited. The Art Therapist had started to hum again as she packed up her things. Handing the Boy the paper, his Father raised his brow in an expression of "well, what do you think about that?" The Boy read the note:

"I need a job. Will you come with me tomorrow to help? I don't know the city very well and I can't use my voice. Be my wingman?" His smile creeping ever larger, the Boy released a massive sigh and briskly nodded. An adventure. He hugged his Father as tightly as he dared. He was very glad to have his family under one roof - most of his family, anyway.

The Nightmare

Walking along through the dimly lit hallway of his school, the Boy felt as if he was the last thing alive on Earth. The scuff-scuff-squeak of his shoes across the waxed linoleum was all that echoed into his eardrums. Peering into Room 103, he saw that the lights were off, chairs were pushed neatly into their desks. He walked past several other doors, including his soon-to-be new homeroom, Room 105, but the breath on the air remained his alone - where was everybody? To the gymnasium, but nothing - no kids playing Giraffe or anything - perhaps that was a relief, he thought. A faint orange glow sprung from the opposite end of the hallway, towards the Principal's office. He cautiously made his way back along the hall, careful to peek around every corner, for he was certain the Girl was playing an elaborate prank on him.

As he crept closer to the Principal's office, his nostrils detected the odor of bonfire and cigars, growing steadily more concentrated as he entered into the Secretary's waiting room. Underneath the set of heavy double doors, the orange glow flickered and beckoned, a pleasant heat radiating from the Principal's confines. The Boy swallowed hard, gripped the handles, and pulled. A massive plume of dark, toxic blue smoke erupted into his face, encasing his lungs and squeezing them mercilessly. Coughing and sputtering and terrified, the Boy collapsed onto the ground as white-hot flames began to trickle and dance around him, cackling cruelly and feeding upon his fear. Taking the deepest breath possible, he frantically crawled on his belly out of the room, back into the hallway. Gasping and hacking, he stood and ran through the smoke. As he stumbled forward, he glanced back over his shoulder to witness the blue-black whirling smoke begin to coalesce. It was forming into something… two smokey horns spiraling outwards from its gaseous forehead, a pair of glowing red eyes fixating on him - it was a bull. A burst of hot white ash exploded from its nostrils like the sound of a locomotive slowly starting its steam engine. A sudden eruption of flame from its throat - the smoke monster began to charge furiously down the hallway after the Boy, careening off lockers, dissolving and reforming itself at whim.

Rushing into the gymnasium, the Boy slammed the doors closed, and turned to find somewhere - anywhere to hide. Slipping on the wooden floor, he sprawled face-forward as the roar of the smoke hissed behind him - louder... louder... Cast gray in the low-light of the flickering fluorescent lamps above, the aluminum bleachers offered the only immediate shelter. A tendril of smoke plucked at his shoelaces and tugged viciously, ripping the shoe off of his foot in one fell swoop. As he glanced back, he saw the pair of demon-red eyes glaring at him through the gymnasium door, as a deep rumbling snort shook the school walls. The Boy, deafened by his own racing heartbeat, half-crawled, half-leapt behind the set of bleachers and slid up against the cache of stale chewing gum wadded up and stuck to a support beam - the site of the ant project. He closed his eyes and desperately wished he could become an ant again - so small, that this smoke creature would never find him.

A hot blast of acrid air forced him back further, reeling into the cold metal steps of his pathetic asylum. Daring his eyes open to a mere squint, the Boy screamed, for he was greeted by a pair of huge red flames mere inches from his face. The fireballs danced in chaos, contorting and narrowing as they relayed the only message that they could possibly convey.

"You are mine," the smoke growled. A low rumble and hiss grew from the bowels of the black smoke head, as it opened its jaws and revealed a single white flame at its heart. In one sudden lunging motion, the smoke monster's maw grew impossibly wide as it dove over the top of the Boy, swallowing him whole. Smoke fingers strangled his throat, pricked his pores, gouged his eyes, and pulled his hair. The Boy screamed.

"Schwark..." he managed to choke out before the smoke sealed his lips. If only the Schwark were here, none of this would have happened, he thought. He screamed again, but knew that no one would hear him, as all of his senses dulled and died and he entered into the deepest of darknesses.

And then... he awoke.

~~~

Blinded and suffocated, he believed for a moment that he might still be in the digestive system of the smoke monster. Removing the quilt from his face, he gazed up at the artificial city lights glaring through the small rectangular window above his bed - he had never felt so grateful for that polluted light. He needed a drink of water. He needed to feel alive.

Carefully and quietly opening the creaky bedroom door, he noticed that a light in the kitchen was on. Tip-toeing forward, he nearly gasped at the sight of a shadowy figure hunched over at the shaky card table, holding its head beneath a new, now much brighter, lightbulb. His Father, he
~~~

recognized. The floorboards betrayed the Boy, and the two victims of midnight wearily looked at each other through empathetic, tired eyes.

"I had a nightmare," whispered the Boy, sitting down next to the man.

"Me too," mouthed his Father, shaking his head in shared misery.

"My school was on fire, and the smoke chased and ate me," the Boy recounted, his breathing still increased, his nerves slightly unsure of reality, ready to bolt at a moment's notice. His Father places a hand on the Boy's back and patted him gently, just enough to allow his adrenal glands to cool. Then, the man took out a pad of paper and began to scribble.

"I had nearly the same nightmare. I dreamed that the hospital was on fire, and a smoke creature chased me through the hallway, down the elevator, into the parking garage. It almost ate me, too, but I escaped back into the forest," the Boy read aloud. They looked at each other in silence until they breathed at ease. Together, they felt safe in the sanctuary of the shoddy card table.

"I wish I had the Schwark back. Then neither of us would have had those nightmares," said the Boy in earnest. His Father searched his son's face and nodded his agreement. He wrote a few more lines on the paper.

"We have each other. We will learn to adapt here. That is our nature. We survive," the note read. The Boy nodded. He had heard this advice many times since the fire, but somehow having it come from his Father added a much-needed boost of confidence to the Boy's spirit.

"Let's sleep" mouthed his Father with a satisfied smile. With that, they drifted back to their beds and fell into a dreamless, soundless slumber.

The Dock

In the frosty predawn autumn fog, a line of figures bundled in thick fleece-lined jackets and oily overalls with ratty leather gloves sticking out from back pockets wrapped around the side of the dingy brick building. Some had brought small boxes of odd tools, others simply blew into their exposed hands to keep them from going numb - they would need them to sign up for the same-day labor listings released in the next several minutes. Towards the middle of the sulking mass, the Boy stood with his silent Father, both of them ignoring the cold, for the chill of the anxiety was worse. At eight o'clock sharp, a rotund man with a red nose and grey beard waddled out of the double-wide trailer with a clipboard and a roster. Whistling off-key, he tacked a large sheet of paper to side of some molding particle board - the jobs. Next to each was a small description, expectations, necessary training, and a blank line for one's name. Glancing behind his Father, the Boy saw that the line inched around the corner of the city block and back into the alley where the Captain once lived. He knew that on the other side of this double-wide, sat the thrift store, and perhaps (although he felt it impossible) the Schwark. A voice in the back of his mind suddenly urged him to run, run, run to the donations bin, dive into it, rip apart anything and everything until he found it. He took a breath, looked at his Father, and…

"Well, look who it is!" chirped a familiar gruff voice. "So... yer' lookin' for work, are ya, son?" The Captain strode up to the Boy, squatted, and gave him a hearty smack on the back with one hand, a rough and tumble tussle of his hair with the other. Any inkling of running away now was totally stifled. He was grateful for that, he thought. The Captain was in high-spirits and looked spry and healthy. "This your ol' man?" said the Captain standing to face the Boy's Father. "Howdy, buddy! Great kid ya got there! Saved me... a couple times, actually!" he said sticking out his hand. His Father accepted it and shook firmly, a slightly confused but equally friendly smile growing. He slowly turned his head from side to side, pointed to his throat, and drew a 'slash' sign across it, finishing with a slight shrug.

"Lost your voice, eh?" replied the Captain. "Too much partyin'! I know the feelin'. No worries, mate. Ya lookin' for a job today?" The Boy and Father both nodded together.

"Ya know how to weld?" the Captain said with a sly tilt of his head and squinted eye - the perfect caricature of a pirate, the Boy decided. The Boy and Father nodded again, more eagerly this time.

"Well, heck! I've got the job for you then my friend!" the Captain announced, clapping his hands and skipping into the air. He slapped the Boy's Father on the back and led him to the front of the line. "See, I just now drove up from the new docks they're puttin' in - I'm recruitin' for some new welders today. Not many around these days. I'll sign you up personally, how about that? Got a truck parked round back." And with that, his Father followed the Captain past several disgruntled laborers - most muttering unpleasantries loud enough to be enjoyed by both men. Signing his name in fine cursive and listing his welding experience on the side of the job description, he gave a curt nod to the red-nosed, gray-bearded man who stamped his approval on the sheet.

"Awfully handy for being so new around here," the red nosed man smiled to the Captain. Rounding the back of the double-wide with the two men, the Boy froze. Across the street, a neon sign blinked, 'Thrift.'. His eyes wide and mouth gaping, he would have almost been run over by a taxi if his Father had not returned to pluck him from the side of the street. Giving the Boy a stern look, he took out a small flip notebook and started scribbling.

"What's wrong? What are you looking at?" the note said. Pointing across the street, the Boy signaled to his Father.

"That's where the Schwark is...er, was… I don't know." His Father exhaled deeply and squatted next to the Boy.

"Maybe tomorrow" he mouthed. The Boy was having none of it. Here, in this place, at this moment, he had a chance to reclaim his lost family member. Fists balled up, lips curled into a snarl, he released his war-cry. "No!" he screamed, racing past his Father, through two lanes of traffic, up to the glass walls of the thrift. Reaching the automatic doors, he paused briefly - they were not responding. Yanking on the door handles, he felt the give and pull of a deadbolt locking them in place. He looked around frantically for another way in. A small sheet in the window stated the hours - he was too early. Collapsing onto the cement curb, he covered his face and balled.

"Thh-wackl!" A black walnut fell beside him and cracked into three pieces. A swoosh of air above him, as a pitter-patter of tiny awkward feet click-clacked behind, followed by an inquisitive 'caw.' A crow - a very unsympathetic crow.

"Get out of here, bird," the infuriated Boy swatted and spat. The crow easily dodged his lazy attempt to shoo it away, and simply rolled the innards of the nut a few feet away and began to eat.

"Pretty neat, huh!" piped the second very familiar voice of the morning. "Just an hour's worth of training, and now most of the crows around here know how to eat the nuts! Just gotta get them to move back to the forests and parks. I think they look a lot healthier, don't you?" it finished, in quite the proud tone. The Girl. The Boy blinked and stared up at her, as the crows assembled on the power line behind her. She threw a few nuts and giggled with delight as the murder descended to claim their prizes.

"Aren't you supposed to be in school?" asked the Boy.

"Yup. I am in school. This is much more exciting and fun, don't you think? I don't learn anything in the classroom anyway. Plus, I sort of missed my adventure buddy, and thought - sort of hoped - you'd be out here, too!" she smiled.

"My Mom donated the Schwark," the Boy didn't know how else to respond - he had to tell her. "She thought it was distracting me from school. She thought it was the reason why I kept getting in trouble." He had a feeling the Girl knew how important the Schwark had been to him, and his intuition was proved right with her sudden expression of shock and dismay.

"That's terrible!" she started, eyes searching the cement sidewalk for an answer. "Is it... in there? Can we get it back?"

"Not open for an hour er' two," replied the Captain, his lips balancing a freshly rolled, unlit cigarette. How long had he been standing there? His Father was beside him intently watching the conversation between the Boy and Girl. He occasionally looked at the growing number of crows above and scratched his head. He had much to learn, the Boy decided.

"Hey Cap!" squealed the Girl. "Are you going to the docks today? I want to go!" she said, jumping up and down.

"All depends" the Captain replied, with a silly wink. "Did ya bring the goods?" The girl pulled out a baggy stuffed full of plump radishes and soft cheese and handed it to the Captain.

"Absolutely, positively hated this stuff the first time. But, boy, does it grow on ya!" the Captain replied, crunching half a radish between his teeth. "Okidokie hokie schmokie - jump in the truck, seems we're all headed to the docks today!" The gaggle of unlikely misfits walked one behind the other over to the dock company's truck and got in, his Father riding shotgun, the Boy and Girl in the back bench of the cab. A chubby crow landed on the bed of the truck and gave a slight, perplexed croak. The Captain turned the ignition and the truck belched and shuddered for a few seconds before rumbling down the city street towards the river - the dock - to where the Captain's new groove lie.

His Father looked in the side-mirror at the reflection of his son and smiled.

"Here we go!" he mouthed. His smile was a toast to new beginnings.

The Girl was overcome with excitement and the thrill of the adventure. She watched the crow in the back and wondered if it would teach the birds by the river the same trick.

The Boy looked back at the thrift store.

"Tomorrow," he thought.

~~~

As the truck tipped down the gravel-paved access road, the massive port came into view - stacks of shipping containers of every color piled in every corner like some unfinished Lego project. Huge moving equipment grasped the containers like the claw game at the supermarket and whisked them to awaiting train cars or ship beds. Construction cranes, their raised necks looming into the low clouds and disappearing, dangled hooks and bobbed beams of steel at the site of a new dock being constructed at the river's edge.

"It looks like angels or gods or something trying to fish," said the Girl, watching the thin threads of cable and chain stretch and dangle from the bottom of the clouds, eventually latching onto various pallets and loads.

"That's where we're headed, gang," announced the Captain, "the new dock. Gotta get those beams situated with some serious welds. Glad to have a new friend along for the work!" he said, punching the Boy's Father playfully in the side of the arm. His Father smiled and punched the Captain back. Parking the truck next to a giant transformer that whizzed and surged with current, the Captain sprang out and greeted several workers. A large team of welders was working on securing the steel skeleton of the dock. The Boy watched as the Captain introduced his Father and discussed how he couldn't really speak much at the moment because of some "party" he
~~~

had likely attended. After a hearty laugh, his Father was handed a welder's mask, apron, and gloves and was led off with a site manager to assess his skill. The Captain waltzed over to the truck, whistling a goofy but familiar melody, and kneeled by the Boy and Girl.

"Alrighty! We're going to work! You two - I'd say 'stay out of trouble' - but that's what you do best! Ha!" he joked. He was about to leave it at that, but thought better and turned back to the Girl. "You know what? I've got a science experiment for ya - a step up from crows. Certainly light-years from ants!" Her eyes bulged at the notion.

"Yes ma'am, need yer' help. Need a top notch scientist for this one." the Captain continued. "See, we got lots of ships 'round here. And with that, you've got rats. And I mean, *huge*, giant, bloodsucking rats!" he said, miming saucer eyes and ferocious claws, digging into the air this way and that. "They chew holes in stuff, make nests where they shouldn't be, and just cause a general nuisance to everyone who works here. Your mission: get the rats outta here. That's it!" He shook his head and laughed mightily. "Oh, and if you happen to come across a welder, don't look at the spark - you'll blind yourself. Okay! That's it! See you at five o'clock!" he clapped his hands, twirled on his heels and jogged back over to see how the Boy's Father was getting along.

The Boy and Girl looked at each other and grinned.

This would be their biggest project yet.

~~~

The rats were mutants. Monstrous, dark-eyed bandits that were paradoxically very cute-appearing, but incredibly crafty. Nimble and ferocious when they fought each other, they resisted every attempt to be lured by food - seemingly wisened from prior traps the dockworkers had set. They could sprint, long-jump, swim, tunnel, and the Boy swore he saw one fly. Olympic athletes with savant-level intelligence - formidable creature, he decided.

"These guys are super cool, eh?" thought the Girl, frustrated and enamored by her newest subjects. She had already named several of the rats: Slim, Fats, One-Eye, and Sparky, who loved to sneak into welder's bags and chew on their sweaty gloves.

"I don't know if we can trick them to actually go anywhere," the Boy responded, sitting down on a an unattached beam in slight frustration. "they seem to really like it here - there's plenty of food and shelter." The
~~~

Girl considered that and sat down next to him in silence for a few moments.

"Maybe they are overpopulated - no natural predators. I wonder why there's no cats!" she said suddenly. The Boy could hear the gears and cogs whirring and spinning in the her brain. She was definitely a child of the wilderness, of nature, like him.

"I think I have an idea," she finally said, with a thoughtful eyebrow raised towards a particularly mischievous rat - probably Sparky, decided the Boy.

~~~

For the rest of the afternoon, the two split up - the Girl hyper-focused on locating rat nests and rat mazes and rat hideouts and everything else rat-related - the Boy interested in how his Father was doing - his first real work in the city. Following the raucous laughter of the Captain from inside the partially assembled ribcage of the steel dock, the Boy soon found his Father straddling a gargantuan column, about to set a long, horizontal weld. The Captain was crouched nearby, ready to observe. Both men flipped down their masks, as his Father gripped the welding gun. Molten metal bubbled and spit at the site of the spark, expelling a shower of incandescent droplets every which way. Fortunately, a pair of beams obstructed the potentially blinding spark and the Boy was grateful he wouldn't be blind for the rest of the day. He sat and watched as the miniature meteor shower rained down upon his Father and crew. Donning large black leather hoods and aprons, the men had the appearance of some sort of evil astronaut gang.

"That's a great weld, man! Perfect layers. You haven't lost the touch, that's for sure," commented a dockworker to the Boy's Father. The Boy, beaming in admiration, unconsciously hooted and hollered. Grinning up at the Boy, The Captain shot him his idiosyncratic wrinkled wink.

~~~

As the day came to a close, the group reassembled by the old company pickup truck and piled in.

"I'll take you guys back to your car in the city. And you, missy, I can drop you off at your home. Your parents, uh, will probably want some sort of explanation," said the Captain, with a nervous chuckle. The Girl crossed her arms.

"Oh, I go on adventures all the time. I used to get in trouble, but as long as I tell them where I'm going and as long as I am back for dinner, they don't get too upset," she said matter-of-factly.

"And so where did you tell them you were going today?" asked the Captain, sarcastically suspicious.

"I said I was going near the school to work on the crow project - that's not a lie! Now the project is even bigger!" she pleaded. Eyes widening, she seemed to remember something rather important then. "Do you know where I can find a bunch of cats, Cap?" she queried.

"A bunch of cats," he repeated, starting the truck's lethargic engine, revving the gas it a bit too for encouragement. "And why would you want a bunch of cats, may I ask?"

"For the rats! Obviously!" the Girl responded, exasperated by so many questions.

"I see," said the Captain, stroking his beard, considering the idea. "You think you could train em' to catch those suckers, eh? Won't be no cinnamon-and-socks trick this time around, sister." he said, wagging a finger as he adjusted pulled the transmission into reverse." But, yeah, I know a lady. Has tons of cats - sort of. Not sure if they are hers, or what. It's on the way back, we can stop real quick. That okay with you boys?" he offered to the Boy and his Father. Both quickly nodded, clearly intrigued by this strange development.

The truck chugged and blurched up the gravel drive and onto the main city street. After a few miles, the Captain began to follow the signs pointing to the city's main park. Following a winding road down to a small pond surrounded by Japanese Maple, he parked the truck in the empty lot and turned off the ignition. The sun was beginning to set, and cast a pink-orange glow over the still-as-glass pond - the two flaming orbs seemed to be on a silent, peaceful collision course at the horizon.

"Okidoke. Here we are - they call this place, 'The Sacred Garden.' Supposed to be 'Home of The Most Beautiful Tree In The World. Or so they say. Heh." snorted the Captain, clearly skeptical. "Cat Lady likes to sit at the end of the pond at sunset. Used to trade cigarettes for cans of tuna with her back in the day - which wasn't very long ago, actually," he reflected. The four figures exited the truck and hiked the circuitous path along the southern border of the small pond towards the western end where a woman sat hunched over, alone on a bench. The setting sun encompassing her head like an old portrait of a saint, or maybe an alien. Around her, small bodies slithered and stalked, whispering tails flicking this way and that, perching on her shoulders and knees and curling up near her feet. The smell of processed tuna wafted towards them as a gentle breeze blew off the glass pond. Here was The Cat Lady.

"Hello there, stranger," purred the Cat Lady, back still turned to the approaching gaggle. "Could hear you coming a mile away! You still talk too loud! And ya stink - nothing new there," she said with a hearty laugh. A black and white cat nuzzled up against her face, and she, in turn, rubbed her cheek back upon it. Cat Lady, indeed, decided the Boy.

"Well nice to see you too!" replied the Captain slumping down next to her with a great yawn and sigh. He scratched a cat between the ears with a single finger and grinned as it purred its acceptance of him. "Brought some folks that may be interested in your line of work." The Cat Lady looked over her shoulder at the remaining three and gave a curt smile and wave.

"*My* line of work?" she echoed, "You mean, 'how to make terrible decisions?'" she said with a sarcastic grin. A tabby cat was hogging a tin of tuna on the ground and she shooed it away gently to allow a small kitten unbridled access. "You mean, 'how to beg for money everyday to buy tuna for a bunch of cats?' Yup, if so, then I'm your gal." she announced with a down-trodden sniff. The Girl approached the Cat Lady slowly. She was clearly mesmerized by the puddle of felines patrolling the bench.

"Well," the Girl timidly began, holding her up-turned palm to an inquisitive tabby. "I was wondering.. if we could borrow some? To take the dock. They have a lot of rats there, and no cats. So the ecosystem isn't balanced," he explained. The tabby leapt onto the Girl's shoulder and was now vigorously rubbing at the nape of her neck. She giggled. The Cat Lady laughed and slapped her thigh.

"Sure, sure! Is the ecosystem ever really balanced? Hasn't been that balanced for me, in, oh, in forever?" she recounted. The Girl gave the woman a confused look.

"Tell you what kiddo: you prove that you can love these cats and that they love you, and I think you can borrow a few to take back with our mutual friend here," the Cat Lady bargained, poking the Captain in the shoulder. Sitting cross-legged on the grass, The Girl considered the cats. They looked back at her with cautious, unsure, liquid yellow eyes, bodies tucked behind the safe confines of the Cat Lady's legs, bellies guarding half-eaten cans of cheap tuna fish. Closing her eyes and raising her hands to rest on each knee, the Girl turned her palms up and brought her thumbs to her index fingers in a classic meditative pose. A deep, exaggerated purring began to vibrate from the back of her throat. The Captain and the Cat Lady began to laugh hysterically, sending cats leaping off of their laps in hysteria.

"What in the…" chuckled the Captain. Keeping her focus, the Girl purred in a slightly lower octave. The cats, clearly agitated from the Cat Lady's laughter, began to creep closer to the perfectly still Girl. A pint-sized, black-as-night feline dared to confidently strut up to her left knee, gave it a curt sniff, and rubbed its back against her, testing the waters. The Girl did not move. Another cat - a white, elderly lady with pink paws and glossy gray eyes - waltzed over and lay at her side. The Girl did not move. A minute later, and the Girl had garnered a superficial bridge of trust with over ten cats, who laid about and upon her in various lazy poses. As she unhinged her eyes, her purring slowed and slowly faded. Twenty yellow eyeballs suddenly turned their whiskered faces towards hers - and began to gently purr back. Stroking their necks and scratching behind their ears, the Girl looked up at the Cat Lady and the Captain and smiled.

"A real Buddha, I guess," said the Cat Lady, shaking her head with a smirk.

"Some kinda animal whisperer, I think," replied the Captain.

"She's a scientist, actually," the Boy clarified. It was the second time that day he had felt immense pride in someone else's courage and skill.

~~~

As they walked back to the truck on the north side of the pond, the Captain promised the Girl that he would bring a few cats to the dock tomorrow.

"If this thing works, maybe we can even make the lady a few bucks! Hire her on at the dock as the official 'Cat Caretaker' or something like that," the Captain suggested, a twinkle in his eye. As the Boy looked over to ask his Father what he thought, he was interrupted by an all-too-recognizable 'caw.' and looked up to find the Runt perched a few feet above.

"Woah," gasped the Boy, freezing mid-stride. The single crow sat on a low branch of the largest Japanese Maple tree the Boy had ever seen. Perhaps one-hundred feet tall, and equally as wide, the tree's infinite
~~~

spiraling branches held leaves of every burnt hue - smoky orange, blood red, sun yellow. As the sunset breeze blew over the pond, the tree became a living firestorm of color - a sensuous rustling that made the hair on his arms stand. The Most Beautiful Tree In The World.

"Caw!" the Runt considered the four humans as it dropped a large nut from a claw, silently taking wing. Falling to the ground in slow-motion, the black nut impacted upon a jagged edge of basalt, exploding into four perfectly symmetric quadrants. Suddenly, hundreds of tiny black sugar ants poured from each quartered section and raced along the wood-chipped trail towards the feet of the Girl. Letting out a gasp, she stumbled backwards and tripped, falling onto the Boy, sending them sprawling onto the earth. The ants continued their charge. As the Boy helped the Girl back to her feet, he felt a convulsive wriggling coming from the front pocket of her oversized sweatshirt. As she attempted to conceal the source, a crooked calico-patterned tail draped out of the left-hand side, as a scruffy pair of triangular ears poked out from the other. Before the Girl had a chance to explain, the animal leapt from her sweatshirt cocoon, onto the ground, and pranced towards the onslaught of ants. Sitting on its haunches and licking its paw, the cat patiently waited as the ants careened towards it. Neither Captain, nor Father, nor Girl, nor Boy dared to move a muscle at the fascinating spectacle. As if running straight into a glass screen, the ants abruptly stopped. Piling on top of each other, they began to form a rising volcano of constantly eroding, constantly growing miniature tectonic madness. As the mountain of arthropods reached eye-level with the cat, a few unfortunate and unlucky ant-souls toppled off the summit and fell within a paw's grasp.

"Meoww!" Springing onto all fours, the cat let out an almighty hiss, its energy reverberating across the soil, causing the ant-pile to erupt and explode, scattering tiny bodies every which way. Slinking back to the Girl, the Cat softly purred and begged its way into the pouch of her sweatshirt. In seconds, it appeared to have fallen asleep.

"Her name is Grandma," whispered the Girl. "The Cat Lady said she's really old, and really wise - magical even! She's the one that told the Cat Lady to move here in the first place! She said Grandma needs a safe home, too. I think she knows about balancing ecosystems. I'll take care of her, okay?" explained the Girl, stroking Grandma's coat. It was not a question, but a simple assertion, thought the Boy. He looked to the horizon just as the blazing autumn sun dipped below the distant hills - a brilliant green fluorescent flash appeared - for just a millisecond.

<p style="text-align:center">~~~</p>

"This your place, kiddo?" asked the sleepy Captain as he plunged the transmission into park - it had been a long day, indeed. The Girl nodded. Looking out the foggy truck cabin window, the Boy tried to conceal his shock at the size of the Girl's home - a literal mansion, he decided. A three car garage, two story brick home that seemed to stretch itself into the length of a city block. A rushing sense of disappointment and embarrassment ran through his heart in that moment - he wanted her to be like him: poor, displaced, disadvantaged... or did he? His confliction made him anxious, and he barely heard her when she said goodbye.

"Thanks for the great adventure! Grandma is going to love it here," she said, giving each of the three a bear-hug, careful not to squish the hitchhiker in her sweatshirt. Smiling at the Boy, she waved and ran towards her house. He sighed - how wonderful it was to have a friend like the Girl. The pickup coughed into drive, as they began the journey back towards the city.

<p style="text-align:center">~~~</p>

"Good first day on the job, partner," yawned the Captain as he pulled up alongside their station wagon. "No need to come back here lookin' for work," he said, motioning to the job signup trailer, "dock's boss-man likes ya plenty. You're hired buddy! Just come on down to the dock by eight o'clock tomorrow and we'll make it official," he finished, slapping the Boy's Father on his back.

"Thank you," mouthed his Father.

"Oh my pleasure," responded the Captain, now looking at the Boy. "Least I could do... for an old friend," he grinned. The Boy caught a glimpse of his Father giving a confused, but amused look at the two of them. He decided he better not start to explain that story - not yet, anyway. As his Father opened the rusted driver's side door on their wagon, the Boy heard the jingle of bells rattling against glass. Across the street, he watched an elderly man pull down a set of steel security bars across the front entrance to the thrift store. Feeling a quick pat on his shoulder, he glanced up at his Father who simply nodded - "Go."

Sprinting over the desolate city street, the Boy yelled after the Shopkeep.

"Excuse me! Wait!" he panted. The Shopkeep turned and flashed
the Boy a smile with several twinkling golden teeth.

"All closed, son" he said with a shrug, dusting his hands off on his
jeans. "Come back tomorrow morning 'round ten." The Boy wouldn't have
it.

"No!" he impulsively replied. The Shopkeep startled and turned.
"Sorry, I just have a question. About something dropped off here," the Boy
pleaded. The elderly man looked across the street and saw the Boy's Father
leaning against the station wagon, watching patiently.

"Tons and tons a' things come rollin' through our place everyday.
No way I'm gonna remember a single item -, sorry kid," he said, palms
held high to the dreary night sky. "Ought to get back to your old man, son.
I gotta get home to my family, too."

"It's a Schwark!" exclaimed the desperate Boy.

The Shopkeep paused, and flashed his golden smile again. "A
what? A 'Shoe-Wart?" he asked.

"A Schwark! A stuffed animal. It's part whale, part shark, part otter,
part fox, and, uh, part lots of things, I guess," the Boy clarified in rapid-fire
manner.

The Shopkeep starred at the Boy for a few moments, a blank affect
across his face. Slowly considering the description of the creature the Boy
had described, he looked up at the fresh mist raining down and smiled
again - golden moonbeams glinting off of his teeth.

"You know what..." he began, "Yeah... I do remember a weird
thing like that. A lady dropped it off in a hurry, all by itself in a paper bag.
Sort of strange." The Boy could hardly contain his ecstasy.

"Do you still have it? Is it in there? Can I get it? It's mine!" he
implored. The Shopkeep kicked a broken nut off the sidewalk.

"I'm sorry, son. The Chaplain came by yesterday - comes by every
week for a big ol' pile of stuff. Took that Shoe-Wart up to his mission on
the hill, I'm pretty sure," he said, thumbing in the direction they had just
driven from. Shaking his head softly and offering his nonverbal
sympathies, the Shopkeep got into his van, started the engine, and rolled
down the window. The Boy had not moved.

"Son, if the Chaplain's the man I know, then take comfort in
knowin' that your toy? It's gonna bring some hope and joy to another boy
or girl. Just think of that," finished the Shopkeep, pulling away with a
pointed salute to the Boy's Father. Trudging back to the station wagon with
angry and frustrated tears in his eyes, the Boy slammed the car door shut

and squeezed his empty backpack to his chest. His Father placed a comforting, calloused palm on the Boy's leg, diffusing his rage and grief ever so slightly, as only a Father could. As the car coughed into drive, the two locked eyes.

"What's a 'mission?'" the Boy asked.

The Astronaut

"Three... two... one..." Three beings strapped into upside down chairs, donning massive gray puffed up suits and silver reflective helmets, sat in silence in a completely dark room.

"Liftoff," announced the flat static voice. An incredible surge rattled the figures in their seats. If the room was illuminated, each of the astronauts would have been able to see the eyelids and cheeks of their comrades pulled back in hilarious and frightening fashion as the impossible acceleration ripped them away from gravity. The Boy sat comfortably in the center of the room in his pajamas, seemingly unaffected by the turmoil. As flickers of light from their control-paneled confines began to fluoresce the cabin in dull reds and greens, the Boy examined each of the three faces - none appeared familiar to him in the least.

"Where am I?" he thought silently. Seconds later, all of calm. The roar of the mighty engines had ceased, as gravity left the cabin entirely Unbuckling from their rigid chairs, the astronauts began levitate around the cramped vessel. Out of a small porthole about the size of an apple, the Boy caught a glimpse of the blue-green sphere he knew was home, as the sun crossed the planet's watery horizon and shimmered brilliantly. A stirring in the cabin, as one of the astronauts began to remove its heavy helmet and thick gloves. Floating over towards the same miniature window occupied by the Boy, he examined the Earth, and then casually looked directly into the Boy's eyes and smiled - subtly, but knowingly. The Boy gasped, for the Astronaut had the most pale gray eyes the Boy had ever seen - like perfect crystalline ice.

"Well wasn't that heckin' somethin'?" the Astronaut exclaimed to his comrades - and to the Boy - chuckling into the recycled spaceship air. *Heckin.'*

"Haven't I heard that before?" thought the Boy. A sudden blur of color and sound and light. A stretching sensation within his mind. A queasiness in his stomach as he dealt with the sensation of simultaneously existing in two different points in time and space, receiving sensory inputs from both in an overwhelming chaos: Monotone static radio communications blipping and bleeping... then, dirty dishes being washed and scrubbed and clinked and clanked... now, bright bursts of blue hydrogen-fueled plasma pulses from an interplanetary engine... finally, bright red and white holiday lights flickering on and off above a softly glowing fireplace mantle. Screaming into the vacuum, the Boy shut his eyes and hugged his knees as he tumbled headlong through the inter-dimensional whirlpool of his mind.

~~~

Falling out of nothingness, the Boy collapsed onto a glossy, tiled kitchen floor. A jazzy swing tune was playing on a scratchy set of speakers somewhere nearby. Standing beside him was a figure with its back turned to the Boy, vigorously scrubbing a cast iron pot while whistling off-key to the old-timey song. Two children sat at the dining room table playing checkers, while a middle-aged woman knitted a rainbow-colored scarf. The doorbell suddenly rang, and the house fell eerily silent. The faucet abruptly turned off, albeit for a residual drip-drip-drip. The figure - a man - with ice-gray eyes - stopped whistling and looked to the woman - his wife. She nodded. His large Adam's apple rising and falling, he nodded back and strode to the door.

"Same-day mail," announced a delivery man wearing navy blue and a pointed cap. "Sign here, please, sir." he explained, passing a small, sealed envelope with the words 'Extremely Urgent' tattooed on its side. The two nodded curtly, as the ice-gray eyed man shut the door gently. A trio of soft snowflakes had drifted in at the last moment. Holding the envelope with his slightly trembling hand, the man returned to the table and sat down, four pairs of eyes staring and silently imagining what it may contain. The fifth pair - the Boy's - simply confused. With perfect precision, the man sliced the envelope longitudinally with a golden letter opener and pulled out a single sheet of heavy-weighted paper, folded in half once. A red waxed seal of some sort was affixed to the bottom. Clearing his throat, he considered reading the message aloud, the room seemingly holding its own breath.

"Congratulations," he began, "You've been selected as a candidate for group number thirty-three." A single, quick breath - the man immediately dropped the paper on the table. Tears of pride, of joy, of anxiety, of unknown fear fell from the faces of his son, his daughter, his wife, himself. His family huddled around him, hugging him tightly. Over the top of their heads, his ice eyes peered at the Boy still sitting on the kitchen floor, a sliver of near-frozen water glimmering like a diamond from his cheek. He smiled at the Boy, winking out the tear.

"Alright, buddies..." the Astronaut whispered. The Boy's eyes went wide.
~~~

"Buddies?" the Boy considered, searching his memories in random
fashion. Just as he was about to retrieve the memory from the tip of his
tongue, the visual frame of the Astronaut and his family sitting at the table
began to rapidly stretch and warp towards a single bright pinprick of light.
Feeling himself accelerate in every direction at once, the Boy instinctively
curled into a ball as his stomach and intestines and spleen searched for a
way out through his mouth. The adrenaline of riding the top of a massive
wave before suddenly falling down the backside filled his head with a
nauseating floating sensation. Peer over his kneecaps, he watched as the
universe blurred past incoherently.

~~~

"Roger, Bravo Two-Niner. This is Tiger Lead. Throttle up and
bank left to heading six-four, eight-six on my count," came the static-
riddled canned voice in his head. The Boy was strapped into a narrow steel
seat surrounded by a thick canopy of glass. The stretching and blurring and
distorted sense of time had vanished, but the nausea and sense of crushing
gravity seemed to only worsen.

"Three. Two. One. Push it." A massive roar and explosion of
orange flame ignited the boy's periphery, as a shaking terrible force held
him against the seat, preventing even a finger from being raised in protest.
His chest wall paralyzed, he struggled to exhale. As the fighter jet leveled
off, gravity released its grip from its pajama-clad passenger, and a pair of
ice cold eyes twinkled at him from the rear-view mirror of the pilot who sat
in front of him.

"Howdy, partner!" said the Astronaut's chipper voice through the
plane's internal communications line. The Boy blinked back at the eyes.
Suddenly, the fighter jet rolled left, and with it, flung the Boy sideways
through the curtain of space and time and into a sea of cacophonous
clapping and whistling.

~~~

Sitting on the edge of a stage, the Boy looked outwards at the
hundreds of faces beaming back - not at him, but at the sixty-odd figures
standing behind him. Dark, oversized, baggy black robes swung
awkwardly from their teenage frames, square caps and turquoise tassels
tickled their necks. Screeching feedback from a microphone, and then a

soft sound, a name was read from a scroll. A raucous applause, a handshake, a diploma. Repeat. The Boy sat watching - who's graduation was this?

Finally, the last name was called. A tall boy confidently strode to the podium, gave the customary handshake and accepted his leather-bound, oversized diploma. He remained standing as the throngs of adults in the audience stood and clapped wildly for several minutes. Stepping to the podium, he gave a short speech.

"I am honored to be your valedictorian," said the boy with ice-gray eyes. "None of this would have been possible without the support of my parents, the encouragement of my teachers, or the strength of my friends," he finished to another standing ovation. "Or without the kindness of a stranger," the Astronaut whispered down to his side, out of range of the microphone. He was smiling at the Boy sitting on the stage.

"Who are you?" the Boy whispered back. The cheering and clapping grew louder and more shrill, blending and culminating into a whining white static that began to coalesce and fragment the figures on the stage. Arms and legs and caps and gowns began to crumble and de-pixelate into crystals of fine sand that began to drift into fine plumes, the winds of time scattering them haphazardly forwards and backwards and sideways. A rainbow of circulating colors churned and wailed, ensnaring the Boy in an infinitely massive mound of quicksand, sucking him towards its conical bottom. Arms pinned to his sides by an impossible weight, he took a final breath as his head dipped below the multicolored granular surface.

~~~

As he rapidly slid and squirmed downwards toward a pinpoint singularity of soft white light, the Boy swore he heard the faint mellow rumble of a baritone saxophone, the relaxed vibrations of an accompanying clarinet. Through the singularity he stretched, his body elongating into a string of a trillion quarks, the haunting, floating jazz riffs squeezing through alongside. Falling gently now, he felt the blue and green and orange crystalline sand raining down upon his head as he came to rest in a small plastic neon-yellow chair, his legs cramped under a miniature desk. Piles of sand began to reform in front of his eyes as he took in this new place… or was it an old place? Other desks, some with smaller children in their seats began to materialize, as did a stout, elderly woman at the front
~~~

of what was slowly recognizable as a classroom - Room 103, he suddenly realized.

"Yesterday, we all started working on composing a poem about something important in our lives," began the Teacher." This morning we are going to be sharing our masterpieces. Are there any volunteers to start us off?" A flanneled arm shot up in front of the Boy, its hand waving frantically. The student in front of him wore a bright yellow knit beanie atop a mop of brown hair.

"Our newest student. Of course," smiled the Teacher, "come on up." Diving into a forest-green canvas backpack with brown leather trim, the student retrieved a slightly crumpled piece of paper, zipped up the bag, and hurried to the front, he shoes squeaking on the linoleum. A faint pulsating glow illuminated the interior of the backpack ever so briefly. The Boy's heart skipped a beat. Waves of stomach-churning déjà vu swept over him in that moment as the flanneled student smoothed out the edges of his poem. That flannel - something so familiar. That beanie - and that backpack…

"Those are mine," though the Boy. "Were mine?" he corrected, brow wrinkled. Was he watching himself in some alternate timeline? Some other dimension where he actually completed his homework? The student at the front of the class turned and faced the judging glares of his peers, his ice-gray eyes radiating confidence and filling the room with anticipation. A soft saxophone began to play in the background of the classroom - could no one hear it? Clearing his throat, the Astronaut began his poem.

"My New Old Friend.

From out of the mist, and between the drops,
A familiar face walks... and then stops.
Smile. Nod. Hello. How are you?
I've seen you before, and you know that it's true.

We aren't so different, you and I.
Remembering Home often makes us cry.
But inside our dreams, free hearts do soar,
Led by the Creature, we sing, dance, and roar!

Awakened minds, we're up for the test,
To lead family and friend towards their best.

Silence. A smattering of awkward confused claps. A mandatory 'Thank-you, next-please' from his Teacher. Shuffling footsteps returning to the desk. A slow turn of the head. The Astronaut's eyes glowed an icy-soft gray as he looked at the Boy, a slow, slight smile and a subtle nod. For once, the Boy returned the smile, for he was beginning to understand. As the classroom grew brighter, and the figures within dimmer, the Boy bowed his head and shut his eyes in anxious anticipation for the next stretch, dive, tumble, or tear. Relinquishing his fear, he inhaled deeply, and began to hum a familiar melody to himself, the warmth of the notes wrapping his mind in acceptance and appreciation of the mysterious journey that is time.

Silence.

A soft, pleasant nothingness.

The Boy opened his eyes.

Awake or not, he awoke.

The Plan

"What is this?" mouthed his Father, holding the golden disc under the kitchen light. "Space food - or something like that" answered the Boy, between mouthfuls of syrup and gummy starch. Maneuvering the circular sponge through the air like some sort of out-of-control UFO, he suddenly brought it to a sustained hover over his plate and pretended to abduct a bent fork. His Father smirked, joining his own partially eaten space-waffles in assembly of a miniature syrupy star fleet. Breakfast hadn't been so much fun since before the great fire, thought the Boy. A great sigh emptied out upon the table, quenching the giggles and make-believe rocket-engine noises - his Mother. She sat, hunched forward, poking at her breakfast, a tremendous gray, dull cloak hovering invisibly over her heavy shoulders. A hand clutched at her chest - her empty, forlorn sternum - no purple aura in sight. The Boy swallowed his bolus of anxiety. His Father furrowed his brow and placed a gentle hand over his Mother's.

"What happened?" he mimed. A deep, staccato breath. A perfect stillness, and then… a deep, terrible sobbing filled the hollow dining room, flexing the yellowed drywall as it reverberated back and forth. The Boy watched in horror, as his heroine - his pillar of strength - his Mother - wailed into the early morning mustiness of the dingy apartment, her hair dipping into pools of stagnant syrup and berry juice as she wept.

"I... it…" she managed, choking on her words. "I spilled a tray of ketchup and mustard all over myself. Had to… had to change my apron," she explained, her bottom lip trembling. "The manager was so *angry* for some reason, told me, 'Hurry up and change or you are out of here.'" The Boy saw his Father's eyes furrow - how could anyone say such a thing to the Boy's Mother? "So I… I flung the apron off - the necklace, oh!" her chest heaving erratically as she covered her face with both hands. "It… must have come right off with it - onto the floor, under a table or chair, who knows?" she whispered. The Boy pushed his chair out abruptly.

"Have you checked?" he frantically asked. "You searched all over the place?" A great sigh came as his response.

"Yes… of course I did," she replied, head bent forward again. "It was gone." At that, his Mother stood and cleared their dishes, busying herself to forget her sorrow. Placing the sticky dishes into the sink, she suddenly turned to face the Boy and his Father. "Listen: if it returns to me - to us - then so be it. If not, then it is what it is," her face a stoic shield. The two at the table sat motionless. "You two get going - I'll take a taxi today," she replied in even flatness to their silence. For once, the Boy wished he could go with her - to help her look again, to console her, to empathize. After all, the loss of something sacred was a topic he knew all too well.

~~~

The Principal hummed a light-hearted tune as he escorted the nervous Boy to Room 105. Two sturdy, dramatic knocks, and suddenly, the door swung open with a great bravado, revealing the embarrassed, pale-faced grimace of the new student. Thirty pairs of bored, tired eyes yawned at him - they had been prepped regarding his arrival, he figured. Skipping two grades had its short-comings - especially when one was already a bit short. Sulking to his position in the back of the classroom, the Boy realized that he was now no more than half the height of the average student in the room. Sitting at his new desk, he glanced out of his periphery to check for any sneers or tongues poking out in his direction - there were none. The children of Room 105 couldn't have cared less that he was amongst them - two years younger, and clearly from another planet, he thought they would assume. Instinctively, he reached into his backpack for the familiar, reassuring soft fleece body, furry flippers, and ticklish whiskers, only to find a sad, cold brown bag half full of carrots, hummus, and stale sourdough. Needing desperate confidence, he found profound loneliness in that moment. He missed the Girl. He missed the Schwark.

His new teacher was a bald, thin man with a gray handlebar mustache that he itched every few minutes. The Boy quickly realized that the man had clearly been informed about the Boy's past misadventures, for he seemed to have half an eye constantly affixed in his general direction. Immediately after the lunch bell rang out, the Boy requested to join Room 103 for a few minutes and was promptly and flatly denied. At physical education class, he was ordered to stay within the basketball court, explicitly instructed not to wander behind the bleachers or near the alley door. He was only allowed bathroom breaks as long as he went with a "buddy" - a prospect so terrifying, he held his bladder the entire day, nearly peeing his pants before the final bell signaled his surrender. Once at after-school recess, he was "encouraged" by the chaperone to spend his time completing his homework. When he protested and asked to join the other in free-time at the gymnasium, he was told that "new rules" existed for students in Room 105 - homework first. Opening his Math textbook, he sighed at the problems that snickered and glared back at him - not because
~~~

of their level of difficulty, but rather the sheer quantity of them. After an hour of mindless, repetitive scribbling, he was permitted to join the Girl as she sat on highest row of bleachers, whispering into her backpack.

"Hi-ya Mr. Smarty-Pants! How's Room 105 with Mr. Mustache-McGee?" she chirped, hands caressing a frantic wriggling inside her sweatshirt. The Boy smiled and told her about the boring classes and "bathroom buddy" situation, at which she laughed mightily. Just then, a small crooked tail poked out of her shirt pocket - just long enough for the Boy raise his eyebrows. Quickly tucking the furry finger back into place, the Girl peered over her shoulder in a cute sort of paranoia.

"Grandma slept all day. She's nocturnal," she stated, in a motherly sort of proud way. The Boy watched as she inserted two small and soggy rectangles into the front pouch where the cat lay. "I brought her some fish sticks that I microwaved at home - I hope she likes them." The soft smacking sound of the feline's strange breakfast was just audible over the echoing of bounced basketballs and screaming kids below them. "Do you think the port cats will be alright?" she asked the Boy, changing subjects only slightly. "I think I'm going to go down there this weekend and check - want to come with?" she asked, eyes wide with excited anticipation. She lived for adventure, just as him.

"I was actually going to propose my own adventure to you," replied the Boy, holding back a sneaky grin. She listened intently as he told her about the encounter with the Shopkeeper the previous night. The Schwark was on a mission, or in a mission, or at a mission - with a Chaplain - up near the Girl's home. He lamented to her about the loneliness and shunned feeling he felt in Room 105, and knew the Schwark would help him cope. The Girl nodded wholeheartedly in earnest agreement.

"I know that mission!" the Girl erupted, clapping her hands. Grandma meowed loudly in protest. "There's a camp of homeless folks right behind the building - they actually have a pretty nice little tent village. There's a kitchen, and bathrooms, and a medical clinic - and I think my dad said they even have a mayor!" she recalled. "On the weekend, people come volunteer there. My mom cooked soup there a few times," she finished, sitting in silence scratching a white spot between Grandma's eyes, deep in thought about something from long ago - or maybe long ahead. The Boy let the Scientist ponder, her motor whirring a million miles per hour. Finally, turning to the Boy, eyes on fire, a soft pale yellow haze surrounding her figure, she laid out their plan.

"If we go to the dock that morning, I bet we can convince the Captain to drive us to that mission afterwards! It'll be an epic adventure!" The Boy's heart skipped several beats. He wanted to hug the Girl right then, but feared he would disturb Grandma and her meal. How did she keep that cat so secret all day, he wondered? For the rest of the late afternoon, the Boy and Girl hashed out the details of their grand scheme. It would truly be epic, he decided.

The Amanita

The soft, dew-licked moss cushioned and wrapped the Boy's body softer than the finest spider silk. A waxy green umbrella of humongous fern fronds patch-worked themselves over the Boy's face allowing only the tightest of morning sunbeams through. Slowly pushing himself upright, his face poking through the gentle plants, he realized he was amongst the largest old growth Douglas Fir he had ever seen - their trunks wider than their station wagon, their branches thicker than most other trees, for that matter. As he turned to greet the morning sun, a fine white mist serpentined through the underbrush and beckoned him dreamily towards a small single-track that had suddenly appeared between two stands of manzanita. Setting foot on the perfectly cleared dirt path, the Boy jumped, for a small shaggy-mane mushroom had suddenly sprouted a few feet ahead of him, its white elongated cap swaying to a silent fungal beat. At the beckoning of the forest, the Boy began to walk.

Gliding through patches of snowberry that lined the winding path, the Boy summited a small ravine was immediately met by a curious fork in the trail. At the intersection, a comically large Amanita sat brooding, its white polka-dotted candy-red cap large enough to serve dinner upon. As he admired the toxic mushroom, a quick trot-trot-trot came rustling forth from the left side of the fork - a slender red-furred creature, nimble and sly, came to a halt in front of him. The Fox!

"Hello, friend," the smooth voice purred, as its stealthy body came to rest upon its haunches alongside the toadstool, grinning mischievously at the confused Boy. A slower, thicker clop-clop-clop of dirty boots came reverberating up the right-side of the fork - a tree-rubbing of creaky leather-on-leather accompanying it in grungy chorus. As the Fox whined in anxious, joyous anticipation, a faint sweet odor of tobacco smoke wafted through the pine needles. A smoke ring preceded her figure and encircled the Boy in a gentle ephemeral snare. The Scavenger.

"Hey kid," she smirked, squatting down next to the Fox, stroking its forehead with her calloused, yellow fingers. Leaning into the scratch, the animal closed its eyes in sheer bliss. The Scavenger extended her other palm towards the Boy, inviting him to take a seat next to them under the pulsating gills of the great mushroom. The Boy had so many questions for both of these visitors, that his mind became a jumbled buzzing of nonsense. Instead, he decided to sit quietly and focus on the rustling breeze as it zig-zagged through the underbrush. Slowly pivoting his head, his gaze fell upon the intersection ahead of him. Breaking the tranquil silence that danced around them, he sighed deeply.

"I'm not sure which way to go," he finally admitted. "Is there a wrong way?" A soft chuckle arose from his left.

"What is wrong and what is right?" replied the Fox in typical riddled fashion. A puff of smoke floated over the Boy's right shoulder.

"And if it doesn't feel right, maybe it feels left?" shrugged the Scavenger.

"I wish the Schwark was here - it would sort this out for me," the frustrated Boy murmured.

"It's not here?" replied the Fox and Scavenger in unison searching over head, a thick blue haze building above their faces. The Boy followed their gazes - nothing but the dark canopy of Fir rustling in the twilight air.

"Have you two seen the Girl?" the Boy whispered, "I wish she was here, too - she'd do some experiment to test each choice." The Fox and Scavenger looked at each other and shrugged before turning back to the Boy, whose brow narrowed in confusion.

"You do," emphatically replied his friends. The Fox tepidly placed a paw upon the Scavenger's dirty jeans and was immediately invited up upon her lap. Curling into a ball, it draped its tail plume of wiry hair over its eyes and promptly fell asleep. Taking this as a hint, the Boy fixated upon the intersection. Was the Schwark really here? The Girl, too? Closing his eyes, he allowed himself to focus on his breathing as his mind slipped sideways.

~~~

He felt the warmth immediately. The forest floor was radiating the most inviting heat as the Amanita's mycelial core metabolized the detritus of the dead back into the vibrant beats of life. As he sat, the pulsating rhythm of root and fungi danced beneath him - a duet of violin and cello, accompanying and leading each other to and fro. Time passed - perhaps seconds, maybe years. Opening his eyes, the Boy was met by a silent snowfall that sprinkled down upon him from the massive pearl-white gills of the Amanita. Cupping his hands, a velvety soft pile of cotton-candy pink spores accumulated and tumbled between his fingers. Gently blowing the rest off from his palms, the Boy suddenly squinted as the spores reacted to his breath and fluoresced wildly in the midnight darkness rife. As he crawled out from the mushroom's sanctuary, the Boy convulsed with an
~~~

intense fit of sneezing. Moonbeams and starlight refracted off of his watery eyes as he refocused on his surroundings. The Scavenger and Fox had disappeared.

Suddenly, a stabbing pain of extreme hunger gripped every inch of his body. Woozily standing to his feet, he swayed in the twilight and frantically looked for anything edible. His eyes fell to the mushroom as his mouth swelled with saliva. Toxic - terribly toxic, he knew. But only in large quantities, his Mother had explained. Or was that Angel Wings? He couldn't recall, the hunger now hijacking his memories. No, he knew this: sometimes they would boil the Amanita - three times - to dilute the poison. Surely, a small nibble wouldn't hurt him… He broke a few inches off the polka-dotted cap and stared at the pink flesh inside, the invigorating earthen odor calling to the empty pit of his stomach. Raising the fungal fruit to his lips, he took a bite, chewed and swallowed. Uncooked, it was unpleasant and bitter - but his hunger was insatiable. Another piece, surely, not that much. He broke off another piece from the monstrous cap and crammed the entire portion into his greedy mouth. As he was about to reach for a third, an unpleasant heat prickled at his toes, rose up through his legs, crept into his pelvis and torso, and dove deep inside his brain. Nausea crippled him in half as he heaved and wretched, the pain coming in waves of excruciating aches and stabs.

"What have I done?" he repeated over and over into his tormented mind. "What have I done?" Receding just as quickly as it had approached, the sickness seemed to sublimate off of his skin and into the night sky, leaving the Boy with the strange sensation that he was floating. Looking back towards the fork in the trail, the Fox's path began to suddenly wriggle and warble, reminding the Boy of how the heating vents at school made the windows seem like a mirage. Rubbing his eyes, he looked to the Scavenger's rightward trail, which inexplicably seemed to stretch and shrink in no particular rhythm, almost as if it were alive and breathing. Neither path seemed particularly appropriate, the Boy decided.

As he contemplated his options, a soft purple-green glow began to pulse from the partially eaten Amanita, illuminating the trunk of the Fir tree behind it. The looming giant wore a thick coat of moss like a rain soaked sweater - except for a peculiar thin spiral, completely vacant of the hyper-green plant. It was… another trail... leading upwards? Approaching the dark trunk, the Boy felt the heat of the golden light that formed the tortuous path to the top of the conifer, dodging and weaving around massive branches. Hand cautiously extended, he touched the narrow striations of bark as his periphery hazed and warped. The entire forest had suddenly tilted ninety degrees, knocking him over onto his back. A flurry of silver butterflies, no larger than a thumbnail, flittered past him, as he planted his feet to stand - on the tree. Disoriented, the Boy rose to a careful wobbly stance and took a step. He was now walking *up* the tree, or, rather, *across* the tree, from his point of view. Above and below, trunks protruded from the massive wall of earth behind him, arranged like thousands of pins in a pin cushion. Turning towards the opposite wall of starlit sky, the great Fir's pointed tip at the horizon, he tiptoed along the rounded trunk, suppressing a newly realized vertigo.

Slowly, carefully, he advanced through the vertical stalagmites of needled branches. In perfect synchronicity, the trunk of the tree rose and sank with every one of his own breaths. The moss lining the path enveloped the Boy in golden light that dimmed and brightened with his every heartbeat. He had always loved the towering Douglas Firs and coastal redwoods and giant sequoias of his home, but never had he felt so intimately connected to a tree in all of his life. Nearing the end of the golden tree-path, the Boy froze as a bitterly cold wind howled across his neck. A dark figure flapped and whooshed inches over his head and nestled on an outstretched vein of fireless smoke that hovered on the final rubbery branch of the tree.

"Ca-Caw!" clacked the crow, all but invisible against the ink-black backdrop of the sky.

"Hey, dude!" called the Ghost, slowly materializing from the smoke. He scratched the bird on the forehead gently, as it cooed and croaked in return. The Runt.

"Um, hello again," replied the Boy. "Is this the, uh, right path, to… wherever I'm going?" he inquired. A curious silver-lined butterfly perched on his shoulder.

"'*Where*' you are going?" replied the Ghost, slightly amused, "I'm not sure if there ever was a '*where.*' I mean, you are just *going*, that much is for sure," he finished, releasing the Runt back into the night. The Boy thought about that for a moment. Going - he was going; to where, he did not know, and perhaps, it did not matter. Maybe it was the going that was the most important. He felt a funny sort of peacefulness settle into his soul with that idea, and he sat next to the Ghost in silence, looking out over a setting moon and rising Milky Way. In the distance - far, far below him, actually - a great canyon revealed the dim reflection of a crookedly traveling river. A small pier poked out into one of the eddies and a wooden boat bobbed around gently in the swirling waters.

"I'd like to keep going, I think," said the Boy to the Ghost, to the wilderness, to himself. The Ghost giggled as he extended his translucent arm for the returning Runt. As it landed, the Boy noticed it carried a large dark nut in its beak. Instinctively, the Ghost began to stroke the bird's silken feathers, sending it into pleasured convulsions of clicks and clacks as it threw its head back and puffed out its chest. Once it was satisfied, the bird hopped over to the Boy's lap and scrutinized his face as only a crow could do. Peering into its infinitely black beady eyes, the Boy watched as his reflection slowly morphed into that of the Girl. His mouth gaped open. Her tiny figure smiled in response. The Runt gingerly placed the nut into the Boy's upturned palm and dove off into the fir-lined abyss. He examined the gift.

The weight of the dark sphere was immense, its outer shell the consistency of a petrified brain. Suddenly, it began to vibrate rapidly, a high-pitched ringing pierced the Boy's head. Cracking along its equator, a burst of metallic light beams shot out in various directions, impossible to look at directly. With a final novel "pop," the nut fell into two symmetrical halves as thousands of miniature silver butterflies poured from its confines and enshrouded the Boy. Tiny wings beating and tickling against his skin in chaos, the insects awkwardly swarmed and stumbled all around him. Transfixed by the butterflies' mesmerizing silver aura, the Boy was reminded of his best friend's funny hair-clips, and he let out a joyous laugh without abandon.

"They will take you, if you trust them," suggested the Ghost, slowly sublimating back into a stagnant blue smoke. The Boy watched as the amorphous cloud drifted out over the forest, only to vanish entirely amongst the needles and leaves. Standing at the edge of the horizontal Fir, the Boy squinted down far into the distance at the little dinghy and its dock. Maybe miles away, he thought. No matter - he had decided. Extending his arms out to his sides, he felt the gentle pressure of a thousand small arms and legs and bodies amplify in concerted effort. A thrumming of wings reverberated more intensely now, as he suddenly felt his body leave the moss-riddled bark of the great Fir. Slowly, the Boy and a thousand silver butterflies descended across the forest canopy, ducked into a slot canyon, and glided down to the small pier. The Boy imagined how the spectacle most have looked to the passing squirrels - like a slow-motion meteorite streaking through the sky - like a great bottle-rocket with a thousand sparklers attached to it in grand finale fashion - like the world's largest firefly descending to find its mate. He touched down on the wooden pier without a sound. The silvery glow rapidly faded as the butterflies dispersed into the canyon brush and fell quiet. As he cautiously tested the strength of the creaky and weathered wooden floorboards of the pier, a voice calmly greeted him from the dinghy. A shadowed figure sat hunched at the bow.

"Fancy seein' you here, kid - hop on in, let's get 'er goin," said the gruff, familiar voice that wore a scraggly beard and soggy sweater. The Boy didn't need to see the face to know its owner.

"Evening, Cap," he replied, stepping into the shallow dinghy. He was going.

The Last Day

Four impossibly long and torturously boring days plagued the Boy as he sat in Room 105 and marched in step with his peers. For the first time, he completed every homework assignment, even scribbling out the proofs in perfect penmanship. While the algebraic expressions were certainly more complicated than long division, his intuition would provide the answer near instantaneously - why prove what he intrinsically knew to be right? He deeply despised the wasted paper required for such exercises, so he would often cram every problem onto a single sheet of paper, much to the consternation of his farsighted Teacher. Playing along with the institution's game, its incarceration of his creativity and individualism, the Boy understood he would need to pay this price to avoid any disruptions to the Plan he and the Girl had settled on for that weekend. Everything seemed balanced on a razor-sharp knife edge: his Father's job, his Mother's love, the Girl's experiment, the Principal's promise - Forest School.

On the final evening before the Plan, the two friends sat on the bleachers at after school and reviewed their strategy. He would hitch a ride with his Father to the dock. She would take the city bus and meet him there. Together, they would ride to this Mission and investigate the whereabouts of the Schwark.

"Last bus back to the dock from the Mission departs at four o'clock," the Girl had researched, "so we'll have at least six hours to search." She was enthusiastic and excited. The Boy was nervous - not about concealing the Plan from his Mother, who already had a weary but steady eye upon him these days, but of riding the bus. He was flummoxed how the Girl could be so comfortable and confident in riding around in such a massively confusing concrete jungle.

"I wonder how those cats are doing at the port. Haven't seen the Captain anywhere. Can we check on them tomorrow?" begged the Girl, "after the Mission?"

"If there's time - sure," he cautiously replied, feeling the heat of his Mother's omnipresent gaze. If they missed the bus back to the port, if they lost track of time searching for cats, if his Father could not find him after work… Better not to think about these things, he decided. Time to change the subject. "Have you ever eaten an amanita before?" Her face contorted through several strange expressions as she tried out the word.

"Am-a-need-ya? What the heck's that?" she asked.

"Just a spotted mushroom," the Boy clarified, "I thought they were toxic. But now I'm not so sure. I'll show them to you one day." The Boy missed the forest in that moment, flashing back to mornings of foraging with his Mother.

"Why did the mushroom get invited to all the parties?" the Girl interjected, her cheeks battling back a creeping, maniacal grin. The Boy shrugged. "Because he was a fun-guy! Get it?" she giggled, as a stray basketball rolled up to their feet.

"Want to play a game of… 'Fungi?'" suggested the Boy. It was her turn to return the blank face. This would take some explaining, he realized. "Its like 'Horse,' which is like 'Giraffe,' but its 'Fungi.'" he started. "Never mind, I'll teach you," he said, giving a soft tug to her sweatshirt, leading the way to an empty half court. For the rest of the afternoon, the two friends made the worst basketball shots ever attempted while screaming out the letters 'F-U-N-G-I,' over and over and over. With every terribly wayward shot, they would collapse onto the waxy gym floorboards in fits of laughter. It was the most fun the two had ever had while staying inside the actual school.

~~~

The final bell rang. Students donned their raincoats and zipped up their backpacks. The Boy and Girl left together towards the semi-circle pick-up lot. Between the bitter early winter raindrops and rays of fluorescent street lamp light, the two friends waved good-bye, as the Boy opened the door to the rusted station wagon.

"You're all chipper," started his smiling Mother, "Good day today? Or happy for the weekend? Or both?" The Boy considered this.

"Both," he replied, setting his backpack crammed with math and literature books on the back seat. His Mother gave an approving nod, squeezed his shoulder, and pushed the old car's transmission into drive. Arriving home that evening, they found his Father sitting proudly at the dining room table. He had prepared an old favorite - forest mushroom soup. Still unable to speak, he had mastered the art of nonverbal communication and facial expressions, raising eyebrows and wiggling ears in such a way to ask,

"Well, what do you think?" or "Did you have a good day today?" The Boy hugged him mightily as an answer to both. Looking up at his Father's beaming face, the Boy smiled.
~~~

"Can I go to the dock with you tomorrow?" he asked, trying his hardest to sound nonchalant. His parents looked at each other suspiciously, but shrugged simultaneously.

"That's fine with me," said his Mother " I've got an interview for a new job, so I'll be gone most of the time. Behave yourself," she finished with a wink. The Boy's mouth gaped open.

"What kind of job?" he exclaimed.

"Don't worry. It's a good one - not bartending or waitressing - something more... *my* style. I don't want to jinx it just yet though, so I'll only talk about it more if I get the gig." Before the Boy could follow up with more questions, she skipped into the bedroom to change out of her grease-laden apron. When she returned, the Boy caught his Father sharing a knowing smirk with her, before masking it away with a mouthful of rehydrated porcini.

"Try your soup before it cools," his Mother said lovingly, her hand scratching to back the Boy's neck. Something was up - he could sense it. He decided he would find out eventually - there was enough on his mind as it were.

The River

Creaking and sighing, the bones of the ancient drift boat alternated between protesting and resting as the invisible hand of the eddy fence held its wayward passengers in check at the banks of the wild river. Whitecaps danced in single file through the black tongue of the moonlit current just off the starboard side. His eyes reflected the subtle purple and pink glare of the rising Milky Way overhead, instilling grimaces of prior nightmares and grins of future adventures upon his bearded face. Standing at the bow of the boat, the Captain smirked at the Boy and pointed to the pair of worn and weathered oars stacked at his feet. Nodding to the locks on either side of the vessel, the Captain reached down and helped the Boy hoist the heavy wooden blades into their sturdy steel sockets with a satisfying 'ka-thunk.'

"All yours, son," murmured the Captain.

"I've never paddled a drift, Cap - let alone at night. And this is white water!" yelled the Boy over the rushing rapids. Running a hand down the massive oar grips in a state of confused anxiety and awe, he could feel his fear of the unknown building and tumbling and transforming itself into a small flame of intense excitement.

"You know what you *know*," started the Captain, planting himself firmly into the seat at the bow, "and you know what you *don't*!" he continued, plunging his feet under a pair of partially concealed straps on the deck of the boat. "The unknown? You'll know how to know - eventually!" he finished, suddenly grabbing the handles of the oars from the Boy. Lurching forward and encircling the Boy between his two sea-strong shoulders, the Captain bellowed a mighty groan as he single-handedly reverse-paddled the wooden drift boat straight through the seemingly impenetrable eddy fence and off into a swiftly moving black blood that rocked and reeled and hissed and sputtered.

"Grab the oars!" The Captain howled, releasing the oars as he jumped to the stern. Laughing hysterically, the man almost fell overboard as the boat rode upon a series of chaotic wave-trains and errant boils. Frantically clutching for the oversized wooden shafts as they bobbed and jolted in their locks, the Boy finally latched on and brought the blades out of the water. He quickly discovered that the only way he could maneuver with enough room to range his short, stubby arms was by actually standing in the center of the clumsy vessel.

"Keep 'er pointed forward, son," snorted the Captain, grinning ear-to-ear. Waxy-leaved manzanita and rhododendron lined the banks of the crooked river and reflected the soft purple and orange glow of the constellations as they reflected across the eddies and slippery rocks strewn throughout the water. As his retinas adjusted to the low-light contrast, the Boy began to read the river for what was not there - an absence of ripples signaling shallow water, a pinecone off the port side whizzing past in the opposite direction serving as a hint of a powerful recirculating eddy, and a sudden dark drop in the horizon line... the encroaching growl of nothingness... a rapid! Spittle frothed and foamed up from the unknown depths beyond the invisible drop-line as the dory screamed forward, overtaken by the accelerating current. The bald heads of two gigantic granite boulders began to emerge, flanking the dark purple and green tongue of the river on either side - two trolls guarding their pass. The Boy would have to be precise, for the gap was just slightly larger than the wooden row boat.

"Thread the needle, kid - otherwise we're in the drink!" the Captain commanded with a hiccup - he was clearly enjoying this. With as big of strokes as he could manage, the Boy steered the careening dory straight down the tongue and tucked the oars into the sides. Holding his breath as the boat accepted its final trajectory, he gripped the rails and prepared for the worst. Slipping past the boulders in uneventful silence, the Boy exhaled and let out a maniacal scream.

"Whooo-ooop!" he exclaimed.

"Whooo-ooop!" the Captain hollered back. They were two rogue hyenas riding the white water of a nameless river down a nameless canyon on a nameless night. Gazing into the Milky Way above, their eyes were suddenly drawn towards a massive meteor as it slowly streaked over the canyon. From left to right, its lingering orange fireball left tracers and afterglow in the Boy's vision, its faint low rumble echoing down from the stratosphere seconds later. The light from the meteor was just enough of a flare for the Boy to gain a temporary view of the river downstream. He swallowed hard as the light dimmed back to baseline. The quarter-mile of rock-strewn tumultuous tumbling white water that lie ahead also faded into darkness. As the dory began to pick up speed, the roar began to vibrate in their ears, in their minds, in their bones. The steady current became rough, bouncing the boat between powerful and unforgiving eddy walls as the Boy attempted to keep the bow pointed forward. Ahead, at the top of the rapid, he could see that a house-sized rock split the current into two forks. The river-left option seemed the best at first, until a huge downed fir tree emerged into the starlight - a massive strainer - caught up directly in the main current. The tree would crush the boat and likely drown the two riders.

"Guess the meteor knew the way, too," murmured the Captain, eyeing the same dilemma. As he attempted to push the oars forwards to turn to dory, the Boy found that the building momentum was too much for his kid-strength, and the boat started to drift towards the left.

"Turn around!" yelled the Captain. "Pull, kid! Pull! Don't push!" he exclaimed. Spinning himself around, the Boy grasped the oar handles and reversed motion - plunging the oars down in front of his chest, extending his elbows, dipping the blades back into the chilly waters and pulling backwards with all his might - his legs exploding from underneath as he fought the waves. To his surprise, the dory began to turn - the wrong way.

"Look over yer' shoulder! You gotta see where yer goin' kid!" the Captain blasted, startled with a mixture of amusement and disbelief. The Boy attempted to pull the starboard oar harder to turn the dory, but he was no match for the incredible force of the river - the tongue had split, and they were headed towards the strainer.

"I can't do it! Cap! We're headed for the tree!" the Boy screamed, as the boat rose and sank between a train of five-foot waves. Off the port side of the dory, a bright purple hazy glow emerged from behind an eddy fence. Moving undeterred through the barrier of back-current and whirlpool, the purple glow grew brighter and began to pulse gently as it formed a half-crescent around the side of the wooden death-trap. Peering over the rails, the Boy caught a glimpse of a furry clawed flipper pressed up against the side of the wood paneling. Another flipper joined this one, and another - all down the side of the boat. A rounded whiskered face emerged between a set of flippers - small black beady eyes reflecting the starlit white caps back up to the Boy. Winking at the Boy, the Otter sunk its head beneath the river as the purple pulsing light grew blindingly bright. The boat began to lurch, steadily ferrying across the current. Approaching rapidly, the monstrous strainer was but a few seconds from devouring its waterborne meal. A massive lurch sent the Boy and Captain sprawling on top of each other - the otters had suddenly pushed the vessel up and over a rock garden separating the two tongues of the river. As the dory pin-balled over the top of several shallow boulders, a sudden eerie calmness beset the boat. They were river-right. Impossible. Peering over the side of the saved dory, the Boy watched as the half-moon of glowing furry flippers released their grasp and dispersed back into the darkening waters like the last embers of a bonfire. Looking up at the scraggly beard and rosy cheeks of the Captain, the Boy's eyes were met by a simple shrug and knowing smirk.

"Clever critters, they are, eh?" was all the man could say. As they continued down the river, its waters mellowing, the rocks and boulders and eddies becoming more sparse, the Boy's proficiency at the oars increased. On a particularly long, calm stretch, he brought the blades into the boat and sat down for the first time in a long while, sighing deeply. The Captain had fallen asleep and was snoozing and snoring, an arm loosely draped over his eyes, the other dragging it's fingertips along in the still waters off the port side. Fluttering down from the basalt cliffs overhead, a large crow came swooping down, landing on the Captain's right shoulder. Barely aware of his role as the bird's new perch, he let out a huff and a gurgle and remained deeply consigned to slumber. The crow cooed and purred softly, cocking an eye at the Boy. The Captain really did look like a river pirate, he decided.

Just then, the crow turned its attention to a sudden minuscule movement creeping out and over the Captain's sweater - a sugar ant. Meandering its way up the soggy fibers, the insect was totally unaware of the crow's presence until it was too late - with one lighting-quick peck, the ant vanished, as the bird squawked and ruffled in delight with itself. After several moments, the crow became increasingly shifty and squirmy, shuffling side-to-side over the Captain's shoulder, until two soft beams of white light emanated from its nostrils. Shaking its head violently, the crow cawed, and the Boy saw that the light was indeed coming from down the birds gullet. A sudden heave and chortle as the crow choked, as it finally belched up a beautiful fluttering silver butterfly. Hovering briefly to admire its new world, the butterfly landed gently on the Captain's nose as both Boy and crow looked on in befuddled amazement.

"Ahh-choo!" Sneezing so hard that the dory rocked from side to side, the Captain exploded from his sleep and gazed perplexingly at the soft glowing white insect fluttering away over a nearby eddy, disappearing behind a passing cottonwood. Rising higher and higher over the boat, the crow cawed and clacked at the Captain and the Boy as it rode an invisible thermal pocket and soared out over the river, upstream and away from the slowly awakening sun. Looking at the Captain, the Boy was about to ask, 'what next?' - but was interrupted by a fine spray of mist and a surge of current that sent him reeling back into an oarlock. The two sailors scanned down river as the dory rounded a bend, their eyes greeted by an impossible site. A green-blue river, rushing and roiling, seemingly flowed directly into the red glowing orb of fresh grapefruit sun - and disappeared. An early morning pink sky grasped the fine tendrils of white water mist as it vaporized on contact with the fire in the sky. A rising sense of anxiety told the Boy that this was merely an illusion, for even the trees seemed to drop away from their banks... everything, it seemed, dropped and fell away, like a...

"Waterfall!" howled the Captain, holding onto the bow as the dory rocketed down the narrowing river, the mist and froth drenching the two riders. The Boy dropped the oars into the straining river and fought back the surge of adrenaline pumping through his arteries and veins. As they neared the precipice, he could see that the drop was taller than his apartment building - perhaps five or six stories. Frantically, he searched the sides of the hopeless drift boat, wishing and hoping for the faint glow of purple salvation to once again rise from the depths and miraculously guide the wayward souls back to the safety of the forested banks. Tears in his eyes, the Boy looked at the Captain - a surreal foam-crusted grin glared back.

"Just gotta roll with it!" he thundered over the growling of the gaining waterfall. "Live or die, not for you to decide right now, son!" he bellowed, turning to face the the last few hundred feet of river, his body outlined by the orange and yellow glare of the morning sun. "Only thing you can do - decide how much hootin' and hollerin' you're gonna do when we take the plunge! You'll never be more alive, kid!" he finished, raising his arms to the sky. As shock, rage, and resentment wheeled and washed up around his mind, nearly drowning him in a sea of fear and despair, the Boy took a deep breath and realized that the Captain was right - even in the most dire of circumstances, it truly was his choice to let the darkness in. He would not, he decided, let that happen again. Rising from his seat, he joined the Captain and thrust two fists high above his head. As the bow of the dory cleared the event horizon of the monstrous waterfall, its two passengers screamed into oblivion, their voices thick with the ecstasy of mayhem and certain death.

"Whoop-woop-woop!" cackled the Captain, still clutching the rails of the wooden dory as it sailed downwards, lost in a vertical wall of mist and torrential power.

"Cow-ahhh-bungaa!" exclaimed the Boy, his mouth open, drinking in the blissful energy that came with escaping time. He was present, and the world was beautiful. Closing his eyes, he allowed his feet to leave the wooden planks of the boat as he wrapped himself in the heat of the morning's sun, the frigidness of the river's glacial water, the dankness of the cliffside's sea of mosses, the calmness in the moment's chaos. He could have stayed there forever, he thought.

~~~

Opening his eyes, the Boy began to cough violently, heaving great spews of icy water. The sun was at its apex in the cloudless noon-sky, welcoming him back to life - or whatever, wherever, this might be. As he placed his hands onto what he was sure was a riverside beach, his fingers instead sank into a great fur comforter that gently expanded and shrank in small undulations under his back and his legs. He was floating again. A hazy purple aura refracted from the eddy in which he drifted, as a pair of wiry whiskers rose next to his furry floating raft. An Otter.

"I've been here before" chirped the Otter, smiling at the Boy. "A long time ago. After a great storm. I drifted here. Had to find my way out - to my family. I know the way in which you seek," it finished. The Boy stared at the Otter quizzically. He realized he was indeed riding upon the bellies of twenty-some-odd otters, a stray flipper poking up here and there to scratch an itch.

"What do I seek?" replied the Boy. The Otter spat a thin jet of water at the Boy's face and laughed, ducking beneath the mellow waters, quickly resurfacing near the opposite side of the raft, near an eddy fence.

"Your home," it answered, winking at the Boy before slapping the water with its tail flippers. Suddenly, the living raft on which he rode began to strum and roll in unison, as the mass of fur and Boy easily floated into the gentle current.

"Otter! Hey! Have you seen the Captain?" the Boy exclaimed, searching both shorelines for the scraggly bearded man. The Otter poked its whiskered face out from the center of the living raft, its black eyes locked onto the Boy's.

"We all have our paths," said the Otter, before rolling over and dipping beneath a small wave.

~~~

The Boy floated silently along for several hours. The banks grew further and further apart, and the sun began to twinkle a burnt orange and peaceful pink - sunset approached. He contemplated his friend, the

Captain. Was he really gone? It didn't feel like it, so he must not be, the Boy decided. He reflected on his friend, the Schwark, and decided the same. His thoughts dove deeper. Did something need to be alive to be present? As he mulled this over in his mind, the raft of otters beneath him began to quietly disperse, releasing the Boy into a few inches of warm bubbling water tucked into a small rocky cove - a hot spring. He crawled up the thin pebbly beach and turned towards his cadre of otters.

Twenty whiskered faces bobbed up and down in the gentle eddy - collectively, they smiled at the Boy. As he waved and nodded his gratitude to his furred rescue team, they twitched their whiskered noses back in silence, and, one-by-one, rolled and sank back into the current, their purple aura filling the emerald green waters with a vibrant palpable energy. Salted breeze peppered his nose, beckoning him to turn and face the what he knew lay downstream - the great ocean. Just a bit further lived the estuary, and beyond that, the open waters he had always known and deeply loved. Closing his eyes, he inhaled the world and sighed. He would walk the banks to the cove on his own now.

As he approached the estuary, a soft bristling sensation nuzzled against his damp skin and sent goose-bumps up his arms. Jumping backwards in fright, he stumbled and splashed back into the spring. Looking up at the bank of the briny mollusk covered shoreline, a pair of yellow eyes stared down at him, black vertical slits interrogating his soul.

"Meow?" the feline called to him, cocking its head to one side, tail held high and swishing to and fro. Suddenly turning to sit on its haunches, the animal began to lick its paws and stare out at the sea, giving the impression of complete ambivalence and disinterest in the Boy. Rising back up to stand in the shallow water, he glared at the back of the feline.

"Hey! Cat! Where did you come from?" the Boy yelled, hands on hips, saltwater dripping from his brow, an incredulous look in his eye.

In silent response, the cat looked over its shoulder back at the Boy and darted behind a rocky outcropping, out of sight. Clamoring up onto the sharp lava rock, the Boy found the sneaking creature near a tide pool, pawing at a large purple starfish, just out of reach. Suddenly, a blur out of the periphery of his vision came streaking over the shallow rocks - another cat, joining the first in a half-hearted attempt to claw out the spiny starfish. The nearby sea anemone community, with their translucent nuclear green tentacles, contracted and expanded with each swiping paw, unsure as to what sort of strange lazy threat the cats posed. As the seconds ticked by, cats began to appear from every direction - tabby and calico and speckled and Maine coon and dwarf. After the final cat had taken up its ranks around the tide pool, the first cat, completely black and supremely confident in its strut, approached the Boy again, scent-marking the Boy's legs with its forehead

"Grandma?" called the Boy, suddenly recognizing the animal.

'Follow me' said the cat's perfumed musk, curling into the Boy's olfactory senses, latching onto his subconscious, and pulling him along by the soggy shirt collar. Up over the tide pools and along the narrow cliff line, Grandma led him to the wide mouth of a large cave, the blood orange sunset beaming off the hexagonal angles of the glassy columnar basalt formations that flanked it's entrance. A soft flickering light undulated and danced deep in the throat of the cave, while a huddle of shadows gathered around its uvular warmth.

"Meow," whispered Grandma, prancing into the darkening maw of the rocks, making sure the Boy was following. Without warning, the cat sprinted to the four dark figures. The Boy could make out four pairs of raised palms, warming themselves to the glow of a small driftwood bonfire. Ten paces from the silent party, the Boy stopped, eyes wide, for he knew the cave dwellers well.

"Hello again, my friend," said the smoky voice of the Scavenger.

"Howdy, kid! You pry thought I was a goner, huh?" chuckled the Captain.

"Hi pal!" chimed the ice-eyed, yellow-beanie-wearing Astronaut.

"Hey Mr smarty-Pants!" smiled the Girl, her attention scored down the middle, torn between him and the stalking cat. The group of four shuffled around the flickering flames to make room for the Boy. As he approached, he looked to the walls of the cave, for the shadows of his four acquaintances seemed starkly different than their hosts. A great bear, standing tall, mouth open to the sky, seemed to two-step behind the Captain. A stealthy Coyote, slinked and crouched and leapt to the figure of the Scavenger. A huge eagle spread its wings, unfurled its razor talons, and clacked its knife-edge beak as the Astronaut stretched and yawned and smiled at the Boy. A mighty elephant ruffled its oversized ears and with its inquisitive, rubbery snout, probed the air over the top of the Girl. He decided not to look at his own shadow, for fear that it would be anything other than the Schwark.

"Warm yourself, but don't stay too long," started the Scavenger.

"Ya gotta get back out there, partner - journey's not over yet," the Captain elaborated.

"I'll come with, you won't be alone," promised the Astronaut.

"You'll need an adventure buddy - hope you don't mind me tagging along," finished the Girl. Too exhausted for questions, the Boy simply nodded, smiled, and stepped up to the heat, warming his skin and bones and heart and mind. How good it felt, he thought, to stand around a meager fire in a dreary cave on the edge of a desolate midnight beach with those who cared for him, and he for them. For the second time in that day, or year, or dream, or life, he decided that he could stay in that moment forever. He laughed gently, and was met with a chorus of similar giggles and smirks in reply. They sat in silence for hours around the flame, watching the embers settle and rest only to roar back to life in their final gasps of life, or death, or something in between.

"It's time," announced the Scavenger, looking to the Captain, his hand clasped with hers - similar calloused, heavy fingers interwoven.

"Off ya go! You know where to find me!" said the Captain with a wink. Where, exactly, would he find him, thought the Boy? The dock? The alley? On the road with the Scavenger? The Captain, sensing the Boy's confusion, placed a hand over his own burly chest and lightly tapped the rhythm of his heartbeat.

"See you there," smiled the Boy.

~~~

As they faced the still, open ocean, pelicans and other harriers whisked and dove amongst the glowing predawn air, whistling through the gentle rolling swells that were building just off shore. The Girl scurried about on hands and knees, examining potential shellfish breathing holes, humming quietly to herself. The Boy and Astronaut stood barefoot at the edge of the frothy ebbing waves, taking in the expansive unknowns on their own accords.

"Do we... go out there?" asked the Boy, hesitant excitement in his tone.

"Yes," replied the smaller boy, a piercing twinkle from his ice-gray eyes.

"How... do we get out?" the Boy inquired, for the dory had surely been pulverized, and there were no rafts or boats on the beach.

"However you want," the Astronaut answered, somewhat perplexed by the Boy's question. "You'll figure it out" he finished with a subtle smirk, slowly closing his eyelids tight, his forehead bowing to the
~~~

sea. The Boy followed suit and closed his own two eyes, opening up a third. How to get out - any way he wanted. Reflecting back on his life and dreams and thoughts and fantasies, he realized he did, indeed, know - he had simply been out of practice. Relaxing every fiber of his self, he allowed the forest green aura to explode outwards, a massive pulse of reverberating bass riding the shock wave in toe. Squinting into the sunrise, the Boy crossed his legs and waited for a response…

"Look," whispered the Astronaut, his index finger pointed to the horizon. A flash of dark against the sun's rays, followed by a soundless splash back into the sea. And then, another. And another. A pod of bottlenose. The Boy smiled as tears appeared in the corners of his eyes - he had been heard. An answer approached. Schwark or no Schwark, his reality and unreality was entirely at his control. Pulsing wildly under the still green twilight waters, the yellow strobing of the bottlenose dolphins reflected off the damp sand and ignited the beachfront in fantastic shades of orange and red. A rostrum protruded from the surface of the sea and opened slightly.

"Eee! Eee!" the Dolphin called.

"Eee! Eee!" replied the Girl, her voice cracking, her nose pointed up to the setting moon. She splashed into the tide, eee-eee-ing as she hopped and skipped over larger breaks to greet their guests.

"Good choice," replied the Astronaut, tugging at the Boy's arm. Together, the three waded into the sunrise sea to meet their porpoise entourage. Suddenly, the golden yellow aura rapidly expanded, forming a tight semicircle around the three bipedal figures. At the apex of the ring of dolphin, at precisely the position where the break became the deep, dark ocean beyond, a string of tiny bubbles gurgled and boiled. White-water surged and sheared as a monstrous black stone emerged like a great submarine, rising high above the waves and the three spectators. Reflecting the moon from one half, the sun from the other, the great stone revealed itself as a barnacle studded, seaweed-draped shell.

"A Leatherback!" blurted out the Girl. As if on cue, a massive reptilian head, spotted and speckled, rose gently in front of the three. On its forehead and upon its throat, it wore a smear of bright pink pigment that glowed softly as it lazily blinked through black-holed eyes. Wrinkling its stubby neck and chewing the breeze with beak held together in a slight overbite, the great Turtle examined and considered each of the figures that huddled before it.

"Its humongous!" said the Astronaut.

"Its beautiful!" whispered the Girl.

"It's… our way out, I think," pondered the Boy, raising a hand towards the rough skin of the Turtle's wizened face. Sandpapery and warm, it radiated a sense of safety and serenity that reminded the Boy of the otters. With a blast of cool air and sea-foam spritzing from its nostrils, the Leatherback lower its head and submerged itself slightly. A sudden nudging at their ankles caused the three preflight passengers to jump backwards, for a particularly impatient bottlenose was prodding them forward. With mild trepidation, the Boy stepped upon the Turtle's gigantic flipper, and carefully clamored up the side of its shell. Hoisting the others up one by one, the Boy sighed a sense of relief - he was going again.

"Now I know where they get the name!" said the Girl, using handholds of wrinkled reptile in her ascent. Atop the giant shell, the three found ample room in the nape of the beast's neck to sit comfortably, as the Turtle began a one-hundred-and-eighty degree turn. The Boy was brought back to memories of riding the Schwark through infinite coral reefs and towering kelp forests. Before he had time for his eyes to water, another passenger chimed in, keenly in tune with the sensation of déjà vu.

"Not as comfortable as that one spot behind the rainbow blowhole, but it'll do, eh?" the Astronaut suggested. The Boy looked back, eyes wide and dumb-founded, heart beating wildly with shock and joy, for here was another person who shared his reality beyond the real, who lived in that space between wakefulness and dreamscape. With a great surge forward from its immense flippers, the Turtle broke through the surf with ease, trailing a golden aura of weaving a jumping porpoises as its contrail. Looking back over his shoulder at the mouth of river, the Boy noticed two figures standing in the knee-high dune grass, arm-in-arm - the Captain and the Scavenger. They each raised a palm and silently waved after the three departing riders. Extending his hands into the air, the Boy yelled into the sea breeze.

"Goodbye!" he bellowed, knowing his voice would be drowned out in the waves.

"Good luck!" waved the Girl in solidarity. They looked over at the Astronaut - he hadn't budged. His focus was uniformly forward, away from the beach.

"You're not waving? Aren't you sad to be leaving them?" asked the Girl. The ice-gray eyes slowly pivoted towards her.

"Leaving? No one's leaving anyone, though…" he replied, confused by his passengers' dismay.

"I think I know what you mean,'" realized the Boy, feeling the energy of the ocean, of the Turtle, of his friends, both near and far. The peaceful power of such a revelation surged through his fingertips, into his chest, pierced his heart, entered his mind and enveloped his soul. He was beginning to know, he decided.

The Mission

Cloudless, perfect, uniform blue blossomed forth from between the city's apartment buildings and office sky-rises. Burning furiously and beautifully overhead, the sun beamed confident radiance into the Boy's soul as he closed his eyes to feel the heat enter his pores and fill his heart. The day had finally arrived - the Mission. Today, he would find the Schwark again - he was sure of it. Packing his damp raincoat into his overflowing backpack, he took a survey of the day's supplies: three almond butter and marionberry jam sandwiches, three apples, and a steel canister of water. He had prepared for the very real possibility that he may not return that evening. After all, he the Girl had casually warned him of the odds, and he wasn't one to argue with a scientist.

A gentle, calloused hand gripped his shoulder. Gazing down upon him was the stubbled face of his Father - that smirk ever-present. Had he seen the Boy's excessive cache of food? Did he suspect something? Walking to the station wagon over steamy evaporating rain puddles that reflected the sun into miniature rainbows that floated around their ankles, the Boy said nothing. His Father said nothing as well, of course. Something in the energy between them - that parent-child magnetosphere - tipped his Father's hand, for the Boy gradually became aware that his Father knew something was amiss. The fact that the man did not inquire or gesture about what was up communicated his silent approval, his trust - the Boy was free to adventure. A smile filling his groggy morning face, the Boy tossed his heavy pack in the backseat as he swung himself into the front - today was the day.

As the station wagon bumbled and spluttered through the weekend morning traffic, the Boy observed the scurrying about of hundreds of people and wondered who they were, where they might be going, if any of them were also on some sort of mission. He decided so, for, perhaps, maybe life was actually just one big mission to fulfill several smaller missions - some done in a day, some in a week, others in a year, or a lifetime. Looking at the expressions of men and women and children on the crosswalks that smiled back at him through the breath-frosted window, he thought he might actually know what sort of mission each was on. He hoped they would succeed - maybe not today, but certainly later. Sometimes he felt the urge to roll down the window and shout at the top of lungs, "Good luck! You can do it!" but he felt deep inside that they had already silently heard him - after all, it was a bluebird winter morning, and the sun filled the city with unparalleled energy that day - *the* Day.

Approaching the intersection of his school, the Boy caught site of the Shopkeep at the thrift store, sweeping out the entrance of the store. A murder of crows suddenly dove directly into the center of the road where a clutch of broken walnuts laid, forcing he Boy's Father to bring the clunky station wagon to a screeching halt. The crows didn't budge - instead, they had all turned their feathered heads in unison, seemingly staring directly at the Boy. Swallowing, he looked out the driver's side window and saw that the Shopkeep was smiling and waving maniacally, a golden tooth shimmering in delight. The Boy returned the wave hesitantly, just as the birds awkwardly hopped across to the sidewalk and encircled the Shopkeep. One of the crow's eyes seemed to cast an eerily similar golden reflection back at the Boy, as his Father accelerated through the intersection, past the school. A person in a leather jacket was leaning against the cracked brick in the Captain's alleyway, blowing perfect blue smoke rings. Hidden by the shadows of the school facade, the Boy couldn't make out their face. He didn't need to, he decided - only one person made smoke rings that perfect…

<div style="text-align:center">~~~</div>

Pulling into the gravel parking lot of the Port, the Boy and his Father sat motionless for several seconds. His Father had barely turned off the ignition when a slate black cat suddenly jumped up upon the hood of their car, peering at them both with unblinking quizzical curiosity and slow-motion tail swishes.

"Hey!" rang out from behind their parked car, footsteps shuffling between pickups and cargo vans. "She did that to me when I got here, too!" The Cat Lady says she's actually the queen of all the cats! She's the first to greet all newcomers" exclaimed the Girl, attempting to lure the feline off the station wagon and into her frantically beckoning arms. Grandma did so obligingly, purring and nuzzling the Girl's maroon sweatshirt enthusiastically. The Boy closed the car door and reached out a tentative finger towards the cat's forehead, offering a gentle and subdued scratch - he was never really sure of cats. Grandma suddenly leapt onto his shoulder and began rubbing its face against his green flannel.

"Ha! She approves, I guess" came the gruff voice of the Cat Lady from behind the Girl. She held a large tabby under her left arm. The Boy's

Father, his welding gear in hand, just stood and shook his head in disbelief, mouthing to the Boy,

"You like cats, now, huh?" The Boy shrugged and smiled. The Girl cleared her throat, drawing their attention.

"The Captain says they haven't seen any rats in two days now! He thinks they went into hiding - they stopped eating the welder's lunches and pooping on the freshly welded rafters. And everyone loves the cats!" she proclaimed, looking back at the Cat Lady in admiration. A practical project, thought the Boy - this was certainly a bigger leap forward from ants and socks and crows and nuts.

"That one even offered to put me up in a trailer around back here - 'pest management' he says," started the Cat Lady, pointing at a shadowed figure sitting on an I-beam high above. A scruffy beard protruded from under the helmet as the welder laid a molten bead of steel, throwing a waterfall of bright yellow sparks down upon the lower rafters. "He even convinced the superintendent to give me a small stipend. Things are good here. I'd stay if I could," she finished, with a satisfied smile.

"You... you aren't going to stay here?" asked the Boy, a perplexed eyebrow raising high. The Cat Lady kept her gaze on Grandma as she responded. "Nah. I live with my son up the hill a ways. He's starting school soon, and this place would be too far for him to commute. Wouldn't be right. I'm happy up there anyway." she said, biting her lip. Joining her gaze, the Boy stared at Grandma and contemplated the Cat Lady's predicament. His mind was beginning to spin up solutions when it was abruptly interrupted by a deep baritone laughter coming from high above.

"Hey buddies!" bellowed the barrel-chested voice. The Captain, sitting precariously across the horizontal beam of freshly welded metal, waved down at the group. "We're goin' to high places today, my friends! Strap on your harness and get on up here!" he proclaimed to the Boy's Father. A calico cat stalked and strutted above him, in search of its invisible prey.

"Well, maybe we should, um... get started... on our new project," whispered the Girl to the Boy, picking up his backpack from the ground with a huff.

"Whatcha got in there, kid? A ton of bricks?" queried the Cat Lady. He did his best to look casual, as the beads of sweat formed rapidly across his forehead. Looking instinctively at his Father, his gaze met with the smirk. Taking a knee next to the Boy, his Father cupped hands around his son's ear and breathed almost imperceptibly.

"Be. Care. Full." The Boy felt his heart jump several beats
forward. His Father's first words to him in months - since the Fire. And
they were words of knowing - of permission - of love. Hugging his Father
as tightly as he could manage, the Boy realized he was ready - today was
the Day.

~~~

Pretending to be absorbed in all things cat, the Boy and Girl
secretly watched the Captain gather the welders together and lead them
into the labyrinthian abyss of the dock. With his Father's last eye upon
them fading into the darkness, the Boy turned to the Girl - he could feel the
anticipation building.

"We have five minutes before the next bus - c'mon!" she
exclaimed, launching from her seat, startling Grandma, who dashed off
into the newly constructed steel ruins of the dock. The Boy barely had time
to close his backpack before she began tugging on his flannel sleeve.
Quickly and clumsily, the two made their way through the parking lot,
hiding behind truck beds to dodge any potential witness to their escape.

"Cawww!" came the terrifying cackle of a nearby crow.

"Quiet, Bird! They'll see us!" hissed the Boy. A dark orb whisked
through the air, and the crow was upon it immediately. A nut.

"They've been on to me for awhile" the Girl murmured. The bird
looked back, a golden shimmer in its eye reflecting its acceptance of the
tithe. A familiar bird - a bit plumper than the Boy remembered. Before he
could mention it to the Girl, the Runt grasped the nut in its beak and
flapped silently towards the river. A deep huff of hydraulic brakes pulled
the two back into the moment - the bus was lumbering down the gravel
driveway to their stop. Sprinting without abandon, the Boy and Girl made
it through its doors without a moment to spare.

The white-haired amiable driver offered a confused smile at the two
stragglers as he gently tapped the ticket scanner. The Boy was at a
complete loss - he had no money to speak of. The Mission was going to be
a failure, unless the driver would accept an apple - or a sandwich - or a nut.
Before he could make the ludicrous proposition, the Girl had already
yanked out her bus pass from her pack, scanning it twice. The driver
nodded and set the bus back into drive, nearly knocking the Boy into the
Girl, who nearly fell onto the driver.
~~~

"Haha! Never ridden a bus, huh? No worries, just hold onto the rails!" the Girl instructed, helping the Boy back to his feet. Stumbling to the middle of the bus, the two sat next to each other and took in their fellow passengers: a man speaking loudly on his cellphone, sometimes angrily, about numbers, margins, quotas. He was sweating and appeared very uncomfortable, the Boy thought. Nearby, an elderly woman knitted a scarf expertly, her eyes nearly closed as she rocked and danced to the chaotic rhythm of the city bus.

"Thanks," said the Boy curtly. After all, the Girl had saved him from failure - and embarrassment.

"Oh no problem! My parents gave me the pass - I told them about you, and I know they wouldn't mind that I shared it today with my friend." she replied. She had told someone about him? His friend. He decided when the Mission was over, he would tell his parents about his friend, too.

"Thanks," he said again, "for everything."

~~~

After twenty-some-odd stops, the Girl abruptly stood and pulled the yellow cord that dangled above their heads. A 'ding' rang out throughout the bus, and she summoned him to the backdoor. A quick stop and a garbled voice over the intercom called out a random street name as the double doors hissing open. Stepping out into the early afternoon breeze, the Boy swore he could smell the salted ocean mist and sweet sap of the forest. They were standing on a crooked sidewalk atop a great hill in the middle of the city, the port far below them now, the river winding beneath several bridges and disappearing beyond the horizon. A heavy bell tolled from the squat three-story adobe-style stucco building that stood directly in front of them.

"The Mission," she pointed, "we're here."

~~~

A hazy ribbon of blue-tinged patchouli and sage smoke crept from the half-opened windows that flanked the heavy cedar front door. The Boy, sensing the odor, felt his feet leave the earth for a second as his mind was transported back to his last winter in the woods: his Mother steeping herbal tea, his Father smoking a cigar.

"Achoo!" the girl let out a tremendous sneeze, ripping the Boy from his distant memories, and covering his face in tiny droplets of apple-scented spittle. "Sorry!" the Girl exclaimed, frantically scrubbing the Boy's face with her mitten. They both laughed through their disgusted grimaces as a voice called from behind the cedar door.

"Gesundheit! Salud! Bless you! Bleshoo!" came the echoing tenor voice as the opening to the Mission creaked open. A very tall, dark-skinned, thin man donning a three piece pinstripe suit gave the two a deep and hilariously overly-dramatic bow, the thick dreadlocks atop his head tumbling to the ground like some great magical mop.

"Greetings my friends!" he beamed through pearl-white teeth. His suit was a kaleidoscope of every possible shade and hue of sunrise and sunset, purples adjacent to greens lined up beside whites across from reds and blues in haphazard arrangement and size and width. The suit's dizzying chaos reminded the Boy of the art he had made alongside the Art Therapist at the Hospital - he decided that he trusted this Mission man.

"I sense you've come for some answers, perhaps?" the rainbow-suited gentleman continued through the silence, for the Boy and Girl were speechless in their admiration of his attire. The Boy managed a nod. "Excellent! Outstanding! Fantastic!" the Mission man clapped his hands together and did a small three-step jig. "Well, let me introduce myself! I'm the Chaplain!" he announced, taking a knee, palms extended outward in grandiose fashion. "You can call me whatever you'd like though! To some, I'm 'Father,' to others, 'Mister' for little ones I am 'Pappy.' I've gone by 'Friend,' 'Buddy,' and 'Dude.' Heck, you could call me 'Potato' and I'd love you. Come in! Come in!" the Chaplain beckoned. Dumbstruck and profoundly curious, the two small visitors tip-toed into the Mission behind their waltzing host, entranced by the sights, smells, and energy of the mystical place. The main hallway quickly opened up into a massive rotunda, its ceiling made of glass, its perfect white walls and brightly stained wooden rafters covered in a contiguously creeping dark green philodendron that made the air both crisp and clean feeling. In the center of the round room stood what the Boy could only assume was a pulpit for lecturing or speaking. He frowned.

He had been in a church - exactly once - with his grandmother. He remembered the stifling humidity, a hundred some-odd people sitting on benches in silence - no smiling. There was an old balding man in baggy robes with a purple scarf that reached to the floor who drawled on and on in a low moaning voice about terrible things: temptation, testing, sinning and confessing; about death, death, death, and then eternal life - but only if if one 'believed;' and then, about hypocritical tolerance and forgiveness for those who did not 'believe.' He remembered leaving the strange morning ceremony sad and tired and depressed. He wasn't quite sure what he was supposed to believe in, whatever it was - he was worried he wasn't qualified. This Mission, though... this was not the same as that church - he was almost certain. It was the smell, the silent pulsating energy of the place. The soft green aura that emanated from the Chaplain, as well as the building itself. Still, though, he had to be totally sure.

"Are you... a church?" he asked timidly, gazing down at his shoes, unsure if he should be embarrassed.
A mighty laugh echoed through the rotunda.

"Oh! Ha ha! A church? Why, what do you think about churches?" bellowed the Chaplain, "Have you been in one before? How about a temple? A monastery? A shrine?" he asked intently, half-way attending to one of the philodendrons that needed its vines trained. The Boy shrugged.

"I've been in one before. I've heard about the others. People pray and stuff," he began to reflect, "to gods, and statues, and books and things. They look sad. I think... I think churches are..." he hesitated, biting his lip instead.

"Weird!" answered the Girl for him. The Boy's mouth gaped open in shock. Surely, this Chaplain would kick them out of his Mission for insulting his hospitality and his home. A low rumbling chuckle. A scratch at his chin. A flick of the dreadlocks over his shoulder. A thoughtful smile. The Chaplain knelt next to the Boy and Girl at the foot of the pulpit, sunlight shining in various directions as it snuck through the indoor jungle's living canopy. He clasped his hands together and closed his eyes, drawing in a deep breath.

"People need *something* to believe in," the Chaplain began, "they always have, they always will. Whether that something is a god, a ghost, an Allah, a Buddha, a Yahweh, a Vishnu, an ancestor, a star, a moon, a tree, or an atom. They search for answers," he elaborated, standing now, facing the open door of the Mission - the clouds had turned pink outside. "So what does it matter - and who am *I* to judge - what *you* choose, what script *you* follow?" Here, he paused, turned, and placed gentle hands on the shoulders of the Boy and the Girl, squeezing lightly, sighing deeply. "As long as you believe in the goodness within yourselves first... and seek kindness in each other... that is *all* that truly matters." His dreadlocks floated softly in the soft green haze that radiated around him.

"Be kind," whispered the Girl. "My Dad always told me that was all I had to do, and the rest would fall into place - as long as I can remember to always 'be kind.'" Nodding slowly and smiling ecstatically, the Chaplain locked eyes with the Girl.

"Yes! 'Be kind!' To yourself, to others - human, and non-human - organic, and inorganic - that is what we celebrate here, in this place, this '*Mission*,' as you call it," finished the Chaplain. The Boy felt the thin tingling tendrils of green static tickle his skin as the Chaplain released their shoulders. Rising back up, the Chaplain turned his face to the noon sun overhead and breathed in its rays and heat and life. "In this place, we simply advocate just that - being kind. We have no holy books, no idols, nor do we have ceremonies or holidays. We simply celebrate our lives together. We sing, we dance, we eat, we tell stories of our struggles and our fortunes. We help each other live life to its fullest. We take care of our home, and of each other's homes." he spoke softly. "That's it."

"Like a family?" asked the Girl, turning her face to sunbeams in mimicry of the Chaplain, a smile growing upon her face. Her yellow aura melded with his green, forming a cloud of fluorescent lime green that brightened the Mission walls ever so slightly.

"Yes. We are a family. All of us. Even you - and we just met!" replied the Chaplain, clapping his hands and spinning slowly in place, the colors of his suit dancing madly around his thin frame. "You see, for every difference between you and I, there are one thousand similarities. It is so easy to see the differences, but that is not what we should be focusing on! When you can appreciate that we are all part of this reality together, then you can understand that we are all One." The Boy thought about that - was this what he had been coming to understand over the past several weeks? Was this what the Schwark had helped him understand?

"You and I... we... us, here," the Boy tested, mulling the words over and over, "we... are all the same 'One?' he half-asked, half-asserted. The Chaplain gazed down at the Boy with a look of pure joyous glee.

"Close your eyes, Boy," commanded the man. "Now, one at a time. Open up your heart. Who is it that you love the most? Who of us on this Earth give you love in return?" the Chaplain began, his hand over his chest. "Ready? Open your mind. Who provides you real knowledge and strength? Who do you teach in return?" kneeling now, the Chaplain softly removed the Boy's yellow beanie and tapped gently on his forehead with a long bony finger. "Finally, open your Great Eye. You feel it, I know you do. We have never met here... but we have in other places... in other...

times." His two conscious eyes closed, the Boy did as instructed and opened his third.

~~~

As his consciousness rapidly expanded and melded with the deep ocean of his unconscious, a great foggy nothingness overcame him. He was simultaneously everywhere and nowhere. From out of the colorless mist, the face of the Chaplain emerged, silently walking towards him. The pearly-white teeth gleaming, the dread-locks perfectly wrapped - slowly, the face of the man began to subtly change… to metamorphosize. Red, wiry hair replaced black, thick ropes of hair. Sharp, pointed teeth shaved down from perfect white, squared incisors and molars emerged. A set of sleek arms and legs and paws replaced pin-stripe suit, cuffs and pants. A pointed snout between a pair of narrow dark eyes smiled back at the Boy - the smile, unchanged. He knew this smile from eons ago - the Fox. Snapping open his real eyes, the Boy gasped. The Chaplain - the Fox - gazed down knowingly at the Boy.

"We have always known each other, Boy. And we always will. I am a part of you, as you are of me."

A pair of tears dropped from the corners of the Boy's eyes and fell onto the lapels of his flannel shirt. Stepping to the Chaplain, he wrapped his arms around the technicolored jacket, and hugged him deeply. A heavy hand rested upon his head and patted him lightly. To his surprise a second pair of arms joined in - one half around the Boy, the other around the Chaplain. The Girl. In the center of the softly lit, philodendron-filled rotunda, the three held each other in silent celebration of their knowingness, of their interconnectedness, of their understanding of the mission - the Mission - *their* Mission. With a sigh and a whisper, the Chaplain slowly released the Boy and Girl and spoke.

"As I said, I know why you have come, of course," he grinned. "I would like you to meet someone. Would you follow me, please?"

~~~

Low-hanging purple clouds whisped and wandered just beyond the cityscape that vibrated and buzzed far below them from atop the hill. Warm sun-soaked breeze wrinkled the blades of grass and swayed the thick branches of the nearby elm trees. A raven, clacking happily, rode a thermal wave of invisible pressure, rising rapidly above the Mission without a single flap of it' wings. Small patches of fairy-ring mushrooms grew nearby, and the Boy could smell their pleasant earthiness. The Chaplain led them down a wood-chipped path to a large meadow hidden just beyond the view from the bus stop. A small village of beige tents flapped and fluttered. The Boy could see a few people milling about - some children playing tag in the center. As they approached the perimeter, the Chaplain stopped and spoke to his two visitors.

"At some point in life, a person needs a helping, caring hand. It may be when you are very young, or perhaps when you are very old. Sometimes it happens right in the middle," he explained. "A lost job, a lost family, a lost purpose, a lost sense of control. It does not matter. We do not judge. That is not our place. We simply extend a hand. That is *this* place" he signaled, hand raised towards the tents.

"Be kind," summarized the Boy. From his periphery, he could see that the Girl was smiling at him. They entered the village. As they passed several larger dwellings with signs on their outer aspects that read "Clinic" or "Library" or "Store," the people idly standing nearby perked up and grinned at the site of the Chaplain.

"What's up my main man? Lookin' fine as always," called an elderly woman sitting in a rocking chair. She was stitching a pair of broken boots back together, a set of flirtatious dimples raised at the passing Chaplain.

"Father Rainbow - how's it hangin'? Who ya got with ya?" inquired a younger man, hanging clothes to dry in the breeze.

"Yo, Dreads! Thanks for arranging those extra cans of soup - we're goin' big tonight for supper! Miss Kitty's gonna be cookin' up her rolls again, so come on by!" offered another. A large silver Maine coon strutted past the three and stretched its back long enough to strategically entice the Girl to reach down and stroke its long hide.

"You have cats, too!" she exclaimed.

"Sure do," replied the Chaplain. "Miss Kitty's cats. She gets 'em from the alleys in the city. Takes 'em down to the free vet clinic every other Sunday to get all tuned up. She trains 'em somehow to be really nice. They keep out the pests and such. Great lady. Heard she got a new job - but I think you already knew that," he finished, a grand wink projected at the Girl, a massive sparkle in his eye. Both Boy and Girl gawked at the Chaplain. He was talking about the Cat Lady, no doubt. Surely, it had to be her. Rapidly, the pieces of the puzzle began to fall into place for the Boy.

The Cat Lady lived in the Village at the Mission. She had a son, who must live here, too - who would be starting school soon. Perhaps this was even the place where she and the Captain had first met. Feeling as if he had found ground zero for the center of his universe, the Boy suddenly had an incredible impulse he knew he needed to fulfill.

"Can we... meet Miss Kitty? And her son?" asked the Boy, cautiously. Somehow, he felt this was the next bend in the river, the next switchback in the trail to take. The Chaplain smiled and laughed a short few bursts of 'I knew it, I knew it'-type laughs.

"Of course, they live right over this way. She's probably still at work, but her kiddo? He's probably playing with some of the new toys we picked up from the thrift store the other day."

The Girl gasped.

The Chaplain bit back his grin.

The Boy swore he could hear the drifting melody of a saxophone.

~~~

As the trio proceeded through the narrow paths between the tents, a small clowder of felines began assembling behind them. Black and white and tabby and calico and silver and hairless - an amber glow began to form around the meandering creatures. The Girl could not have been more pleased.

"They know we're going to their home!" she hypothesized. Rounding the final corner, the gaggle of humans and cat compatriots were met by a woman laying out cans of tuna and cat kibble around the outer aspect of her tent - the Cat Lady.

"Why Miss Kitty, you're back early today," greeted the Chaplain. The cats surged past the group and began to assemble around the fresh food.

"Took the noon bus. Have to get the kid all ready for his big day tomorrow," replied the gruff voice, "First day of school and all," the Cat Lady finished. She looked at the Boy and Girl and widened her eyes. "Now what are you two doing way out *here*? Does your Father know about this?" she asked, half-scolding, half-suppressing her amusement. The Boy nodded - his Father *did* know the Boy was at least not at the port. He wasn't lying, he decided. The Maine Coon crept up to his feet and meowed loudly, rubbing its large head against his ankles. He leaned down and stroked its forehead.
~~~

"I believe these two would like to say 'Hello' to your kiddo, Miss Kitty - he around?" asked the Chaplain, looking at the Boy, smiling at the Girl. The Cat Lady nodded and thumbed towards the closed tent door. "He's playing with that new toy he picked out. Strange looking thing. He's got quite the imagination these days."
The Boy swallowed his heart back into the pit of his stomach. The adrenaline was almost too much - he was visibly shaking. Today was the Day.

"Well, I'm going to head back to the building to water the plants - you two come say 'good-bye' before you leave," instructed the Chaplain to his visitors, who nodded adamantly.

"I'm going to go feed the cats around the perimeter of the tents," started the Cat Lady. "Gotta drop a can here and there - helps keep scuffles over the tuna to a minimum."

"Cat gangs?" inquired the Girl, eyes bulging with curiosity. "Can... Can I come with? I'd love to ask you some questions about how you train them." She looked at the Boy and felt a wave of building disappointment surging overhead - she could see it, could feel the heat of his anxiety.

"I'll come right back! I promise!" she stammered. A steady calmness suddenly flushed across the Boy's mind and heart. Of course - this was *his* mission, now. The Girl had gotten him this far, and her path forked at this junction. Her journey went elsewhere, and he would have to be content with that. Time to go it alone, he decided.

"Take good notes," the Boy said to his best friend, smiling with an expression that said both 'I'll be fine' and 'thank you' simultaneously. The Girl blushed slightly as she scooped up the Maine coon - it was literally half her size. Walking beside the Cat Lady, she began a litany of questions that blurred together and faded as the two walked behind the row of tents. Over his shoulder, the Boy watched as the technicolor Chaplain skipped up the oak-chipped path, ducking into a small stand of old-growth Fir - a steady green haze enshrouding his movement. As he continued to stare, the Boy could have sworn he saw the blur of a foxtail slinking through the sword ferns. Rubbing his eyes, he turned to face the tent doors. The soft hum of jazzy alto saxophone percolated through the heavy canvas and onto his eager eardrums. He knocked on the aluminum center post of the tent.

"Come in!" called a small, faint voice. Pulling back the side of the heavy tent awning his eyes were met with a constellation of dimly pulsating bioluminescence - shades of every color cast along the floor. He took a step inside the tent. Today was the Day.

<div align="center">~~~</div>

"Could you pass the cranberries, please?" came the all-too-familiar goofy voice. In the corner of the large tent space, a small child - his back facing the Boy - held a small stuffed animal in his lap. Whiskers protruding from its snout, furry flippers front and back, a sharp sharky dorsal fin, its blowhole reverberating blue and green pulsating light in a pleasant manner. The Schwark.

"Schwark!" the Boy exclaimed, feet frozen to the floor of the tent. A blinding brilliance of rainbow light erupted from the creature and filled the tent with a million suns.

"Buddy!" replied the Schwark, "How the heck are ya, Partner? Haven't seen ya in awhile! Come on over, meet my new pal!" it beckoned. Strangely, almost unsettlingly, the smaller child slowly spiraled around to face the Boy. His face expressed supreme calmness, a light smile suggesting a gesture of 'welcome.' An ancient soul in a small boy's body. Flashing his gaze onto the Boy, the two locked stares. Ice-gray eyes twinkled for a second, revealing a millennium.

"It told me about you," whispered the Astronaut, petting the felty back of the Schwark. "And I told it that I had already met you," he finished, eyes reflecting the swirls of pulsing fluorescence wildly. "I suppose you want it back now, since it's yours to begin with." The ice-gray eyes held constant - not even a blink. The Boy clenched his fists to settle his tremulousness and knelt to sit on the floor of the tent, for the flood of emotions in his brain was starting to make him woozy.

"You... call it Schwark, too?" was the first thought he could iterate, ignoring the question of ownership for the time being. The Astronaut nodded.

"That's what it said I could call it. In a dream. We dream a lot now. I'm starting to see things differently."
The Boy scuffled a bit closer to the Astronaut, his eyes drawn to the Schwark, but his hand too hesitant to touch it just yet.

"What do you mean - 'differently?'" he inquired of the ice-gray eyed boy. The Astronaut picked up the Schwark and stared at its beady black eyes for several moments, his breath long and deep. Finally, a great sigh.

"A long time ago - before all of this - my mom and I were forced to move. My dad left us. We didn't have any money. We used to live in a great place. I had friends," began the Astronaut, bringing the Schwark closer to his chest with every sentence. "Then one morning, my mom found this really old black cat - we named her Grandma. My mom dreamed that Grandma told her to come to this place." the Boy held his breath - this was too much. Before he could say anything, the Astronaut continued.

"We begged for money for awhile… then my mom's friend here, an old sailor, he asked if she could work at the dock. Suddenly things were moving so fast. I'm starting school. And then…" he looked up at the Boy, the ice melting from his irises. "Then, Father Rainbow came to visit me one night. He had a present - said 'this has been looking for you.' It was the Schwark!" he revealed, voice trembling. "And now? Now, I see that things *can* be better, as long as I think about them a little differently. The Schwark shows me the nice things amongst the dark things. It finds the fun in the sea of boredom and gloominess. I'm happier I think. Tomorrow I'm even going to school." The Astronaut finished, his eyes beaming brighter at the thought.

"Aww shucks. Just doin' my best, guys!" the Schwark acknowledged. The Boy suddenly realized with great clarity why it was that he and the Astronaut had come to know each other outside of this place. Through their uniquely painful tribulations, they shared incredibly similar unconscious thoughts and worries, as well as conscious dreams and desires.

"Do you remember meeting... in the... other place?" asked the Boy. The Astronaut blinked and slowly shook his head. "I remember who you are, and that we've met... somewhere. Somewhere dark. We were looking through a window together. But that is all I can remember." The Boy smiled greatly at that.

"I remember more. I remember that you are going to do some very important things in the future," he riddled. The Astronaut laughed at that and rubbed his eyes.

"I'm serious!" continued the Boy.

"That he is!" supported the Schwark. The Astronaut shook his head in disbelief.

"That's funny. I dreamed the same about you," he replied. For several minutes, the three beings sat on the wooden floorboards inside a tent, at a Mission atop a hill, in the city by the woods - and simply inhaled, considered the present moment, and exhaled. An idea came to the Boy in that moment: had the Schwark known all of this already? Did it arrange for these particular fates, or was it all simply coincidence? The Boy decided it was a question better left unanswered. Reaching out, he touched the fleeced front flipper of the Schwark and moved to scratch it behind the dorsal fin.

"Ohh that's the spot" the Schwark moaned, its voice melting into sublime relaxation. "Now if you could just flip me a cranberry or two, we'd be set, know what I'm sayin'?" The Boy put a hand on the shoulder of the Astronaut.

"I know how it feels to lose your home," he started, "to have to start life again in a strange place. I also know that as excited as you may be to start school, there must be a terrible anxiety welling up inside of you - same as me." The Astronaut blinked away his tears and looked to his feet, swallowing down his refusal and boyish pride.

"I *am* scared, actually," he softly admitted. In that moment, the Boy realized what his Mission was truly all about. Sliding off his backpack, he unbuttoned his flannel jacket and took off his yellow knit hat, laying the items beside the Astronaut.

"You know, I think that the Schwark really does belong with you now," the Boy realized aloud. "You'll need its help along this journey you're about to start - especially the first few weeks. You'll also need this backpack to bring home your books. And this jacket and hat - that way you can blend in with the environment a bit better." He bopped the Schwark on the snout and smiled. He had never felt so confident - so right in his entire life. Echoing his convictions, the Schwark radiated with a tremendous purple-green, the tent growing warmer, the two boys floating a few inches from the floor.

"Thank you," sniffled the younger to the elder. "Thank you..." The Boy stood and looked at his mystical friend, the Schwark, for a final time. "Goodbye Schwark. You were a great pal," he eulogized. A flash of hot white exploded throughout the tent.

"Excuse me, Buddy!" an irritated Schwark erupted, "Did you say, '*were*?' C'mon partner - you should know better than that by now!" the creature scolded, its luminescent blowhole whirring a thousand miles an hour. "I am *now*, and always *will* be, a 'great pal!' And by the way, friend, you already know where you can find me, whenever or wherever that may be! I'll always be there for ya." With that, a burst of alternating red-white-red-white burst forth from the creature, a fine beam splitting into two parts; the first landing onto the Boy's chest, his heart; the second resting upon his forehead, the portal into his mind. The Astronaut smiled up at the Boy.

"Schwark's right, you know," he said.

"I know," replied the Boy. "I know."

~~~

On leaving the tent, the Boy found the Girl sitting cross-legged at the entrance, no less than six cats curled up on or beside her. She looked at him quizzically and with anticipation.

"Well?" she finally blurted, "Did you find it?" The Boy nodded and sighed.

"Someone else needs the Schwark more than I do," he explained. "Besides, I have everything it taught me in *here,* and in *here,*" he said, tapping his temple and his chest. "It will always live on in there, I guess." The Girl slowly stood, removing several cats from her lap, and faced the Boy, her bottom lip trembling, the late afternoon winter sun reflecting from her eyes.

"You're part Schwark now!" she giggled. The Boy decided he liked the sound of that. He liked it quite a bit. The two friends walked back towards the Mission and boarded the four o'clock bus back to the Port - just as planned. The Girl talked continuously about cat behavior as the Boy sat in silence and listened, a perpetual smile upon his face.. As the bus rolled down the hill, a wiry fox and a elderly black cat sat hidden amongst a cluster of sword ferns and recalled the day's events, laughing and crying with unparalleled joy, for the world they knew was truly a marvelous place to be alive.
~~~

The Atoll

Rhythmically pulsing across the glassy stillness of the open ocean, the massive turtle effortlessly glided towards the burning sunset as it dipped a solar toe into the horizon. The three passengers sat huddled together atop the great shell, silent in their spoken words, but brimming in a shared wonder and joyousness of the life that danced and swirled and dove all around them. Pointing to the aft of the Turtle, the Girl sucked in her breath in a great excited gasp. A school of flying fish furiously beat their fins and skittered and skipped and hovered and flashed across the lazy mountains of wake the Turtle left in its path. Fluorescent pinks and purples reflected off the silvery lining of the bullet-shaped fish, giving the impression of a frenetic cloud of brilliant diamonds sparkling like contrails to the steady course of the rising moon.

As the hours aboard the Turtle passed, their escort of golden-hued bottlenose dolphins handed off duties to a new entourage: a band of heavily whiskered and generously plump sea lions. Whistling and barking madly in swirling chaos around the metronomic forward energy of the Turtle, the sea lions turned out to be a real gang of tricksters. No sooner had the three riders clapped and applauded the antics of the flipping and hooting pinnipeds, then a sudden cold spurt of high-pressure ocean water exploded across the side of the Astronaut's face, nearly hurtling him off port side of the Turtle - a potential three story fall.

"Hey!" he exclaimed, rubbing the salt from his ice-gray eyes. The Boy and Girl attempted to suppress their obvious amusement through short snorts of laughter and covered grins, but in the end, were spared no mercy, as the entire raft of sea lions rose off the starboard nose of the Turtle and unleashed a flurry of spittled seawater at the two onlookers. Immediately knocked into the air, the two grasped for any sort of reptilian hand or foothold, and instead latched onto the poor, soaking wet Astronaut, dragging him down the slippery shell into the twilight ocean waters below. A great series of splashes, followed by muffled silence as the three victims came to their senses several meters below the surface. Stroking and clawing furiously upwards, the refracted moonlight above momentarily flickered as the silhouettes of snarky sea lions darted overhead. With great gasps, the three paddled back to the monstrous outline of the Turtle, its shell simultaneously casting a pitch black semi-circle against the sky and darkened shadow upon the sea in which they swam. It had slowed to a drift, thankfully. As the three comrades clamored across its front flipper, they took a few seconds to catch their heavy breath, smiling at each other's irrationally terrified faces. To their relief, the massive rubbery turtle fin provided a small relief on which they could stand, waist-deep in stagnant foamy sea. Several bald, brown heads bobbed to the surface in front of them, whiskered cheeks bulging with a fresh salvo, black, beady eyes glittering and sparkling as only a prankster's could.

"Hey, you jerks!" exclaimed the Astronaut. "You're supposed to be helping us out, not causing trouble!" He was answered with a playful burst of sea lion spray as his tormentors dove and whistled and reemerged behind the Boy.

"Hello! Do you guys, um, know the... the Schwark?" queried the cautious Boy, gasping and holding his breath, ready to duck at the slightest suggestion of another assault. The pair of bobbing sea lion heads looked at each other for a moment, blubbering and flapping their whiskered lips back and forth before sucking in great heaps of sea, their cheeks bulging.

"Wait!" yelled the Boy. "We just want to find the Schwa.." Before he could finish his words, his mouth was filled with the stale warmness of the ocean, preheated by the jowls of the sea lions. Choking and hacking, he clung to the Astronaut for stability as he fought for another breath. The sea lions drifted below the surface, their muffled hooting and barking vibrating against the legs of their final victim - the Girl. Unbeknownst to the sea lions, the Girl had been making very careful observations and calculations. As the slippery sea dogs confidently rose above the surface, they were met with the wide-eyed ferocious face of the Girl just inches from their own - her cheeks fasciculating under the pressure of a great gulp of seawater.

"Phewwppff!" came the sound of spurting foam impacting the snouts of the shocked sea lions as the Girl emptied a seemingly endless spurt upon their faces. Sneezing and coughing, the sea lions attempted to awkwardly wipe their whiskers clean with their stubby front flippers as the Girl prepared for round two - a second fire-hydrant spray that sent the ocean-going jesters back under the cover of the purple and midnight sea.

"You got 'em!" congratulated the Astronaut. No sooner had he spoken than a growing rumble of crazed bubbles erupted in a frenetic circle around the three, a steady barking emerging louder and louder beneath the great Turtle flipper on which they stood. From beyond the safety and confines of the Turtle, two dozen dark brown heads rocketed to the surface, shaking their whiskers in silence. What had started as a playful practical joke now began to take on the specter of something more sinister, decided the Boy. He swallowed and looked to the neck of their ship - could they climb it quickly enough? Six eyes stared down forty-eight in the shadow of the great Turtle as the moon hovered above in glowing anticipation.

"Ark-ark-ark!" exploded forth from all directions as the raft of sea lions began to laugh hysterically. Some were bellowing and hooting so hard they had to float onto their backs, blubbery bellies facing the sky, flippers covering their eyes as their chests buckled and rose in great heaving fits of hilarity. "Ark-ark-ark!" they rang out, drifting all around the mass of the Turtle and their three terrified guests.

"Are they... laughing at us?" murmured the Astronaut, a hint of disgust in his voice.

"Maybe they think we're funny?" thought out the Boy, an inkling of belief that they were in no real danger after all.

"Ark-ark-ark!" echoed the Girl, her eyes squeezed shut, her neck arched back in mimicry of the slippery beasts. "Ark-ark-ark!" she barked, a great smile forming as her outstretched arms smacked the surface of the sea, sending random waves in all directions. The lions responded in kind, smashing the still surface with their powerful flippers, creating a virtual whirlpool around the apathetic Turtle. A particularly brave sea lion drifted over to the Astronaut, rolling onto its back to gaze at the ice-gray eyes - a ridiculous stare-down, decided the Boy.

"Whewww!" whistled the sea lion. An absurd grin crossed the face of the Astronaut.

"Whewww!" he squealed back. The whiskered face rustled its rubbery lips and displayed its pointed canines in a sort of fantastically terrifying smile. Rolling back onto its chest, the sea lion beat its tail fins and returned to its friends. In a burst of high-frequency staccato whistling, the sea lion summoned the raft of fellow lions together in a tight mass of brown squirming skin. As the three looked on, the lions began to layer themselves at the base of the Turtle's neck - eight bodies in parallel as six more dove on top, arranged at ninety degrees to the first. Four more lions managed to bounce and wriggle to the top of these six, and so on, until a great ramp of blubbered bodies sat floating alongside the turtle.

"They're being friendly! They made us a way back up!" clapped the Girl, trampolining off the Turtle's flipper, breast-stroking over to the living tower of hairless leathery flesh. The Boy looked at the Astronaut as both shrugged in silence and followed the Girl in pursuit. Ascending the ramp of sea lions, the three were careful not to unintentionally use a loose jowl or whiskered lip as a handhold. Nearing the top, the Boy slipped and fell onto a lower tier of belly-up sea lions, sending up a commotion of barks and hoots and whistles. One of the sea lions smacked him on the backside with its flipper - he'd be sure not to fall again, he decided. Reaching the summit, he was able to easily scramble to his post alongside his friends atop the Turtle's shell, tucked into the front of the carapace. Down below, the great sea lion tower collapsed and fell back into the still ocean in a series of terrific nose-dives, belly-flops, and somersaults.

"Ark-ark-ark!" called out the three friends in chorus, acknowledging the peaceful treaty reached with their strange escort.

"Ark-ark-ark!" replied the raft of sea lions, humored and satisfied by their funny guests. In a single great lurching motion, the Turtle began its huge strokes forward. Had it even perceived their ridiculous pit-stop with the lions, or was time something else entirely to such an amazing creature? The Boy considered that thought, as the barking and whistling subsided into the starlit distance. The three passengers rode in silence for another hour as their bodies dried amongst the mysteriously warm ocean breeze. Despite the day's incredible distance traveled, the Boy found himself unusually alert and energized. Did the others feel the same, he wondered? As he gazed at the faces of his friends, he saw a faint emerald green emerge and flicker across their glassy eyes.

"What's that?" whispered the Astronaut.

"It's a... a mirage?" replied the Girl, hesitant and unsure. She stood on the slick shell and balanced herself between the shoulders of her comrades. "No trees. Just... sand. It's an... atoll!" she announced proudly. The great Turtle seemed to be heading directly towards the small pitch of land, if it could even be described as such. A beam of blue-green light birthed from the center of the circular sand bar, its rays piercing the black of the night like some fantastic searchlight. The Boy could make out three faint figures hunched over in a tight circle, gathered around the source of the illumination. They seemed to be dangling something from their hands directly into the center of the light.

"There are people on the island!" announced the Astronaut.

"How would anyone get out here, anyway?" mused the Girl, who was met with smirking grins from her right and left. "Oh," she replied, smiling through her embarrassment at the obvious impossible answer to her impossible question.

"I think... I know who they are," whispered the Boy. They were clearly too far out yet for any distinguishing features to be relied upon, but... it was a feeling he had - an aura he sensed - a sound he heard - an amalgamation of sounds, really.

As the Turtle slowed its strokes and pivoted around several shallow reefs, the three riders gripped its shell and hunkered down, careful not to be tossed into the jagged elk horn coral protrusions that broke the white wash far below. Suddenly, the great beast surged forward in a furious final turn of its flippers, hydroplaning across the inch or so of sea-foam that coated the firm compacted sand. In a final perfectly calculated maneuver, the great Turtle spun ninety degrees and turned its head ever so slightly, as to casually slide its three passengers off its leathery neck and onto a soft pillow of windswept dune grass just a few feet below.

"Hey-oh!" hooted the Astronaut, who somersaulted in slow-motion across the mound of sand, clearly enjoying this newest pitstop on their journey. Or perhaps this was the destination? Did it matter? The Boy decided that it probably did not. A pair of hands appeared in front of his upside-down face - he had landed in a very peculiar position, and was awkwardly sliding down the backside of the beach dune head-first, the brilliant beam of atoll light surging over his head.

"Let me help you up!" came her voice, followed shortly thereafter by two great, strong pulls up onto his feet. "I think I recognize the atoll people - at least a couple of them! C'mon!" beckoned the Girl, nearly ripping the Boy's shoulders from their sockets. Dusting off the sand that had crept into every crevice and pore, the three passengers signed simultaneously as they took in the atoll: a perfect circle, maybe four or five acres in size. The great Turtle now occupied approximately a third of the sand mass - it appeared to be sleeping? One couldn't be certain with such beasts, thought the Boy. In the very center of the atoll, a separate set of figures sat cross-legged around the spotlight - a pool, actually. They appeared to be holding long bamboo-styled fishing poles. The thin line dangling from each seemed to vibrate in a subtly melodious frequency. As he walked with his friends towards the fishing people, The Boy recognized each of their faces immediately.

The long perfectly symmetric dreadlocks swooshed and swirled around the forehead of the Chaplain as he raised his brow to greet the newest arrivals.

"Welcome friends! Please! Come, have a seat around the Hole!" An impossibly colored blanket sat partially unfurled at his side, a million colors refracting the blue-green light emanating from the pool in a way that made the cloth seem to hover a few millimeters off the sand.

"Well, howdy everybody! Wow! What an awesome Turtle you got to ride in on!" said the glowing face of the Ghost. Several plastic action figures were strewn around his position on the edge of the Hole.

"You kids again, eh?" snorted the Cat Lady, smiling through her faux-annoyance. "Guess you'll haveta come on over here and help entertain ol' Granny," she said, as the large yellow-eyed black cat slithered forth from her lap and silently strode towards the approaching guests with all the confidence that one would expect from the queen of cats. One by one, the arrival party took their seats next to the Atoll Keepers, the Hole Fishers - their friends.

The blue-green light that emerged from the perfectly still pool was mesmerizing, entrancing - the Boy could hardly turn his gaze from its depths. Between his breaths, he swore he could detect the muffled notes of clarinet, bass guitar, maybe even a snare drum - a jazz ensemble? In a slightly paranoid manner, he looked over his shoulder back at the Turtle and the sea. The sounds were certainly not coming from the crashing waves or the snoring Turtle. He looked at the dangling fishing lines and saw they were vibrating to the same beat as the subtle jazz licks filling his head. It was music - deep down, in that great atoll Hole that blazed with surreal bands of interwoven forest green and royal blue. Had he heard this song before? It was too distorted to clearly make out. His concentration was quickly broken when the Girl began to ask her usual questions.

"How did you all get here? Where'd you get that bamboo fishing rod? There aren't *any* trees here! Did you catch anything? What's down that hole?" she blurted, hardly able to contain her excitement. The Chaplain began a deep, booming laugh that reached a grand crescendo before finally subsiding.

"You ask a'lotta questions, young one - that's a good thing! People don't ask enough questions these days," he began. "The answers you seek are down the Hole" he pointed with a nod of his head, his moon-white teeth glimmering in the midnight reflection of the Milky Way racing overhead.

"Into your fishing hole?" asked the Astronaut, peering over the side of the circular pool. "It's so clear! I can see maybe a hundred feet down!" he exclaimed. A living wall of miniature coral fans and limestone formations rippled across the walls of the Hole, as small parrot fish and clownfish darted into and out of shadowed dwellings, investigating the new faces that had emerged around the surface of their abode.

"Something's wrong with your lures, I think," the Boy murmured. Vibrations from the fine translucent wire had made him think that perhaps they were, in fact, getting nibbles from some unknown creature lurking below. As he traced the ends of the line into an abrupt end of several metal sinkers and weights bundled together a few feet below the surface, he shook his head. What were these three doing? "You don't have any hooks on your lines?" he half-questioned, half-asserted.

"Hooks? For what?" replied the Ghost, a concerned look across his face. "To... catch things? Like fish? Those beautiful guys down there?" He was clearly upset by the suggestion. The Cat Lady chuckled.

"Oh, we're fishin' alright" she started. "Just not for fish. Or sharks. Or lobsters. Or any other thing like that. Don't know if you've noticed, but ya don't need to do that sorta thing in this place," she finished with a wink. Grandma was purring loudly on her lap again. His upturned, outstretched palm intensely glowing as it hovered over the water, the Chaplain happily sighed and closed his eyes.

"I'll let you in on our lil' secret," the Chaplain hushed. "Please, friends - dip your ear into the water. Just one. Close your eyes, open your minds - and listen," he stressed. Watching as the Girl and the Astronaut lowered their heads, the Boy could clearly hear the steady rhythm of a snare drum - had it grown louder just now? As her ear canal broke the surface tension, the Girl gasped. The Astronaut's ice-gray eyes exploded into a widened expression of awe. Carefully, the Boy lay upon his stomach, turned his head to face the smiling Chaplain, and plunged his ear into the surprisingly warm and soothing water of the sparkling Hole.

Instantaneously magnified by the perfect fluidity and viscosity of the seawater, streams of infinitely relaxing and comforting music enveloped and washed over his brain. A vinyl record of three jazz musicians playing in perfect concert with one another: an electric guitar, a stand-up bass, and simple drum set - snare, cymbal, and kick drum. He couldn't help himself - taking a deep breath and plunging his entire head under the surface, the Boy opened his eyes and explored the world of the Hole. Slowly, fish reemerged from their hideouts and reentered their previous musings in exact synchronicity with the music that reverberated and filled the entirety of the Hole. A school of baby zebrafish floated inches from his face, swaying to the groove of a gentle uplifting guitar riff. A rock lobster clicked and clacked its claws in rhythm to the bass that strummed steadily and diligently forward, framing the music for its companions. Bioluminescent shrimp pulsed and darted up and down and sideways with the sudden repetitive 'rat-a-tat-tat' of the snare. Turning his gaze star-wards, the Boy saw the three fishing lines pulsating with their acoustics - each clearly in tune to a separate instrument. Suddenly fearing for his breath, he pulled his head from the water and gasped mightily.

"You three!" he began, wiping the beads of water from his mouth, "you're making all that music down there?" Dipping a foot into the Hole, he could feel the sonic impulses on his skin, the mellow comfort of it all sending goosebumps up his legs and into his heart. The Chaplain, the Cat Lady, the Ghost all looked at their three new compatriots and smiled in silence.

"Are we?" suggested the Cat Lady through mysteriously narrowed eyes.

"Of course you are!" replied the Astronaut "Best folk music I've heard in... forever! A banjo, a violin - heck - even a slide-guitar!" The Boy and the Girl looked at him, mouths open in utter confusion.

"What are you talking about? Folk music? There's clearly a bass and snare drum - all the fish are swooning to the jazz coming from those guitar licks," corrected the Boy. The Ghost laughed uncontrollably at that. The Chaplain's smile had grown even larger.

"Well, what do you hear?" asked the Astronaut of the Girl. Looking hesitantly away from their gazes, she began to bite the corner of her thumbnail instinctively.

"Metal," she murmured. "Death metal, actually." Even the Chaplain's eyes went wide with that.

"No. Way." replied the Astronaut.

"I like you, kid," chirped the Cat Lady, one thumb up in the Girl's direction. All eyes drifted back to the raging blue-green glare from the Hole, all ears transfixed to a tune unto themselves, all minds open to the infinite.

"Perhaps we are 'fishing' - in a sense," started the Chaplain. "'Fishing,' in that we are here, dangling an extension of ourselves into a mysterious abyss, searching and hoping to find and share in its energies, its wisdoms, its mysteries, its impossibilities. And voilà! What do we find, but our own rhythm - our own beat!"

"And," echoed the Ghost, "we don't need to 'catch' anything - except maybe ourselves." The Cat Lady nodded at that.

"What you hear and see and feel and think beneath the surface of the Hole is a reflection of yourself at your most comfortable, most happy state of... well, of just *being*," she explained. Impulsively, the Boy slowly reached out to lay a hand across the Girl's closed fist - a test, of sorts. As their skin connected, the Boy was met with a furious riff of face-melting guitar solos blistering through half his mind, oddly placing him in a trance of supreme ease and relaxation. Blinking away the heavy reverb and double-bass pedals, he turned to face the Astronaut. Releasing his hand from the Girl, he touched the younger boy on the shoulder. Sudden twangy, plucky notes off a four-string banjo square-danced around with the overlaying melody of a bright violin. The Boy removed his hand, shook his head, and refocused on the Hole, allowing the flow of his jazz to return.

"Ah. You felt it, eh?" the Chaplain nudged, clearly watching the Boy's experiment. "You finally opened your ears a bit more." The Cat Lady cleared her throat.

"Not just hearing each other's rhythms either. If you listen - *truly* listen - you'll hear more. You'll hear their feelings. You'll feel their love, taste their fear, smell their knowledge, and see their mind. But first - you 'listen.'" The six figures sat in silence for many moments - hundreds of breaths - millions of thoughts - listening to each other with one, singular mind.

"Do you think we can 'listen' to the animals and plants and all the other living things?" asked the Girl to the group. A soft sigh from the Chaplain.

"Why don't you go and see?" he offered, his hands and eyes open towards the Hole. The Boy, Girl, and Astronaut felt each others' hearts race at the suggestion, the smell of adventure, a taste of mystery, the glow of blue-green life around their hearts. As each of the three slowly lowered themselves into the watery welcome of the Hole, the Ghost called out.

"Nothing scary down there, don't worry! Oh, and in this place, you won't need to worry about your breath. You'll see," he smiled. The Astronaut took a huge breath and dove. The Girl breathed in a reserved amount of air and slowly sank. The Boy laughed. He remembered places like this. An old friend had shown him such tricks in another time. Exhaling all of his air, he looked to the ice-gray eyes and slowly submerged himself.

"Cowabunga, dude!" said the Boy, dipping below the surface, the sultry, smoky jazz scales pulling him downwards towards his friends.

~~~
~~~

Spinning slowly through the depths of the Hole, the three were gradually made aware of the presence of their co-inhabitants. A pair of rainbow-colored mantis shrimp poked their monstrous, multifaceted compound eyes out of a fire coral crevasse to examine the Girl first. As she extended a finger, the Boy could hear her amazement in the form of chugging power chords roaring forth from her outstretched arm. The mantis shrimp, in turn, replied back with dual electric guitar solos that rose over the Girl's chords in powerful precision and aggressive beauty. Raising their massive shrimpy arms to meet the Girl's finger, a mighty bass began to thwump-thwump through the Hole. A passing group of light-blue jacks paused to appreciate the duet, and began to bob their narrow heads to the building anthem. As claw met flesh, an explosion of blinding blue-green light burst from every living cell in the Hole, sending a wave of terrific, death-metal tinged energy moon-wards.

The three swam on.

"I didn't know mantis shrimp loved metal as much as I do!" exclaimed the Girl. "I could feel their joy - I could hear it!" Suddenly, a humongous mustard-yellow eel wriggled and wrapped itself around the Astronaut, its menacing toothy grin and pale purple eye considering his presence. Hovering inches from his face, the eel stared at ice-gray eyes and suddenly cocked its slithery head. An acoustic guitar strummed softly as a mandolin began its graceful scaled interlude with an accompanying fiddle. Floating in near stillness, the Astronaut let the earthy rhythms of wood and twine penetrate his soul, as he began a slow-motion underwater jig. Alternating heel kicks and swaying shoulder-blades were met in synch with the eel, for it, too, had begun to jive and sway.

As the Girl and Boy stamped their feet on invisible watery floorboards, the Astronaut and the eel spun and twirled around each other to the building banjo riffs wailing around them. Starfish on the adjacent walls flapped their legs in coordination with the four-four time of a washboard bridge leading to a chorus of slide-guitar and juggy percussion. Sea anemones pulsed inwards and outwards with the bassy echo of the dreadnought rhythm guitar. After many measures and a dizzying amount of spinning in place, the Astronaut threw his head back in joyous laughter and opened both arms towards the eel. Almost immediately, the creature darted forward, encircling the Astronaut, its face nuzzling against the crook of his neck. An eruption of folksy blue-green flared brighter than the sun as the two energies became one.

The three swam on.

"I could hear its love for the sea, for the reef, for small caves, starlit nights, good company, and foot-tapping, finger-pricking, folk music. Who would have ever known?" the Astronaut said aloud. Downward they dared, until the depths became darker yet, the walls of the Hole gradually vanishing and blending into the still darkness. Suddenly, the Boy felt a ticklish tap on his shoulder, sending him careening off the Astronaut and into a shelf of brain corals, his arms paddling frantically.

"Was that you?" he exclaimed towards the Girl. She responded with a shrug. Another spooky tap - this time, at his left foot. He caught a glimpse of an orange tendril zooming into the abyss - the brief residual glow and hum of a woodwind trailing behind it - he knew that sound. Closing his eyes, the Boy focused on the jazz ebbing and flowing through his veins and mind and whatever else he was. Trickling through the quick percussion of the snare and high-hat, bleeding underneath the minor scales perfectly picked from the electric guitar, swimming alongside the immensely deep echo of the stand up bass, came the rapidly growing flame of his favorite jazz instrument - a clarinet. He opened his eyes to the sight of eight undulating bright orange tentacles.

"Why, hello there," said the Boy to the octopus. "Glad you could join in." The cephalopod fluttered fluorescent shades of pink and purple and yellow as it stretched its arms into a vertical array, as if holding a miniature clarinet. The Boy mimicked the same, his fingers depressing and releasing valves as he swayed to the changing time signature of the new vibe the octopus had introduced. As the guitar and snare cooled off, the Boy and octopus began to belt out an uncanny clarinet duet together, sending shivers up and down the spines and spineless-spines of the onlooking creatures in the Hole. As bass and guitar began to pick up the slack, and snare and kick-drum resumed their neat, down-tempo, easy-styled sway, the octopus extended all eight of its tentacles and started lightly snapping in time to the cooled beat of the night. Joining in, the Boy snapped both thumbs against middle finger and was surprised how perfect the sound filled the ensemble. As he looked over his shoulder, he saw that the Girl and Astronaut had joined in, as had every starfish, lobster, crab, shrimp, clam, scallop, and even sea cucumber. The pure electricity that the octopus jazz generated opened doors in the Boy's mind that he had not known existed, for he was truly *listening* now - he decided. He could hear the life pulsating around him - that shared energy that not only charged his heart, but also connected him into the hearts of so many more. As the octopus began its frenetic blue-green fluorescence, the Boy could feel the light building around him, awaiting his signal to be released.

"Now?" he silently asked the octopus.

"Now," signaled the creature, spiraling away into the lightless abyss below.

<p style="text-align:center">~~~</p>

Bobbing gently back to the surface of the Hole, the three explorers were met by the grand applause and whistles of the Chaplain, Cat Lady, and Ghost, all of whom still sat dangling their reeds into the mystic waters. The sun was rising and the heat of the morning felt incredible to the dive team. Taking her seat next to the Chaplain, the Girl remained silent - upon her face, an expression of utter contentedness.

"Any questions?" the Chaplain whispered, winking at the three. The Girl thought on that for a few moments, before widening her smile.

"May I hold the fishing pole, please?" she requested. Laughing and shaking his head, the Chaplain happily obliged. Anything for a scientist, thought the Boy.

"Looks like you'll be staying a while, eh?" remarked the Chaplain. Biting her lip, she looked at the Boy.

"I need to be here. For myself," she attempted to explain. "This place... this is where I will find my answers. I think you will find yours out there," she finished, pointing out to the open sea. The Boy followed her finger and sighed. He nodded - he could hear the determination and the resounding happiness in her decision and in her conviction, and it was this that filled him, too, with joy - for her. He smiled. He decided this was the place for her, indeed. Her mission. His mission. As he rose from his position alongside the Hole, the Astronaut also stood.

"I'm coming with you," he announced. "I'm supposed to. I know it," his ice-gray eyes glowing with supreme confidence. Striding alongside the Boy, the Astronaut looked out to the open sea. The great Turtle had vanished from the beach, but neither boy was particularly worried, for they knew their journey would continue by any means necessary.

"I've got an idea," smirked the Astronaut. The Boy sat atop the small sand dune and watched as the younger child waltzed up to the receding tide line, unzipped a concealed jacket pocket, and removed a small plastic baggy containing some sort of small dark marble-shaped object. Emptying the contents onto the beach and reforming them into a neat pile, the Astronaut skipped up to the dune and sat, lightly punching his friend in the arm.

"Schwark bait," he said, raising his eyebrows.

"Cranberries?" asked the disbelieving older boy.

"Cranberries," affirmed the younger.

"So now we... wait?" inquired the Boy, smiling at the clever plan.

"We wait," replied the ice-gray eyes.

~~~

The sun had barely risen another inch by the time the distinctly familiar sound blew through the steady ocean breeze - so subtle, so faint, and yet... so idiosyncratic. The two looked at each other through ecstatic eyes.

"Saxophone!" they simultaneously shouted, surprised and relieved to know that the other heard the same sound in this instance. Standing as tall as they could on the tiny atoll, the Boy and the Astronaut scanned the horizon, blinded by the radiance of the burning flames of the morning sun. A small silver butterfly landed on the Boy's shoulder and fluttered back out to sea. The saxophone grew louder. From under the sun, beneath the waves, a powerful swirling constellation of colors emerged. And then...

A breach!

Bursting from the surface, the rainbowed bioluminescent blowhole and stubbly whiskered face of the Schwark barrel-rolled over the waves before crashing back into the sea. The two boys jumped into the air, hooting and hollering wildly.

Another leap!

Furry flippers beating at the whitewater and sharp dorsal fin splicing through the waves, the Schwark slid into the shallows of the atoll and breathed a mighty sigh. Hundreds of butterflies began to land on its back as the blowhole began to pulse a steady blue-green.

"Howdy, buddies!" exclaimed the Schwark. "C'mon over you two, and hop on! We've got places to go!"
~~~

The Promise

Wafting through the early morning light came the soft alluring tendrils of invisible odors from the kitchen, creeping under the doorframe, along the walls, up against the bedpost, across his semi-conscious body and into his nostrils. His eyes closed but his mind fully awoken, the Boy inhaled deeply and exhaled a gratified smile, for the finest of breakfast odors rode the air that early hour - his favorite smell of them all, in fact. Opening his ears a bit wider, he allowed the hiss and fizzle and pop to drift in, playing rhythm to the clang-clanging of the cast iron pan against the cheap aluminum electric stovetop. His Father's breakfast; a meal the Boy had not had since the Fire. Flinging his eyes open, he exploded from the heavy comforter and nearly tripped over a pile of laundry in the darkness before ripping open the bedroom door. Ping-ponging off the hallway walls as he careened towards the kitchen, the Boy could hardly contain his excitement.

At the table sat a fantastic heap of scrambled eggs mixed with a variety of crunchy green and orange peppers, extra firm tofu, and raw red onion. Strips of toasted maple tempeh were meticulously balancing off to the side. His Father wore his mother's cooking apron and did a small jig at the stove, spinning and bowing greatly towards the Boy in a grandiose 'good morning' gesture. The Boy laughed and returned the bow before scrapping a shaky folding chair across the kitchen floor in anxious anticipation of his favorite meal. Removing a small stack of oiled toast from the oven, his Father sat alongside the Boy and rubbed his hands together vigorously before snatching up some utensils - he was just as excited as his son.

"Let's eat!" his Father mouthed. The Boy could have sworn he heard a faint voice behind those silent lips, but he couldn't be certain. After several mouthfuls of glorious eggs and sourdough, the Boy began to glance continuously towards his parents' bedroom.

"Mom?" he asked, eyebrows raised. How could she miss a meal like this, he wondered - it must have cost them a considerable amount, for fresh eggs and vegetables were inhumanely more expensive here in the city.

"At work!" his Father enthusiastically and dramatically lipped, knife and fork raised to the ceiling overhead. "Got the job!" he finished. The Boy blinked and stared at his Father. Had he forgotten what she had been interviewing for? No - he had never really been told. Should he have asked? He had thought it too sensitive a question. Perhaps she had been promoted to a manager at the restaurant? Whatever it was, his Father was definitely celebrating this morning, and the Boy had no intention of spoiling the festivities. He would keep his mouth shut, he decided. Chewing a final bite of peppered tofu, he set his utensils down, climbed off the rickety chair, and hugged his Father as hard as he could manage. Wrapping a thick and sinued arm around the Boy's small frame, his Father smiled... and ever so softly… sighed aloud.

"Your voice!" the Boy exclaimed, "I heard it!" Locking eyes with his Father, the Boy felt a hot tear slide into the sides of his eyes.

"Go get your stuff" his Father mouthed. "I'll be dropping you off at school."

~~~

Mist floated in and out of city blocks, as sunlight dribbled through alleyways, randomly illuminating garbage dumpsters and fire hydrants and parked cars in no particular worry or care. The station wagon coughed and sputtered onto the uneven city side-street and lurched down its familiar route towards the Boy's school. His Father examined the Boy with a half-glance and furrowed his brow quizzically.

"Yellow hat?" he inquired. "Green flannel?" he spoke silently. The Boy noticed a twitch at the side of his Father's mouth - he was clearly trying to suppress a grin, and doing a very poor job of it. Self-conscious, the Boy placed a hand over the front of his old, frayed, gray sweatshirt, thumbing the slightly peeling iron-on logo that proclaimed "National Parks Are For Lovers" with a silhouette of a giant Sequoia, a sandstone arch, a Joshua tree, and a massive half-dome of granite. Having known one or likely both of his parents would be wondering what had happened to his new clothes and backpack, the Boy had prepared a speech, of sorts - a great, long-winded explanation and saga about how these items had been compromised, donated, exchanged or stolen. In the heat of the moment, though, none of these false statements made any sense. He stared out the passenger window and simply shrugged. If his Father could see his face, he would see a poorly hidden grin of his own, attempting to wriggle free.

The Boy looked down at his feet at the paper grocery bag full of heavy textbooks, haphazardly arranged folders of completed homework, and grungy crinkled lunch bag, thankful that his Father appeared to have ended the unusually brief interrogation. The Boy knew his Father
~~~

suspected some sort of shenanigans had occurred yesterday, but could he possibly also know of the Mission - *his* mission? He decided not to overthink it. Pulling into the school rotunda, the station wagon came to an abrupt halt, jerking and jostling both passengers violently from side to side, sending up a wave of laughter from the two. As he opened the creaky car door, the Boy turned his head and nodded a 'good-bye' towards the driver.

"See you soon!" his Father mutely proclaimed, a sparkle in his winking eye. The Boy stared back as the car sped away. His Father had never picked him up from school before - did he mean 'soon' as in his Mother would still be at work? 'Soon' as in dinnertime? 'Soon' meant an impossible number of things at that moment. As he walked down the hallway to Room 105, the Boy decided that he had a few questions to clarify with his parents that evening.

~~~

A furious chaotic ringing of the first period bell signaled a review of last week's algebra lesson, a pop-quiz, and doling out of fifty problems as homework. As the rest of the class recorded the assignment into their planners, the Boy glanced over half of the night's work, immediately surmising the answer in his head without a moment's hesitation. He would still do the mindless work, he decided, for this was the game he must play - after all, he had made a promise.

As the start of his second period literature class began, a wadded up piece of notebook paper smacked him in the right shoulder and fell into his grocery bag full of folders - the third one that morning. Sighing deeply, he opted to leave it be, for he knew its message already. For what could it possibly contribute to the prior messages of "Nice backpack loser" or "Where did you get that dirty sweatshirt, a dumpster?" Biting his lip, he closed his eyes and allowed the faint sound of a saxophone to drift through his mind. Lunchtime couldn't come soon enough.

"Page 985, everyone," announced the nasally voice of his Teacher, who must have had a case of sinus congestion that morning. Flipping through the massive textbook to the appropriate page, the Boy suddenly stopped as a great squirrelly clattering squeaked from beneath the classroom's door. As the door crept open, a pair of pointed pleather shoes emerged into the fluorescent colorless light, followed by a well-groomed hefty beard that seemed to probe the air before allowing the thin face to
~~~

enter. The Principal's mighty grin stared straight at the Boy, orange glowing eyes haunting and yet inviting.

"Hello everyone, I'm so sorry to interrupt," began the Principal, "but I'd like to have a word with one of our students," he finished with unusual excitement. An upturned palm extended into the classroom and beckoned the Boy, as thirty pairs of narrowed judgmental eyes silently snickered at the strange situation affecting their favorite target of jealous bullying. Rising from his plastic chair, the Boy casually picked up his paper sack of books and strode to the front of the room, placing the wads of paper insults on his Teacher's desk before exiting through the classroom door, his face an expressionless gray mask of apathy. Just another day at school, he decided, following the Principal back to his office. Perhaps he would finally be expelled, he thought.

<p style="text-align:center">~~~</p>

Whistling while he waltzed down the polished empty school hallway, the Principal seemed to be in an exceptionally good mood for whatever terrible news he was about to deliver, thought the Boy. Perhaps he was daydreaming of not having to worry about students sneaking out of the building to interact with the homeless, or feed nuts to crows, or empty their dirty socks onto the asphalt. Or maybe he was exhausted from dealing with his teachers, proclaiming that the Boy never did his homework, but knew all the answers.

"He must be cheating," he had overheard one instructor say to the other at recess a few days prior. Strange how they always suspected the worst from him, even when he was now actually committed to completing the useless assignments. Perfect scores could only mean one thing - he was no good. A hand gripped his shoulder and jerked him from his doldrum thoughts.

"No need to be so dreary, my Boy!" chirped the Principal. "I've got some news for you that I think will turn that frown upside down," he finished with a wink, holding the door ajar for the Boy to proceed into the Secretary's waiting room. Taking a breath, the Boy stepped towards the massive set of wooden doors and paused, glancing at the Secretary. She peered back at him over the rim of her lime green rimmed glasses, her hair recently dyed a similar hue. Smacking away at a piece of gum, she blew a baseball-sized bubble that unexpectedly exploded upon its recall, splattering her nose and chin with chunks of pink goo. Stifling a sudden burst of laughter, the Boy was surprised to see that the Secretary laughed along with him, pulling the glop from her face in small pieces.

"Guess you can't help but laugh at the sticky situations," remarked the Principal, who chuckled at his own corny pun. The Secretary and the Boy simultaneously nodded, unsure of who the comment was directed at. Pushing the creaking mahogany doors aside, the pointy-shoed bearded man led the Boy inside and beckoned him to the chair in front of his desk. Across its impressive surface stood a newly arranged series of miniature figurines, half-robot, half-machine.

"Some of my son's favorites," the Principal explained, obviously aware of the Boy's stare. "Camouflaged and hidden in plain site as normal everyday cars, trucks, planes, or bulldozers, they are all secretly robots ready to transform to save the world at a moment's notice," he continued, picking up a semi-truck that held an oversized sword over its head. "My son always loved to imagine that everything around him could transformer like that. Anything - even a human - was ready to change into its proper form to do good." Sighing as he collapsed into his dusty armchair, the Principal replaced the semi-truck robot and locked eyes with the Boy for several breaths. The mellow bassy strum of a cello reverberated through the room as a smooth and gentle purple wave cradled the Boy's consciousness like an otter adrift in a tide pool. He thought about the Ghost. He smiled. Kicking his feet up onto the desk, a finger and thumb stroking his beard into a fine point, the Principal seemed to be nodding along to the same rhythm of the cello, before drawing in a great breath.

"I think you are actually one of them - a transformer," the Principal said softly, caringly. The Boy blinked, his brow raised slightly in confusion as he examined his hands and feet - definitely still flesh and bone, he hoped. Chuckling in his chair, the Principal slapped his desk in amusement. "Ha! No, no, you're not a robot... but you are a transformer, son." Rising from his desk, the Principal slowly approached the Boy and knelt alongside his chair.

"I realized it over the weekend: you are camouflaged here, at this particular school, as an ordinary boy. You try to go about the normal routine: finish homework, ace quizzes, take notes, march to the beat of the bell. But that's not who you really are, is it?" The Boy blinked. A soft, relaxed piano melody had joint the cello in the background of his mind. The Principal continued.

"No... deep down, you are something else entirely, aren't you? You can feel it. When someone needs a hand, you're there - you *transform* into the *real* you. And I've come to understand something," he said, eyes wide, head tilted forward, a hand on the Boy's shoulder, "that *real* you - that *transformed* you - it might not be so good at trying to hide and blend in to life here at this school, but it sure is amazing at bringing about kindness and hope in the world outside of here." The Principal stood and clutched a small airplane. Slowly, he manipulated it into a robot that carried a shield.

"The *transformed* you - that's the you I, and so many others, want to live and thrive at all hours of the day. No need to camouflage anymore, son." The Principal finished, handing the Boy the transformed toy. Looking up at the man, the Boy allowed a humble smile - he was not used to being complimented like this. The Principal nodded, his eyes drifting to the set of heavy doors. Following his gaze, the Boy suddenly became aware of a faint red-blue-red-blue pulsating glow that seemed to be emanating from the door's frame. Flinging open the doors, the Principal stood aside to allow the familiar figure of an ancient friend to fill the space.

"Hey-ya, kiddo!" bellowed the Captain, jaunting across the creaky floorboards and plucking the Boy from his seat in a single great motion, swallowing him in a ferociously friendly bearhug.

"Cap. I. Can't. Breath," choked the Boy, squeezing the man's muscular shoulders in both appreciation and frantic plea for release. The Captain laughed heartily and set the wrinkled Boy back into his chair.

"My boy, I gotta hand it to ya - you changed me. Transformed me, even!" exclaimed the Box Man, the Captain, the Welder, the friend. "'Showed me the light,' or so they say, ha!" Opening his jacket, he removed a greasy, oil-stained envelope and placed it on the Boy's lap.

"What's this?" asked the Boy, hesitant to open the letter.

"Heard through the grapevine from your Pops about this particular place you were tryin'a get to - a 'Forest School' or somethin' to that nature." The Boy heart began to rapidly accelerate, his vision tunneling and his palms trembling. An easy-going trumpet had formed a trio with the piano and cello, swirling jazz measures around the Principal's office. Swallowing his adrenaline, he blinked and nodded back in silence.

"Well, me and the guys at the docks decided to pay our respects, in whatever little way we could," he began. "Everyone's a little happier without all the rats around, anyway! So we worked a some extra overtime - few hours here and there this week. Cat Lady even pitched in - put on a 'Cat Talent Show' after work one evening - we all chipped in a bit for that - an 'admission fee,' so to speak.Cats jumpin' through hoops and over rafters and catching little fake mice and the like - sort of weird, but fun to watch!"

continued the Captain, twirling and spinning through the room like some great drunken tiger bobbing and weaving around invisible poles and hoops. The Boy hoped they could have another talent show - it seemed like something the Girl would dream about.

"Anyway! From all of us down there at the dock - we'd like to give you that there lil' 'donation' towards your tuition. Cheers pal!" he finished, tussling the Boy's hair. Peeking inside the envelope, the Boy saw a thick stack of money - perhaps in the hundreds of dollars. Tears welling in his eyes, his cheeks growing flushed, the Boy raced from the chair and hugged the Captain mightily.

"I've got something for you, as well, Transformer," announced the Principal, his pointed shoes squeaking across the room to his desk. The sound of a small steel key unlocking a small wooden drawer, a shuffling of papers, the sliding friction of a thin, crisp manilla folder being removed from its confines and pushed silently across the desk - the sounds lingered and lasted a lifetime as the Boy patiently sat glued to his seat. "For you," encouraged the Principal. The opened the perfectly rectangular file to reveal a single piece of paper decorated in excessive cursive declarations across its top half. Holding it against his chest, the Boy could not bare to read it. The Principal drew in a breath.

"I had a small dinner party at my home the other night," he began, "told my friends about a certain, exceptional boy, in need of being set free. One of my guests is a physician at the hospital - a burn specialist. He remember you immediately." Silent elevator rides, squeaking, polished sterile floors, tubes, lights, bleeps and blips and bandages - the images raced across the Boy's memories as he relived the last several months in the span of several seconds. Nearly too much for his mind to contemplate, he began to feel mildly nauseated. The Principal continued.

"This doctor said, 'I'll match anything you all come up with this evening.' And just like that, we collected enough for six month's tuition at The Forest School." Turning the piece of heavy-weighted paper around, the Boy could see it was, in fact, a check - its line of repeating zeros making him woozy. His breaths came shallow and fierce now - was this really happening?

"There's more, son," whispered the Principal. "This doctor told the burn unit about your situation, and one particular staff member - an Art Therapist, I believe - was adamant that you receive this." Handing the Boy a small black card, the Principal returned to his chair and smiled at the Captain. Flipping the card over to its front, the Boy immediately recognized a spiral of flaming brilliant color burning brightly in the center. A soft familiar song - a humming - echoed from inside the card and crept into his fingers, through his nerves and into his mind. Opening the card, he did not need to read its contents, for the words poured into his ears as a roaring whisper:

"Choose Happiness," they read, as a folded check floated out and perched atop his shoes. The echoing staccato of a bongo solo interlaced with the jazz trio playing in perfect time. As he bent over to retrieve the paper, a creak-creak-creak of well-worn rain-soaked leather-on-leather reverberated from the Secretary's room. A subtle sweet-tobacco odor tickled his nostrils as a smokey voice called from the doorway.

"Hey kid," The Scavenger. "How've you been?" she asked, pulling out a half-smoked cigarette from a tasseled chest pocket.

"Ma'am," warned the Principal, curtly yet sternly.

"Alright, alright, pal, no worries," she apologized, stuffing the butt behind her right ear, wiping her runny nose on her sleeve.

"Hey, I-I'll smoke that with ya outside on our w-way out?" the Captain stammered, not one to typically stutter. The Boy couldn't help but acknowledge how enamored the Captain was in that moment - bulging eyes and boyish grin barely contained. The Scavenger nodded and smiled back. The Boy was certain they recognized each other…

"Listen Kid: my old friend told me you were in a pinch," started the Scavenger. "You know her - rescues cats and the like." The Captain and the Boy stared at each other and silently shared a laugh. The Scavenger looked at both slightly suspiciously, but continued. "She told me you had sort of had a hand in getting her a place at the dock to work. Says you even came to visit up at the Mission. Gave her kid the clothes off your own back. That true? That's something, man," she smirked. The Boy thought of the ice-gray eyed Astronaut. Had he started school today? He hoped so.

"Her kid's a special kid, too. Like you." The Scavenger reflected aloud. "No surprise he ended up with that creature I gave you," she finished, tobacco-stained teeth fully revealed behind sun-dried lips. The Schwark. Flipping through the chapters of his life, the Boy was riding to the bottom of the sea, floating through empty space, connecting to worlds and spaces and times near and far and everywhere in between. The Schwark.

"The Schwark" he barely spoke.

"The, sch-what?" replied the Scavenger.

"The Schwark," he said loudly and confidently, now standing in the center of the Principal's office. "The creature that you gave to me. I don't know how to explain it, but it changed me. It... transformed me. Thank you." The Scavenger nodded.

"Of course, kid. Of course." She casually creaked over to the Boy. "I've got something else here for you - for your next adventure, you might say." From an inside pocket, she withdrew a rubber-banded wad of bills and slapped them into the Boy's hand. "Sold some trinkets. Thought I'd make a donation to your cause. 'Good karma,' you know," she explained. Turning to walk back out the door, the Scavenger suddenly spun on her heels and quickly returned to the motionless Boy. Plunging her hand into a back pocket, she removed an item that gave off an intense purple glow.

"Oh, almost forgot!" she began. "I happened to come across this little something at a resale shop a few hundred miles south of here, out in the middle of nowhere. My kind of place. Well, I recognized this thing immediately." she opened her hand. Exploding into a brilliant, blinding purple-white radiance, the Boy felt his heart fill with immediate warmth and sense of home. The necklace - his Mother's necklace.

"Maybe surprise her some day," winked the Scavenger. The Boy had no time to express his gratitude, as she was already striding out of the room, a cigarette in between her fingers and a smile aimed at the love-struck Captain who stumbled and nearly tripped as he floated on after her. The Principal cleared his throat and brought the Boy's focus back into the present.

"So do we have enough, Transformer?" Pulling up a chair next to the Boy, the two began to add up the sum-total of his donations. Sitting back with a satisfied sigh, the Principal nodded and squeezed the Boy's shoulder. "That'll do for the next year, at least, son!" announced the Principal, releasing a long satisfied breath. The Boy was beside himself, for the tidal wave of emotions was approaching near-drowning levels. Ecstasy, joy, gratitude, love, happiness flooded his mind. The Forest School! So many mystical and fantastical thoughts and dreams had been born and recirculated with the concept of such a school - out in the wilderness! He knew he should have felt supreme, unrivaled happiness. Instead, his skeptical mind had risen and separated from his optimistic heart, creating a rift through his soul that left him equal parts worried and distraught. For above this sea of new fantastic feelings floated a white-cap of crushing anxiety: one year. He had enough funding for one year... and then what?

"How... how long is Forest School?" he asked the Principal timidly, eyes fixated to the floor, terrified of the answer he had already surmised. The Principal did not speak for several moments. He clearly sensed the Boy's apprehension and fear: to start another school only to be ripped away after a year. Surely his parents would not be able to afford it, and he would never dare burden them with such a request.

"It's three years long, son. Three years," answered the Principal finally. Biting his bearded lip, he tipped the Boy's chin up to meet his eyes - they were sparkling with a cryptic energy, a secret not yet revealed. Had he expected the Boy's question? In almost perfect concert, the Principal spoke.

"There is one more guest for us this afternoon," he smiled, breaking his gaze with the Boy to call towards the Secretary's waiting room. "Come on in, Father!" the Principal beckoned. As the Boy spun in his seat, a tendril of pachouli dribbled in through the doorway accompanied by the distant vibration of a clarinet warming itself with a fluttery C-scale. A neatly groomed crop of dreadlocks poked through the door, illuminated by a set of perfectly pearly-white teeth that grinned like a cheshire cat at the Boy. The Chaplain.

"Well hello! Howdy! Good day! What's up! How are my good friends?" Trouncing into the room decked out in an expertly starched dark blue three-piece suit accented along the cuffs and inseams with inch-wide rainbow trim came the Chaplain, his hands outstretched, a deep, beautiful chuckle rumbling from his chest. In his right hand, he carried an intricately carved cane made up of interwoven, curving and interlaced pieces of wood that gave it the appearance of tree roots, or a double helix, or a bed of capillaries. Leaning against the Principal's desk, the Chaplain began to rotate the cane around his index finger in perfect ringmaster fashion as he stared at the Boy and grinned. As the Chaplain blinked between the revolutions of the cane, the Boy could have sworn he saw his eyes rapidly alternate colors; their normal deep hazy blue suddenly flickering into the candlelight yellow of a fox, with black vertical slits for pupils. Suddenly, Father Rainbow closed his eyes and simultaneously caught the spinning cane with his left hand, rapping it into the floorboards with a satisfying thud.

"I believe congratulations are in order!" began the Chaplain. "The Forest School - a wonderful place, for wondrous people! You deserve it, my friend. You deserve it!" Leaping from his stance against the desk, the man took a step and sank to a knee in front of the Boy, the pachouli filling the small space between them with an intoxicating aura of relaxed comfort and mysterious hope. Gingerly extending the wooden cane towards the Boy, the Chaplain's face grew somber and quiet, his voice dropping to a whisper.

"Look carefully, my boy… what is it that you see?" hushed the man, as he pushed the fantastically decorated cane closer towards the Boy. Squinting his eyes, the Boy realized that the cane was not merely a single piece of wood, but several. At least ten strands of slightly different grains, colors, striations, and thicknesses. An amalgamation of fir and pine and oak and maple and elm and many others. As the Chaplain slowly rotated the cane on its long axis, the Boy suddenly saw that a twine of darkly stained cedar had a small message etched into it.

"Together, we are One," the Boy softly spoke. Immediately, the words began to glow a burning sunset orange, an intense but pleasant warmth quickly folding over the Boy's face. As Father Rainbow continued to gently spin the staff, the Boy recognized several other carvings and whittled words, each on a different type of wood, each about the same length, but all in different languages. The Chaplain began to whisper them off, one by one.

"Juntos somos uno," erupted in fluorescent Spanish green.

"Razem jesteśmy jednym," glowed a perfect bright Polish red.

"Ensemble nous sommes un," pulsed in brilliant French blue.

"Zusammen sind wir Eins," breathed a fiery German yellow. The Chaplain's smile grew ear-to-ear as he spun the cane upon the final engraving.

"And how we say where I am from," he started, eyes wide, "Ansanm, nou se youn!" The words exploded into a visual smorgasbord of every hue and shade and color - a terrific Haitian-Creole rainbow. The Chaplain locked eyes with the Boy over the spectral lights enveloping their two figures.

"Place your hand here, Boy… what is it you feel?" beckoned the man, shifting his hands apart to make room for a single fist in the center of the staff. Without hesitation, the Boy slowly extended his palm towards the interwoven wood, his flesh parting the softly glimmering beams of light still flowing from the engraved words. As his hand inched closer, he could suddenly sense a pulling - a magnetic, anticipatory calling to his deeper self that seemed to echo from somewhere beyond the cane, the Chaplain, the Principal's room, and in fact, the world. Grasping the staff, the boy felt a massive tidal wave crash down upon him as his world went completely dark.

~~~

"Open your eyes, Boy," the soothing, familiar voice called. "It's your turn, anyway." A clarinet solo hopped and skipped over the spicy notes of patchouli aroma. Confused and disoriented, the Boy fluttered open his eyelids, only to be met by the candlelight eyes of the Fox starring over a pawful of cards.

"I remember this place," the Boy recalled, as a small translucent yellow butterfly landed on the edge of free-floating card table.

"'Déjà vu,' you might say!" replied the Fox. "Although there is a good reason for that feeling, as you know." He squinted at the Fox, who seemed to be hiding a sly grin. "You're Father Rainbow?" he asked in knowing disbelief. The Fox snorted a quick laugh. "Oh, I'm many things, my Boy! Many things, in many places. But you already know those things, don't you?" The Boy supposed he, in fact, did. Suddenly, a bristling of soft fur brushed against his shins. A soft purring reverberated up from underneath the card table. Peering between his knees, the Boy was met by two perfect yellow orbs.

"Meow?" He knew this cat, its perfect black coat, it's endlessly inquisitive nature. Smiling at the little beast, the Boy invited the feline onto his lap. In a single silent hop, the cat pounced upon his shoulder and began to nuzzle his cheeks.

"Grandma, you sneak!" giggled the Boy as the cat leaped onto the table, disturbing a few cards with a quick swish of its tail.

"Ah, my good friend," said the Fox, its wiry eyebrow raised. Grandma fearlessly stretched out in front of the Fox as he scratched between her eyes with a single claw. The Boy gasped.

"You know Grandma?" hey blurted incredulously. The Fox smirked.

"Of course - she's my sister," the Fox casually replied. "When we lived on the island together - my original home - she was a priestess, a real queen."

"I think she still is?" the Boy cautiously replied. The Fox laughed. Grandma purred loudly.

"She is a seamstress now," continued the Fox. "Sometimes, she will still make a blessing on one of her works." He stopped scratching. The two furry siblings turned in unison to look at the Boy. "I believe - if I'm
~~~

not mistaken - she's even made *you* a blessing." His mind racing through the past, the massive black tornado, the Scavenger, the paper bag...

"The... Schwark?" whispered the Boy. He could have sworn Grandma smiled at him in that moment. A flurry of a distant saxophone dribbled overhead - just a few ephemeral notes before vanishing.

"You call it what you call it, Boy," shrugged the Fox. "It goes by infinite names, by infinite people, from as far back and far forward as you could possibly imagine." Completely entranced by this new knowledge, it took all the energy the Boy could muster to simply just breath. To be part of something so big, so beyond himself, so... connected.

"I've been watching you," started the Fox, laying down his hand of cards, "from the beginning, to the end, back to the beginning again. In this place, and in that place." he continued in typical cryptic fashion. "Tell me, Boy. The people you have met. How do they make you feel?" inquired the Fox, cocking its furry ears forward, the clarinet holding a long, deep chord that vibrated the soft haze around them. Laying down his own hand, the Boy swallowed and thought about the faces of his friends: The Girl. The Astronaut. The Ghost. The Captain. The Cat Lady. The Scavenger. The Art Therapist. The Principal. The Chaplain. His Mother. His Father. The Schwark.

"Happy," the Boy answered, taking a breath. The Fox did not blink, anticipating more.

"Loved," he continued, closing his eyes. The Chaplain grinned - awaiting another answer.

"Connected," finished the Boy, releasing a great sigh. Grandma began to purr.

"Yes," replied the Fox - Father Rainbow - with an elegant whisper. "You feel it now - that energy, that indescribable thing that surrounds us all. The Great Connection." The two card players stared at each other, unblinking. Smiles slowly cracking across each of their faces, they spoke their shared thoughts in synchrony:

"Together, We are One" the spirits sounded together. The butterfly on the edge of the table began to flap its fragile wings, luminescing a great furious light. Grandma lazily swatted at the creature, prompting it to take flight. As it floated higher and higher above the table, a warm darkness soaked in around the Boy. When the last drop of color vanished from his vision, he allowed his eyes to close. Content. Connected.

~~~
~~~

Releasing the cane, the Boy collapsed back into the chair at the center of the Principal's room. A small plume of royal blue smoke puffed from the staff and sank to the floor as the clarinet's sultry hum slowly faded into the distance.

"Connected," the Boy repeated, his smile drifting between the Chaplain and the Principal. "That is what I feel." Standing tall, tossing the wooden cane up onto his shoulder, Father Rainbow changed tones, back into his typical chirpy self.

"Excellent! Yes! What a *connected* world it is, eh?" he repeated, head bobbing side to side. "In fact, you probably wouldn't even be surprised if I told you that my good, gracious cousin is the director of that Forest School!" His widened eyes rolled from the ceiling back down to the Boy in dramatic expression. Sitting rigid now, the Boy invoked every conscious effort not to show his hand and reveal his shock, but it was clearly too late.

"Ha! Yes, to answer your question!" clapped the Chaplain. "Of course I spoke to him about you. And the lovely things you've been up to, the terrific adventures you've been on, and the beautiful people you've befriended - who are, of course, my friends, too." he continued, winking at the Principal.

"I told him he absolutely, positively, one-hundred-percently has to have a student like you at the Forest School, and he absolutely, positively, one-hundred-percently agreed!" said Father Rainbow, slowly sliding a hand into a suit vest pocket. With great flare, he suddenly flicked his wrist, sending none other than a rainbow-colored envelope whizzing through the air, expertly landing on the Boy's lap.

"Read it!" encouraged the Chaplain. With trembling hands, the Boy unfastened the back of the perfectly crisp envelop and removed a small piece of coniferous bark, its sharp ridges and scales still fresh on the outer side. Turning it over to the smooth, waxy inner surface, the Boy saw a small message scrawled in shimmering silver ink:

To a very special spirit,
Welcome!
- The Director

PS - Your last two years are on us.

As fresh hot tears rolled down his cheeks, the Boy looked at the grinning faces of his friends and began to laugh - a laugh of every feeling, of every memory, of every dream. He laughed because he was happy, and he laughed because he was loved. But most of all, he laughed because he was connected.

~~~

Floating out of the Principal's office, the Boy must have worn the biggest smile of his life, for the Secretary could barely contain her giggling between mouthfuls of bubble gum. Gazing down the hallway of the school - his old school - the Boy paused and scratched his head. Was there a point to returning to class? Suddenly the entire building, its walls, its lights, its lockers, everything - seemed incredibly foreign to him. Sensing this development, the Principal placed a gentle hand on his shoulder and chuckled.

"No need to head back that way, my friend. Why don't you take the rest of the day off? Tomorrow's going to be a big one." he finished with a wink. A wave of relief washed over the Boy, but what exactly did the Principal mean, 'Take the day off?' Again, the universe seemed to read his mind as the answer approached him from the school's massive front doors. A hazy orange aura encircled the approaching figure, quiet ascending arpeggios of piano trickling in from all sides. His Mother.

"Mom!" the Boy exulted, as he sprinted into her open arms, squeezing her as tightly as her could. She smelled of lavender and dirt and car exhaust and he loved it. Holding him by the arms, she stared into his eyes, her own filling with tears of joy. She knew.

"My son," she whispered, "what a tremendous gift you have been given today." Wiping the rivulets of jubilation from the Boy's face, she stood and nodded to his Principal. Placing a hand on his shoulder, his Mother continued.

"You have made some truly incredible friends," she spoke, "and now you have this new journey to begin. I am so very proud of the Boy - the Spirit - you have become." Hugging her once more as mightily as he dared, the Boy sensed her stoic energy flowing and cradling his own, in constant support, forever nurturing, forever connected. As the two turned, hand-in-hand, and proceeded to take their final walk through the school's doors, the Boy suddenly stopped, his eyes wide, his breath held, his heart stopped, time itself on pause. He had nearly forgotten.
~~~

"I… I have one more thing I have to do!" he declared, pivoting and leaping across the waxed tiled floor. The Principal and his Mother looked at each other quizzically, brows raised, knowing smirks subtly growing - they simply watched as the Boy raced down the empty hallway with reckless abandon. Past the Principal's office. Past Room 101. Past Room 102. Stopping abruptly, nearly falling over, his shoes squeaking in protest - Room 103.

Too short to spy through the door's high window, and too desperate to wait for the end of the period, the Boy grasped the cold steel door handle and froze. Thoughts racing, words tumbling over themselves in frantic, crazed chaos. *How* would he tell her? *What*, exactly, would he tell her? His dream had come true, and all he could feel in this moment was the deepest despair and loss. His best friend - he would be leaving her tomorrow in this… non-school. His friendship forever altered… but never over, he decided. Expelling all of his anxiety away with a great breath, the Boy closed his eyes and focused. He knew he would always carry a part of the Girl with him - wherever he went.

"Thank you," he whispered to himself, for that is exactly what he needed to say to her. That was the most important thing he could ever say, perhaps to anyone. He opened his eyes. As he flung the heavy door to the side, the Boy stood motionless as it crashed into its stopper below. Thirty pairs of wide, white eyes and open, shocked mouths greeted him, as expected. Sixth row back, two seats from the wall. Her chair.

It was empty.

The Schwark

Riding side by side, the open ocean breeze steady on their faces, the Boy and the Astronaut silently swayed to the rhythmic strokes of the Schwark as the great beast paddled confidently forward into the twilight horizon. As the fiery sun dipped a hesitant toe into the infinite purple ocean, the jazzy saxophone riffs rippling out from all directions intensified. The Schwark responded in kind by pulsing a burning orange hue from its luminescent blowhole. Its passengers smiled a great contentedness - this was the journey that could last forever, they had both decided. The Astronaut was the first to finally break the silence.

"Schwark! Where are we off to next? What's our next adventure?" the ice-gray eyed boy hollered into the pointed fox ears.

"Well, buddy, where would you guys like to go? What is it that you feel you have not seen yet?" replied the creature, playfully splashing a few accompanying dolphins with its great furry flipper. The Astronaut considered the question for a few moments, glancing at the Boy for any suggestions. The Boy simply returned a smile and shrugged - he understood now, that it was the journey and not the destination that mattered. This was not something he could casually say to the Astronaut, though - some lessons are best learned on one's own, the Boy decided.

"I... I want to see the world, Schwark," exclaimed the Astronaut. "The whole world! No leaf unturned, no rock unearthed!" he finished. For several unspoken seconds, the Schwark seemed not to respond at all - just the steady up-down-up-down as it beat its muscular tail through the small white caps far below. And then... the world dissolved.

Beginning as a soft, ticklish static under their legs and feet, the Schwark's skin began to rapidly vibrate and melt, spreading out across the sea - trillions upon trillions of fine gray particles replacing the water molecules of the ocean. A bed of pint-sized prickly hairs rising and spreading as far as their eyes could see, a meadow of alien grass waving back and forth with the unrelenting breeze. Suddenly, groves of massive, brick-red, wiry-haired stalagmites began erupting haphazardly around the gray landscape, rising twenty, thirty, forty feet high - a forest of fox ears, each occasionally wriggling and squirming from invisible itches. The Boy and the Astronaut watched, mouths gaping, as the dark blue sky above ignited into a brilliant spectrum of rainbow, spanning from horizon to horizon - no moon, no sun, just pure and radiant color. Slowly, the technicolor sky began to spin clockwise. A saxophone solo floated its notes across a gust of wind. Looking at each other in disbelief, the two passengers were suddenly knocked to the floor of stubby gray grass as the entire world seemed to take a monstrous inhalation, ear-trees rising into the swirling colored sky above. Standing cautiously, the two collapsed back on top of each other as their new foreign planet rumbled and exhaled and sank beneath their feet - the universe was breathing. From all around them came the booming familiar voice.

"Well, fellas! Here ya go! The *entire* world!" announced the Schwark, from everywhere and nowhere. The sky began to pulse and swirl more intensely, its vertiginous revolutions making the Boy dizzy.

"Schwark?" replied the two simultaneously.

"You... *are* the world?" asked the Astronaut in astonished, confused disbelief. Minor earthquakes shook the ground in quick succession, as a guttural deep chuckle reverberated through the air and rattled the boys' teeth in their skulls.

"Ha! Oh! Me? The *world*?" replied the Schwark, "Well, I guess I am now! But now that I think about, I always was! I am the world, and the world is me! And so are you! Catch my drift?" the creature finished. The Boy could not see its eyes, but he knew one of them was winking at him in that moment.

"Schwark riddles!" murmured the Astronaut to the Boy. "It really doesn't like straight-forward answers, does it?" The Boy grinned again - perhaps the Astronaut would need a few more adventures with the Schwark to understand. In seemingly silent response to the Astronaut's playful ribbing, a blindingly bright yellow beam illuminated upon the the Schwark-scape directly ahead of them, between a distant pair of fox ears. Shielding their eyes as the light dimmed, the two passengers softly gasped at the sudden appearance of a massive tree. Not just any tree - a walnut tree. This tree, wearing a coat of golden tapered leaves that shimmered and rustled in the wind like a high-hat cymbal, wielding limbs that extended and sagged with the weight of thousands of black walnuts, was the largest tree either boy had ever seen. On the highest branch of the walnut tree, a midnight-black bird flapped its wings and cawed mightily as it took flight, diving straight down towards the two onlookers.

"It's coming straight for us!" exclaimed the Astronaut, who anxiously looked at the stoic Boy for any hint of retreat. A reassuring hand rested upon the Astronaut's shoulder as the Boy's calm and confident eyes eased the other's worry. The great crow landed a few paces ahead and considered each of the two carefully with a sideways black eye.

"Ca-caw!" called the Runt, dipping its breast with every exclamation.

"Hello friend," replied the Boy, his voice soft as smoke. "It's good to see you again." The Runt cooed and clacked and stomped its tiny ragged feet into the grey ground. Slowly lowering to his knees, the Boy extended an upturned palm towards the bird and smiled.

"Caw?" replied the curious bird, as it awkwardly hopped and waddled towards the Boy. As it closed to within inches of the empty hand, the crow lowered its head and sat on its legs. Cautiously extending a finger, the Boy began to lovingly scratch the bird's neck. Ruffling its feathers and shivering to what the Boy suspected were goosebumps - maybe crow-bumps - the Runt pushed into the scratch and nuzzled the empty hand with its pointed black beak.

"It likes it," called the Astronaut in delight. The Boy smiled. Suddenly, the Runt backed away from the hand and bowed its head. In almost slow motion, it keeled to one side, laying on its wing. Heavy breaths ensued… a final great breath… its dark eyes closed. Sitting back onto his feet, the Boy dropped his hand and lowered his head. Anticipating crushing sadness and terrible grief, the Boy was surprised to find neither building in his chest. Instead a curious energy of hope began to brew and bubble forth from his heart.

"It... it died?" whimpered the Astronaut, clearly distraught. Diamond tears dripped from his ice-gray eyes and soaked a patch of Schwark grass beneath him. As he desperately searched the Boy's face for affirming clues and much-needed solace, the breeze turned warm and comforting, like an infinitely soft quilt being drawn up around the Astronaut.

"I don't think it's really died," answered the Boy, his conviction of the idea growing more confident by the second. "Well, maybe its body - *this* body, anyway - has died. But I don't think the crow is actually gone."

"You sound like the Schwark," responded the Astronaut, wiping the tears from his eyes on his flannel sleeve. No sooner had he finished his last sniffle, when the rainbow sky began to pinwheel and propeller into a steady blurred kaleidoscopic madness.

"Look!" cried the Astronaut, pointing to the figure of the deceased crow. Incredibly, the Runt's body began to rapidly decompose - feathers ripped away by the wind, skin worn thin and dry from the light above, organs shriveling and darkening, bones collapsing at the joints. Just as the fast-forwarded decay seemed to be complete, a rupture and fissure in the ground emerged. In seconds, a glowing purple mushroom stipe pushed up through the bird's carcass, burrowing directly into the cadaverous heart. Bursting forth from the rib cage, the grand pulsating cap twisted and opened its pink veil, casting an umbrellaed shadow over the crow. With every millimeter of fungal growth upwards and outwards, the remaining bird bones seemed to fracture and dissolve Entranced by the mushroom, the Boy realized he had seen this species only once before…

"The necklace," he whispered under his breath. Just as quickly as it had grown, the fungus suddenly twitched and sagged, darkening into a brown, slimy thing that draped over the side of the remaining flesh and bone. Immediately, a single-file line of black dots approached from the fissured Schwark-earth - ants. Encircling the mushroom, each tiny speck rose onto its back legs and dismembered a microscopic-sized chunk of the decay, returning to a small but rapidly enlarging anthill several feet away. When the entire mass of mushroom and crow was recycled, the ants amassed into a monstrous amorphous roaming black amoebae that wound its way towards the golden walnut tree in the distance.

Within seconds, the chaotic conglomerate of insects returned from the tree, carrying a single black walnut on their backs. Disappearing into their buggy abode with their grand prize, the ants grew silent as the Schwark-scape grew still. Then… a rumble… crack, a groan, a sudden star-bursting of the gray-haired ground that radiated in all directions from the anthill. As the hill suddenly collapsed into itself, a gigantic trunk erupted from its center, rocketing towards the rainbow ceiling. Branches birthed and budded, bifurcating rapidly into smaller and thinner limbs - a net of capillaries and neurons reaching out from their central vessel. Gargantuan roots wormed and rolled across the ground. Golden leaves flashed onto the blank wooden canvas as black orbs expanded and dangled in random fashion - walnuts.

"Up there!" exclaimed the Boy. Pointing to one of the higher, thicker limbs, the Boy held his amazement in his lungs as long as he dared, for there appeared to be a small nest spiraling into existence. And then, an egg. A second later, a tiny beak emerged from the top of the egg, which rapidly began to shatter and fall away in chunks, revealing a hatchling - a pink, naked, newborn crow. The boys silently observed as the hatchling rapidly grew into a nestling, puffy feathers sprouting from its pores. In a breath, the nestling became a fledgling. A final cautious step from the nest, one reckless terrifying leap, and what was once an awkward flailing creature plummeting to certain death, had instantly matured into the sleek, slate black arrow of a proud crow. Expertly swooping inches from the ground, quickly rising through the gaps in the yellow-leaved canopy, the bird silently landed on the highest branch and let out its call of the wild - its call to life.

"Ca-caw!" the Runt proclaimed, high and mighty and alive one more.

"Ca-caw!" screamed the Astronaut, his spirit soaring with amazement.

"Ca-caw!" echoed the Boy, his heart reverberating with a certain knowing. As the whirring sky slowed, time began to approach relative normalcy on the Schwark-scape. The Runt dropped from its perch and dove towards the boys. The Astronaut - any remaining anxious fears totally dissolved - laughed with delight. The Boy, a curious sense of déjà vu itching the back of his mind, raised his brow in suspicion. Hovering an inch above the ground, the crow's flapping wings began to beat in slow-motion as the rainbow pinwheel came to a near halt. As the bird's talon nestled in between miniature grey Schwark hairs, it suddenly froze. The sky stopped, the wind held its breath, the saxophone paused its rhythmic melody.

"What's happening?" whispered the Astronaut. In a great flash of light, the rainbow swirl overhead launched into a ferocious counter-clockwise motion, blurring all colors into a single bright pure whiteness. The frozen crow began to flap backwards, retreating rapidly back to its perch, down to its branch, and into its nest. Shrinking in size, the crow, now nestling, became enveloped by a reorganizing white shell. Soon, the egg vanished, as did the nest. Leaves and nuts shriveled back into their respective limbs, branches retracting back towards the central great trunk. In the span of several seconds, the massive walnut tree repackaged itself inside the small circular black nut. The anthill reformatted itself around its prize as roots retreated and cracked ground flattened. The two boys watched as the ants marched their nut back to the original golden tree far in the distance, only to return empty-handed to a growing heap of bones and fungal flesh. As the ants pieced the mushroom back together, it valiantly rose in defiance of the possible, a shimmering purple aura glowing brighter and brighter. A reconstructed ribcage and skull materialized at the base of the thick stipe. With veil closing, the mushroom quickly shrank back through the shriveled crow heart and retreated into the ground. Liver and kidneys and brain began to swell as cellular structures became bloated with water.

Vessels feeding organs and muscles.
Ligaments linking joints.
Skin enshrouding the body.
Heart pumping life.
Eyes opening mind.

"Ca-caw!" cooed the Runt. Fluorescing and pulsating in reds through violets, the sky calmed as the call of the saxophone floated on. The bird returned to its high perch atop the great walnut tree. The Astronaut smiled forwards at his friend. The Boy smiled backwards.

"Thank you, Schwark," quietly spoke the Astronaut into the sky. "I have seen the world, and now I understand." Instantly, the ground sighed as red-eared fox-trees retreated and were replaced by the fluid, rolling waves of the sea. Back atop the creature, the two boys rode on, a deep knowledge - a knowing - now shared between them forever.

~~~

The red wolf moon rose magnificently above the sea-sky boundary behind the two travelers, casting a hazy bon-fire-like glow across the waves. As he gazed into the distance, the Boy took note of the white water crashing and crescendoing against a dark pillar in the distance - the coast.

"Hey! Is that land?" exclaimed the Astronaut, who was now precariously standing on the back of Schwark, gripping the rough skin of the towering dorsal fin for balance. Reflecting in brilliant yellow, a soft strand of beach peeked through a low fog. Two great points flanked a natural bay that housed the beach, its waters calm and protected, with neat perfect rolling waves crashing gently across the sand. A delicate lacy waterfall trickled into a tidal pool on the left side of the beach; a fine, narrow trail leading into a stand of old-growth fir on the right.

"I know this place," recalled the Boy, his excitement growing exponentially. "I've been here before - so many times!" As the Schwark swam parallel to the coast, the Boy's eyes traced the forested path upwards until it disappeared. If this was truly where he thought he was, a light should be just visible... there! An almost imperceptible glow pulsed from a grove of slightly taller redwood deep on the rising hill behind the beach.

Without a word, and barely a breath, the Boy leapt off the back of the Schwark and crashed into the building swell below, the water's familiar coolness sparking a thousand memories. Furiously swimming towards the shore, he suddenly remembered the familiar sandbar that lie smack-dab in
~~~

the middle of the bay - it would produce a perfect leftward-breaking wave that he could ride into shore effortlessly. Looking over his shoulder, he saw the familiar rising wall of water quickly climb above his head. One stroke. Two strokes. A frantic kick of his legs. Caught in its immense power, the Boy toppled head over heels in the chaos, holding his breath as he somersaulted under the waves, his breath demanding escape. Upside-down or right-side-up, he swam toward the stars and gasped ferociously above the ebb of the swell. His Father's words spoke to him in that moment.

"You swim, or you dive, or you ride. That is all there is. Whether you are catching the power of a wave, or the power of life - they are the same," his Father had once explained to him on their first surf outing at the bay. Steeling his face, and clenching his jaw, the Boy paddled hard for the break. Too far on the inside of the wave - he was forced to duck-dive under its colossal force. Another wave - a frantic freestyle over the top, nearly dropping off the lip as the monstrous wave began to crest. A breath between the lulls. Focusing his intent, his spirit, his mind, the Boy stared at the horizon and saw the darkness approach. The gentle rippling of the surface gave way to a perfect swell, with the Boy in its prime breaking position. Closing his eyes, the Boy relied on the innate sensation of the water to guide his timing. A subtle rise in his abdomen, a sudden tipping point reached - he exploded forward in line with the swell, every aching ounce of muscle fiber engaged, his smile the only energy exceeding his strength. Extending his back, he allowed the wave to lift his body and spirit up above the water as he began to glide down the face on his chest, the ecstasy of catching his favorite wave holding him in the present. Misty saltwater spray congratulated him as the mighty wave barreled overhead. As he hydroplaned down the face of the mighty wave, time slowed as the Boy entered a perfect moment of peace. As he exited the barrel, the wall of water crashed unto itself, morphing from perfection to chaos once again. Into the whitewater the Boy spilled, head held under for a brief joyous second, forced to pay respects to the wild waters he so loved and cherished. As he waded ashore, panting and laughing and crying, he pulled himself to a stand and turned to face the moon.

Drifting a few yards out was the Schwark - it had followed him in, through the swell and the surf. As the wind settled, the waters calmed, and a deep baritone saxophone dripped from the sky. The huge, sharply shaped dorsal fin cut into the stars above as two wiry red fox ears laid submissively down to the sides. Furry flippers idled at rest, gently rippling the waist-high waters. Stepping back into the warm, still sea, the Boy slowly stepped towards the massive beast, its huge eyes staring down upon him. The Boy extended his arm, and rested his hand on the Schwark's soft nose, causing its whiskers to twitch. The bioluminescent blowhole glowed in steadily alternating colors, sharing its energy with the Boy through each pulse. Two spirits, intertwined through time, through space, through each other, through all others. Connected.

"Thank you, Schwark," whispered the Boy, finally removing his hand. To his great relief, he continued to feel the immense connection in his fingers, in his bones, in his mind, in his heart. No tears fell, for the Boy understood this was not the end - it was never 'the end.' It was simply a transformation. The happiness, the love, the connection that they shared - those things, that energy, would endear for eternity. Perhaps it always had, the Boy decided.

"Cowabunga," the Boy said softly to the rider atop the great Schwark. Gazing up at the Astronaut who sat motionless and pensive, the Boy saluted a farewell. After several moments, the ice-gray eyed boy bowed his head deeply towards the Boy, slowly raising his neck back up to reveal a gracious smile. The Boy closed his eyes and bowed in response, thankful for this friendship, content with this journey they shared together. By the time he opened his eyes, the Schwark and its rider had vanished back into the sea.

Walking along the yellow sand beach towards the ribbon of trail that wove into the midnight woods, the Boy heard the distant saxophone build in quick intensity, ripening for sweet release. Feeling the sudden urge to look out across the bay's white-capped horizon, he saw it: the silent massive silhouette of the Schwark, breaching up against the glowing backdrop of the blood red moon. A final blinding pulse of rainbow-colored light radiated across the beach, as the great creature splashed back into the sea and onto another time and place.

~~~

Navigating through the forest up alongside mighty fir and pointed sword-fern, the Boy realized he remembered every inch of this well-trodden dirt trail. He knew that around the next rightward bend, an ancient, huge shelf mushroom dwelt ten feet in the air upon a moss-laden cedar. He recalled that in half a mile, there would be a stream to his left where steelhead and chinook would begin their journey a thousand miles inland
~~~

to breed. But most importantly, he knew that at the end of the trail, lay a certain clearing.

As he climbed higher, he looked back - the bay was slowly emerging behind the lower canopy, the beach glimmering like stars amongst the Milky Way. He could have painted this view from memory, for this was the view he experienced nearly every morning before the Fire. He walked onwards. What would he find in the clearing? His heart quickened as he steeled his mind against every possibility.

A half mile to go. The salted sea breeze giving way to a sultry fireplace smoke that permeated and caressed the trunks of the fir trees around him.

A quarter mile left. A faint rhythmic creaking drifted in and out, sometimes muted by the dribbling of the adjacent stream or his own footsteps on freshly fallen leaves. It sounded like... swinging. No - tree-rubs, he decided, trying his best to quell the surge of adrenaline.

A hundred feet to the clearing. Faint laughter. A clinking of glass. Gentle sighs. Sprinting through the gap in the saplings, the Boy burst onto freshly cut grass, caught in the shadow of his old home.

"Hello there," called his Mother gently. "We've been waiting for you," she said, sipping a glass of wine on the porch swing, his Father's arm draped around her neck.

"Mom! Dad!" the Boy cried, leaping over the garden boxes, skipping up the front steps, and crashing into the awaiting arms of his parents.

"I knew it!" The Boy sobbed, face pressed into the shared crook formed by his parents adjoining shoulders. "I knew I would find you here!"

"Of course you did," spoke his Father. "We've never left. Neither have you." The Boy looked to each of his parents, their faces a beacon of perfect calmness and serenity, beaming constant guiding confidence into his soul. He could sense, though, that his own face still portrayed a feeling of great worry. His Mother wiped the tears from his cheeks and smoothed the wayward hairs behind his ears, her glowing orange aura of warmth and comfort blanketing the three figures in its love. She took a breath.

"Son, this place will always be here," she explained. "You. I. Your Father. Our home. This Forest. All of this will *always* exist - if you let it."

Let it exist.

In your mind.

In your heart.

In your spirit.

Of course - the Boy knew this all along, he decided.

"Well," started his Father with a slight grin, "Will you let it?" The Boy took a great breath in and gazed at his loving parents.

"We have always existed," he replied, "and we always will."

The Sequoia

Awakening to the gentle, effervescent pressure from her fingertips as they swiped back the sleepy hairs that dangled over his forehead, the Boy let out a satisfied yawn and smiled up at his Mother's sparkling eyes.

"I almost didn't want to wake you," she spoke softly, carefully removing the comforter back from his protesting shoulders. "You were in such a pleasant dream, weren't you?" His smile stretching wider, the Boy rubbed his eyelids and nodded.

"I was," he said, pausing to reflect on his mind's journey, recollecting his senses into the present, realizing how wonderful it was to be in that moment: to share a smile with his Mother, to hear his Father whistling in the kitchen, to smell the nutty, sweet odor of breakfast wafting through the apartment.

"I think I still am" he finished thoughtfully.

~~~

"Good morning, pal!" whispered his Father, his voice an excited hoarseness that nearly brought tears to the Boy's eyes. Today would likely be a day of many wonderful tears, he decided, as he took a seat at the beloved rickety, wobbly table beside his Mother.

"Eat up! Big Day!" his Father encouraged, scooping an enormous pile of chia seed pudding into the Boy's bowl. Roasted hazelnuts, sliced almonds, fresh marionberries, and crisp apple slices decorated the top of one of his favorite breakfasts - one he had not had in ages. Wandering back in time, he recalled mornings at their forest home that began this way: hearty breakfasts followed by a long day's work outside chopping wood, gathering berries, filling water basins, clearing paths, turning soil. The very notion that morning's before Forest School could potentially begin this way filled his heart with bursting joy.

"I have something for you," his Father announced between great mouthfuls of pudding. "Since you'll be outside all day now, I thought you could use a new coat," he winked, pointing over to the closet near their apartment's front door. Scrambling out of his seat, the Boy flew to the entryway and yanked the sliding doors of the closet nearly off their hinges. Next to his Father's bulky, oil-greased, tan-colored jacket hung a miniature version of the same. Ripping the coat from its hangers, the Boy swung the fleece-lined innards over his shoulders and buried his arms through the
~~~

immensely soft sleeves. Clapping her hands and giggling, his Mother stood to examine the Boy.

"You look just like your Father now!" she chirped.

"*Almost* like me," his Father clarified, jokingly, "just needs one more thing," he finished, reaching onto the top shelf of the closet to find a brand new burgundy beanie. Folding it onto the Boy's head and rolling it just over his earlobes, he chuckled. "Now you're ready - go get 'em, buddy."

~~~

As the station wagon choked and sputtered and roared to life, the Boy watched as his Father climbed into the Captain's pickup and drove off towards the dock. His Mother sighed - a pleasant, content sound.

"That man your Father is friend's with - he's a good man," she spoke, patting the Boy on the shoulder pad of his new coat. "Hope you don't mind me taking you to school from now on." she finished. The Boy detected a faint hint of something hidden just beneath the surface of those words. He looked at his Mother for any sign, any show of her cards, but she remained as stoic as ever. The car backed out onto the city side-street, and proceeded down the pot-holed asphalt, headed in a direction completely foreign to the Boy. High-rises and tucked away coffee shops and restaurants too expensive for his family to ever set foot in gave way to crumbling brick convenience stores and graffiti-tagged dilapidated warehouses. Garbage-strewn junk yards, metal recyclers, and twenty-four hour diners dotted the sides of the single-lane highway. His Mother pointed to one particular greasy spoon.

"That's where I worked," she said, neutral and flat. Suddenly, it dawned on the Boy - his Mother had a new job. What was it again? Surely they had told him. He casually glanced at her outfit for clues. Thick, high-ankle hiking boots, heavy canvas brown pants, a knit sweater with a rain-coat loosely zipped over the top. Wherever she was working, it certainly wasn't at another diner, the Boy decided. After several more miles,, the woods began to finally reclaim their lost territory, with only the rare gas station appearing from time to time. Thick groves of replanted fir and cedar, only a few decades old, gathered and spread across the rolling hills as far as the Boy could see. Cracking the car window, he allowed the chilled wind to fill his soul with the essences of moist dirt and dew dropped moss. He closed his eyes and inhaled - the smell of Home.
~~~

"We're close now - are you excited?" inquired his Mother. The Boy nodded furiously, his mind seething with infinite thoughts and preconceptions of his new school, his new classmates, his new teachers. How different things would be. He reflected on his old school, and suddenly, strangely, felt sadness creeping in. He never had a chance to say 'goodbye' to her. Perhaps she knew. Of course she would have deduced this, the Boy decided - she was a scientist after all.

The station wagon's funny-sounding turn signal came on, popping rapidly on and off as his Mother turned the cranky old car onto a soft dirt road. Winding between massive trunks of old growth fir and sword ferns as tall as his Father, the skinny single-lane wove its way through a mist-laden valley, paralleling the rushing whitewater of an adjacent creek. On the final turn, a fantastic wooden archway appeared over the washboard road, dark green ivy and philodendron lazily hanging from its struts.

"'The Forest School,'" his Mother read aloud. Holding his breath as they drove under the entrance and into the small parking lot, the Boy thought he heard the drifting notes of bass guitar mellowly warming up. "We're here," his Mother announced.

~~~

As the two walked up the set of basalt steps flanked by meticulously manicured Japanese maples, the Boy clutched his Mother's hand tightly. She responded in kind with a bright, cheery burst of excited squeezes, just as the light tap-tap-tap of a snare drum joined the bass in a gentle duet. Atop the stairs, a short wooden walkway led to a gigantic rotunda as large as several of his old school's classrooms - bigger even than the gymnasium. Standing under its confines were perhaps twenty other boys and girls his age, some with their parents, some gathering closely together, examining an object with great interest.

"I'm going to sign you into class," his Mother started. "Why don't you go over and introduce yourself to those kids, see what they're up to?" she suggested, dropping his hand and walking briskly over to another woman near a desk. Slightly older, her hair graying and tied into a neat bun, this other woman wore a pair of overalls decorated in a psychedelic arrangement of colored flowers. The Boy watched as the two embraced - had they met before? His curiosity was cut short by a sudden voice calling in his direction.
~~~

"Hey! Kid! You in the beanie!" the friendly voice called. "Come on over, New guy! We're looking at some fossils!" Swallowing his anxiety, the Boy smiled and hustled over to join the gaggle, his confidence surging.

"It looks like part of a mandibles" suggested one girl, her incredibly thick-lensed glasses falling down her nose.

"Like a mammal? Or a dinosaur?" asked another boy, who seemed to be drawing a sketch of the chunk of rock that stood on a mantle in front of them.

"Jurassic - or maybe Cretaceous?" chimed in another voice, squeaky and cracking often.

"Can't be that old," started another boy with a long ponytail, "they found this on the other side of the mountains - it's all lava beds over there. so has to be a more recent period. Maybe the Paleogene - like 40 million years ago."

"Nope! Definitely Neogene!" replied an incredibly familiar voice from behind the Boy. He turned around rapidly, but was surrounded by taller children that blocked his view. A small monarch butterfly fluttered above the gaggle. The voice continued.

"If it was Paleogene, it would have more shale and siltstone and the like - that's what the lava's flow left behind then." An electric guitar riff came hurtling out from the ceiling of the rotunda. The soft voice spoke in perfect time with the music.

"This has a bunch of layers: red ash, pea-green clay, yellow and orange sediment flows. It's like a rainbow!" The voice pushed to the front of the group and peered inches away from the fossil, her butterfly clips dangling from her braided hair. "Yup - just like the ones I saw at the museum," she elaborated, spinning to face the Boy.

"Probably a saber tooth tiger jaw, I suspect," finished the Girl, a huge grin across her face as she stared at the Boy. The group of students voiced their agreement and disbanded, leaving the two old friends alone together. With time and space perfectly still, the Boy took a breath. And then a step. Two more. Throwing his arms around the Girl, the Boy hugged her as tightly as he could, lifting her off the ground in a fit of mutually shared laughter and love.

"Wh-what are you d-doing here?" he exclaimed, releasing her from the bear-hug, his hands on her shoulders. Slapping his sides, she giggled and shook her head.

"Let's just say that the Principal suggested to my parents that I transfer," she said, biting her lower lip with a mischievous smirk. "Once you told me about the Forest School, I begged my parents to let me go, too. The rest is history," she finished, shrugging her shoulders.

"Guess we're meant to be here together," wondered the Boy to his friend.

"Ha!" replied the Girl to her friend, "You know, good friends are always together, no matter where they might be," she finished with a tilt of her head. The Boy nodded. She was connected, too.

~~~

Soft, calming drones of sound bowls echoed from the center of the rotunda as a large metallic gong was rung, sending gentle vibrations through the moist morning air. School had begun. Finding his Mother near the Teacher's desk, he looked into her soothing eyes as a clarinet picked up the rhythm in the background, swinging solos with the bass. She knelt beside her son and placed a hand on his head.

"This is the right place for you, bud," she whispered. "Are you ready?" Blinking away the warm tears, the Boy slowly and meaningfully hugged his Mother deeply. Hard work. Determination. Sacrifice. He realized in that moment how many extraordinary lessons she had taught him through her own example while they struggled in the city together.

"Thank you," he replied, his face buried into her sweater. Now, he decided, was the right time. Reaching into his back pocket, he removed the item, its energy pulsing bright and wild. Fastening the necklace around her neck, he backed away and wiped away his tears as her brilliant purple aura hazed back into life. Trembling hands clutching the heart-shaped piece of metal, she allowed her own tears to drift to the wooden rotunda floor.

"Where... where did you..." she started.

"A friend found it," the Boy finished, wiping her face with his coat sleeve. He stared at the necklace.

"You've never seen what's in this, have you?" his Mother realized, her voice choked with emotion and the shock of sudden realization. Fumbling with the latch, she suddenly stopped and instead tipped the Boy's chin up to meet her eyes. "In here is a reminder of the day that I felt infinite love and happiness and connection enter my life." As she opened the amulet, the Boy squinted to see that it contained but three small strands of hair, all different hues: the dark black of his Mother's, the white of his Father's, the light brown of his own - all tied together with a single purple ribbon.
~~~

"Sometimes," his Mother began, "when life is particularly hard, or depressing, or frustrating, it's nice to have a memento, a beacon, a light to hold onto in the dark." Carefully tucking the hairs back into their heart-shaped abode, she stood and held the Boy's hand. "But I've realized that all I really need is the presence, the smile, the touch of someone who I love - who loves me." Brilliant purple pulsing light twirled and poured from all around his Mother as the two slowly walked to the center of the rotunda. A trumpet had joined the chorus and intricately supported the other instruments in perfect melodious concert. The Teacher began to speak.

"Forest School has begun for the day. Class, please welcome our newest two students," the Teacher announced, palms upturned towards the Boy and Girl.

"Welcome to the woods, friends," chimed twenty soft voices in simultaneous harmony. Wonderful surges of ecstatic adrenaline pumped through the Boy's heart and mind, as he shared a smile with the Girl, her own excited energy rippling outwards and casting him in its warmth.

"And let's not forget to welcome our newest assistant instructor to our pack," continued the Teacher, pivoting towards the Boy. Her eyes caught his... and then trailed up and over his shoulder to meet his Mother's.

"Welcome to the woods, friend," sang out the students once more. The Boy stared at his Mother, who gazed down upon him with the grandest of all smiles, a proud, radiant sparkle twinkling in each eye. Hand on his back, she leaned down to whisper into his ear.

"Told you I found a new job," she giggled.

~~~

As the winter sun burnt high and bright above the interlaced canopy of Douglas fir and red cedar, the fine string of students marched down a single-track of beaten clay. In the middle of the pack walked two best friends, clutching their new notebooks and freshly sharpened pencils, absorbing the words of their teachers as intently as they inhaled the earth around them. Arriving at a small clearing alongside the trickling stream, the students fanned out and quietly unrolled their bamboo mats. It was time for their first class of the day. At the base of a massive sequoia stood the lead Teacher and the Boy's Mother.

"Today, we're going to start with a lesson on ecology," explained the Teacher, removing a small notebook from her flowered-overalls. "To
~~~

start, let's review the life cycle of this tree in front of us - who knows its genus and species?"

"Sequoiadendron giganteum!" most of the class responded in enthusiastic unison.

"Good. And what is its relationship with fire?" asked their Teacher. The class fell silent for a moment.

"Why is it's bark so soft?" hinted the Boy's Mother.

"It's super-thick, and water-logged," answered the Girl. "Highly fire resistant," she finished.

"That's right," clapped the Teacher, "and if you look up its huge trunk a few meters, you'll see the blackened scorch marks of prior fires - and you know what? The tree is doing just fine! It's adapted and evolved to co-exist *with* fire, with destruction, with turmoil," she elaborated.

"I don't see any plants around the tree," commented the Girl. "No sword-fern, no rhododendron, no fir saplings."

"Excellent observation," proclaimed the Boy's Mother. "This tree, the Great Sequoia, needs fire - needs death - to reproduce. The fires clear out all of the competing plants and small trees. At the same time, the intense heat stimulates the release of thousands of pine cones and seeds. Those seeds land on a blank canvas of a forest floor and take root!" she explained, arms outstretched towards the massive trunk.

"Life from death," summarized the Teacher. "What else do we know creates life from death?" she queried with a smile.

"Mushrooms!" exclaimed every student - the Boy and Girl included.

"Yes!" confirmed his Mother. "Nature's ultimate recyclers - breaking down death and decay to revive our living soils and allow trees like this Sequoia to prosper." Walking over to a large bolete mushroom, his Mother cut the fruit at its stipe, and held it up in the air. Its underside glimmered a golden yellow as she spun it slowly in the afternoon light.

"This Porcini was born from the atoms and molecules and proteins of so many other things that lived and then died," his Mother continued.

"Like logs and bushes and leaves?" suggested the girl with thick glasses.

"Like birds, and bugs, and mice?" added another.

"What about wolves, and bears, and cougars?" asked the boy with the ponytail.

"All of those things!" their Teacher confirmed. "Everything that lives must die, only to be newly remade into something else alive."

"Even people?" asked one especially timid boy.

"Even people," replied the Teacher.

"So does that mean that any one of us - me, you, anybody - could have been part of a mushroom once?" asked the Girl.

"Most certainly!" the Boy's Mother replied. "And how wonderful it would be to be a golden chanterelle, or a black morel, or even a lobster mushroom!" she daydreamed, placing the porcini into her backpack. "All of you have been a part of so many other things before becoming who you are right now."

"I could have been a wolf?" one girl excitedly mused.

"I think I was a bear!" exclaimed the ponytail boy.

"I was certainly an owl, stated the Girl with the utmost confidence. Somehow, the Boy knew this to be completely true. She had definitely been an owl before.

"You were each part of those things," his Mother explained, lowering her voice to a gentle soothing pitch as she knelt on her mat in the center of the students.

"You were each *all* of those things - the animals, the trees, the plants, the mushroom, the soil, the earth." Taking a deep breath, she sighed and smiled, looking at each of their entranced faces as she continued. "Later, in time, you will become part of them once again." Silence fell upon the Forest School as a warm, sun-drenched breeze washed over the semi-circle of young spirits, bathing their budding knowledge in love and light. They were unafraid of this revelation. They understood. The Girl spoke.

"Then some of us right here might be made from parts of the same tree - maybe even the same giant sequoia - from a thousand years ago," she hypothesized, "and some of us might become one together in another thousand years." As she finished her thought, the Girl's eyes widening in the wake of her theory. She looked to the Boy and smiled. How nice it would be to be part of a giant sequoia with her, he decided. His Mother sighed aloud.

"When you look at this tree now, what do you see?" she asked, arms outstretched overhead, fingers widened like the great Sequoia's branches hundreds of feet up.

"I see my Grandpa," hummed the girl with thick glasses, hugging herself, rocking gently.

"I see the stars," proclaimed the boy with a ponytail, gazing out over the canopy's horizon, his mind drifting across the universe.

"I see the future," said the timid boy, laying on his back, heart wandering through time.

"I see you," said the Teacher, smiling back at the Boy's Mother.

"I see me," said the Girl, a supremely satisfied glow emanating from her smile.

"I see everything," whispered the Boy, "for everything is connected."